The Sorcerers' Plague

Tor Books by David B. Coe

Blood of the Southlands

The Sorcerers' Plague
The Horsemen's Gambit (2008)

The Lon Tobyn Chronicle

Children of Amarid
The Outlanders
Eagle-Sage

Winds of the Forelands

Rules of Ascension
Seeds of Betrayal
Bonds of Vengeance
Shapers of Darkness
Weavers of War

The Sorcerers' Plague

Book One of Blood of the Southlands

David B. Coe

A Tom Doherty Associates Book
New York

THE SORCERERS' PLAGUE

Copyright © 2007 by David B. Coe

Edited by James Frenkel
Book design by Spring Hoteling
Maps by Ellisa Mitchell

A Tor Book
Published by Tom Doherty Associates, LLC
175 Fifth Avenue
New York, NY 10010

www.tor.com

Tor® is a registered trademark of Tom Doherty Associates, LLC.

Library of Congress Cataloging-in-Publication Data

Coe, David B.
  The sorcerers' plague / David B. Coe.—1st ed.
      p. cm.—(Blood of the southlands ; bk. 1)
  "A Tom Doherty Associates book."
  ISBN-13: 978-0-7653-1638-7
  ISBN-10: 0-7653-1638-2
  I. Title.

PS3553.O343S67   2007
813'.54—d22   2007025656

First Edition: December 2007

Printed in the United States of America

0 9 8 7 6 5 4 3 2 1

For Nancy,
who took me halfway around the world to explore a new land;
this is the place I discovered while we were there.

Acknowledgments

Again, many thanks to my terrific agent, Lucienne Diver; my publisher, Tom Doherty; the great people at Tor Books, in particular Liz Gorinsky and Irene Gallo and her art staff; Terry McGarry for her friendship and thorough copyediting; my fine editor and good friend, Jim Frenkel; his assistant, Melissa Faliveno, and his interns, Ben Freund, Mark Kleinhaus, Brianna Pintens, Merrill Hill, and Alan Rubsam.

As always, I'm most grateful to Nancy, Alex, and Erin, for their love and patience.

D.B.C.

The Southlands

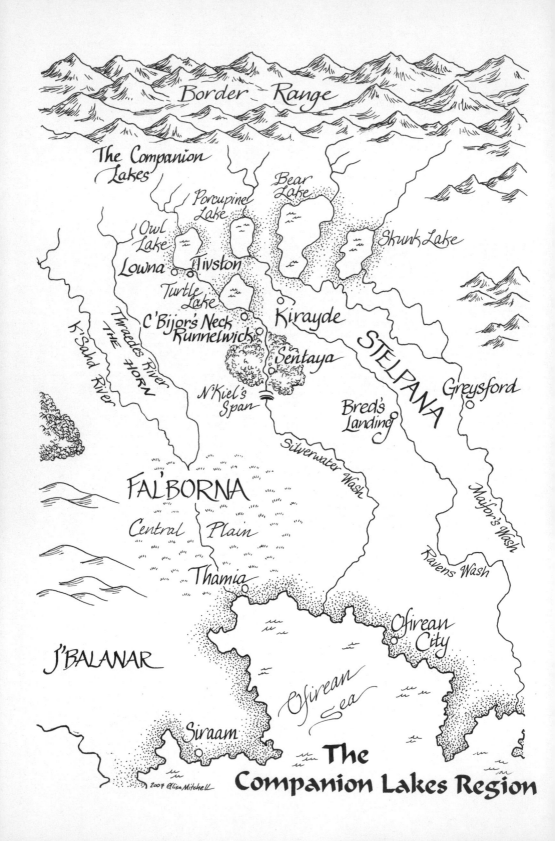

Border Range

The Companion Lakes

Porcupine Lake

Bear Lake

Owl Lake

Skunk Lake

Lowna

Tivston

Turtle Lake

C'Bijor's Neck

Kirayde

Runnelwich

STELPANA

Thraedes River

THE HORN

K'Sahd River

Sentaya

N'Kiel's Span

Greysford

Bred's Landing

Silverwater Wash

FAL'BORNA

Central Plain

Major's Wash

Ravens Wash

Thamia

Ofirean City

J'BALANAR

Ofirean Sea

Siraam

2007 Elisa Mitchell

The Companion Lakes Region

The Sorcerers' Plague

Prologue

✦✤✦

She could hear the last of the thunder rumbling in the distance; she could feel it pulsing in the ground beneath her feet, as if the earth itself trembled at the storm's fury. The forest flickered with lightning, strange, frightening shapes flashing before her and then vanishing like wraiths. The rain had ceased long ago, but a cool wind swept among the trees, carving through her damp clothes, chilling her like death.

She still carried the torch, though it offered no light. She didn't remember it dying out. She should have thrown it away, but she couldn't bring herself to let go of it. There was comfort to be found in the feel of that rough wood, in the faint smell of oil that still lingered in the burned remnants of cloth. She should have taken something from the house. There were clothes she might need, toys she still loved, tokens that would help her remember Mama and Papa, Kytha and Baetri. As if she could forget.

Fear had kept her from going inside. She'd gone in once, seen that they were dead. She hadn't found the courage to go in a second time. Then Mama had died, the last of them, and she had run from the village. Was it even a village anymore? The houses remained. The lanes, the marketplace, the garden plots. But with everyone dead, was it still a village?

A moment later she was crying again. How many tears could a girl shed in one night? Did grief and shame know any limits? Did fear and rage?

She didn't know where she was going. She knew only that there was nothing left for her here, and that she couldn't go to the white-hairs again. Not after what had happened this night.

She crumpled to the ground, overcome once more with anguish. She wanted to be sick or to scream or simply to die. Yes, that would have been easiest. Better death than living with the knowledge of what she had done, and what had been done to her. There was no one left to mourn her, and there was nothing left for her but to mourn the others. What kind of life was that?

She knew that she couldn't take a blade to herself. She wasn't brave enough for that. But she could throw herself in the wash. Or could she? Even that thought made her quail.

Maybe if she went back. Maybe if she returned to the house and laid herself down beside her dead sisters and her father. Maybe that would be enough to kill her.

Another gust of wind made her shiver, made her teeth chatter. Perhaps she didn't have to move at all. She'd heard of people dying in the wild, killed by cold and hunger and thirst and wild dogs. That could be her.

But just thinking it made her sit up straight and grip her torch tighter. Even wanting to die, she was too much a coward to do anything but survive. She felt that she was betraying those who were gone, though Mama and Papa wouldn't have seen it that way. Young as she was, she knew that much. They would tell her to get up, to start walking again. *It doesn't matter where*, they would say. *Just walk. Find another village. Live!*

They were dead because of her. The taste of failure in her mouth was enough to make her gag.

"It wasn't just me," she said aloud, angry, hurt, desperate to believe it. "It's their fault, too. Maybe even more than mine."

Then why did you lie to Mama?

"I didn't mean to lie," she whispered, tears streaking her face.

Lightning flashed overhead, illuminating the wood and making her flinch. Pale faces seemed to loom among the trees, watching her, laughing. She covered her ears and closed her eyes, but it was several moments before the thunder finally rumbled its answer. Eventually she opened her eyes again and her hands dropped to her side.

She sat there for what seemed a long time. Lightning lit the forest several times more, and still the thunder retreated. No more rain fell. Even the storm was leaving her. How she wanted to lie down and close her eyes and never wake again. But as frightened as she was of being alone, death scared her more.

Eventually she climbed to her feet, and still gripping that dead torch, she started down the path once more. *Yes, walk*, the voices said, urging her on. *Find another village. Live.*

Chapter 1

+I+

What are we, Grandfather?"

Besh sat back on his heels, wiping beads of sweat from his brow with the back of his hand and looking over at the boy. "What are we?" he repeated. "We're sheep, of course. Why else would we live in the highlands and eat roots and greens?"

Mihas giggled, but quickly grew serious again. Whatever had taken hold of the boy's curiosity didn't want to let go.

"You know what I mean," he said. "What kind of people are we?"

The old man leaned forward again, his knees and elbows cushioned in the soft black earth as he pulled clover and thin sprays of grass out of his garden. The goldroot looked healthy, the tops of the tubers firm and plump. In another half turn he'd harvest them. The time for pulling weeds had long since passed. Was it then vanity that had him crawling about in the dirt, peering into the shadows of the root greens? Ema would have thought so. She would have teased him day and night had she seen him now, an old man too proud to share the earth with clover and grass.

"Grandfather?"

"We are Mettai, Mihas. You know that."

"But what does that mean?"

Besh sat up again. "Why are you asking me this?"

Mihas looked down at the ground, kicking at a clod of dirt with his bare foot. His fine long hair, black as a raven's feathers, hung over his forehead, concealing his eyes.

"Do you remember the peddler who came through here just after the dark of the moons?" the boy asked.

"The old Qirsi?"

"Yes, him. He said something."

"Come here," Besh said, waving the boy over to him.

Mihas walked to where his grandfather was kneeling and sat beside him, looking solemn.

Besh smiled to show the boy he wasn't angry with him. "What did he say to you?"

"He said we were like the creyvnal, that we really didn't know what we were."

"Perhaps he meant it as a compliment. The creyvnal is a powerful beast. Wouldn't you like to have the body of a lion and the head of a wolf?"

He smiled; Mihas didn't.

"The creyvnal isn't real, Grandfather. Even I know that."

"You're right. It's not real. But still, the peddler was also right, in a way. The Mettai are like the creyvnal."

"How?"

"Well, we're Eandi. We have dark hair and dark eyes, we live long lives, we're strong like other Eandi. But like the Qirsi, we can use magic."

"But did he mean that we're not real? I mean, I know we are. But was he saying that our powers aren't real?"

Besh eyed Mihas briefly. Then he reached for one of the clovers he had pulled from the ground and held it out to the boy.

Mihas frowned.

"Take it," the old man said.

The boy held out his hand and Besh placed the clover in his palm.

"What does 'mettai' mean?" he asked. "Do you know?"

"You mean the word?"

"Yes."

"It means blood of the earth."

"Good. Put some dirt in your hand with the clover."

As Mihas did this, Besh pulled his knife from the sheath on his belt and dragged the blade across the back of his own hand. His skin there, tanned and brown from the Growing sun, was scored with dozens of thin white lines, all of them running parallel to the cut he had just made; evidence of a life spent drawing upon earth magic. Like rings within the trunks of the great firs and cedars growing in the forests around Ki-rayde, the lines on a Mettai's hand could be used to judge his or her age.

A man could even trace the history of all his years, if only he could recall the conjuring made whole by the blood that flowed from each of those scars. Some would claim that unnecessary conjurings like this one were a waste of blood and earth, that they were frivolous expressions of Mettai power. But wasn't there value in helping a boy find pride in his heritage and in the power that flowed in his veins? Besh had been conjuring for most of his sixty-four years. This, it seemed to the old man, was as valid a reason as any for drawing forth his blood.

He let the blood well from the wound for several moments before carefully gathering some on the flat of his blade. He held the knife over Mihas's hand, balancing the blood on the steel.

"Blood to earth," he murmured. "Life to power, power to thought, color to clover."

He tipped the blade, allowing the blood to drip off the knife and onto the boy's hand, where it mingled with the earth and the flower. For a moment nothing happened. Then the blood and soil, blended together now in what looked like rich crimson mud, began to swirl slowly in the palm of the boy's hand. Four times it went around, and then it vanished into the roots of the flower.

An instant later, the soft pink hue of the clover gave way to brilliant sapphire. The flower appeared to come to life again, its color dazzling, its leaves opening once more. In the center of the bloom, amid the blue, there appeared a small spot of bright yellow, as perfect and round as the sun in Morna's sky.

Mihas laughed aloud.

"If our magic isn't real," Besh said, "how do you explain that?"

The boy reached for another clover. "Do it again, Grandfather!"

"No. Once is enough. One should never trifle with Mettai magic."

"Can you teach me?"

"Not yet. You know that. When you begin your fourth four you can start to learn. And when you complete that four, you'll have earned your blade. All right?"

Mihas nodded, looking glum. No doubt five years seemed an eternity to the child. Little did he know how quickly the time would pass.

Besh glanced at his hand. The bleeding had slowed. Another scar to mark the years.

Sixteen fours. How quickly they'd gone by. Many among his people lived to be this old. He wasn't so unusual in that respect. If anything, he was more fit than most. Sixty-four was said to be a powerful age for those who reached it, a time of wisdom and enhanced magic. For most it was actually a year of endings. How many men had he seen live out their sixteenth four only to weaken and die soon after?

Besh had no intention of being one of them. He planned to guide Mihas into his power. Better him than Sirj, the boy's father. The man would make a mess of it, and in the process he'd do the same to the boy. Besh had never liked Sirj's father—he was as stubborn as he was stupid, and he could never manage to keep his mouth shut. It was bad enough that the man had built his house just next to Besh and Ema's back when she still lived and Besh still worked as the village cooper. But that Elica should marry the man's son . . . Besh shook his head. He would have spit at the thought of Elica's fool of a husband had Mihas not been there, watching him. No, Besh couldn't die yet. Once Mihas came of age he could go and join Ema in the Underrealm, but not before.

He licked the blood from the back of his hand and from his blade, as was proper. A Mettai never wasted blood, and by licking the wound, he stopped the bleeding. From what he'd heard over the years, he gathered that this wasn't true for other Eandi or for the sorcerer race. But it worked for a Mettai every time.

"Can I see your knife again, Grandfather?"

"Have a care with it," he said, handing it to Mihas, hilt first.

Mihas's brown eyes danced in the sunlight. "I always do. You're the one who's always cutting himself."

Besh had to laugh.

Clever boy. His mother's child. Dark-skinned and long-limbed, like Elica and like Ema, and as quick as both of them. Ema would say that the father of such a child couldn't be all bad. As far as Besh was concerned it meant only that Elica's blood was stronger than her husband's.

The old man turned his attention back to the clover and grasses intruding upon his goldroot, and for a long time he and the boy said nothing. The sun burned a lazy arc across the sky, blue save for a few feathered clouds. Swallows darted overhead, wheeling in the light wind, chattering and scolding like children at play.

"Are you the oldest person in Kirayde?" Mihas asked suddenly.

The boy was sitting in the dirt, still toying with the knife. The blue-and-gold clover lay on his knee, a prize that he would show his mother and father.

Besh laughed at the question. "No," he said. "I'm not the oldest."

He turned and sat, stretching out his stiff legs. *An old man shouldn't kneel for so long,* Ema's voice scolded in his head. *If you're not careful, you'll wind up bent and lame.*

"That little girl you play with, the one with so many older brothers."

"Nissa?"

"Yes, Nissa."

"She only has four brothers."

"Only four?" Besh said. "I thought it was more than that. Anyway, her grandmother is older than I am. And so is the herbmistress."

"She is?"

Besh raised his eyebrows. "Is that so hard to believe?"

"Not really. I just . . ." Mihas shrugged. "If you're not the oldest, then why are you one of the village elders? Nissa's grandmother isn't."

"No, she's not, but the herbmistress is. Truly, Mihas, I don't know why the other elders chose me to join their circle. But I do know that there's more to the choice than just a person's age."

"Oh." Mihas turned the knife over in his hands. "What about Old Lici? Is she older than you?"

Besh glanced at the boy again, but Mihas seemed intent on the blade. Most likely he was curious and nothing more. Besh had seen several children shouting taunts at the old woman just a few days before, and he had warned Mihas to stay away from her. When the boy had asked him why, he hadn't been able to give a good reason. This was the first time either of them had mentioned the woman since then.

"I believe she is older," Besh said, trying to keep his tone light.

Apparently he failed.

"You don't like her, do you, Grandfather?"

"I don't really care for her one way or another."

"It seems like you don't like her."

Clever indeed.

Mihas was right. Besh didn't like the old witch who lived at the southern edge of their village. Or more to the point, he didn't trust her. He might even have been afraid of her. Besh had been no more than a babe suckling at his mother's breast when Lici first came to Kirayde, but he'd heard others speak of her arrival enough times that he could almost claim as his own other people's memories of that cool Harvest day.

Lici was but eight years old at the time, a pretty girl with long black hair and fair features. But something dark lurked in her green eyes—the memory of tragedy, some said—and for some time she refused to speak. It was clear to all that she had wandered alone in the wild for many, many days, perhaps as long as an entire turn of the moons, and that she had been without proper food and clothing for all that time. She was emaciated. Her arms and legs were covered with insect bites and scarred as if from brambles, and her hair was matted with filth. Most likely she had kept herself alive by eating what roots and berries she could find.

Many speculated on what might have happened to her. Some assumed that she had survived an outbreak of the pestilence that claimed the rest of her family and village. Others wondered if she'd been the lone survivor of an attack by brigands. There were darker suggestions as well—even then, when Lici was but a child, a few wondered if she might have been responsible for whatever doom had befallen the rest of her people.

To Besh's knowledge, though, the full tale of Lici's past was known only to two people: Lici, of course, and a woman named Sylpa.

Sylpa had been the leader of the village elders at the time Lici came to Kirayde. That first day she took Lici in, and during the years that followed raised the girl as she would a daughter. Gradually, as Lici's strength returned, and the memories of whatever tragedy she had endured faded, she began to speak. She took her lessons with the other children and grew to womanhood. Besh remembered thinking her beautiful when he was a small boy and easily impressed by long silken hair and eyes that sparkled like emeralds. But he also recalled that, even then, he never spoke with her, or rather, that Lici never spoke with anyone other than Sylpa.

She rarely smiled, and she had a discomfiting habit of looking a person directly in the eye as she walked past in utter silence. Though Besh dreamed of marrying her, he also began to fear her.

Over time his fascination with her waned. He married Ema, had children of his own, made a name for himself among the Mettai as a skilled cooper and wise leader, and eventually was selected as one of the elders. Lici never married. She had suitors, including an Eandi merchant who saw her one morning as he drove a cart loaded with his wares into the village marketplace. He returned to Kirayde several times during that one

Planting season, hoping that this dark, beautiful Mettai woman might deign to speak with him. She did not. After a time, he stopped coming.

When Sylpa died, Lici left the house they had shared and built for herself a small hut in a lonely corner of the village, near what villagers called the South Rill. She still spoke with no one, but she began to teach herself to weave baskets. The Mettai of the northern highlands had long been known for their basketwork, and Kirayde had a master basketmaker who could have offered her an apprenticeship. But as with everything else, Lici did this alone. And she did it brilliantly. Within only a few years, her craft rivaled that of the village's master. Soon, peddlers were coming from all over the Southlands to buy Lici's baskets.

Some in the village began to say that the woman was growing rich off her craft, that she hoarded gold and silver pieces the way a mouse hoards grain for the Snows. It may well have been true, at least for a time. Nevertheless, Lici remained in her tiny hut, wearing old clothes that had once been Sylpa's, and eating the roots and greens she grew in her small garden plot. Then abruptly, just a few years ago, she began to turn the peddlers away. Suddenly it seemed that she had no interest in trading any of her baskets. The peddlers offered more gold. They offered jewels and silverwork from the Iejony Peninsula, and blankets from the cloth crafters of Qosantia. They stood outside her door and pleaded with her for just one simple trade. Lici refused them all.

To this day, no one in the village knew why.

Besh thought it a fitting end to her years of prosperity, and he was surprised that others didn't recognize it as such. The old woman had spent her entire life in shadow, marked by the gods for some dark fate. Perhaps she meant well. Perhaps she chose solitude and behaved as she did because she never had the chance to learn any other way. Truth be told, Besh didn't care.

He didn't want to have anything to do with her, and he certainly didn't want Mihas going near her.

"It's not that I don't like Lici," he told the boy at last, watching the swallows dance overhead. "I just think you'd be better off staying away from her."

"But why?"

"It's hard to explain. She's . . . odd."

"Is it because her parents died?"

Besh looked at the boy, wondering how much he had heard about Lici's past.

Mihas leaned closer to him, as if fearing that others might hear what he said next. "Nissa's father says that wherever she walks, four ravens circle above her."

Four ravens. The Mettai death omen. That was as apt as anything Besh might have thought to say about her.

"Nissa's father may be right."

"Then why is she still alive?"

"There are many deaths, Mihas. Some are slower than others."

The boy frowned. "I don't understand."

"That's all right. Just do as I say and stay away from Old Lici."

"Yes, Grandfather."

Besh stood slowly, stretching his back and legs. "We should go home," he said.

Mihas scrambled to his feet. "Are the roots ready yet?"

"Not quite. Next turn, perhaps."

The boy nodded and handed Besh the knife.

They started walking back toward the house Besh shared with his daughter's family. They hadn't gone far, however, when Mihas suddenly halted.

"Oh, no!" the boy said, and ran back toward the garden.

"What's the matter?" Besh called after him.

Mihas stopped beside the goldroot, bent down, and lifted something carefully out of the dirt. Then he started back toward Besh.

"What did you forget?"

"My clover," the boy said, holding it up proudly for Besh to see. One might have thought that Mihas himself had changed its color. "I want to show Mama."

Besh knew what the boy's mother would say about the flower, but he kept his silence and they walked back home.

The house stood in a grove of cedar on a small hill just east of the marketplace. It was larger than most houses in Kirayde, though to an outsider, someone from one of the Qirsi settlements along the wash, it would have seemed modest at best. A thin ribbon of pale grey smoke rose from the chimney, and two small children chased each other among the trees, giggling and shrieking breathlessly as they ran.

As Besh and Mihas drew near, Elica emerged from the house bearing an empty bucket, her long hair stirring in the breeze.

"It's about time," she said, glancing at Mihas and then fixing Besh with a hard glare. "What were you doing all this time?"

"Taking care of the goldroot. Can't an old man tend his garden without being questioned so by his daughter?"

"Not when there are more pressing chores to be done." She held out the bucket to Mihas. "Fetch some water from the rill, Mihas. Quickly. Supper's going to be late as it is."

The boy stopped just in front of her, but instead of taking the bucket, he held up the clover, beaming at her.

"What's this?" she asked, taking the flower and examining it.

"Grandfather did it!" Mihas told her. "It was a clover and I asked him whether our magic is real and he did that!"

Elica fixed Besh with a dark look, but then smiled at her son. "It's lovely. Such a bright color. Now, please, Mihas. The water."

"All right, Mama."

He grabbed the bucket and ran off, still clutching the clover in his free hand.

"You should know better, Father!" Elica said, sounding cross, as if she were speaking to one of her children. "No good can come of teaching the boy empty magic. And anyway, he's too young to be learning blood craft."

Sometimes Besh thought that Elica might be just a bit too much like her mother.

"I taught him nothing," he said. "I showed him a bit of magic. And it wasn't empty. That Qirsi peddler who came through here earlier in the waxing had him wondering if Mettai magic could do anything at all. I wanted him to see that it could."

"So show him something useful. You could have brought him back here and started my fire. You could have healed one of the children's cuts or scrapes. Elined knows they have enough between them to keep you bleeding for half a turn. But no. You choose to color a flower."

Sirj, Elica's husband, stepped around from the back of the house, his shirt soaked with sweat, a load of unsplit logs in his arms. He wasn't a big man—he was only slightly taller than Elica—nor was he particularly broad. But he was lean and strong, like a wildcat in the warmer turns.

"What are you going on about, Elica? I could hear you all the way back at the woodpile."

"It's nothing," she said.

Sirj didn't say anything. He put down the wood and regarded them both, waiting. His house, his question. He was entitled to an answer and both of them knew it.

"I colored a flower for Mihas," Besh finally told him. "I wanted to show him some magic. He was asking if Mettai powers were real."

Sirj eyed the old man briefly, his expression revealing little. It might have been that he knew Besh didn't like him, or maybe he was no more fond of Besh than the old man was of him. Whatever the reason, theirs had never been an easy relationship. But after a moment, Sirj merely shrugged and continued past Besh and Elica into the house. "No harm in that," he murmured.

Besh and Elica exchanged a look before following him inside.

Their supper consisted of smoked fish, boiled greens, and bread. Annze and Cam, the young ones, spent much of the meal teasing one another across the table and, after being chastised for that, feeding their fish to one of the dogs that ran wild through the village and in and out of nearly everyone's home. Except Lici's, of course. Even the dogs knew better than to bother her.

After they had finished and Mihas and the little ones had been put to bed, Besh lit his pipe and went out to smoke it in the cool evening air. He walked to the stump Sirj used for chopping wood, sat down, and gazed up into a darkening sky. Panya was already climbing into the night, her milky glow obscuring all but the brightest stars. No doubt red Ilias was up as well, following her across the soft indigo, but Besh couldn't see the second moon for the trees.

After a short while, Elica came out, walked to where he sat, and rested a hand easily on his shoulder.

"It's a clear night," she said.

"For now. The fog will come up before long. It always does this time of year."

She nodded. Then, "I'm sorry about before, Father. I shouldn't have said what I did. Sirj is right. There's no harm in showing Mihas some magic now and then." She kissed the top of his head. "Sometimes I wonder if I'm too much like Mother."

Besh smiled. "There are worse things."

"I suppose."

Elica started to walk away.

"He asked me about Lici."

She stopped, turned. "What did you tell him?"

"Same thing I always do: Stay away from her. But he won't be satisfied with that for much longer."

"She won't be alive much longer," Elica muttered. Immediately she covered her mouth with a hand, her eyes wide as she stared down at Besh.

"Forgive me, Father. I shouldn't have said that. It was cruel. And I didn't mean that because she was old—"

Besh began to laugh.

"You think it's funny?"

The old man nodded. "Yes, in a way. Mihas asked me today if I was the oldest person in Kirayde. That's how we ended up speaking of Lici." He took Elica's hand. "It's all right, child. You're right: She won't be with us much longer. And—Bian forgive me for saying so—perhaps that's for the best." He gave his daughter a sly look. "I, on the other hand, intend to stay around for a good many years. So don't go selling off my pipeweed any time soon."

She kissed him again. "Good night, Father. Don't stay out too long. It's getting cold."

Besh gave her hand a squeeze, then watched her walk away. After some time his pipe burned out, but still the old man sat, enjoying the air, and the darkness, and the sounds of the night. A few crickets, the last of the season, chirped nearby, and off in the distance a wolf howled. In recent nights Besh had heard an owl calling from the hills north of the village, but not tonight.

Eventually he began to see thin strands of mist drifting among the dark trunks of the firs and cedars, and he stood. The cold night breezes were one thing, but as Besh had grown older he'd found that the nighttime fogs chilled him, bone and blood. He retreated into the house and made his way to bed.

None of the rest would remember.

Why should they? Most hadn't even been alive at the time; those who were had been too young to understand.

But she knew. Oh, yes, Lici knew.

She could still see it all. She could see houses that had long since been broken by storms and snows and howling winds. She could see copses and clearings that had since given way to homes and garden plots. She could close her eyes and summon an image of Kirayde just as it had appeared that first day. She could walk the lanes past house and plot and tell any who cared to listen when each had been built or first tilled. She could go to any person in the village and give the year, turn, and day of his or her birth.

Lici remembered all of it.

They thought her crazed. She never married or had children, she didn't speak to them, she refused to prattle on about nothing or smile greetings that she didn't mean. And so they called her mad, they called her a witch. The children mocked her and their parents scolded them in turn. But then those same mothers and fathers ignored her, as if she were nothing more than a spider spinning webs in her tiny corner of the village. Did they really think that was better? Would they have chosen silence over taunts had silence been all they knew?

How long would it take them to realize that she was gone? Who would be the first to notice? Would they think that she had wandered off by accident? Would they think that she had drowned herself in the rill or gotten lost in the night mists? Or would they know that she left them by choice? Might there be one among them who would even guess her purpose? Would any of them know why she had chosen this night? Probably not. But it amused her to imagine the possibilities.

Sixteen fours. Sixty-four years. To the very day. That was long enough for anyone to stay in one place, to live among the same people, to turn over in one's head the same thought again and again, to direct every moment of every day toward a single purpose. Sixteen fours. Some said there was power in the very number. Indeed. Lici had power in abundance. And she would need all of it.

She had learned her craft well. Not basketmaking, though she also had much skill at that, but rather the blood craft, the magic of her people. The white-hairs thought that Qirsi magic reigned supreme in the Southlands, and perhaps they were right. But the magic of the Mettai was no trifle. And in the hands of a master, even one as old as she, it could be a mighty weapon.

At last her waiting had come to an end. She had planned and waited, she had suffered indignities both glaring and subtle, she had trained herself in both her crafts, pushing herself harder than any master would push even his most prized apprentice. All in preparation for this night, which was both an ending and a beginning. Kirayde would be lost to her forever, and despite all that she had endured here, the thought saddened her. This had been Sylpa's home and so had been as much a home to Lici as she could have expected after Sentaya. Now, though, she would begin a new journey, a new life, if one as old as she could ask for such a thing. She had hungered for this countless long years.

From her hut by the rill she could see the mist gathering about the village, shifting and elusive, glowing like a horde of wraiths in the white and red radiance of the two moons. It was nearly time. She had her baskets packed and ready in her old cart. She could see the nag from her doorway, gleaming white in the moonglow, shaking her head impatiently, ready to be on her way. The creature would be a good companion in these last days.

She had enough food to keep her going until she could trade for more. And though she tried to think of items she would need that she might be leaving behind, she knew there was nothing.

She had but one purpose now. That was all that remained. She could almost smell the Silverwater and the trees that surrounded the place. The gods knew she remembered the way, even after all this time.

Some things could never be forgotten. Or forgiven.

Chapter 2

✦❉✦

Sunlight sparkled on the windblown waters of the wash, shifting and dancing like stars in Morna's sky, so bright that Giraan had to shield his eyes from the glare as he checked his traps at the water's edge. The first two of his eight traps were empty. One of them had been robbed of its bait. He doubted that he'd find much in the others either. This trade was still new to him, and he knew better than to expect success to come quickly.

The gods rewarded labor. They found virtue in the struggle to perfect new skills. Giraan had spent sixteen years making his living as a wheelwright, and he had mastered the saw and the rasp, the plane and the hammer. In return, the gods had given him a strong back and a steady hand. They had given him a beautiful wife and four fine children. And they had granted him long life, so that he might see his sons and his daughter take the first steps into their adult lives. They had seen to it that he and Aiva wanted for nothing.

If anything, they had made life too comfortable, too easy. It almost seemed to Giraan that they were telling him to try his hand at something new. So after four fours as a wheelwright he passed the business on to Oren, his eldest, and he started teaching himself to trap. He bought one trap from a peddler who had passed through Runnelwick just after the thaw. The rest he built himself, copying that first one as closely as he could. It took him two or three tries to get it right, but in time he had his eight traps.

Qirsi in other villages would have thought him a fool, of course, struggling with his tools when he possessed shaping magic. But such was the way of the Y'Qatt. His people understood that the V'Tol, the Life Power—what others called magic—was a gift from Qirsar, one that was not to be squandered out of indolence. He'd heard the names by which others called the Y'Qatt: ascetics, fanatics, lunatics. Even the name Y'Qatt had once been meant as an epithet, for it was believed that the Y'Qatt, an ancient Qirsi clan, who had refused to fight in the early Blood Wars, had been driven by cowardice. But it wasn't that they were craven; they had been opposed to war itself, seeing it as evil, a misuse of Qirsi power. And so those who, like Giraan, refused to wield their power for any purpose embraced the name, seeing in the principled stand of these ancients an echo of their own piety.

Giraan had argued with the Qirsi peddlers who occasionally stopped in the village to sell their wares. He'd been called all the usual names. And always he silenced them with the same question: *If Qirsar had intended for us to expend our V'Tol on acts of magic, why would he shorten our lives every time we use it?*

No one had ever been able to answer to his satisfaction, because, quite simply, there was no good response they could offer. Throughout the Southlands, magic was killing the people of his race. It was a slow death, imperceptible to some, but real nevertheless. In recent years, as the number of Eandi in the land increased and the number of Qirsi dwindled, others had begun to realize this as well. Already the Eandi lived longer than did the men and women of his race. What sense was there in adding to this disparity by using magic frivolously, by relying on V'Tol to do what might also be accomplished with some physical effort, with sweat and muscle and skill? More and more Qirsi were asking themselves this same question; the Y'Qatt movement was growing.

The next two traps Giraan checked were empty as well, and he walked on to where he'd set the third pair. As he drew near, he saw that the nearer of the two had something in it. A beaver. The gods had been generous. Beaver skins fetched a fair bit of gold from most merchants— at least, the peddlers he'd seen trying to sell them had been asking quite a lot. He'd made a deal with Sedi, the old tanner. Sedi would skin and treat any animals Giraan managed to trap, and in return Giraan would make any repairs that Sedi's wagons might ever need, free of charge. Sedi had agreed to the exchange with a chuckle and a shake of his bald head, no doubt thinking that he had won the old wheelwright's services at no cost to himself. He was going to be disappointed.

When Giraan finally started back toward the village, he was as giddy as a child. He'd caught a stoat in the seventh trap. By the end of this day,

Sedi would be trying to change the terms of their bargain, or he'd be looking for a way to be done with it altogether. Angry as Sedi would be, though, they'd have a good laugh over it before the night was through.

On his way back home, he walked past the village plantings and checked to see how the crops in his and Aiva's plot were faring. It had been a fine Growing season—warm, with enough rain to keep Elined's earth moist and dark. It would be another turn before the goldroot was ready, but they might be able to begin picking the vine beans in half that time. Whenever it finally began, Giraan was certain that this would be a generous Harvest.

His home stood near the southern edge of the village. It was no larger than any other house in the village, but it wasn't small either. And now that all the children had been joined and had built their own houses, it felt almost spacious, like one of the great palaces in which the Qirsi clan lords lived.

Aiva sat out front, sharpening the blades she used in the kitchen. Her white hair was pulled back into a plait, and she wore a simple brown dress. She'd been a beauty as a youth, with long, thick hair and eyes as pale as bark on an aspen. As far as he was concerned, she'd lost nothing to age. As he drew near she looked up and waved. Giraan held up the two animals he'd trapped and laughed at what he saw on her face: her widened eyes, her mouth agape and covered with a slender hand.

"Two of them!" she said, breathless.

"A beaver and a stoat." He couldn't keep the pride from his voice. In truth, he didn't even try. Where was the harm in letting his beloved Aiva see how pleased he was?

"Does Sedi know?"

"Not yet." He smiled. "But he will soon enough."

"He'll be angry."

Giraan shook his head, the smile lingering. "He'll act angry at first, but he won't really mind. He knows that it was a fair bargain we struck."

"I hope you're right." She stood and looked at the stoat and then the beaver. "They're fine animals, Giraan. You should be very proud."

"I doubt that either one is fit for eating."

"We both know that you didn't trap them for their meat. You trapped them for gold, and for the sheer challenge of it."

Giraan frowned. "You sound as though you disapprove."

"Not at all. Just don't be talking about the lack of meat as if that makes you less thrilled about the catch than you really are."

She smiled to soften the words. Then she raised herself onto her tip-toes and kissed his cheek. "Take them to Sedi," she said. "I don't want them in my kitchen."

He had to grin. "Yes, my lady."

It usually made her laugh when he addressed her so, but suddenly Aiva was looking past him, toward the path that wound by their house to the marketplace. He turned to look.

An old woman had paused on the track to watch them. Her hair was as white as that of any Qirsi, but the darkness of her skin and eyes marked her as one of Ean's children. She wore a simple brown dress much like Aiva's except that this one was frayed and tattered. Though the day was warm, she also wore a faded green wrap around her bent shoulders. She carried two large baskets, one under each arm, both of them covered with small blankets that concealed their contents. She also wore a carry sack on her back.

"Hello," Giraan called, raising a hand in greeting as he stepped around Aiva to put himself between this stranger and his love.

"This house is new," the woman said, her voice so low that for a moment he wondered if he'd heard her correctly.

"I'm sorry, but I believe you're mistaken. My wife and I built this house ourselves nearly sixteen years ago."

The woman stared at him a moment. Then a faint smile crept over her face. "Yes," she said. "And to me, that would make it new."

"You were here that long ago?" Aiva asked, taking a step forward.

"It's been sixteen fours," the woman said. "I was just a child."

"Sixteen fours!" Aiva said. "Truly the gods have blessed you!"

The woman grinned, revealing sharp yellow teeth. "Yes, they have."

"You live near here?" Giraan asked.

"I did once. We lived . . . we lived south of here. But my people moved about a good deal."

"You're Mettai," he said.

She stared at him for several moments, her smile fading slowly. "We are," she answered, ice in her voice.

Giraan shook his head. "I'm sorry. I didn't mean to offend you."

"Why should I be offended? You merely told me what I already know. I'm Mettai."

"Yes, of course. But I . . ."

"When you said I was Mettai, did you mean to insult me?"

It almost seemed that she was trying to confound him with her words and her indignation. "Not at all," Giraan said, smiling, trying to mollify her.

"But you know that we are hated by Eandi and Qirsi alike, and so you feared that I would take offense. If you were to see a one-legged beggar in a marketplace, you would not say to him, 'You're a cripple.' You would ignore his infirmity, or at least pretend to. But you would slip a silver into his cup as a gesture of pity, and feel that you had done a good turn. So it is with the Mettai. You spoke without thinking, stating what was obvious, and now you fear that you have reminded me of my infirmity."

"I assure you—"

Aiva laid a hand on Giraan's arm, silencing him.

"I'm afraid you've misunderstood my husband, good lady," she said. "He simply apologized because we do not judge people by their race or even their clan, and he feared that you would think he was doing just that. We are Y'Qatt. We know as well as anyone what it is to be shunned by one's people. You would be welcome here no matter your clan or your nation." She beckoned to the woman with an open hand. "Please. Come and sit with us. No doubt you've traveled far. You must be weary. We haven't much, but we can offer you food and drink."

"My lady is most kind, but I should be getting on to your market-place. The day's nearly half gone, and I've farther to go."

"What is it you're selling?" Giraan regretted the question as soon as the words crossed his lips. He would have preferred that this strange woman move on and leave them in peace. But he was curious about those overlarge baskets she carried, and he couldn't help but give voice to that curiosity.

She smiled again, and he thought he saw a flash of malice in her dark eyes. He knew what she was thinking. He and Aiva would buy something from her now, or at least agree to a trade. He'd asked the question. But more than that, he was still stinging from what she'd said earlier. They'd barter over price and he'd convince himself that he needed whatever she might be selling. But in the end, no matter how much he gave her, it would be the same as that silver slipped into a beggar's cup: a token of his pity, a way to assuage his guilt. For the truth was, as soon as he said that she was Mettai, he had cringed inwardly. Her infirmity. He would never have phrased it that way, but yes, that was just how he thought of it. Whatever Aiva might have said, being Y'Qatt was nothing like being Mettai.

He and his people chose to live as they did because they knew that in resisting the urge to use their powers, they were acceding to Qirsar's wishes. Their way of life honored the Qirsi god. The Mettai, on the other hand, were born to their fate. Some said that they were created by the Eandi god, Ean, to mock Qirsar. Here, Ean seemed to be saying, I give you Eandi sorcerers who are neither frail of body nor cursed with brief lives. Others claimed the opposite. Qirsar made them, these people said, to show Ean how his children might have been if only he'd been able to give them the gift of magic. Either way, the Mettai were mongrels, or worse, the bastard offspring of some rivalry between the gods. In a sense, they were the embodiment of the Blood Wars, the violent conflicts that had been fought throughout the history of the Southlands.

More to the point, though, they used blood magic, opening their veins for every act of sorcery. They were as different from the Y'Qatt as the darkest, coldest night of the Snows was from the bright warmth of this fine day.

"You'd like to see what I'm carrying?" the old woman asked, tilting her head to the side as might a mischievous child.

Aiva nodded, no doubt eager to end the unpleasantness. She hated it so when anyone failed to get along. "Yes, please."

"All right, then." The woman placed both baskets on the ground and stretched. Even without her burden, her back remained bent, her shoulders rounded.

Then she removed the blankets that covered the two baskets, and Giraan forgot everything else. The strange awkwardness that had made him wary of the stranger just moments before seemed to vanish, as if swept away by magic. Within the large baskets were smaller ones of all sizes, shapes, and colors. Basketry was the one craft for which the Mettai were renowned throughout the land, and clearly this woman had mastered the art as few others had.

"They're beautiful!" Aiva whispered.

The woman smiled and inclined her head. "Thank you, my lady."

"You made all of them yourself?"

"I did."

"There are so many. It must have taken you years."

"Several, yes."

Giraan looked at her. "Haven't you been selling them all along?"

"I promised myself that I would see as much of the land as possible before Bian called me to his side. So I made these baskets and set them aside from those I sold day to day. I trade these for food and gold, sometimes even for a night's sleep in a warm bed. As you can see, there are plenty here, and they're of good quality. And if need be, I can make more. Osiers are easy enough to find."

The smile remained on her tanned, wrinkled face, and she didn't shy away from his gaze. But something about what she was telling them struck Giraan as odd. Still, even if the woman was half mad, there could be no denying the worth of her wares.

Aiva had already chosen two baskets, one that was shallow and round, and another with steeper edges and a braided handle.

"You've chosen well, my lady," the woman said. "Those are two of my favorites."

She might have been strange, but clearly the woman had been peddling for a long time. She knew this craft as well.

"How much for the two of them?" Giraan asked, reverting to the tone he had used in his shop when negotiating the price of a new wheel for a cart, or the repair of a broken rim. "We don't have much gold."

"I don't need gold; only something else I can trade in another village." She nodded toward the beaver and stoat that he still carried. "I'd trade them for pelts if you have any."

"I'm afraid I don't."

"Food then. Salted meat? Cheese? A loaf or two of bread?"

"Baskets such as these would fetch a fair bit in the marketplace. I'm not sure that we can spare so much from our kitchen."

"I'm an old woman, sir. I don't eat much, and I'm not trying to grow fat and rich in my last years. As I've told you, I seek only enough so that I can continue my travels. Surely you and the lady would be able to part with one loaf of bread and half a wheel of cheese."

"You'd trade the baskets for so little?"

She frowned, seeming to consider this. "I don't suppose you have any wine as well?" She glanced at Aiva, the grin returning. "I might be old, but that doesn't mean I've forsaken all my old pleasures."

"Of course you haven't," Aiva said kindly. "But I'm afraid we have no wine. Perhaps some smoked fish. We've been preparing it for the colder turns, but we already have a good deal, and we've time to catch and smoke more."

Aiva looked at Giraan, a question in her eyes. He was reluctant to part with the fish, but he could see that she wanted the baskets, and she was right: They did have time before the end of the Harvest. They could catch more fish.

"Three whole fish," he said, facing the old woman. "In addition to the cheese and bread."

She nodded. "Done."

They stood in silence a moment, the woman eyeing him expectantly. Then he realized that Aiva was already holding the baskets she had chosen, and the stranger was waiting for her payment.

"Right," he said. "I'll get the food."

He turned, walked into the house, and quickly gathered the fish, cheese, and bread, wrapping them in an old cloth, as ragged as the woman's dress. When he stepped back outside, he heard Aiva speaking to the stranger. It took him only a moment to understand that his wife was trying to make conversation, and that the old woman was doing little to encourage her.

". . . with your family when you came here?"

"I believe so. I was very young."

"Do you remember how old you were?"

"No."

"But you remember the village. You said so. Is it so different now? Have we changed that much?"

At that the woman looked up, gazing first at Giraan, who had paused on the top step, and then at Aiva. "No," she said. "I don't think your people have changed at all."

She swung the carry sack off her shoulders and held out a thin, roughened hand for the food.

Giraan walked to where she stood and handed it to her.

"Thank you, sir," she said, placing the bundle carefully in her sack and shouldering the burden again. She looked briefly at Aiva. "My lady. I hope you find good use for the baskets."

With that, she started off into the village. She didn't so much as glance back at them.

"I'm glad to see her go," Giraan said.

Aiva nodded absently, admiring her new baskets. "She is odd. But she does fine work."

"I suppose."

She glanced at him. "Go find Sedi. Get your animals skinned and tanned. You'll feel better."

Giraan laughed. "You're right." He started for his friend's house. "I won't be long."

He walked slowly, having no desire to catch up with the old woman. He even stopped briefly by the wash, just to sit and watch the water flow by before continuing on his way. By the time he reached Sedi's home, at the west end of Runnelwick, he felt reasonably certain that the stranger had seen to her business in the marketplace and moved on.

Sedi glanced up from his work as Giraan entered the shop. An instant later, his eyes snapped up a second time, fixing on the two animals Giraan carried.

"I don't believe it!" he said, setting aside his work and standing. "Two already? And a stoat, no less!"

"Both in need of your skills, my friend."

The tanner shook his head, a smile on his thin face. "I should have known better than to make such a bargain with you, Giraan. I've known you for more than eight fours, and you've always managed to best me in everything."

"Not everything," Giraan said. "You've always been the better fisherman, and our garden never looks as fine as yours."

Sedi nodded, conceding the point. "Almost everything, then."

"You know that I'll gladly do whatever work your wagons ever need."

"Of course, and I'm happy to treat your skins."

Giraan handed him the rope on which he'd tied the animals.

"That's a good-sized beaver," Sedi said. "It should fetch a fair price when the next peddlers come through from the sovereignties."

"The sovereignties?"

"Yes. Wait for an Eandi. No matter how much a Qirsi peddler offers you, an Eandi will beat the price. Particularly if he's headed for Qosantia or Tordjanne."

Giraan knew immediately that this was sound advice. It made sense, really. Since the end of the Blood Wars, the Eandi nations bordering Qirsi lands—Stelpana and Naqbae—had remained hostile to anyone or anything having to do with the Qirsi, even outcasts like the Y'Qatt. The people of Aelea were much the same way. The wealthier nations of the lowlands, however, seemed more than happy to trade in Qirsi goods, and in fact, according to many of the peddlers who came through Runnelwick during the course of the year, they often sought out certain items from the Qirsi clans—baskets, blankets, the fine light wines of the H'Bel and the Talm'Orast. It shouldn't have surprised him that they would also covet the fine animal pelts found in the northern lands near the Companion Lakes.

"All right, then. Thanks for the advice," Giraan said.

Sedi grinned. "You sure you should trust me? We're competitors now."

Giraan had to laugh. "Hardly." He turned to leave the shop. "Thank you, my friend."

"My pleasure. I won't get to them today, and they'll need a few days to dry once I've done the work. Give me until the beginning of the waning."

"Of course." Giraan opened the door, but then paused on the threshold. After a moment he faced the tanner again. "Aiva and I had a strange encounter today. A Mettai woman along the road."

"The one peddling baskets?"

"You saw her, too."

Sedi shook his head, light from the doorway shining in his bright yellow eyes. "No. But I've heard others speaking of her. Of her baskets, to be more precise."

"What are they saying?"

The tanner shrugged. "That her baskets are the finest to be seen here in anyone's memory."

"But what about her?" Giraan demanded, his voice rising. "What are they saying about the woman?"

Sedi frowned. "I've heard nothing about her. Why?"

Giraan sighed, then took a long breath, trying to calm himself. Why, indeed? He wasn't sure himself. "Forgive me. I found the woman . . . odd. Disturbingly so. But I said something foolish when first I saw her, and it may just be that she didn't like me very much."

"What did you say?"

"It doesn't matter." Giraan forced a smile, embarrassed by the memory. "Forget that I mentioned it." He left Sedi's shop, intending to walk back home. Instead, not quite knowing why, he turned and walked to the marketplace, scanning the stalls, peddlers' carts, and byways for the old woman. He didn't see her, but he soon realized that her baskets were everywhere. Or rather, not everywhere, but present in numbers enough to be noticeable. Several of his fellow villagers had already purchased their own, and a number of sellers had traded for others and were peddling them along with their wares.

Wherever she was now, the old woman's purse had to be bulging with Runnelwick's gold. Giraan wasn't certain why this disturbed him so, or why he should begrudge the stranger her success. What was the old woman to him? Yes, she was strange, not to mention rude. But even he could see that her baskets were lovely. No wonder so many of his neighbors wanted them. Hadn't Aiva herself traded for two of them? After some time he shook his head and turned for home. This was too fine a day to waste brooding over a strange old Mettai witch.

Giraan and Aiva ate a modest supper of smoked fish, black bread, and steamed greens. They had their meal outside, on the steps of the house, where they could enjoy the cool evening air. Still, throughout the meal, despite his best efforts, Giraan could think of little besides his encounter with the Mettai woman. And each time he relived their conversation, the memory of it grew darker, until he began to wonder if he should burn the baskets she had given them and run through the village shouting for his neighbors and friends to do the same. He tried to laugh off his fears, but they clung stubbornly to his mind, souring his mood.

So it was that he didn't notice how quiet Aiva had been during the evening until she actually said something.

"I don't feel well."

He looked at her. "What?"

She'd barely touched her food, and her face looked pale in the shadows of the cedars and hemlocks growing beside the house.

"I feel ill. My stomach."

"Maybe you're hungry. You haven't—"

"No, that's not it."

He held the back of his hand to her brow. "You're burning up!"

"Damn," she whispered. She stood abruptly, spilling the plate that had been resting on her lap, and ran around to the side of the house. Giraan heard her vomit.

He put his plate aside and followed her. His hands were trembling; was it a response to hearing her be sick, or was he starting to feel ill as well?

"Maybe I didn't smoke the fish enough," he said.

She shook her head. "You said I was feverish."

"That damned woman brought the pestilence. She'll be the death of us all."

"Don't be a fool, Giraan," she said through clenched teeth, breathing hard. "She wasn't sick at all. A woman that old. She wouldn't have been able to walk."

She spun away and retched again.

"Should I get the healer?"

Aiva nodded, her back still to him.

He strode away, making his way quickly toward old Besse's home, west of the marketplace. Was that ache in the pit of his stomach fear or illness?

The walk seemed to take ages, but at last he came within sight of the small cottage. The healer's door was open and a thin, curving line of blue-grey smoke rose from her chimney, but Giraan saw no sign of Besse herself.

He stopped a short distance from the house. "Healer?" he called.

After a few seconds, she emerged from the house, straight-backed and alert, in spite of the deep lines on her face.

"That you, Giraan?"

"Yes. Aiva's sick. I think . . . I don't know . . . It might be the pestilence."

She nodded once. "I'll come with you. Just let me get my herbs."

Besse disappeared into the house.

Giraan took a deep breath and closed his eyes briefly. If anyone could help Aiva, it was the old healer. She'd been caring for the people of

Runnelwick since before Giraan had finished his fourth four. Always she had put the needs of the village ahead of her own. She had never been joined to anyone, though he knew there had been men in her life. She'd never had children of her own, though she'd been there for nearly every birth in the village for the last twenty years. Even now, hearing Giraan say that the pestilence might have come to his home, she didn't hesitate to follow him to Aiva's side.

She stepped out of the house and bounded down the stairs as if she were closer to five fours than ten. Giraan actually had to hurry to catch up to her as she strode up the path toward his house. As he did, he noticed that she bore her herbs and oils in a new basket. His heart sank.

"What are her symptoms?" Besse asked, whatever fear she might have felt masked by the crispness of her voice.

"She's vomiting and she's burning with fever."

Besse nodded once. "And you? Are you feeling ill, too?"

He was. His stomach was churning and he could almost feel the bile rising in his throat. But was he imagining it all? "I don't know," he finally said.

Giraan had expected that she'd think him a fool, or worse, a coward. But she merely patted his arm and nodded again. "I know," she said. "Our minds do strange things at times like these." Then, almost as an afterthought, she raised her hand to his brow. Immediately, she frowned. "You're warm. Hot really."

He felt his innards turn to water. It seemed he really was a coward. For all his concern about Aiva, it was the prospect of his own death that brought panic.

"I'll come see Aiva, but then I have to leave you. The elders need to be told."

"Yes, of course," he whispered. His eyes flicked to her basket, and he almost said something about the old Mettai woman. But she would probably think him foolish, just as Aiva had.

"It might be something else, Giraan. I'm not certain yet that it's the pestilence. But even the possibility . . ." She exhaled. "You understand."

He nodded, fighting to keep from being ill right there on the path.

They walked the rest of the way in silence. By the time they reached Giraan's house it was growing dark. A faint light shone from within the house, and the door still stood open, but there was no other sign of life.

They hurried up the stairs, and found Aiva lying in bed, her face damp with sweat, her eyes half closed. A single candle burned on the small table beside her.

Besse sat on the edge of the bed and laid a hand on her brow. After a moment, she leaned closer and looked at her eyes.

"How are you feeling, Aiva?" she asked.

"Great," Aiva said weakly. "You?"

Besse grinned briefly. "Good for you. I deserved that."

Aiva squeezed her eyes shut and grimaced. "It's getting worse."

"What is?"

"The pain."

"In your stomach?"

She shook her head slightly, her eyes still closed. "No. My head. My head is hurting."

Besse frowned. "Your head?"

Aiva pulled a trembling hand free from the blanket, and raised it to her temple. "Right here. And the other side, too."

"What does that mean?" Giraan asked.

Besse didn't even look at him. "I don't know."

She lifted the blankets off of Aiva and began to examine her limbs. "Light another candle," she said. "I want to see if I can find evidence of a bite."

"A bite?"

"The pestilence comes from vermin, and it often begins with a flea bite." After several moments she shook her head. "But I don't see anything."

"Maybe she caught it from someone else."

"No one else in the village is ill."

"Maybe it wasn't someone in the village."

"Oh, Giraan," Aiva said. "Not this again."

"What?" Besse demanded, looking from one of them to the other.

"That Mettai woman," Giraan said. "The one who made the basket you're carrying. I . . . I think she brought the pestilence to Runnelwick."

"Impossible," Besse told him. "A woman that old wouldn't have been able to walk had she been as sick as Aiva. And you can't pass the pestilence to anyone until you have it yourself."

Giraan knew that she was right. She had to be. Besse knew far more about these matters than anyone else in the village. But still, he couldn't let go of his suspicions. He fully intended to argue the point further. But in that moment, he felt his gut spasm. He stood and lurched to the door, just barely making it outside before emptying his stomach.

He leaned on the railing of his small porch, retching until his body was sore. Eventually, as the spasms passed, he realized that Besse was with him, steadying him.

"Come on," she said. "You need to lie down."

She led him back into the house and soon had him lying beside Aiva, cold, damp cloths on both of their brows. "I need to speak with the elders," she said, "but I'll send for Oren."

"No!" Aiva said. Giraan felt how her body tensed, but she could barely manage more than an airy whisper. "I don't want him coming near us."

"He's grown now," Besse said. "I'll leave that choice to him."

Before Aiva could argue more, the healer had gone.

"He'll come," Aiva whispered. "If she tells him to, he'll come. That's the kind of boy he is."

"He's not a boy anymore. He'll have a child of his own before long."

"All the more reason to keep him away from here."

"So he should let us die alone?"

"Of course, if that's the choice."

Giraan knew that he should have been thinking the same thing. Again, he wondered at his own cowardice, his willingness to save himself at the expense of those he supposedly loved.

"You're right," he said, hot tears running down into his white hair. "Forgive me."

She took his hand.

He could feel the pain building in his temples now, just as Aiva had described. *I'm dying*, he told himself. *In these last hours, I must make peace with that.* He heard Aiva's breathing slow, felt her grip slacken. She had fallen asleep. He wondered if she'd ever wake again. He almost woke her then. Perhaps sleep would hasten death's advance. Perhaps he was merely afraid to be alone.

He must have fallen asleep himself, for the next thing he knew, Oren was there, sitting beside him on the bed, trying to spoon hot broth into his mouth. Giraan tried to swallow one mouthful, but as soon as the liquid hit his stomach, it started back up again. He turned his head and retched onto the floor. After a moment he settled back onto his pillow.

"I'm sorry," he said. He could barely hear his own voice.

"It's all right," Oren told him. "Mama couldn't keep it down either. My cooking isn't as good as hers." He tried to smile, but there were tears on his cheeks. "Seslanne has it, too."

"You should be with her," Aiva said.

"I have been. Her mother and father are there now. But I wanted to see you."

"Did she see the Mettai woman?" Giraan asked, his heart laboring.

Oren narrowed his pale eyes. "What?"

"Seslanne. Did she buy a basket from a Mettai woman today?"

"No. Well, she bought a basket, but from one of the peddlers in the marketplace. She said nothing about a Mettai woman. Why?"

Giraan opened his mouth to explain, but at that moment Aiva went rigid beside him. For a moment Giraan thought she was going to be sick again. But she didn't so much as move.

"Oren, you must leave at once!" she said, her teeth clenched.

"But, Mama—"

"Leave! Now! I beg you!"

"Aiva—" Giraan began. But in that instant he felt it, too.

It had been so long since he'd even reached for his magic, since it had occurred to him to wonder how powerful he was, or even to think of himself as a sorcerer. He was Y'Qatt. As a boy, of course, he had dreamed of wielding his magic in battle or perhaps using it to save the village from brigands. No doubt all children did, including those in an Y'Qatt village. But he hadn't yet come into his powers then—he hadn't known that he was a shaper, that he could bend matter to his will, or that he could call to the wild creatures of the wood with language of beasts. Once he was old enough to understand what it was to be Y'Qatt, he had put such notions out of his mind. The urge to use his magic had left him years ago.

Or so he had thought. For suddenly, he felt power building inside of him, like floodwaters gathering behind an earthen dam. He tried to resist. Qirsar knew he did. He had spent years disciplining himself, refusing to give in to the temptation to use his powers. But that had been a matter of choice, of denying himself the luxury of laziness. This was something else entirely, like holding one's breath until the urge to breathe overmastered one's will. He struggled against it, but he knew from the start that he would fail in the end. It was too much; there seemed to be a greater force at work, as if the god had chosen to punish him for a lifetime of abnegation.

"She's right, Oren!" he managed to say. "You must leave! Now!"

"But, Papa—"

"You feel it, too?" Aiva asked. He could hear the strain in her voice.

"Yes. I can't fight it much longer."

"Fight what?" Oren asked, gaping at both of them, looking so terribly young.

Before Giraan could answer, a wind began to rise, making the candle flames dance and rattling the chairs and tables. Aiva's wind. That was one of her powers: mists and winds. And fire.

"Leave now!" Giraan shouted, though it took all his strength to make himself heard over what was fast becoming a gale. And in making that effort, he felt his control over the storm of magic raging within him waver. It was only for an instant, but that was enough. He heard the rending of wood as if it were thunder, and he saw a crack open in the roof of his home.

Aiva's wind keened like a wild beast, extinguishing the candles, so that the only light in the house came from Panya, the pale moon, whose glow filtered through the trees.

Oren was on his feet, his eyes wide with fear, but still he wouldn't leave. "What's happening?" he cried. "I don't understand!"

"The fever is attacking our magic," Giraan said. Again his grip on the power failed. It was all he could do to direct the magic at the table by the bed and not at his son. The table crumbled as if hammered by some unseen demon. "We can't control it!"

"My god!" Oren whispered. "Seslanne!" He backed toward the door. "I'm sorry . . ."

"Don't apologize!" Aiva told him. "Go to her!"

Giraan tried to pour out the magic inside him by calling upon his other power, knowing that he could do no further damage to the house with language of beasts. But he hadn't the control. He knew that he was speaking gibberish to the wild creatures in the woods around Runnelwick, but still shaping power coursed through his body. So he wasn't at all surprised when the ball of fire flew from Aiva's side of the bed and crashed against the opposite wall. Immediately, flames started to climb the wood, licking at the ceiling and filling the room with thick smoke. Between her fire and winds and his shaping, their home would soon be a pile of charred ruins.

"We have to get out of here!" he said, taking her hand.

"What's the use?" she said, coughing.

"Maybe Besse can find a way to help us."

"Besse will be sick before long."

Rather than argue the point further, he pulled her out of the bed and toward the doorway. More power slipped out, but he managed to direct it. He heard the ceiling above the bed groan and collapse. Another fireball crashed into the floor near them. The wind howled at their backs. They made it outside, though not before both of them had been singed. Aiva fell to the ground, gasping for breath, and Giraan dropped to his knees beside her.

He could feel his power spilling over and it was all he could do to keep directing his shaping magic at something other than himself or Aiva. All around him tree limbs were shattering, splinters of wood floating down like snow. He could hear birds crying out. Wolves howled in the distance. Fire shot into the sky from Aiva's hands and still the wind blew, buffeting the trees. Looking toward the marketplace, Giraan saw that the sky was aglow with fire magic. Voices cried out in pain or fear or both.

"How many are sick?" he whispered.

"Giraan."

He crawled to Aiva's side. Her eyes were fixed on the sky above her, but he wasn't sure that she could see anything.

"I can't stop it," she said. "I'm so tired, but I can't stop. It's like I'm bleeding."

He couldn't either. The dam had broken. Trying to stop the flow of power now would be like standing in the center of Silverwater Wash at the height of the thaw, and trying to hold back the waters with his hands. His shaping magic still battered the trees and the remains of his home, but he could feel it weakening. The fire rising from his beloved was dimming; her wind had slackened.

"Aiva, no! Fight it!"

"I don't know how, Giraan! Do you? Can't you help me?"

She sounded so frightened, so weak, so far away. Clenching his fists, feeling tears on his cheeks, the wheelwright looked up at the fiery orange sky and roared in his anguish. Because he didn't know how. He couldn't stop his own magic from flowing, much less hers. He couldn't stop any of it. It seemed that his entire village was at war with a foe they couldn't see or understand. He could hear it so clearly now: the screams and the rending of wood; the sounds of a town under siege. His nostrils stung with the smoke of a hundred fires. And he could do nothing but kneel there watching the light in Aiva's eyes die away. After years of holding his magic inside, he could feel it lashing out at his home, at his trees, at the earth beneath him. But it was of no use to him in this fight.

He saw Aiva's lips moving. *Giraan.* She was saying his name, but she hadn't the strength to make herself heard.

"Yes, my love. I'm here." But even as he said it, he felt himself fall onto his side. He was too weak to kneel anymore. V'Tol. Magic. Life. It was leaving him. He was nothing but an empty vessel, a husk.

"Why, Qirsar? Wasn't it your will that we live thus? Did we fail you in some way?"

But no answer came. Just the cries from the village marketplace, and that baleful orange glow flickering above the trees.

She sat on a small rise overlooking the river, gazing northward, her hands working the rushes into place. Occasionally she reached for her blade to thin a strand or cut off a frayed end. But she never looked away. She didn't have to, not with hands as deft and sure as hers. She'd been weaving baskets for more years than she cared to count. She knew her craft. Just as she knew magic.

From her perch above the gently flowing waters, she could see and hear her spell at work. Let the Qirsi dismiss Mettai blood magic as a lesser power. Let the Eandi—her own people—make outcasts of the Mettai. Lici knew just how potent her magic could be.

Now the people of Runnelwick knew it as well. Their cries floated up to her. The glow of their fires danced in the night sky. The forest swayed with their winds and shuddered with the power of their shaping magic. All because Lici had decided that it should be so. They were her puppets, her playthings. She could make them do anything she wanted.

She lifted a hand. "Look," she whispered to the night. "No strings." Then she laughed.

Her cart horse stamped and shook her head. Lici had left the cart outside the village, venturing into its lanes on foot. That way they'd think her poor, they'd buy her baskets out of pity, out of desire to do good. That was what she had decided, and she'd been right. They were as stupid as they were weak, and now, because of this, they were suffering the fate their kind had earned so long ago.

She was but a feeble, old woman—a Mettai, no less—and she had done this to an entire village of Y'Qatt. One small cut on her hand. One among so many. Yes, let them laugh at blood magic. Soon enough every Y'Qatt in the Southlands would be trembling.

Chapter 3

Kirayde

It began as a rumor passed among the children of the village. They spoke of it in hushed tones during their lessons in the small sanctuary at the north end of the marketplace; they conjured wild explanations for it as they walked together back to their homes. Before long their parents heard the whispers as well, and though the men and women of Kirayde might normally have frowned upon such gossip, in this case the tale told by their sons and daughters was so extraordinary that they couldn't resist.

Old Lici was gone.

Nobody could say with any certainty on what day she left the village. Such was the nature of the woman and her standing in Kirayde. Sometimes, even when she hadn't gone away, Besh went for ten or twelve days without seeing her. At other times it seemed that she was dogging his every step, so often did he cross her path. No doubt it was the same for the others in the village. He preferred to ignore and avoid her, and yet in a settlement so small that was not always his choice to make.

For his part, Besh heard of the old witch's disappearance only a few days after speaking of her with Mihas. He was working in his garden again, waiting for his grandson to meet him there after his lessons with the prior. Usually the boy could hardly draw breath for all the things he wished to tell Besh about what he had learned and what games he and his friends had played in between lessons, and this day was no different. Except, the old man soon realized, nothing that the boy was saying had anything to do with lessons or games or the other children.

"Slow down a moment, Mihas," he said at last, holding up a dirty hand to silence the boy and settling back on his heels. "What is it you're talking about?"

"Her house!" the boy said. "It's just empty!"

"Whose house?"

"Old Lici's!" he said, as if Besh were the most foolish man on Elined's earth.

"What were you doing at her house?"

"I told you, it wasn't me. It was Keff and Vad."

"And they are?"

Mihas rolled his eyes. "Nissa's brothers, the two oldest ones."

Besh considered this for a moment. "She's gone, you say?"

"Yes! Her horse and cart are gone, too. No one's seen her in days."

"How many days?"

The boy shrugged. "I don't know. A lot."

"She's left before, you know. There was a time when she'd go to other villages to sell her baskets. Sometimes she'd be gone for more than half a turn."

The boy frowned, his excitement dampened for the moment. "I didn't know that," he said.

And with good reason. She hadn't done it for many years, since well before Mihas was born. In truth, it struck Besh as odd that she'd leave her hut at all. He'd never thought that he would see the day when she left the village for any length of time. It wasn't that she was bound to Kirayde or any of its people—aside from Sylpa, long dead and buried, Lici had no real friends, and of course, she'd lost her family before coming to the village. But had she wanted to leave, she would have done so long ago. Instead, she'd made a point of remaining, of enduring the taunts of children and the silence of their parents, of staying right here, just where she knew she wasn't wanted. Besh had assumed that she would die here, if for no other reason than to burden those who would have to dig her grave.

On the other hand, he'd heard of old men and women from other Mettai villages simply going off into the wilderness to die when they thought that their time had come. As far as Besh knew, that had never been common practice here in Kirayde, but perhaps it had been in whatever village she'd come from.

He shook his head slowly. He couldn't imagine Lici doing anything so . . . quiet. For years he had expected that when her time finally did come, the entire village would know about it.

"What is it, Grandfather?"

He looked at Mihas. "Nothing. I'm just not ready to assume that Lici is gone for good. Not after only a few days."

"Keff and Vad are. They think that her hut is filled with gold and silver from all the baskets she used to make. They're talking about going there when both moons are full and searching for it."

"Are they?" Besh said. "Well, you tell them that if anyone—anyone at all—takes even one grain of river sand from Lici's hut, I'll hold the two of them responsible."

"But, Grandfather, if I say all that to them, they'll think that I told you everything!"

"You did tell me," he said mildly.

"Yes, but . . ." The boy shook his head. "Never mind." He started to walk away.

"Mihas."

The boy faced him again, looking sullen.

"If somehow those boys don't get my message, I'll hold you responsible. Do you understand?"

"Yes, Grandfather."

Besh chuckled as he watched the lad go. Next time, Mihas would think twice before relating to him all that he and his friends said. That was regrettable, but this was too important. Even if Lici had left the village for good, it was not the place of two boys to root through her belongings.

Over the next several days, the old man began to listen more closely to the tales bandied about in the village, hoping that he might hear something that would help him make sense of Lici's disappearance. But with each day that went by, the stories about her grew ever more wild. A man from her past, perhaps that Eandi merchant who had once tried so hard to win her affections, had returned one night and taken her away. Lici herself had used magic to shed the burdens of old age, transforming herself into a beautiful young woman who then ran off to find a new life in some other village. Sylpa, her old mentor, had returned from Bian's realm and had turned Lici into a wraith so that together they might haunt the woods surrounding Kirayde. One man, who was nearly as old as Lici, swore that he'd seen her in the forest late one night, running with a pack of wolves.

Half a turn went by, and still she did not return. Gradually the power of Besh's threat faded, and the older children began once more to eye the old witch's house, wondering what riches were hidden within. At Besh's urging, the village elders had a guard placed at the house day and night. Several of the men living in the village took turns at this, including Sirj, Elica's husband. But even this precaution, though extraordinary in such a small village, did little to ease the growing tension. If anything, it made matters worse, by drawing attention to the fact that Lici had gone, leaving a house filled with who knew what. Soon it wasn't just the children who were expressing eagerness to get inside.

"She's not coming back," Geovri, the wheelwright, was heard to say again and again.

Lerris, an older man, almost as old as Besh himself, was said to agree with the wheelwright. "She might well be dead by now. If she left gold in there it ought to be ours. All of ours," he was always quick to add. "It should be divided among all the families in Kirayde."

By the end of the Dreaming Moon's waxing, the village elders found themselves with little choice but to do something.

They met just before sundown on the last day of the waxing. Both moons would be full this night; only half a turn remained until the rise of the Reaping Moon and the beginning of the Harvest. This year's crops looked healthy; Besh was certain that his people had no cause to fear a bad Harvest. But this was always an anxious time in the village. The colder turns in the highlands could be harsh and a poor Harvest might mean lean, perhaps even desperate times when the Snows began. The clamor for Lici's supposed riches would only get worse. Walking past the marketplace on his way to the sanctuary, where the elders usually met, Besh couldn't help thinking it odd that a woman like Lici, who throughout her life had shunned the company of others and had been shunned in turn, should cause such a stir simply by leaving.

The elders had decided to meet in closed session, fearing that an open discussion attended by all in the village might turn ugly. As it was, a crowd had already gathered outside the sanctuary when Besh arrived, and though most of those milling about in the lane seemed more curious than angry, he was troubled by their presence.

"We know you'll do the right thing, Besh," someone called as he climbed the steps to the oaken doors.

Several others murmured their agreement.

He knew that he should let the remark pass—perhaps as a younger man he would have. But as he had lost his hair and his strength, he had also lost his ability to suffer fools.

"And what is the right thing?" he asked, turning to face them. "Do you mean the right thing for you, or for Lici?"

"But she's gone."

"Yes, Geovri, she's gone. I seem to remember that you ventured west last year to trade blankets to the Fal'Borna. You were gone more than a turn. Should we have divided up the goods in your house while you were gone?"

"That's different! I left Kisa here. And the children."

"So that's what gives you the right to take Lici's things? The fact that she wasn't blessed with a fine family as you were?"

"No, that's not . . ." He frowned. "That's not what I meant," he muttered.

"Remember," Besh said, raising his voice and looking at all of them. "Whatever we decide to do with Lici's things can one day be done with yours as well. What we do as a community we do to the community."

Silence. He turned once more and pulled open one of the double doors.

"She was a curse on this village from the moment she arrived here," someone shouted at his back, someone who sounded far too young to have known anything of her arrival.

Besh ignored the comment and entered the building.

The others were waiting for him in the main chamber, their chairs arranged in a tight circle beneath the small stained-glass window at the far end.

Pyav, the head of their council—eldest of the village, as he was called—turned in his chair and raised a meaty hand in greeting. He was a big man, a blacksmith. His shoulders and chest were broad, his arms and neck as thick as Besh's thighs. But for all his brawn, he had the temperament of a cleric. He spoke softly, even when angry, and while he might not have been the most learned man in Kirayde, he might well have been the wisest.

"We heard you talking to them," he said, as Besh took his seat.

"It was foolish of me. I should have ignored them."

"Perhaps," the blacksmith said, grinning. "If for no other reason than to leave us in suspense as to how you might vote on the matter."

A few of the others laughed, but not all. This would be a difficult discussion, even without the rest of the villagers awaiting their decision.

Tashya, the youngest in their circle, fixed him with a hard glare. "You think she's coming back."

Besh gave a small shrug. "I don't know. That, I believe, is the point. None of us knows."

He expected an argument, but she merely nodded. She was in her eleventh four, her second as a widow. Her husband died of a fever soon after the birth of their seventh child, and though the years since had been trying for her, she remained beautiful, with glossy raven black hair and pale green eyes. Many men in Kirayde had hoped that she would choose to marry again after a suitable time of grieving, Besh among them. But she had made it clear to all that she neither needed nor wanted another man in her life.

She could be stubborn at times and she had a fiery temper, but most in the village admired her strength. That was why they had chosen her as an elder at such a tender age.

"Where do you think she's gone then?" she asked after a brief silence.

Besh wasn't certain how he had become the village authority on Old Lici, but they were all watching him, awaiting his answer. It really had been a mistake to say anything to the crowd.

"I don't know. It had occurred to me to wonder if she might have gone off to die. But that doesn't sound like Lici to me."

"Nor to me," Tashya said. "It's more likely that she's moved on and is making mischief for others. Which, as far as I'm concerned, means that she's no longer our problem."

Pyav grinned again. "The fact that we're here would seem to belie that last statement."

Tashya gave him a sour look, but said nothing.

Marivasse, the old herbmistress, looked at Besh, and then at the eldest. "Why does it matter where she's gone?" she asked. "We don't meet to discuss the comings and goings of others who live in the village. Nor do we find ourselves forced to post guards at their houses. Lici should be no different from the rest of us."

"But she is different," Pyav said gently. "She has no family. More to the point—and may the gods forgive me for saying this—she has no friends. If something has happened to her, if she's not coming back, then it falls to us to take care of her belongings and her home. That's why we're here."

"There's more to it than that, my friend," Besh said. "You know it as well as I. That crowd outside has heard rumors of Lici's wealth. All of us have. Even if everything else about her was the same, take away the belief that she's hidden her riches away in that house of hers, and we'd all be home, preparing our evening meals."

Pyav smiled wanly. "I suppose. But even with that, if she had family it would be none of our affair." He raised his eyebrows. "Unfortunately, that blade is double-edged. She has no family or friends, so we have to take responsibility in her absence, but since there's no one who can tell us why she's gone, we don't know what her absence means."

Tashya nodded. "Then it falls to us to decide exactly that." She glared at all of them, as if challenging them to disagree.

"That may well be true," Besh said evenly. "But we have to err on the side of caution or else every time future elders decide as we have, using what we do here as justification, our children's children will curse us for our haste."

She appeared to consider this, and when at last she asked "How long do you think we should wait?" there was no hint of ire or mockery in her tone.

"I don't know."

"She's been gone for more than a turn," said one of the others. "She left her garden plot untended. It won't be long before all her crops are lost."

Tashya looked around the table. "So do we wait until the rise of the Reaping Moon?"

"That's half a turn," Besh said, shaking his head. "That seems awfully soon."

"By that time she'll have been gone for nearly two turns. At her age, that's an eternity."

Pyav pressed his fingertips together. "Has she ever been gone for this long before?"

"When she was a younger woman," Marivasse said. "She used to go on journeys with Sylpa. They'd go to the shores of the Ofirean Sea, even as far as the Qosantian Lowlands. It wasn't unusual for them to be gone for an entire season."

"What about since Sylpa died?"

"She never went as far after that. But still, she'd go to trade with the Fal'Borna or the people of Aelea."

"And yet," Besh said, "even that's more than she's done over the past ten years."

Marivasse turned to face him. "True. But isn't it possible that in her last years, she seeks to return to some of the places she visited in her youth? The only times I knew her to be happy were those she shared with Sylpa. Couldn't it be that she's gone back to the sea or even to Qosantia?"

"The question isn't so much where she's gone," Tashya said, sounding impatient once more. "Will she return? That's what I want to know. And if she's gone that far, I'd have to say that I doubt it. I think it's also possible that we could learn more about her intentions by searching her hut. Perhaps if we knew what she took with her, we'd have a better sense of when and if she plans to return."

Pyav nodded slowly. "That seems a fair point."

Even the notion of a simple search of her home made Besh uncomfortable, but if Pyav supported the idea, the rest would as well. There seemed little point in arguing against it.

"So who would do this?" he asked instead.

"You," Tashya said, without hesitation.

"Me?"

She smiled. "Given your scruples with regard to this whole matter, there's no one I'd trust more."

The eldest nodded and grinned. "I'm inclined to agree."

"So am I," Marivasse said.

In the end, the choice was unanimous, but only because they wouldn't let Besh vote. He had no desire to get anywhere near Old Lici's house. Not only did he disapprove of what they were having him do, he still wanted nothing to do with the woman, even after all these years, even though she was probably a hundred leagues away, or dead. Especially because she might be dead.

Besh rubbed a hand over his face, wishing he were digging in his garden, or smoking his pipe on that old stump, or fishing along the banks of the wash. "How soon do you want me to do this?"

"Those people outside want us to do something," Tashya said. "Anything. We shouldn't make them wait long."

"Tomorrow," Pyav told him. "I'll come with you if you'd like. I have a couple of jobs to finish at the forge, but I should be ready before the morning's out. Come by and we'll walk over together."

Besh smiled. "Thank you, Eldest. That would make this . . . easier."

The blacksmith stood, and the rest did as well. "I thank all of you for coming on such short notice," he said. "Besh and I will let you know what we find."

They made their way out of the sanctuary, but stopped at the top of the stairs. The crowd was still there, expectant looks on their faces.

"What about it then, Eldest?" asked a fair-haired man in front. Besh thought he recognized him as the father of one of Mihas's friends.

"Besh and I will search Lici's house in the morning."

"Search it?" the man said with a frown. "Why?"

"To see if she left behind anything that might tell us where she's gone or when she intends to return."

"What about her gold?"

"We don't know that there is any gold."

Others started to protest, but Pyav raised both hands, quieting them. "Please, my friends. This is a beginning. We don't know for certain that there is any gold, and we certainly can't simply assume that, if there is, it's ours to do with as we please. She may be on her way back here as we speak. Doesn't she deserve to find her home just as she left it?"

"She's an old witch!" someone else called out. "We'd be better off without her!"

The eldest narrowed his eyes slightly. "All right, let me put it this way. If she does return, which of you wants to explain to her that we took all her possessions for our own?"

That silenced them. Besh struggled to keep the smirk from his lips.

Pyav nodded. "That's what I thought. As I told the other elders a moment ago, we'll let you know what we find."

With that, the blacksmith started down the stairs. The crowd parted to make way for him, and Besh and the others followed in his wake.

"That was well done, my friend," Besh said under his breath.

The eldest nodded, but he looked troubled. "It put them in their places for this evening, but that won't last long. Let's hope that tomorrow's search turns up something definitive one way or another."

The eldest walked off toward his home, and after a moment the rest of the elders did the same, leaving the villagers whispering among themselves. Besh tried to take some satisfaction in the way the eldest had silenced the crowd, but Pyav's words to him still echoed ominously in his mind.

It was nearly dark when he reached the house, and as he wearily climbed the old wooden stairway, the smell of roasted fowl reached him, reminding Besh that he was famished.

They'd started without him, which was just as it should be; he'd told Elica that the children shouldn't go hungry because of all the foolishness surrounding Old Lici. The younger ones had been giggling about something as he climbed the stairs, but as soon as they saw him in the doorway, they fell silent. Actually all of them did. They just stared at him, as if they thought he might have brought Lici with him.

"I'm sorry I'm late," Besh said, taking his place at the table beside Mihas.

Sirj nodded. "It's all right."

No doubt they were bursting with questions for him, but no one said anything as he helped himself to some meat, greens, and bread.

Finally, Cam, the youngest, looked at his grandfather with wide eyes, and asked, "Did you find her?"

Besh couldn't keep from laughing. "Find her? You mean Lici?"

The boy nodded, but by now the others were laughing as well, and his face began to redden.

"No, Cam," Besh said. "We didn't expect to find her. We don't know where she's gone. We were trying to decide what to do with her house and her belongings."

"And what did you decide?" Elica asked.

The younger ones were laughing still, but Elica and Sirj were watching him closely, as was Mihas.

"Pyav and I will search her house in the morning, just to see if we can find something that will tell us why she left."

"Can I come, Grandfather?" Mihas asked.

He shook his head. "No, Mihas. This is no game, nor is it a hunt for hidden treasure. The eldest and I will be the only ones to enter Lici's home."

The boy looked disappointed, but he nodded and said nothing more.

"And her belongings?" Elica asked.

"Are still hers. Until we know for certain that she's not coming back, nothing will be done with her things."

"Good," Sirj muttered.

"Good?" Besh repeated, turning his way.

The man's face colored, just as his son's had a few moments before. Besh wondered if he'd meant to say it aloud.

Sirj took a breath. "Yes, good. I think all this talk about Old Lici's gold has gone on for too long already. You'd think the rest of them were starving, the way they look toward her little hut. It's all nonsense, if you ask me."

"But, Papa," Mihas said. "If she has half as much as they say she does—"

"It's none of our business how much she has. And even if she has more than the five Sovereigns of the Southlands put together, none of us has any claim to a single coin." He looked at Besh. "Forgive me for saying so, but if it comes to it, and the elders have to do something with her home, whatever gold there is should be used for something the whole village needs. A new well, maybe, or repairs to the lane north of the marketplace."

Besh wasn't certain what to say. None of the elders had thought of this, and yet he knew that Sirj had hit upon the perfect solution to their problem. It occurred to him that he had thought the man an idiot for so long that he'd never stopped to consider the possibility that there was a reason Elica had fallen in love with him.

"I guess that makes no sense, does it?" Sirj said, misinterpreting Besh's silence.

"Actually . . ." Besh shifted in his chair. He could feel Elica's eyes on him. "Actually, I was just thinking that it makes a great deal of sense. I'll suggest it the next time the elders meet."

Sirj stared at him briefly, perhaps searching for some sign that Besh was mocking him. Seeing none, he nodded again. "My thanks."

"What do you think you'll find in her hut?" Elica asked after some time.

"I couldn't say," Besh told her. "Probably little of any consequence. But we have nothing else, and the people in this village want us to do something, even if they don't know what." He took a bite of bread.

"There was a crowd outside the sanctuary this evening, waiting to hear what we'd decided."

Elica's eyes widened a bit. "A crowd? How many?"

"At least fifty. Pyav handled them well, but I only remember crowds gathering outside our meetings like that three or four times—usually in times of flood, and once when the pestilence came to Irikston."

"Do they know what you and Pyav intend to do?" Sirj asked.

"We told them, yes."

"Then they'll be there, too. At Lici's house."

Besh knew immediately that he was right about this as well. "What would you do in our position?" he asked, surprising himself as much as Sirj. Well, he thought, grinning inwardly at what he saw on the younger man's face, perhaps not quite as much.

"I don't know," Sirj said quickly. "I didn't mean—"

"I know you didn't," Besh said. "I was asking for your advice. You seem to understand all of this better than I do."

"I doubt that." He ran a hand through his dark hair. "I don't know what I'd do." He glanced at the younger children, who were deep into their own conversation now. "Truth is," he went on, his voice low, "I've been terrified of Lici since I was old enough to walk."

"All of us have been," Elica put in. "I think she wanted it that way."

"I'm not afraid of her," Mihas said, sounding so terribly young. "Neither are Keff and Vad."

Elica glared at him. "Then you're fools. Now, if you've finished your supper go fetch some water."

He stood up slowly. "Yes, Mama."

"Two buckets, Mihas. One for the dishes, and one for you and the young ones."

"But, Mama—"

The expression on Elica's face would have frightened Lici herself. The boy wisely fell silent and did as he was told.

Besh finished his meal while Elica and Sirj cleared the rest of the dishes from the table. When he'd finished, he took his pipe outside and smoked a bit while he watched stars emerge in the night sky. After a time he heard footsteps behind him and felt Elica lay a hand on his shoulder.

"Do you remember some time ago when we last talked about Lici?"

she said, her voice barely more than a whisper. "It's been nearly a turn now. I said that she'd be dead soon."

"I remember," he told her. "I also remember saying myself that maybe her death would be for the best."

"Do you think that . . . that maybe the gods heard us?"

"If the gods heeded what I said to them on matters of life and death, your mother would be sitting by my side." He looked up at her and reached for her hand. "Whatever has become of Lici, it had nothing to do with us. Unless you conjured something without telling me."

She smiled and shook her head, glancing up at the stars. "No." She kissed his cheek. "Good night, Father."

"Good night."

He sat a while longer, waiting for the owl to call. It often did this time of year, usually from up in the hills, its voice carrying down through the village.

"Where are you, Lici," Besh whispered. "Maybe I'm a fool, but I think that if you were dead, I'd know it. So where are you? What is it you're up to?"

He heard no answer, of course, save for a few crickets and the soft gurgle of the wash. Eventually he did hear the owl, although it seemed farther off than usual, its cries thin and mournful, like some wraith summoning the old and infirm to Bian's realm. Besh shivered.

"Do you hear that, Lici? Do you hear the Deceiver's call?"

Standing, he stretched his back and then walked inside. But even after he lay down in his soft bed, Besh couldn't sleep. After a time, he stopped even trying. He merely listened to the owl and stared up into the darkness. And he wondered what he would find in the old woman's hut.

Besh woke up to dark grey clouds that hung low over the hills, faint tendrils of mist nearly brushing the treetops. By the time he dressed, ate breakfast, and checked on his garden, a steady rain had begun to fall. He walked to Pyav's forge and the two of them made their way to the old woman's hut. Despite the rain, the dirt track in front of the hut was choked with townspeople. Besh saw many of the same faces he had seen outside the sanctuary the day before, but this crowd was even bigger than the previous evening's had been.

The townspeople said nothing as Besh and the eldest approached the house, and though Pyav eyed them as the two men walked past, he kept silent as well. Besh followed him to the door. There was no lock and so they simply pushed the door open and stepped inside. Besh took care to close the door behind them, and so he had his back to the main room when he heard the eldest give a low whistle.

"Blood and earth!" Pyav muttered.

Besh turned in time to see the eldest tap two fingers against his lips four times—the warding against evil. An instant later, Besh did the same.

The hut had been left a mess. Flies buzzed around uncleaned pots of stew and dirty bowls that had grown rank with the passage of so much time. Tattered clothes lay in a pile near the unmade bed, and a wash-basin stood half empty in the far corner, a thick grey film floating on the water.

And covering it all, scattered as if they had fallen from the sky in place of rain or snow, were small clippings of willow and rush, cedar bark and vine. They were everywhere, in every corner of the room. In some places they had gathered in small mounds, like drifts of snow on a windy day. A few floated in the basin, others lay on the eating table. The floor, bed, and chairs were all littered with them. They were of different hues, and yet they were all oddly similar. One end of each scrap was un-tamed, while the other had been cut at a precise angle. Some were as long as a man's finger; others were barely longer than a baby's toe. But all had been sliced at that same angle. A craftswoman as skilled as Lici would never have varied such a thing.

Besh could hardly imagine the frenzy of basketweaving that had cre-ated such a sight. She must have worked on the baskets for turn upon turn; it might even have been years. He took a tentative step forward, his foot making a crunching sound, as if he were walking on a forest path covered with dried leaves.

Pyav seemed to start at the sound, as if awakened from some odd trance.

"Are you all right, Eldest?"

"Yes. Yes, I'm fine." He rubbed a hand over his broad face. "From the looks of things I'd say that she was taken against her will."

Besh frowned. "You believe so?"

"You don't? Look at this place."

The old man shook his head slowly. True, the hut was in such disrepair that a person could easily draw such a conclusion. But Besh couldn't imagine Lici being made to do anything against her will. On the other hand, he had no trouble imagining that she lived in this sort of filth, like a wild creature of the wood.

"I think maybe she simply lived this way," he finally said.

Pyav started to answer, but then stopped himself. Clearly he didn't know what to believe.

Besh began to walk around the room, as did the eldest, their steps making a good deal of noise.

Besh didn't touch anything, feeling that it wasn't his place to do so. Pyav was a bit bolder, but not much. It almost seemed that they both expected the old witch to walk in the door at any moment.

"I thought she had stopped making baskets," Besh said after some time.

"Clearly not."

"But have you seen her sell any?"

"Not in many years, no."

Besh opened his hands, indicating the room. For all the cuttings strewn about on the floor and furniture, there wasn't a single basket in sight.

"Then what has she done with them all?"

Pyav just stared at him. "You think she took them with her," he said at length.

Besh nodded. "In which case, she might have just gone to trade with the Qirsi clans, or to sell them in one of the five sovereignties. She could be coming back."

Pyav looked around again, a look of disgust lingering on his features. "But even if she lived this way from day to day, don't you think she would have taken a bit more care before leaving for so long? At least to clean up her cooking, or to throw out her wash water. Something."

"Certainly you and I would do so, my friend. Most people would. But Lici . . . she's never been like other people. At least not in all the years I've known her."

The eldest nodded. "You may be right." But Besh could see that his thoughts had already gone in another direction. "You won't approve,

Besh, but even knowing that she may be alive, that she could return any day now, I want to search this hut a bit more."

"To what end?" Besh asked, doing his best to keep his face and tone neutral.

"For too long, people in this village have been spinning yarns about Lici's treasure. I think it's time we put those stories to rest."

"But what if they're true?"

"Do you really believe they are?"

"I don't know." How many times had Besh said that about Lici in the past few days?

Pyav stood chewing his lip for several moments. "If we find gold," he finally said, "we'll leave it where it is and simply tell everyone that we found nothing. But I fear that eventually those people outside will take matters into their own hands, come in here, and take whatever they can find. And I want to know exactly what's at risk."

"All right," Besh said with a small shrug. He gestured toward the far side of her room, where the bed and washbasin stood. "I'll start over here."

In truth, there weren't many places to look. Lici had little furniture and few belongings of any sort. There was an old wooden chest at the foot of her bed that was covered with scuffs and burn marks, as if it had once stood near a hearth. It had a rusted lock on it, but the lock seemed to have stopped working long ago; Besh had no trouble getting the chest open. Inside he found clothes and a few old bound books that might well have belonged to Sylpa, who used to trade for volumes with the peddlers who came through Kirayde. He found as well several pieces of parchment—letters from the look of them. They were tied together with a yellowed piece of twine; Besh left them as they were.

There was nothing to be found under or behind her bed, and the rest of the floor on this side of the hut was bare, save for the basket cuttings.

Pyav was still searching the kitchen area, so Besh stepped into a small storage room at the back of the house. Here he found several bowls and cups, none of them as clean as the dirtiest dish in Elica's kitchen. He also found a few baskets, though all of them looked old, and even had they not, there weren't nearly enough of them to explain all the mess in the front room.

Most of the shelves were empty, and had been for some time, judging by the thick dust that covered them. But in the back corner on the floor he spied an old wooden crate. He walked to it and knelt down, pulling it out from under the shelves and brushing away dust and spiderwebs.

Opening the box, he saw a canvas sack that might once have been used to carry one stone of grain. It was closed and tied at the top with the same yellow twine that had been used to bind the letters. And when Besh lifted it out of the box, it rang with the sound of coins. He started to call out to Pyav, but then he spotted something else. In the box beneath the sack, hidden from view until now, was a thick leather-bound volume. Besh put the money sack aside and picked up the book, thumbing through it briefly. It was written in a woman's hand and for a moment he wondered if Lici had kept a daybook as a younger woman. It didn't seem like something she would have done, and the neat writing in the book seemed in such contrast to the state of the woman's home that he found it hard to believe they could belong to the same person. Then again, he hadn't known Lici very well.

He opened to the first entry and saw that the date given was "Fire Moon, year 1119."

1119! Nearly a century ago. This had to have been Sylpa's daybook, not Lici's. He was tempted to begin reading it, right there and then. What a treasure he had found—far more so to his mind than whatever coins jingled in the bag beside him. He could learn so much from this volume about the history of Kirayde, perhaps about his own mother and father.

But wouldn't that have been a violation, as well? Sylpa had left this book in Lici's hands, and for whatever reason, Lici had chosen to keep it private. Reluctantly, Besh returned the journal to the box.

"I found it," he called to Pyav.

A moment later the eldest appeared in the doorway. "Did you really?"

Besh held up the sack and shook it.

"Have you opened it?"

"No," Besh said. "It's quite heavy, though. Even if only half of it is gold and the rest silver, I'd say that she's by far the wealthiest person in the village."

"Damn," Pyav said, staring at the sack. "I'd been hoping it wasn't true."

"Do you want to count it?"

The eldest shook his head. "No. The amount is none of our affair. Put it back and let's be done with this place." He glanced over his shoulder. "I keep thinking she's going to walk in on us, and to this day I'm still afraid of the woman."

Besh smiled. "So am I." He put the sack back in the box, and pushed the box back under the shelves. "There was a daybook in that box, too," he said, climbing to his feet stiffly. "I think it might have belonged to Sylpa."

"I'm sure that would make for interesting reading," Pyav said, leading Besh toward the front door of the hut. "I was still shy of three fours when she died, but I always liked Sylpa."

They stepped out of the house and into the rain. The crowd was waiting. Wet pale faces peered at them from under hats and hoods.

"Did you find it?" asked the same fair-haired man who had spoken for them the evening before.

"Find what?" the eldest said, sounding tired.

"Her treasure, of course," came another voice.

"What she considers treasures, you might consider worthless trifles. Remember that, friends."

Several men and women started to object and Pyav raised a hand, silencing them. "I know what it is you want," he said. "And I assure you, Besh and I saw no gold or silver in that house. Now go back to your shops and homes, and leave Lici's house in peace."

It was cleverly done, and Besh wondered if the eldest had anticipated this when he refused to look inside the sack.

"What did you find?" the man asked.

"Cuttings from her basketry," Besh said. "Lots of them. More than I would have thought possible. I'm convinced that she's gone off to trade her baskets with the clans or with the Eandi. And I'm convinced as well that she means to come back."

"There," Pyav said. "I agree with Besh, and I believe that settles things. It's still Lici's house, for better or worse. And unless you want to be pilloried for thieving, you'll stay out of it."

Slowly, and with much grumbling, the mob began to disperse. Pyav and Besh remained in front of the hut until all the villagers had moved off.

"We might want to continue to post a guard," Besh said, watching the last of them walk away. "At least for a time."

"Yes," Pyav said. "For a time." He glanced at Besh, a wry grin on his lips. "I never thought I'd hear myself say this, but I wish Lici would hurry back."

Chapter 4

✦╌╂╌✦

GREENRILL, NEAR TURTLE LAKE

D'Abjan had been working this same piece of wood for the better part of the day, and still it wasn't right. It never would be. Every time he managed to plane it to the right shape, he'd leave too many rough edges. And by the time he smoothed them away, using the chisels, rasps, and smaller planes scattered over his father's workbench, the lines were wrong again. He was covered with wood—curled shavings, small chips, finer dust. So was the workbench, and the floor, and just about everything else in the shop. Yet he was no closer to finishing it than he had been hours ago. It just looked . . . wrong, and if he worked it any more, he'd leave this piece smaller than the matching one his father had already made for the other side of the chair.

He heard the door open and close, but he didn't turn. His father had been in and out all day long, delivering pieces, doing repairs, checking in with D'Abjan's mother and sisters, who were at their table in the marketplace, selling the last of the herbs and dye flowers to have come from their garden this year. Perhaps he'd forgotten something, or had returned for whatever tools he needed for his next repairs. Maybe D'Abjan would have a few moments more of peace before his father saw how poorly he had done. He should have known better.

"Let me see how it's coming along," his father said, trying to sound jovial, or encouraging, or anything other than what he was: resigned to yet another of D'Abjan's failures.

He crossed to where D'Abjan stood and hovered at the boy's shoulder. After a moment, he sighed. D'Abjan didn't need to look at his face to know that he was frowning, calculating the cost of the wasted wood, the delay in hours or days that D'Abjan's poor workmanship would cost him.

"You've tapered it too much," he said at last.

D'Abjan kept his eyes fixed on the workbench. "I know."

"You need to keep the plane level as you work a piece like this. You can't allow it to bite so deeply. A woodworker can always carve away more, but he can never replace what's already been taken out."

"Yes," D'Abjan said as evenly as he could. "You've told me before."

"And yet still you don't heed what I tell you."

"I tried," he said, glaring at his father. "I told you I wasn't ready to do this."

"This is the third year of your four as an apprentice. By my third year, I was making entire pieces. Chairs, tables, benches. I made a wardrobe during my fourth year: top to bottom, all on my own. At this rate you'll still be doing piecework a year from now."

"Well, I guess I'll never be the woodworker you are, will I?"

"That isn't what I meant."

"Isn't it?"

His father looked at him sadly. "Isn't it just as likely that my father was simply a better teacher than yours is?"

D'Abjan dropped his gaze, his cheeks burning. After a moment he shrugged.

His father stepped into the storage room and emerged a moment later with a new piece of the same maple D'Abjan had been working.

"Start it again," his father said. "Try making the shape right first, even if it turns out too big for the chair. We can work on getting it to the right size later. Together. But concentrate on this first."

He nodded. "All right."

His father patted his shoulder and started toward the door again. "I have one more repair to do over at the smithy. I'll be back soon."

"Father."

His father turned.

"Can I take a walk first, get out of here for just a bit?"

"I suppose," his father said, frowning slightly. "Not too long though. Madli's been waiting for her chair long enough."

D'Abjan began to take off his work apron. "I won't take long. I promise."

"Very well."

His father left their house. Moments later D'Abjan was out the door as well, though he took care to go in the opposite direction, away from the marketplace. Away from anyone who might see him.

He remained on the path for just a short while, strolling past the last of the homes on this western edge of Greenrill. Once he couldn't see that last house anymore—and no one there could see him—D'Abjan turned off the lane and ducked into the wood, fighting his way through the brush and pushing past low cedar branches to a small clearing he'd visited before.

There he found a freshly fallen tree limb—cedar, of course; it grew in abundance in this part of the highlands. He took out his pocketknife and peeled away the bark in long, smooth strips. Then he sat in the middle of the clearing and he began to draw upon his magic, his V'Tol. His power. He'd discovered that he could do this only a few turns before. Other boys his age here in the village had been talking about being able to do things. Some could start fires, others could speak with birds and foxes, coaxing them to take food from their hands. D'Abjan could shape. That's what the Qirsi called it. The real Qirsi; the ones who used their powers every day. He'd heard peddlers talking about them, about their powers. Shaping. He was a shaper.

Except that he wasn't. He was Y'Qatt. By using his magic, even once, even for an instant, he was violating the most basic tenets of his faith, going against everything that his mother and father had taught him.

He placed his hands over the wood, as he had so many times before, and he began to shape it, smoothing the edges, narrowing it at one end, turning it into the same chair arm he'd spent the morning trying to create in his father's shop. It was so easy, as natural as breathing, as immediate as thought. Whatever his shortcomings as a woodworker, he had taught himself to be a fine shaper. Too bad his father could never see what he had learned to do.

He'd heard what the Y'Qatt clerics said about V'Tol. Who among the Y'Qatt had not? V'Tol was life, it was the essence of what they were. All Qirsi, not just the Y'Qatt. Those who chose to use their magic as a mere tool, or worse, as a weapon, were squandering the gift of life given to all of Qirsar's children, a gift from the god himself. That was why using their magic weakened a Qirsi. That was why those who spent their power the way men and women of both races spent their coin in a marketplace died at a younger age than did those who held tightly to the V'Tol. It made sense.

But if Qirsar hadn't intended for his children to wield this magic, why had he made it so easy to use, so powerful, so satisfying? Why had he given them different abilities—shaping and fire, language of beasts and mists and winds, gleaning and healing? Why had he made the V'Tol at all? He wanted to ask this of his father and mother, of Greenrill's prior, of anyone who might be willing to give him an answer. But he knew that the question itself would so appall whoever he asked that he was better off remaining silent.

As it was, if his parents ever learned what he did in this clearing, they would be ashamed. They might banish him from their home or even from the village itself. So, after gazing for a few moments at the wood he had shaped, he tossed it onto the ground a few spans from where he sat, and drawing on his magic once again, he shattered the limb into a thousand pieces. This felt satisfying, too, though in an entirely different way. For just an instant, he could imagine himself as a warrior in one of the Blood Wars, fighting against the Eandi sovereignties, wielding this power he possessed in a noble cause. Of course, his parents would have seen this as a betrayal as well, a worse one perhaps than the simple conjuring he had done just a short time before.

D'Abjan exhaled heavily, then climbed to his feet and started back toward the dirt road. His father would be back at their house before long, back in the workshop, and would wonder where he'd gone.

As he approached the road, he peered toward the village, making certain that no one was watching before setting foot on the path. He hadn't taken two steps, however, when he heard a low groan from behind him. He gasped and spun, his heart suddenly pounding in his chest.

But rather than seeing his father, or the prior, or anyone else from Greenrill, as he had feared, he saw a woman he didn't recognize.

She had white hair, and at first D'Abjan assumed that she was Qirsi—a peddler maybe, or an Y'Qatt from another village. But then he realized that her skin was too brown, and that her eyes were so dark that they looked black. An Eandi then, and injured by the look of her.

In that moment, the woman looked up at him and halted. She seemed to teeter briefly, and then she collapsed onto the road.

D'Abjan hurried to her side. There was a knot the size of an egg at her temple. Already it was darkening to a deep angry purple, the color of storm clouds early in the Harvest. Blood oozed from the middle of the lump and there were small pieces of dirt and rock embedded in her skin.

"What's your name?" he asked her, not quite knowing what to do.

She merely groaned.

He looked her over quickly and decided that she had no other wounds. She had been carrying two large baskets, each one covered with a blanket. Peeking inside of them, he saw that both containers were filled with smaller baskets of fine quality. She also wore a carry sack on her back. She was dressed simply, and she wore no jewelry.

"Can you tell me where you've come from?"

Still she didn't answer.

At last, D'Abjan scrambled to his feet. "I'm going to get help," he said, though he wasn't certain she could even hear him. "We're near our village. I won't be long." And with that, he ran back to his father's shop.

His father was waiting there for him, his arms crossed over his chest, a stern look on his round face.

"Where have you been?" he demanded. "Didn't I tell you—?"

"There's a woman!" D'Abjan said. "And she's hurt!"

His eyes narrowed. "What woman? Where?"

"On the road just west of the village."

"What were you doing there?"

"Just walking. She's hurt, Father. She has a bruise on her head and she was unconscious when I left her."

"Who is she? Do you know her?"

D'Abjan shook his head. "She's Eandi. A peddler from the looks of her. I've never seen her before."

"All right," his father said. "We'll get Pritt. Come along."

Pritt had been the healer in Greenrill for longer than D'Abjan had been alive. And he looked it. He was bent and he looked frail, with wispy white hair and a narrow, gaunt face. But he'd seen the village through injuries caused by floods and fires, as well as through several outbreaks of Murnia's pox. And despite his age and appearance, he remained spry. If anyone could help the old woman, he could.

They found the old healer in the marketplace, buying healing herbs from an Eandi peddler.

"Pritt," D'Abjan's father called, approaching the man. "You're needed on the road west of the village."

The old man turned slowly at the sound of his voice and stared in their direction, squinting as if to see. "Who is that?"

"It's Laryn, healer. And my boy, D'Abjan."

"Ah, Laryn," the man said, grinning. "Good to see you. What's this about the road?"

"There's a woman there. Eandi. The boy found her," he added, gesturing toward D'Abjan. "She has a head injury and she's unconscious."

The healer frowned. "All right. Can the two of you manage to carry her to my house?"

D'Abjan's father looked at the boy, a question in his pale eyes.

"I think so," D'Abjan said.

The healer nodded. "Good. Meet me there."

Pritt started to walk toward his home, and D'Abjan and his father hurried back to where the woman lay.

As it turned out, she was so light that Laryn could carry her by himself, leaving it to D'Abjan to carry her baskets and travel sack. He started to lift one of the blankets to look once more at the baskets she carried, but his father spoke his name sharply, stopping him.

"Those aren't yours to look in" was all he said.

D'Abjan nodded and picked up the woman's things.

The stranger moaned once when Laryn lifted her, her eyes fluttering open briefly. But she didn't stir again before they reached the healer's cabin and laid her on a pallet by his hearth.

The old healer shuffled to her side and bent over her, looking intently at the bruise on her head. After some time, he straightened and clicked his tongue twice.

"Laryn," he said. "Put that kettle on the fire and then fetch me a bowl from the kitchen." He glanced at D'Abjan. "There's a bucket out front, boy. Fetch some fresh water from the stream. Not the well, mind you. The stream. Quickly now."

D'Abjan nodded and ran to do as the healer instructed. It was a long walk to the stream, and longer still on the return, carrying a full bucket of water. By the time he returned, the cabin was redolent with the smells of Pritt's healing herbs: comfrey and borage, betony and lavender.

"Ah, good," the healer said, seeing D'Abjan in the doorway. He beckoned to the boy. "Bring the bucket here. Is the water cold?"

"Freezing," D'Abjan said.

"Excellent." He had placed a poultice on the wound, but now he lifted it off and handed a dry cloth to D'Abjan. "Soak this in the water and lay it on the bruise. Refresh it every few moments. With time it ought to bring the swelling down."

"Yes, healer."

D'Abjan pulled a chair over to the side of the pallet and began to apply the cold cloth as the healer had told him. As he did, Pritt and D'Abjan's father moved off a short distance and began to speak in low voices. D'Abjan had to strain to hear them.

"She's taken quite a blow to the head," the healer said, glancing at the woman, his brow furrowed, a frown on his narrow face. "Someone younger, I wouldn't be too concerned. With time, such a wound will heal. But I'd guess this woman is in her seventies. I just don't know if she can recover the way someone younger would."

"How long until you'll know?"

The old man shrugged, glanced at her again. "By morning certainly. If she hasn't woken by then, she might not at all."

Laryn nodded. "Well, let us know how she's doing."

"Why don't you leave the boy with me?"

D'Abjan had taken care not to let the two men see that he was listening, but now he looked up, making no attempt to mask his eagerness.

"He has work to do," his father said, eyeing D'Abjan and clearly intending his remark for him as well.

"I could use the help," Pritt said. "And he was the one who found her. If she survives, it will be largely because of him."

If D'Abjan himself had asked, Laryn would have refused. The boy was certain of it. But refusing the old healer was another matter, and in the end his father relented.

"Fine, then," he said, trying with only some success to keep his tone light. "Stay with her. I'll return later."

"Thank you, Father."

He nodded once as he let himself out of the house, but he said nothing.

Pritt shuffled over to the pallet and watched D'Abjan as he wet the cloth again, wrung it out, and replaced it on the woman's bruise. "Good," the healer said. "Keep doing that. I've a few things to finish in the marketplace. I'll be back shortly. All right?"

"Yes, healer."

Pritt patted his shoulder and left the house.

D'Abjan continued to press the cloth gently to her wound, refreshing it every few moments with the cold water and watching the woman for any sign that she was waking. Seeing none, he heard again the healer's words, spoken quietly to his father. *I just don't know if she can recover. . . .*

Bending to wet the cloth yet again, D'Abjan wondered if Pritt possessed healing magic. Was that why he had become a healer in the first place? Was he capable of saving the woman with his magic, if only he were permitted to wield it? D'Abjan knew that people had died in the healer's care. No doubt this happened to healers all the time. But if Pritt did have healing power, how did it make him feel, watching those in his care die, knowing that he might have been able to heal them? Of all Qirsi magics, surely here was one that Qirsar had to have intended for them to use. How could the god want the Y'Qatt to let others suffer, simply so that his children would preserve their V'Tol for another day? Where was the sense in that? Where was the compassion, the justice?

He was still considering this when the woman finally stirred, another low moan escaping her as her eyes opened slowly. She reached a hand up to her head, and D'Abjan removed the cloth.

"Water?" she whispered.

He jumped up. "Yes, of course." He found a cup in Pritt's kitchen and filled it with cold water from the bucket. He started to hand it to her but then realized she was in no condition to drink it on her own. Unsure of what else to do, D'Abjan put his hand behind her head and gently lifted her while holding the cup to her lips. Her hair felt thick and rough, and with her eyes open, staring sightlessly over the rim of the cup, she looked odd, even vaguely frightening. She took a sip or two before nodding that she had drunk enough. He lowered her head once more.

"Thank you," she said softly.

"You're welcome, good lady."

She looked around the cabin. "What happened to me?"

"I don't know. I saw you on the road leading into our village. You were already hurt. You made a noise, and then you fell down. My father and I brought you here."

"And where is here?"

"This is Pritt's home. He's our healer."

A faint smile touched her lips. "I meant what village."

D'Abjan felt his face color. "My pardon. This is Greenrill."

She shook her head and closed her eyes for a moment. "I don't know that name." After a moment she lifted a hand to her head again, and touched the bruise gingerly. "I take it we're waiting for your healer to come."

"No, good lady. He's already seen you." He lifted up the poultice that had been on her wound. "He prepared this."

"But you look Qirsi," she said.

"We are, good lady."

"So then, your healer has refused to tend to me."

Again he felt his face turning red. Why should it fall to him to explain this, when he had just been asking himself the same question? Was this Qirsar's way of punishing him? Was the god testing his faith by making him explain to this woman what it meant to be Y'Qatt?

"It's not our way to use magic, good lady. We are Y'Qatt. We . . . we believe that the god did not intend for us to use any of our powers."

She watched him with a strange expression—something akin to anger flashed in her dark eyes, and though she said nothing, D'Abjan felt compelled to explain more.

"The more power we use the shorter our lives," he said. "Our V'Tol—that's what we call our magic—it isn't supposed to be used. It's part of our life." He knew he wasn't explaining it well, but still he didn't stop. "We find other ways. We can shape wood with magic, but we use tools instead. We can light fires, but we use a tinder and flint instead. We can heal with magic, but we use herbs and poultices instead." He held up the poultice again, and then the wet cloth he'd been holding to her head. "We haven't neglected you, good lady. We've done our best."

"But without magic."

"Yes." He nodded. "Without magic."

"And what if your herbs and your cloth hadn't helped me?"

He just gaped at her, not knowing how to answer, afraid even to try.

For several moments, neither of them spoke, and D'Abjan found himself glancing toward the door, wishing Pritt would return.

"But they did help me, didn't they?" she finally said, smiling at him.

He grinned, his relief as welcome as sleep after a long day of work. "Yes, good lady."

She closed her eyes for a short time, before suddenly opening them again. "Where are my things?"

"Just over there, good lady," D'Abjan said, pointing to her baskets and carry sack, which sat by the wall near the door.

"Ah, good. Good." She closed her eyes again. "What's your name, boy?" she asked.

"D'Abjan, my lady."

"I'm Licaldi."

"Do you live near here?" he asked.

"I told you, I don't know where here is. But I've lived in the highlands all my life." She opened one eye and looked at him. "I'm Mettai."

He felt his eyes widen.

"You know what that means?"

D'Abjan nodded. He did know, or at least he thought he did. His father had explained to him once about blood magic and the Eandi conjurers and witches who wielded it. He'd listened as he would to a legend told beside a fire during the Festival Moon, but for a long time he'd wondered if such people truly existed. As he'd grown older he'd come to understand that there was truth to the stories, but until now, he'd never met an Eandi sorcerer.

"You fear me now," she said softly, smiling slightly.

"No, good lady. Forgive me. I merely . . . I've never met one of your people before."

"Are we Mettai that odd then? Are Eandi sorcerers any stranger from Qirsi who forswear their magic?"

Before he could answer, the door opened, and Pritt stepped into the house.

"Ah!" he said, seeing that her eyes were open. "You're awake! Excellent!"

"This is the healer," D'Abjan said. "Pritt, this is Licaldi."

"Licaldi, is it?" he asked, crossing to the bed. He glanced at D'Abjan, who stood and got out of the healer's way. Pritt sat and examined her wound. "How are you feeling, Licaldi?"

"A bit dizzy," she said. "And my head aches."

"I imagine. Do you remember what happened?"

"No, I—" She stopped, staring at him. "Yes. Yes, I do. There was a man. No, wait. Two men. One in front of me on the road. The other behind me. They took my gold and they hit me with . . . with something."

"A rock, I'd say, from the look of the wound."

She shook her head, looking like she might cry. "I don't remember. I just know that they took my gold. I've been traveling through the highlands, selling my baskets, living off what I could earn from the trades I made. Now I've nothing again." Her eyes met Pritt's. "I can't pay you, healer. Even without your magic, you've been kind and you've helped me. But I have no gold for you."

Pritt shrugged. "That's all right."

Her face brightened. "But I still have my baskets." She sat up straighter. "Bring me one of those baskets, D'Abjan," she said, motioning for him to hurry.

The healer offered an indulgent smile, even as he shook his head. "Really, there's no need."

D'Abjan carried one of the large baskets to the pallet and laid it on Licaldi's lap. She removed the blanket and started looking through the smaller baskets as if trying to decide which one to give the healer.

Pritt stared at them. "You made all of these?" he asked.

"Yes," she said, not bothering to look up.

D'Abjan stood beside Pritt, also gazing at the treasures in her basket. "They're beautiful."

"Thank you, boy. You can have one, as well. Take it home to your mother and father, and tell them that you earned it with your kindness and good manners."

He smiled. "Yes, good lady." After looking over the baskets for a few moments, D'Abjan selected a deep, oval-shaped one with a braided handle. The rushes from which it had been woven were dyed green and blue—his mother's favorite colors.

"A fine choice," Licaldi said. She looked up at the healer. "And you, healer?"

Pritt shrugged slightly, but then reached for a shallow round basket that had no handle. "This will hold my healing herbs," he said. "And each day I use it, I'll think of you, kind madam."

"You're too kind, healer."

She pushed herself out of the bed and stood.

"What are you doing?" Pritt asked, a frown on his face.

"I have to be on my way. My gold is gone. I can't tarry here earning nothing. I'll stop at your marketplace, and then I'll be on my way."

"But your injury!" the healer said. "You shouldn't be standing, much less wandering the land on your own. At least stay the night. If you're feeling well enough, you can be on your way in the morning."

She smiled at him, as if he were a child and she an indulgent parent. "But, healer, I'm feeling well enough now."

Looking at her, D'Abjan realized that she did look well. Her color had returned, the haze of pain had lifted from her dark eyes, even the swelling at her temple appeared to have gone down. It almost seemed that the god himself had reached down and mended her wound, as if he were determined to prove to D'Abjan that the healer's poultice was enough, and that there was no need to resort to magic.

"Well, I can't keep you here against your will," Pritt told her sourly. "But I fear you're making a terrible mistake."

"I appreciate your concern, healer. If I do myself injury by leaving your care too soon, I'll have no one to blame but myself. You've been clear with your warnings."

"At least let me place a bandage on the wound."

She inclined her head. "I'd be grateful."

It took Pritt only a few moments to bandage her head, and soon the woman was on her way toward the marketplace, her carry sack on her back, one of the great baskets under each arm.

"She's an odd woman," D'Abjan said, standing in the healer's doorway, watching her go.

"She's a fool," the healer muttered. "You'd best get back to your father, boy. Don't forget your basket."

He retrieved his basket from beside the pallet and started back toward Laryn's woodshop. The walk took him through the marketplace and before long he spotted Licaldi. She stood in the middle of the lane, her large baskets resting on the ground as she bartered with at least six peddlers. D'Abjan tried to catch her eye, but she was too intent on her bargaining to notice him. He hurried on, confident that before day's end she would recoup a good deal of the gold she had lost to the road brigands. Within a few days, everyone in Greenrill would have one of the woman's baskets.

As he walked, he couldn't help thinking that by bringing that woman to Greenrill, by allowing D'Abjan to find her as he emerged from the forest, the god had taught him something. Without using magic at all, the healer had saved the old woman's life. More, he had done it with ease. D'Abjan couldn't imagine that magic would work any faster than had the herbs and cold cloth. Surely not all healers could succeed so quickly, but Pritt had been honing his craft for years. And perhaps that was what the god had meant to show him. Of course D'Abjan couldn't expect to be a master craftsman after only three years as his father's apprentice, and yes, right now his magic worked quicker and with greater precision than did his hands. But with time and practice, he could learn to work wood as his father did. Finally he understood why his people refused to squander their V'Tol in order to save time or avoid work. To do so was to reward laziness and ignore the value of mastering a skill.

"I understand, Qirsar," he whispered. And he knew that he had gone to his clearing in the forest for the last time.

It was late when he reached the house. Sunlight angled sharply across the lane, and the air had begun to grow cool. Even from the road, he could hear his father sweeping the floors, a chore Laryn usually left for D'Abjan.

"Want me to finish?" the boy asked as he stepped inside.

"I'm almost done," Laryn said. He didn't sound angry, but neither was there any warmth in his voice. No doubt he was still annoyed with D'Abjan for staying with the healer.

"I'll stay late tomorrow," the boy said. "I'll finish the arm for Madli's chair."

"I did it myself," his father said.

"Then I'll start something new, anything that you want me to work on."

Laryn stopped sweeping and looked at him, his eyes narrowed slightly, a small smile playing at the corners of his mouth. "What's this about?"

D'Abjan couldn't help smiling, too. "Nothing. I just . . . I'm ready to work harder. That's all."

His father held his gaze for several moments, then nodded. "All right then." He glanced at the basket. "What's that?"

"The woman made it. That's what she had in those big baskets. Smaller ones like this. Beautiful ones. She gave one to me and one to Pritt."

"So, she's doing better."

"Much. She's left the healer's house. I passed her in the marketplace trading with several peddlers."

The smile faded from his father's face. "You're not serious."

"Pritt couldn't believe it either."

"He feared she was going to die. He made it sound as though she would. And instead she's already left his cabin?"

"He's a very fine healer."

Laryn stared at the floor. "Yes, or . . ."

"Or what?"

His father shook his head. "I don't know. Nothing." He took the basket from D'Abjan and examined it closely. "She does good work. And your mother will like the colors."

"I know. That's why I chose that one."

Laryn put away the broom and together father and son walked around to the front of the house. As soon as they stepped outside, D'Abjan caught the scent of the evening meal his mother was cooking. It occurred to him then that he hadn't eaten since morning. His stomach grumbled loudly, drawing a grin from his father.

His mother had prepared stewed lamb and herb bread, his favorites, and that night he ate until he was sated and happy.

It wasn't until he was getting into bed that D'Abjan began to feel ill.

Once she was away from the village she reclaimed her cart and steered it as far from Greenrill as daylight would allow. As darkness fell, she made a fire by the wash. Then she removed the bandage and threw it into the flames.

Conjuring the wound had been but a small matter; fooling the Y'Qatt healer had been laughably easy. A real Qirsi healer would have known that her injury was feigned as soon as he or she used magic to heal it. But the Y'Qatt relied on his eyes and his hands, his herbs and his false faith. Whatever qualities he thought to gain by eschewing the use of magic, wisdom and insight were not among them.

The boy had been kind. It was regrettable that he had to die as well. He was as much a victim of the Y'Qatt as she—no doubt his faith had been forced upon him, drummed into his mind until he could recite it by rote. But there was no avoiding it. That was why she had given him a basket. Let the illness come to him early; let him die before the worst of it. For die they would. All of them.

It would be a long night; she looked forward to it. First she would hear the moans of the Y'Qatt, the cries of fear and suffering. *Is it the pestilence that has come?* they would ask each other. *Is it Murnia's pox?* Then the fires would begin. Winds would keen, sweeping dense mists through the village. Homes would crumble in the face of shaping power unleashed. Dogs would howl at the incomprehensible thoughts conveyed to them by those with language of beasts. Then at last, silence would settle over the village as over a tomb.

And she would move on, toward the next Y'Qatt settlement.

Chapter 5

esh was lying in bed when finally it came to him. Since seeing that daybook of Sylpa's, he had been able to think of nothing else. All through dinner, as the young ones played and laughed, and Mihas asked him question after question about the old woman's hut, he could barely keep his thoughts clear enough to respond. Elica finally asked him if he was well, apparently fearing that his long day in the woman's home had left him fevered.

He felt fine, though. It was just that journal. Why did it bother him so? No, not bother. That was the wrong word. It occupied his thoughts, to the exclusion of nearly all else. But why?

Sitting outside on Sirj's stump, as water dripped from the branches overhead and the sky above him began to clear, he tried to recall all he could of Sylpa. He'd known the woman when he was still a child, and had liked her very much. True, she was forever linked to Lici in his mind, but somehow he had managed to hold on to his fondness for her. Sylpa had been a formidable woman and quite beautiful, even after her hair turned white and the lines on her face deepened. Her eyes, large and dark green, had always seemed to be dancing with humor, even when the rest of her face looked solemn. And her laugh—full, unrestrained, loud enough to carry from one end of the marketplace to the other; even after she became eldest of the village and began to carry the cares of all Kirayde on her shoulders, she always kept that laugh.

She never married or had children of her own, but there were rumors, tales told in whispers and with sympathy, of a great love affair that ended in tragedy. According to these stories, Sylpa had loved a boy from Kirayde who left the village to seek his fortune, only to be killed in a flood along Maifor's Wash in Tordjanne. Heartbroken, Sylpa had vowed never to love again. No one remembered the boy's name, and even as a youth, Besh had questioned the verity of the tale. Then again, how else could he explain the fact that this strong, beautiful, kind woman lived alone at the edge of the village?

But there was nothing in the woman's history, or Besh's own, that would explain why the mere sight of her journal should affect him so. He'd never loved Sylpa himself—he'd been far too young. And though he liked her, they had never been close. So why?

Only now, lying in his bed, in the dark and quiet of Elica and Sirj's house, did he finally understand. It wasn't Sylpa who beckoned to him from those journal pages. It was Lici.

1119. That had been the date of that first entry he'd seen when glancing through the volume. Nearly one hundred years ago. Lici had come to the village well after that—probably forty years after. Of course Sylpa would have written about the girl's arrival in Kirayde. She was eldest at the time. And then she had taken the child in, and cared for her as if she were Sylpa's own. How could she have not written about her? It seemed quite likely that Lici's history was in that daybook. All of it, or at least as much as Sylpa had managed to get out of the girl. It might well contain the truth about whatever had befallen her prior to her arrival in Kirayde, leaving her alone in the world. It might explain the woman's strange manner and her stubborn silence.

He doubted that the journal would shed much light on where Lici was now, but it might tell Besh enough to help him piece together the rest of her story.

But just as the other villagers had no claim on Lici's gold, he had no right to read the daybook. True, he was an elder of the village, but that was all the more reason for him to leave the journal where it was. It fell to him, as well as to Pyav, Tashya, and the rest, to set an example for the other villagers. On the other hand, hadn't the people of Kirayde charged the elders with finding out what had become of the old woman? Mightn't the journal help him do just that?

Besh smiled in the darkness and shook his head.

"No, old man," he whispered. "If you're going to do this, don't lie to yourself about the reason."

The truth was Lici had fascinated him since the moment he saw her. At first, he had confused that fascination with love, but even later, when he realized that he wanted nothing to do with her, when he had started a family with Ema and had begun to warn his own children away from the woman, he remained enthralled by her. She had always been beautiful as well as strange. Or perhaps it was because her arrival in the village had come within a turn or two of his birth, forever linking them in the minds of others who had been alive at the time. Whatever the reason, the fascination had never really gone away. Here he was, a man in his sixteenth four, and still thoughts of the woman kept him awake in his bed. Besh couldn't help but laugh at himself.

He knew he was being a fool, and he tried to force thoughts of Lici and the daybook out of his mind. He needed to sleep. In the morning he'd speak with Pyav and together the elders would decide what to do.

After lying still for what seemed the better part of an hour, he gave up on trying to sleep. Now that he had started to imagine what might be in the book, he couldn't stop. He rose, dressed, and took his pipe, smoking weed, and flint out into the chill air. The last of the rain clouds had moved off, leaving a clear sky. It was past midnight, but this late in the waning the moons were just rising, glowing brightly enough to cast pale shadows across Elica's yard and the lane beyond it.

He filled the pipe bowl, but then laid it on Sirj's stump. Taking a deep breath, he gazed up at white Panya, who shone through the trees, gleaming like fresh snow.

"Gods forgive me," he said. And he began to walk south, toward the old woman's hut.

There would be a guard there—hadn't Besh himself recommended to the eldest that they continue to keep watch on Lici's home?—but Besh was an elder. The guard might think it odd that he would come to the house at such a late hour, but he wouldn't hesitate to let Besh enter.

"I have no right to do this," he told himself, remembering how self-righteous he had sounded denouncing those who wanted to divide up her gold. "I'm no better than they are." Still, he kept walking.

Ojan, the village miller, lay on the steps leading up to Lici's door, snoring softly. He was a big man, heavy as well as tall, with a round, fleshy face and jutting brow. Certainly he looked the part of a night watchman. When standing, he cut an imposing figure; anyone from outside the village who came to steal from the old woman's house would have fled at the mere sight of him. Those who lived here, however, knew him to be a gentle man who was no more dangerous awake than he was asleep. He'd been asked to guard the house by Korr, his father, who was also a member of the Council of Elders. Despite the thoughts churning in Besh's mind, the old man smiled to see Ojan sleeping so soundly on his guard duty. Not wishing to startle him, Besh cleared his throat and stepped farther into the circle of light from a torch burning at the top of the stairs.

The miller opened one eye, then sat up and scratched the side of his face. "That you, Besh?"

"Yes, Ojan. Sorry to disturb you."

"Not at all." He frowned. "What's the hour?"

"I don't know. It's late."

"Is something wrong?"

"No," Besh said. He started to say more, then stopped himself. Now that he was here at Lici's house, he wasn't certain how to proceed. He decided, though, that he wouldn't compound his sins by lying about why he had come. "There's nothing wrong. I saw something today when Pyav and I were searching through Lici's things. A daybook. I wanted to take another look at it."

The miller's frown deepened, making him look fierce in the dim light of the moons. "Now?"

"I know it seems strange. But I wasn't able to sleep, so I thought . . ." He trailed off with a small shrug.

Ojan answered with a shrug of his own. "All right." He stood and took the torch out of the makeshift sconce that had been fashioned on one of the beams of Old Lici's porch. "You'll need this," the miller said.

"Won't you?"

Ojan glanced up at the moons. "I daresay there's enough light without it." He shrugged again. "No one ever comes anyway. You're the first in all my nights here."

Besh smiled. "All right then. My thanks."

He took the torch and climbed the stairs to the house. He almost raised his hand to knock, just out of habit. Instead, laughing at himself, but also wiping a sweaty palm on the leg of his trousers, he pushed the door open.

The inside of the house looked just as it had earlier that day. Of course. But somehow the darkened corners and the shifting yellow glow of the torch made the mess Lici had left seem even more menacing than it had in the light of morning. Shadows lurked along the walls. Light re-flected oddly off windows and kitchen pans. He almost backed out of the house—better to leave this until morning.

But again the daybook called to him. He made a point of leaving the door ajar and started toward the back room. Before he was halfway across the house, a small gust of wind made the door slam. Abruptly his heart was racing, like a horse that bolts at a sudden flash of lightning.

"Damn," he muttered, taking a breath.

He continued to the back room and quickly found the journal in that same crate below Lici's sack of coins. He lifted it out and carried it back into the main room. After setting the torch in a pot, he brushed bark cuttings off a chair, sat down, and began to leaf through the volume.

There was much he wanted to look for in the book—information about his parents, about a flood he remembered from his childhood, about the deliberations of the Council of Elders during Sylpa's tenure as eldest. But he remained uncomfortable with what he was doing, and so resolved to look only for information about Lici.

He thumbed through to the middle of the book, and began to scan the pages for any mention of the orphaned girl who came to Kirayde so unexpectedly. Besh knew his letters well enough, but he was not nearly as learned as some, and at first he had some difficulty reading Sylpa's hand. But after some time, he found what he sought.

". . . She can barely speak of the tragedy," Sylpa wrote. "Nor does she cry anymore. She merely stares silently, her expression utterly blank, only the twisting of her pale hands revealing something of the workings of her mind."

Besh turned back a page, and then another, searching for the date of the first entry that mentioned Lici. When he found it, the hairs on his neck and arms stood on end. "Thunder Moon, twelfth day of the wax-ing, 1147."

It wasn't just that Sylpa had written this sixty-four years ago. That he had expected. But the day: the twelfth of the Thunder Moon's wax-ing. That day in this year had to have been around the time Lici disap-peared from the village. He'd seen her earlier in that turn, but he couldn't remember seeing her since the full of both moons. Was it pos-sible that she vanished sixty-four years to the day after arriving in Ki-rayde? If so, was it mere coincidence? Looking around the house, seeing the filth she had left behind, he found it hard to imagine that Lici could track the days so closely.

And yet somehow he knew that she had. For all her odd behavior, which bordered even on madness, Lici was not one to let an anniversary of such significance go unnoticed. If she left Kirayde on the same day she arrived here, she did so with purpose. But what purpose? What might this mean?

He heard a noise outside, like the scuffing of a shoe on wood, and for just an instant he wondered if Lici had returned. But after staring at the door for several moments, waiting for it to open, his expression, no doubt, like that of a child caught stealing a sweet before mealtime, he realized that it was just Ojan shifting his position on the stairs. Turning his attention back to the book, Besh began to read again, starting this time from the beginning of the entry.

Thunder Moon, twelfth day of the waxing, 1147.

It seems the last of the storms has passed. We've had no rain now for three days, and the wash begins to recede from the top of its banks. The flooding was worst at the north end of the village, but even there the damage is only slight. We've been fortunate.

But already, the gods have found a new way to test us. Near midday, a girl wandered into our village from the south. She looks to be eight or nine years old, perhaps ten. She has long limbs and is tall for a girl of that age, but her face still has the delicacy of a young child. In truth, though, it's hard to set her age with any certainty, for she looks a mess and has yet to speak a word to anyone.

Upon her arrival, her clothes were in tatters, her hair was tangled and matted with burrs, leaves, and all manner of filth, and her body and face had not been washed, it seemed, in half a turn, perhaps more. She is painfully thin. Her ribs show plainly through her skin and her arms and legs look like mere sticks. Well fed and healthy, she would look lank. As it is she appears on the edge of starvation. Her cheeks are sunken, her eyes look overlarge in her pinched face.

Yet, for all this, one need only glance at her to see that she is a beautiful girl, a fact confirmed for us after a few of the women managed to get her bathed down at the river. Her hair is raven black and her eyes are brilliant green. Her skin is brown, and though the sunburn on her face tells me that she has been wandering in the wilderness for some time, I believe that the darkness of her skin comes naturally to her. If I had to guess, I'd say that she, too, is Mettai.

For now, however, her appearance and even her ancestry are secondary. Some tragedy has befallen the child. I'm certain of it, and others among the elders agree. She doesn't cry. As far as we know, she's mute. She bears no sign of injury or abuse, save the scrapes and bruises one might expect a child so young to acquire while venturing alone in the wild. But there is something in her eyes, in the way she flinches away from any direct gaze. This girl has wraiths hovering at her shoulder.

The one thing she does do is eat, and it gladdens my heart to see it. Trenna started her on some thin broth, thinking it might take the girl some time to work up to more substantial fare. But she made quick work of the first bowl and then a second. We gave her bread then, and she devoured that as might a wolf. We dare not give her anything more difficult than a bit of fowl, but for now that seems to content her. Broth, bread, and fowl. At least we can sleep tonight knowing that we have done well by the girl, even if the rest of the world has not.

Trenna has offered to take the girl in, but with her three, and Branz away trading with the Fal'Borna, she has her hands full. She will sleep here tonight, and with time maybe she can communicate enough to help us find her way home.

Thunder Moon, thirteenth day of the waxing, 1147.

The girl slept late, as I suspected she would. I can only imagine how terrified she must have been at night in the wild, taking refuge in what shelter she could find, braving the storms that have just recently passed through the highlands. It makes me shudder just to think of it. No doubt it's been an age since last she had a decent night's sleep.

Needless to say, I did nothing to disturb her slumber. I lit a fire outside and took my breakfast in the cool morning air. It's something I should do more often. How strange that this child should come into our lives, and in this very small way force me out of habits I didn't even know I'd acquired. How long has it been since I did something—anything—different? Too long, by the feel of it. I'm too young to have grown so set in my ways. It makes me wonder if the gods have some other purpose in sending this girl to Kirayde, aside from the obvious, of course: that of healing whatever wounds lurk in the mind of this poor creature.

She awoke a bit before midday and called out. I didn't recognize a word in her cry, but it was the first sound she had made since her arrival, and even as I hurried into the house, I took it as a sign of some progress. She was sitting up in her bed, looking around, as if she had no memory of how she had gotten there. Upon seeing me, however, she must have recalled some of yesterday's events, because she immediately calmed down, and actually favored me with a smile. It lasted just a moment, but again, it gave me some hope.

I asked her if she was hungry, and she nodded. Something else I've noticed about her—she says nothing, but she has no trouble hearing and understanding all that we say. This leads me to think that her silence is a response to all she's been through and that her voice will come back to her once she has had time to heal.

After she had eaten again as much as she had the night before, I sat her down outside on the stairs to the house and sat beside her. I took her hand, which she suffered me to hold, and I looked her in the eye.

"You've been through a difficult time, haven't you?" I asked.

She shrank away from me, and even pulled her hand away. For a long time, she wouldn't even meet my gaze.

"I'm sorry," I said. "I'm sorry for what you've been through, whatever it might be, and I'm sorry for asking you about it. I should have begun differently." I waited for her to face me again. When she didn't, I went on anyway. "My name is Sylpa," I said. "I told you that yesterday, but with all that happened, I thought maybe you had forgotten."

At that, she did turn, and after some hesitation, she shook her head.

"You mean you remembered?" I said.

She smiled again and nodded.

"Well, I'm glad," I told her. "Are you ready to tell me your name?"

Her smile vanished, and she shook her head.

"Can you tell me where you're from?"

Again she shook her head.

"Is it that you don't remember?"

No, she indicated, that wasn't the problem.

"Can you not speak?"

She hesitated again, and then nodded, her face brightening. I knew right off that she was lying to me, but I didn't press the matter. When she's ready to tell me these things she will. I'm more sure of that now than ever. In the meantime, she spent the day as my companion, more like a dog than a girl to be sure, but a companion nevertheless. She came with me to the garden, and even helped me weed a bit, after I showed her what I wanted done. She helped me clean my clothes, needing so little instruction that I'm sure she had done as much before.

We ate a quiet supper and even before we'd finished, she was yawning, her eyes drooping as if she could barely keep herself awake. Still, she helped me clear the table and heated water for the dishes before I said that she should get herself to bed and that I would come to her presently to make certain that she was all right. By the time I did as I promised, she had fallen asleep.

Thunder Moon, fourteenth day of the waxing, 1147.

This day began much as yesterday did, with the girl crying out in fear at finding herself in a strange home. I wonder if she awakens from dark dreams, stark visions of whatever horrors have afflicted her. I had hoped that the pleasant day we spent together might start to rid her of such terrors, but I realize now that I was foolish to think it possible. Such things take time.

And, as matters now stand, I realize that I have been fortunate to have made as much progress with her this day as I did. After we had eaten and were on our way to the garden, the girl actually spoke.

"I lied to you," she said suddenly, her eyes trained on the road as we walked.

"I know." I tried to keep any rebuke from my voice, and I believe I succeeded.

"You knew?" she asked.

"Perhaps not for certain, but clearly you heard everything we said to you, and I had the sense at times that you wanted to speak, but were afraid."

She walked for some distance without answering, as if considering what I had said. At length, she looked at me again. "My name is Licaldi."

I stopped and proffered a hand. "Sylpa," I said. "Pleased to meet you."

She shook my hand, then giggled. We resumed our walk to the garden plot, and she said nothing else. I think she was merely relieved to know that she could speak, if she so wished. I made no effort to engage her in conversation, nor did I ply her with questions. At least I didn't then.

As we were on our way back home, I heard my name being called from the marketplace. Looking that way, I saw Trenna waving to me. I told Licaldi to wait for me, but she seemed reluctant to be left alone. Seeing no harm in taking her with me, I started toward the market with my companion in tow.

Much of what transpired in the marketplace is recorded now in the records of the council, and I won't bother with details here, except to say that two peddlers were in dispute over one woman's interest in buying a bolt of Aelean wool. Both claimed that she had promised to buy their cloth; the woman swore that she had made no such promise to either man, but rather intended to look at the wares of all the other peddlers in the marketplace before making her decision. Trenna, of course, had no intention of making the woman buy from either of them. Rather, she remembered a similar matter coming up several turns before, involving the same two men, and she was now convinced that the two were swindlers working in common purpose.

Reminded of the earlier incident I remembered it clearly, and agreed with her. I ordered the men out of the village, threatening to draw upon my magic if they refused. The pair complained loudly, protesting their innocence and vowing never to set foot in Kirayde again, but all the while they were packing their wares and making a most careful count of what gold they had already made that day. In a short while they were gone, and Licaldi and I started once more to make our way home.

"You're the village eldest," she said, as we walked.

At first, still thinking of those men, I answered absently that I was. Then the import of what she had said reached me.

"Did your village have elders as well?"

She nodded, staring straight ahead. It occurred to me that I had said "did" rather than "does," and that the girl hadn't corrected me.

"You're Mettai, aren't you?"

Again she nodded. I could see the color fleeing her cheeks and lips. Her hands trembled and her jaw quivered.

"Can you tell me the name of your village?"

Suddenly her eyes were brimming with tears. "It doesn't matter," she whispered.

I stopped, gently taking hold of her shoulders and making her face me. "Why doesn't it matter? Did you run away? Was someone there cruel to you?"

"No, it wasn't that."

"Then what, Licaldi? Please tell me."

But she wouldn't say more and I knew better than to push her. I'm anxious to know what's befallen the child, not merely because of some dark curiosity, but because I expect the sooner she can speak of it, the sooner she can move beyond it. And, of course, the sooner we know where she belongs, the sooner we can try to reunite her with her family. That last strikes me as being most important, and *yet something tells me that it will prove the most difficult. The question in my mind is no longer where her family might be, but rather how many of them have survived whatever tragedy the girl witnessed.*

Besh turned the page to read more, but a knock at the door stopped him. Looking up, he realized that the sun had risen. The knock came again and he called for whoever it was to enter.

Ojan stepped inside.

"Sorry to disturb you, Besh."

"Nonsense, my friend. This isn't my home. You don't need to knock on my account."

The big man merely shrugged. "I just wanted you to know that I'm headed home now. I've work to get done. I don't know who's coming on next, if anyone, now that it's day. But I can come back tonight, if you and Pyav need me to."

"Thank you, Ojan. I intend to speak with Pyav this morning. If we need you again, we'll let you know."

He raised a hand and nodded. "All right. I'm off then."

Besh watched him from the window. He thought about reading more, but then set the daybook down on the arm of the chair, stood, and stretched. Now that it was light, he was tired. Of course. He'd been a fool not to sleep, and no doubt he'd pay for his folly before the day was out. For now, though, he needed to get home, before Elica made herself sick with worry.

He returned the journal to the box in the back room and, after taking care to close Lici's door, hurried back to Elica's house. Everyone was awake when he got there and the children came running out of the house to greet him, shouting, "Grandfather! Grandfather!"

The young ones each took hold of one of his hands and practically dragged him toward the front stairs, while Mihas walked beside him.

"Where were you, Grandfather?" the boy asked.

"Lici's house."

The boy stared at him briefly, but then looked away again. "Mother wanted Father to go out and look for you, but he said you'd be back when you were ready to come back."

Just as they reached the stairs, Elica emerged from the house, eyes blazing.

"Where have you been?" she demanded, leveling a wooden spoon at his heart as if it were a blade. "I've been worried sick about you! First Lici disappears and then you go off in the dark of night like a thief or a . . . a . . . a who-knows-what! What were you thinking? Were you even thinking at all?"

While she was shouting at Besh, Sirj stepped out of the house. He remained behind her, but after only a few moments of listening to her harangue, he rolled his eyes and walked past her.

"He's back now, Elica. Have done."

"Have done?" she repeated, her voice rising, which Besh hadn't believed possible. "He's too old to be wandering about in the middle of the night!"

Sirj had placed a log on his stump and lifted his ax, but he stopped now, fixing her with a hard look. "He's not that old, and I can tell you now that when I'm his age, you won't be speaking to me in that tone."

For the second time in as many days, Besh found himself thinking that he'd misjudged the man all these years. He could almost hear Ema laughing at him.

Elica eyed her husband a moment longer. Then she faced Besh again, and in a somewhat gentler tone asked, "Where were you, Father?"

"I went to Lici's house."

Sirj split the log with a single blow, and turned to look at him. "Why?"

Besh regarded him briefly. "We found a daybook there yesterday. It belonged to Sylpa, and during the night it occurred to me that it might have something in it that could tell us where Lici's gone."

"Sylpa's been dead for nearly a dozen fours," Elica said. "What could her daybook tell you about where Lici is now?"

"I don't know yet." He scratched the back of his head and glanced over at Sirj, who just stared back at him. "I suppose what I should have said was that it might tell us something more about Lici herself, something that might give us some idea of why she left." He nearly mentioned then his suspicion that she had departed on the anniversary of her arrival in Kirayde, but he didn't know this for certain, and even if it were true, he didn't know yet what it might mean. "Now, if I may," he said instead, climbing the stairs, "I'd like a small something to eat before I go and speak with the eldest."

He brushed past Elica as he entered the house. A half-eaten loaf of bread sat on a counter, and he cut off a slab and covered it with butter. Taking a bite, he turned. His daughter stood in the doorway, watching him.

"Are you all right?" she asked.

"Of course. Don't I look all right?"

"That's not what I mean, and you know it. You may be able to convince Sirj that there's nothing unusual about you going off in the middle of the night to read Sylpa's daybook, but I know you too well. Now, what's this about?"

He opened his mouth to put her off, but then remembered the promise he'd made to himself the night before. He hadn't lied to Ojan; it didn't seem right to tell his own daughter anything less than the truth.

"It's about Lici," he said.

She huffed impatiently and looked away. "I know that."

"No, you don't. All my life I've felt that Lici and I are . . . are linked in some way. She came to Kirayde the same year I was born. As a child I was fascinated by her, and even now, years later, I find myself being pulled into her life. Everyone in the village is so anxious to get at her riches, and for some reason, I'm the only person arguing on her behalf. The others on the council assumed that I should be the one to search her house. And while I was reluctant, I also know that I would have felt wronged if another had been chosen for the task." He broke off, shaking his head, knowing that he wasn't explaining this well.

Elica was looking at him with an expression that was equal parts puzzlement and disgust. "Do you love her?" she finally asked.

Besh actually laughed aloud. "Hardly."

"Then I don't understand."

The old man nodded wearily. He would need a nap before this day was through. What a fool he'd been. "Truth be told, neither do I. It's enough to say that her disappearance . . . troubles me. And until I know why, I won't be able to rest."

"Do you fear for her?"

"I fear everything having to do with her."

Elica nodded at that, appearing to shudder as she did. "Well, the next time you feel the need to leave the house in the dark of night, I hope you'll at least have the decency to wake me, so I know where you're going."

"Agreed. I'm sorry to have frightened you."

She gave another nod and then started to leave the house.

"Elica," he said, stopping her. When she turned to look at him, he grinned. "What would you have done if I'd said I did love her?"

She frowned so deeply that he had to laugh again. "I don't even care to think about it," she said.

Besh finished eating his buttered bread, took a small drink of water, and made his way to Pyav's home.

The eldest was at his forge, his face even ruddier than usual, his brow dripping with sweat. He saw Besh enter and acknowledged him with a raised chin, but he didn't pause in his work. After a few moments he pulled something out of the fire with a long pair of tongs, swung it around to the anvil, and began to hammer at it, the smithy ringing with the clear sound of metal pounding on metal. Besh could see now that he was making a horseshoe, the curved iron still glowing red. At last Pyav took hold of the shoe with his tongs once more and thrust it into a barrel of water, sending a burst of swirling steam up into the rafters.

Only then did he step away from the anvil and cross to where Besh stood waiting.

"Morning, Besh," he said, wiping his forehead with his sleeve. "What can I do for you?"

"Have you spoken to Ojan today?"

Pyav frowned. "Ojan? Did something happen at Lici's last night?"

"In a manner of speaking, yes. I showed up, and I thought he might have mentioned it to you."

"I don't follow. What were you doing there?"

"I wanted to have a look at Sylpa's journal. I thought it would shed some light on how Lici first came here."

"It might at that." He looked at Besh a moment longer, as if expecting the old man to say more. "Is that all?" he finally asked.

"I thought you should know that I was reading the daybook. It's not mine, and I probably have no business looking at it at all."

Pyav chuckled. "Is that why you've come? To have my permission to look at the journal of a woman who's been dead almost half a century?"

"Well, yes. I—"

"It's all right, my friend." He placed a hand on Besh's shoulder. "You're a good man. To be perfectly honest with you, you've been far more scrupulous about all of this than I would have been. And I admire you for it," he added quickly. "Thanks to you, I believe the council is giving Lici the consideration that is her due. But given all that, I can't imagine you doing anything that would need my approval. In this matter, I trust you more than I do myself."

"Thank you, Eldest."

"Let me say this as your friend, and not as your eldest," he went on, his broad hand still resting on Besh's shoulder. "Learn what you can of the woman, but take care that you don't place too much faith in Lici's willingness to return your consideration. Whatever you do, do for yourself and not for her. I know that we have no right to take her gold or allow others to ransack her home, but the woman is a demon. She has been all her life."

Besh offered no response except to thank the eldest for his concern. But as he walked back home, intending to sleep for a short while, he couldn't help thinking that the eldest had to be wrong. No child was born a demon. And that begged the question: What had happened to turn Lici into one?

Chapter 6

Rois Dungar had been captaining merchant ships for thirty years now, almost since the day of his Fating, when the white-hairs in the tent at Bohdan's Revel, with their strange pale eyes and their magical stone, had shown him at the wheel of a vessel. He'd been barely more than a boy then, just a few days past sixteen, and still enchanted by the festival, by the Qirsi fire conjurers and the tumblers and musicians. It hadn't occurred to him then to care that his fate was shown to him by a Qirsi, that somehow through their gleanings at the Revel, the white-hairs had made themselves the arbiters of everyone's future. And by the time it did, he no longer cared.

Thirty years. Long ago he'd made enough gold to quit, had that been his desire. He could have bought a piece of pastureland near Rennach up in the Forelands and raised sheep as his father had done, and his father's father before that. But even before white-hair magic touched his life, Rois had heard the call of the sea. He started his life as a captain by running the short trade routes along the northern coast of the Forelands, learning his craft by navigating the waters around the Wethy Crown and along the Sanbiri coastline. Later, he'd begun to sail the Sea of Stars farther south, past the cities of Sanbira and the lofty peaks of the Border Range to the crimson cliffs of the Aelean shoreline and the prosperous port cities in Tordjanne and Qosantia. There weren't many of his kind—captains who carried trade between the Forelands and the Southlands—but those who were willing to brave the long voyages and the stormy waters of the south were rewarded with riches beyond the imaginings of most common merchants.

Some of those who traded between the two lands stuck strictly to the western waters, just as Rois stuck to the east. They traded with the Braedony empire in the north and with the Qirsi clans of the Southlands.

None of that for Rois. No white-hair trade if he could help it. The eastern realms of the Southlands were held by the Eandi, and they would remain in Eandi hands. That suited him fine.

There'd been a good deal of trouble with the Qirsi in the Forelands in recent turns. There'd been talk of rebellion and war, of a Weaver, one of those white-hairs with all different sorts of Qirsi magic, who was intent on destroying the Eandi courts. Word now was that the war had been fought and won, that this renegade Weaver was dead. But that didn't change much as far as Rois was concerned. There'd be more where this one came from, and there'd be more trouble. They went together, white-hairs and trouble did, just like east winds and rain.

All of which made somewhat curious the fact that he had agreed to give transport to three Qirsi on this run to Aelea. The short answer he gave to any among his crew with nerve enough to ask was that gold was gold, and these white-hairs were paying plenty for the privilege of sailing on the *Fortune Seeker*. The truth might have been harder to explain.

Had it been just any three Qirsi, he would have refused their gold and left them at the dock in Rennach, where they first sought passage on his ship. Three grown Qirsi were more trouble than any gold could cover. But these three weren't grown, leastaways not all of them. This was a family. A man, broader and taller than any Qirsi he'd met before, a woman as pretty as her man was formidable, and a babe who couldn't have been more than six or seven turns old.

Even so, he still might have refused. But there was talk trailing these three, rumor that gave Rois pause and that eventually convinced him to take their gold and allow them aboard his ship. Usually he didn't credit whispers of this sort. The rumors of ignorant men were worth about as much as weather predictions from a land-bound fool. But these rumors came from guards at the Rennach port, and they echoed things he'd heard in Eardley and Thorald as well. A tall Qirsi, his shoulder slightly malformed, traveling with a beautiful woman who bore his child; that's how they described him.

As to what this man had done, well, that was a bit more difficult to figure. Some said he'd killed the renegade Weaver with his bare hands. Others said he'd bested him with magic, proving that he was a Weaver as well. Still others claimed that he'd been in league with the renegades himself, but had turned on them at the last, just like Carthach, the Qirsi

traitor whose betrayal thwarted the first Qirsi invaders, who had come
to the Forelands from the Southlands nine hundred years before. Rois
wasn't sure what he believed, but he felt reasonably certain that the man
was no traitor. He'd seen his share of liars, cheats, and scoundrels in his
time, and all of them had a shifty look to them, something in their face
or bearing or manner that made him uneasy. However imposing this
Qirsi man might have been, he had an open face, and pale yellow eyes
that didn't shy from a direct gaze.

For a time, when he first saw this couple and their child, Rois did
think the man a brute, and the worst kind. The woman's face, pretty as it
was, bore subtle scars, pale thin traces of a razor's blade or a finely honed
dagger. In his day, the merchant had seen men brutalize in the most evil
ways the women they professed to love, and he assumed that this white-
hair was no different. It didn't take long, however, before he realized his
mistake. These two never strayed far from one another, and the man
doted on her constantly, attending to her as if intent on never letting a
moment of pain or fear intrude upon her happiness. And it was no act.
Some loves could be feigned; Rois had seen it done. This was the genuine article.

A story followed the woman as well, one that reached the captain's
ears after he had first started forming an opinion of this odd pair. She
had once been a servant of the evil Weaver and in betraying him had in-
curred his wrath. It was he, and not the man she so clearly loved, who
had given her those scars, despite the fact that she was sheltered at the
time by the king of Eibithar himself. That much Rois could believe, and
it began to make some sense, not only of what he saw between these two,
but also of why they would seek to leave the Forelands for the Southlands. For while he conducted a good deal of trade in both lands, he
rarely carried passengers between them.

In every way then, it was unusual for there to be Qirsi of any kind on
the *Fortune Seeker*. It seemed that Rois carried the gods as familiars on
his shoulder, the way some captains carried birds or other creatures they
found in their travels. Because had it not been for the Qirsi man standing now in the middle of his ship, Rois, his vessel, and his crew would
have been lost hours ago.

Clouds had hung low and menacing over the jagged white peaks of
the Border Range for the better part of a day, but such was the weather

in the highlands, and Rois thought nothing of it as he steered his ship parallel to the coast. But with this day's dawn had come the urgent ringing of the watchman's bell, and shouted warnings from the night crew. The captain could feel that the waters had grown rough, and even before emerging onto the deck from his cabin, he knew that a storm was almost upon them.

Stepping out into a stiff wind and steady rainfall, he saw that it was even closer than he had feared, and that it looked to be a beast of a storm, summoned, it seemed, by Morna herself. The sky was a deep angry purple; the water around them looked as cold and hard as steel. Within moments, a gale began to howl in the sails, nearly tipping the *Fortune Seeker* onto her leeward side. Swells pitched the vessel to and fro as if she were but a toy, and broke over the sides of the ship, dousing the deck and making the crew's work that much more treacherous. Rois shouted for his men to lower the sails and go to sweeps, but he could hear the hull and deck groaning like wraiths, and he knew that they couldn't possibly carry out his orders quickly enough to save the ship.

It was then that he heard the voice at his back, as even and calm as the sea was rough.

"Can I be of assistance, Captain?"

Turning, Rois saw that the white-hair stood just behind him, with his feet spread wide to keep his balance. He hadn't said more than good morning to the man since he first boarded the ship. At that moment he couldn't have recalled his name for all the gold in Tordjanne. More than once he'd regretted taking him and his family on board in the first place. Whatever the Qirsi might have done for the courts in battling that other Weaver, he was still a sorcerer.

Now, though . . .

"Can you tame a wind?"

"I can raise a wind against it. The effect will be much the same."

"Quickly then, man! Before she's torn to pieces!"

The Qirsi stepped past him and closed his eyes, rain running down his face like tears. Almost instantly, Rois felt a wind rise out of the west, an answer to that fierce gale raging across the churning waters. The force of the storm blunted for the moment, the ship righted itself, and several of the crew scrambled up the masts and started lowering the sails.

"I'm grateful t' ye," the captain said, stepping forward to stand beside the man.

The white-hair still had his eyes closed, but he smiled and nodded. "My pleasure. It was getting a bit rough below."

"No doubt. How long can ye hold this wind?"

"That depends on the storm. If it strengthens further, probably not very long. I'd suggest you get your men on their oars and steer us clear."

Rois nodded. He might not have liked Qirsi, but this man at least spoke plainly.

His was a seasoned crew, and they soon had the sweeps out and were rowing toward shore. This took them into the teeth of the storm, at least for a short while, but with the darkest clouds almost upon them, it made no sense to race this monster farther out to sea. Best to steer them to waters that had already seen the worst of the storm. The seas were high, and it was slow going, but the Qirsi held to his wind. Rois no longer feared for his ship. Those men who remained on deck stared at the Qirsi as they stepped past him, but they said nothing to him, and the captain made certain that they didn't disturb the man in any way.

For nearly an hour now, they had been on sweeps, and at last it seemed that the storm was passing. The waters ahead appeared calmer, and just above the line of shore in front of them, Rois could see faint hints of blue sky in among the clouds. He descended the steps from his wheel and walked to the Qirsi. The man looked terribly pale, and he seemed to be trembling, as if chilled to the bone.

"I think ye can stop now," Rois said.

The white-hair opened his eyes and staggered. He would have fallen had the captain not put a steadying arm around him.

"Thank you, Captain," he said hoarsely.

Rois helped him to a barrel, holding on to him until the man was seated.

"Can I get ye somethin'?" the captain asked. "Water? Somethin' stronger?"

The Qirsi shook his head and glanced up at the sky.

"Aye, it's passing. Ye saved us all, and th' ship." He nodded once. "Again, ye have my thanks."

"Perhaps there are advantages to having Qirsi aboard."

Rois grinned. "Could be." He started to walk away, then stopped and turned to look at the man again. "In th' excitement an' all, I's forgotten yer name," he said.

"Grinsa."

"And th' woman?"

"Cresenne. Our daughter is Bryntelle."

"And a beauty she is."

Grinsa smiled. "Thank you."

"Maybe th' three of ye would do me th' honor of supping with me tonight."

"Last I saw of Cresenne she was vowing never to eat again," the Qirsi said. "But I imagine that with the storm passing, she might reconsider. Thank you, Captain. It's a kind invitation, and I accept on their behalf."

"Good. At eight bells then."

"Eight bells." The man climbed to his feet and made his way below, moving stiffly, as if he had just come through a great battle.

Rois watched him go before turning his attention back to his ship. She had come through the storm with relatively little damage, but she looked a mess and he set the crew to cleaning her up.

By eight bells, the skies had cleared and the sun shone from just above the mountains, bathing the sea and ship in hues of gold. The winds had died down as well, and the water's surface reflected the few soft clouds that glided overhead as if it were a looking glass. Looking west, a man might never guess that the Sea of Stars had been roiled by a storm only a few hours before. The sky to the east remained dark, however, and occasionally it flickered with the glow of distant lightning.

The white-hairs arrived for supper just as the peal of the bells faded away. The man looked rested and none the worse for his struggle with the storm. The woman, on the other hand, seemed pale, leading the captain to wonder if she still felt sickened by the motion of the boat.

She smiled, though, as Rois extended a hand to her.

"Thank you for inviting us, Captain," she said. "It's very generous of you."

"It's th' least I can do, ma'am. What with this kind gentleman saving my ship and all."

She smiled, glancing briefly at Grinsa.

"Sit, please," the captain said, stepping back out of the doorway and waving them into the cabin. "There's not a lot o' room, but I daresay it'll do."

They took seats at the table on either side of Rois's chair. She held the babe, who was looking about with wide eyes, her gaze finally coming to rest on the oil lamp burning brightly above the table.

"Cook will be in with th' meal soon enough. I hope bluefish is all right."

"Yes, of course," Grinsa said.

Cresenne smiled, but the captain could see that it was forced. He didn't expect that she'd eat much.

"In th' meantime," he said, "how's about a bit o' wine?"

As Rois filled three glasses with some of the pale golden wine he had traded for during his last visit to Qosantia, his first mate, Pelton Fent, arrived, taking the fourth seat at the table. Usually Pelton ate with the crew, but the captain had asked him to join them. True, Grinsa had saved the ship, but still Rois didn't relish the notion of passing the evening alone with a family of Qirsi.

He introduced Pelton to the white-hairs and poured the man some wine. Then he raised his own glass, and with a glance at Cresenne, offered a toast. "To smooth waters th' rest o' th' way."

The woman smiled. She really was a beauty. "To smooth waters," she repeated.

They all sipped their wine.

"That's very good, Captain," Grinsa said. "Can I ask where it's from?"

"Th' lowlands," Rois said. Seeing the puzzled look on the Qirsi's face, he added, "Qosantia. One o' th' Eandi sovereignties of th' eastern Southlands."

The man and woman exchanged a look before Grinsa faced the captain again.

"Am I to understand, then, that there are separate Qirsi and Eandi sovereignties in the Southlands?"

"Ya didn't know?" Pelton asked in his heavy lowlands accent, eyeing the man.

Grinsa glanced at Cresenne again and shook his head. "No. We were . . . eager to leave the Forelands, and in our haste I'm afraid we didn't learn as much about our new home as we might have otherwise."

"More's a pity," the first mate said. "Ya woulda been better off taking th' otha route down."

The white-hair frowned and looked at Rois.

"What he means is the Qirsi clans hold th' west, th' Eandi th' east. Ye'll have little choice now but t' cross through th' Eandi sovereignties if ye're t' reach Qirsi lands."

"Do no Qirsi live among the Eandi?" the woman asked, her brow creased.

Whatever his feelings about Qirsi, Rois would have liked to find some way to smooth that pale forehead once more. But he wasn't going to lie to them.

"Very few, ma'am. And them that does have a hard time of it, if ye follow me."

"If you knew this when we first—"

The man laid a hand on her arm, silencing her. She continued to glare at Rois for another moment, though, before finally looking away and raking a hand through her long hair. The baby let out a small squeal, but no one else made a sound.

After some time, there was a knock at the door and Cook and his assistant came in bearing the fish and two loaves of bread. The old man had a smile on his face when he opened the door, but seeing the captain's expression and the frowns of his guests, Cook's face fell. He and the boy served everyone quickly and without a word, before fleeing the cabin.

"I swear t' ye, ma'am," Rois said when they were gone, "we thought ye knew."

She stared at her wine, her lips pressed thin, but after a moment she nodded.

"Ye've paid t' go as far as Yorl, in Aelea—"

"And how much farther is that?" Grinsa asked.

"We're about to Redcliff now," Rois said. "With a bit o' luck and a bit o' wind, we'll reach Yorl in the morning. But what I was going t' say is this. Ye having saved my ship and all, and me taking a shine to th' baby there—Bryntelle, isn't it?"

The man smiled. "Yes. Bryntelle."

"With all o' that, I could see clear to take ye south to Shevden, in Tordjanne. Or better still, Ferenham. That's in Qosantia. No charge, o' course."

Grinsa glanced at the woman, who gave a quick shake of her head. He held her gaze, though, and after a moment she shrugged, looking unhappy. "That's a generous offer, Captain," the man went on, facing Rois again. "What would we gain by going farther?"

"Well, some o' th' sovereignties are better fer yer kind than others. Stopping in Aelea, ye'll have t' go through that one and Stelpana before ye reach Qirsi land. Them's two o' th' worst."

"Why are they so bad?" Cresenne asked.

The captain shrugged. "They bore th' brunt o' th' Blood Wars when they was fought. Folks don't forget, even after more than a century." He wasn't sure that either of them knew anything about the Blood Wars, but they didn't ask, and he didn't see any reason to go into it lest it lead to more ugliness. "In any case," he said instead, "once ye're in Qosantia, ye can cross t' th' Ofirean Sea and get passage across t' whichever o' th' clan lands ye want."

Again Grinsa and the woman shared a look. After a few moments, Grinsa actually smiled and reached to take Cresenne's hand.

"Actually," he said, "I'm not certain that we want to spend that much more time aboard any ship, even one as fine as yours, Captain."

Rois nodded. "I think I understand. In that case, let me offer ye this. I know a farrier in Yorl who's always got a few beasts he's tryin' t' sell. I expect I can get ye a pair o' horses at a fair price. Yorl's the farthest point inland on th' Aelean shore. Ye can make for Eagle's Pass and head due west across th' center o' Stelpana. They're no kinder t' Qirsi there, but there's fewer o' them. There's more people in th' north, near the Companion Lakes, and in th' south near th' seacoast. Steer clear o' those areas."

"All right, we will. Thank you."

"How well do ye know th' lay o' th' land?" Rois asked.

The white-hair shook his head. "I'm afraid we don't know it at all. If you have a map we can look at, I'd be most grateful."

"I don't," the captain said. "But I can describe it for ye some." He looked at Cresenne. "Go ahead and eat a bit, ma'am. It'll do ye good t' have a bit in ye."

She gave a tight smile and nodded. And as they all finally tucked into Cook's fish, Rois began to tell Grinsa and the woman about a few of the more important features of the land south of the Border Range. Pelton put in a word or two along the way, and both Qirsi asked questions now and again. Describing a land so large to strangers without the aid of a map was a bit like guiding a blindfolded man through a rocky shoal, but by the end of the meal, both of them seemed to have a better sense of the Southlands.

The woman's anger faded during the course of the supper, but only slowly, and even as the evening was ending, Rois could see that she remained withdrawn.

"Is there anything else you can tell us about these Blood Wars you mentioned earlier?" Grinsa finally asked, as they lingered over one last cup of wine.

Rois shifted in his chair. He felt the first mate staring at him, but he ignored him for the moment. "There's not a lot t' tell," he said. "There've been Blood Wars in th' Southlands for hundreds o' years."

"Some say there were only th' one," Pelton put in.

"But they've been over for a hundred years," Grinsa said, looking from mate to captain.

Pelton nodded. "They 'ave."

"And still it's not safe for us in Eandi lands."

The first mate looked away. "Joost 'cuz th' wars ended doesn't mean folks like white-hairs any more 'an they did."

"Are you from the Southlands, Pelton?"

The first mate pushed out his cheek with his tongue and nodded, his eyes trained on the table. "Naqbae," he said.

Grinsa frowned.

"Th' southernmost sovereignty," Rois told him. "Th' Horsemen, they're called."

"And yet our Horseman is a sailor," Grinsa said.

Pelton looked up at that, a grin on his round face. "I can ride, too. All us Horsemen can."

"But you don't like our people very much, do you?" Cresenne asked him, a guarded look in those ghostly pale eyes.

"Fighting white-hairs is what my kind are famous fer," he said, not shying from her glare. "No other sovereignty has held back th' Qirsi armies th' way th' Naqbae did. When th' Stelpana were bein' pushed back across th' K'Sahd and th' Thraedes and finally th' Silverwater, an' th Qosantians an' Tordjannis were countin' their gold, we were forcin' th' T'Saan back int' th' hills. T' this day, we hold both banks of th' Grand Salt."

"That doesn't answer my question," she said.

"It's as much o' 'n answer as I got," he told her.

The baby had long since fallen asleep, but she stirred now, perhaps sensing her mother's anger, and she began to fuss.

"Perhaps it's time we were getting back to our quarters," Grinsa said, a smile fixed on his lips. "Thank you for a fine meal, Captain, and as well for all you've offered to do on our behalf."

Rois held out a hand, which Grinsa took in a powerful grip. "It's th' least I owed ye." He stood, stepped to the door, and held it open for them. As the woman walked past him, he inclined his head slightly, and said, "Ma'am."

A small smile touched her lips, but she said nothing.

"We'll put int' Yorl by midmornin'," he told Grinsa, as the Qirsi stepped past him. "Once we're in Eagles Inlet, th' waters should be calmer. Th' lady shouldn't have any more troubles, on this trip at least."

"Thank you, Captain. You've been very kind to us." He turned to look at Pelton. "Mister Fent."

The first mate gave a curt nod.

When they'd gone, Rois closed the door and exhaled heavily.

"I'm sorry, Captain," the mate said. "I'd 'ave done better t' keep my mouth shut."

He returned to his seat and poured the rest of the wine into his cup. "Ye did fine." He felt weary. The storm, this supper with the Qirsi—they'd worn him out.

"It could be dangerous for 'em in Aelea," Pelton said. "An' Stelpana's even worse. They should sail farther south."

"I know that," Rois said. "But it seems they've made up their minds." He sipped his wine. "I have th' feeling they can take care o' themselves. Seems they came through all tha' trouble in th' Forelands all right. And I'd wager there's more t' both o' them than meets th' eye."

"Maybe," the first mate said. "But th' Eandi sovereignties are no place for a Qirsi family, 'specially one what doesn' know th' ways o' th' land."

*T*hey walked back to their cramped quarters without saying a word, except for Bryntelle, who fussed and cried and would have given both Cresenne and Grinsa an earful had she been able. Once they were alone, a candle lit and the door closed, Cresenne pulled off her shirt, sat on the small bed, and began to nurse the child. Grinsa stood in the center of the chamber, his eyes trained on the floor. After a moment, he looked up at Cresenne and smiled.

"The captain was right. It's calmer."

"You were nicer to them than I would have been," she said.

"It's really not their fault that we know so little about where we're going. It's mine. Entirely."

He was always doing this: finding reasons to forgive people for their failings, be they friends or utter strangers. It was one of the reasons she loved him, and yet she often found it annoying. She did now.

"I'm not so sure I agree with you. I think they were so eager to take our gold that they gave no thought at all to anything else."

"And they should have?"

She frowned. "Yes! Of course they should have! We have a child with us. It should have been clear to them that we were strangers to the Southlands. Our accents alone mark us as being from the Forelands."

"Yes, they do. But I doubt many people embark on a voyage like this one without learning a bit more about their destination. I certainly wouldn't have had we been given the choice."

Cresenne could hardly argue with that. They'd been forced by circumstance to leave the Forelands. She had once been party to a Qirsi conspiracy that very nearly succeeded in toppling the Forelands' Eandi courts. Grinsa was a Weaver, a sorcerer who could bind together the powers of many Qirsi into a single tool. Or a single weapon. Since the Qirsi invasion of the Forelands nine centuries ago, Weavers had been feared, persecuted, and, when captured, put to death, along with their families. Yes, the two of them had allied themselves with the courts, risking their lives to fight the conspiracy, but the law of the land was clear. Eibithar's king had shielded Cresenne from punishment for her earlier crimes against the courts, and he had refused to treat Grinsa as anything other than the hero he was, but his land was riven by conflict and he could not risk civil war by summarily doing away with nine centuries of legal tradition.

They might have made a life for themselves in another realm of the Forelands, but the other Eandi courts were every bit as fearful of Weavers as was Eibithar. And so they chose the Southlands.

There was something romantic in the notion, something mysterious and wonderful. The Southlands. Home of the first Qirsi to come to the Forelands. True, they had come as would-be conquerors, but that did nothing to diminish the allure of the place, at least not as far as Cresenne was concerned. Perhaps here, Grinsa wouldn't have to hide the fact that he was a Weaver, as he had done in the Forelands, making his way through Eibithar with Bohdan's Revel, pretending to be nothing more than a festival gleaner, a Qirsi who used his power to offer others glimpses of their futures. Perhaps here, if Bryntelle grew up to be a Weaver like her father, she could wield her powers with pride rather than fear. Perhaps here, Cresenne could forget the shame of having been labeled a traitor by Eandi and Qirsi alike, of having joined the movement to overthrow the courts only to realize that the man who led it would prove to be a worse despot than any Eandi monarch in the history of the Forelands. She had such great hopes for this journey, all of which made what they had learned tonight from the captain and his first mate that much more disturbing.

"I'm still angry with them," she said at last. "And I still think you're being too . . ." She trailed off, shaking her head.

Clearly Grinsa knew what she was going to say, because he smiled, looking away.

Too forgiving. That was another of his faults. Cresenne shuddered to think what her life would be like if it wasn't. For he had forgiven her.

Their love had begun as a seduction, an elaborate deception on her part so that she might learn from this man what he knew of the courts and the gleaned fate of one particular noble. Twice, while still a part of the conspiracy, she had sent assassins to kill him, and even after Bryntelle's birth, when she should have been doing all she could to reconcile with Grinsa, she had instead railed at him, calling him a traitor to his people and worse. Yet still he loved her, and she him. She had finally found the strength to admit as much both to him and herself. She had loved him from the start, and—gods be praised—he had forgiven her for all that she had done to deny and destroy that love, which she had once mistaken for a weakness.

"If it makes you feel any better," he said after some time, "I didn't like Pelton any more than you did. But I do feel that the captain was trying to make amends. And I promise to make certain that he gets us those mounts at a fair price."

She had to smile. Would that she could be as fair-minded.

"And will you hold him to his promise of smoother seas?" she asked.

He sat beside her on the bed and kissed her shoulder. "I will. And if he breaks his word, I'll summon a wind and smooth them myself."

"Well, all right then." She looked down at the nursing child. "In that case we'll let him stay, won't we, Bryntelle?"

The baby paused in her suckling to look up at her mother briefly. After just a moment she resumed her meal.

"That's a yes," Cresenne said.

Grinsa laughed. "I'll take your word for it."

For some time, they sat together, watching Bryntelle eat, smiling as the baby's pale eyes gradually closed and she fell into a deep sleep.

Cresenne carried the child to the small crib the captain had found for them before departing Rennach and gently placed her on the bedding, taking care to cover her in case the night turned chill. Then she returned to Grinsa's side and kissed him softly on the lips. She lay down on the bed and pulled him to her.

"Are you feeling well enough?"

She nodded, smiled. "I'm fine, and I have it on good authority that we're done with rough waters."

They kissed again, deeply this time. Then she undressed him, and quietly, tenderly, they made love.

After, as Cresenne rested her head on his chest and stared at the small bright flame atop the candle, she began to ponder once more all they had heard this night about the new land to which they'd sailed.

"It never occurred to me that things might be worse in the Southlands," she murmured.

Grinsa stirred, as if he had nodded off briefly. "What did you say?" he asked, sounding sleepy.

"Nothing. I just was thinking about supper. About what they told us."

"Are you having second thoughts?"

She shrugged. "Would it matter? Where else can we go?"

He seemed to consider this for a few moments. "We could go back to the Forelands," he finally said. "We could find a small town in Sanbira or Caerisse. Some place where they wouldn't know us."

"No. I don't want that. I was just hoping that the Southlands would be different."

He laughed at that. "I gather that it is."

She smiled, too. "You know what I mean. I had hoped that all of this wouldn't be as bad down here, that maybe the races had found a way to live together, without conspiracies or blood wars, or anything else of that sort."

"Well," he said, "from what the captain says I gather the Blood Wars have been over for a long time. There's peace now. Maybe in building separate societies, they've found the answer. It's not what I had in mind either, but it's working. Really, that's all that matters."

She lifted her head and looked at him. "I wouldn't have expected that from you."

"And I wouldn't expect you to mind."

He was right. He had worked so hard to defeat the conspiracy, forging an alliance of loyal Qirsi and Eandi who waged war against the renegades. Since the day she met him, he had devoted himself to bringing the two races together. And though she owed her life to his success, and admired his courage and resolve, she knew that she wouldn't have sacrificed so much for the same ends. She had expected herself to welcome this change in him, seeing in it the promise of a quieter, more peaceful life. Instead, she was unnerved.

"It's not that I mind," she said, holding his gaze. "I'm just not sure that I understand."

"I'm tired, Cresenne. It's that simple. I'm tired. We came here to start over, and that's what I want to do. I don't want to worry about whether the person standing next to me in a marketplace knows that I'm a Weaver. I don't want to spend Bryntelle's childhood worrying all the time about what powers she's going to develop." He reached up and brushed a strand of hair from her brow. "Even Weavers don't live forever. I don't know how many years I have left, but I want to spend them with you, without having to worry all the time about what the rest of the world is doing to destroy itself. If the Qirsi and Eandi of the Southlands have found peace by living separately, so be it."

She gazed at him another moment. Then she kissed him, and once more they gave themselves over to the passion they shared. And for a time she couldn't tell the rhythm of their movements from the gentle motion of the ship as it sailed Amon's waters.

Chapter 7

✦┼✦

True to his word, the captain had steered his ship into Eagles Inlet by the time Grinsa and Cresenne emerged from their quarters the next morning. Cresenne carried Bryntelle up onto the deck; Grinsa bore a travel sack on his shoulders. The remnants of the previous day's storm had long since blown out to sea, and the sky above the inlet was sapphire blue. Sheer red cliffs rose on either side of the channel, their reflections staining the brilliant aqua waters as if with blood. Flocks of gulls circled overhead, their cries echoing off the stone, and cormorants sat on the narrow strip of rocky shore, holding out their wings to dry and eyeing the ship warily.

There was no wind, no ripple upon the water, no sign of any other vessel. Searching the cliff faces, Grinsa saw nothing to indicate that anyone lived here, or ever had. The crew of the *Fortune Seeker* went about their business without a word, and even the captain, apparently seeing no need to shout orders at men who already knew their duties, held his peace. Aside from the calls of the gulls and the rhythmic splashing of the sweeps as the men below rowed the ship through the inlet, all was silent. The effect was both peaceful and eerie, and when at last the ship turned a gentle corner in the channel, revealing a large settlement at the end of the inlet, Grinsa felt himself relax just a bit. Until that moment he hadn't been aware of the tension in his neck and back.

"Yorl," the captain said, breaking the stillness.

Grinsa turned and nodded, before facing forward again.

It was the largest city Grinsa had ever seen, and though it looked welcoming from a distance, the closer they drew to the end of the inlet, the more he came to realize how misleading this initial impression had been. Several wooden piers stood at the water's edge, and boats both large and small were moored beside them. Just behind them, however, a ponderous stone wall guarded the better part of the settlement, its color a match for the great cliffs surrounding the inlet. The terrain behind the wall sloped upward, so that the jumble of buildings and homes comprising the town seemed to have spilled haphazardly from the highlands above. Near the top of the dale a great fortress stood watch over the city, its towers built of the same red stone, its walls as massive as those of any castle in Eibithar or Aneira or any of the other realms of the Forelands.

A pair of flags, one of them purple and gold, the other blue and red, flew above the towers of the fortress, stirring lazily in the light wind. Soldiers stood on the ramparts of the fortress, their helms and spears glinting in the morning sun, but Grinsa couldn't imagine an enemy daring to attack such a place.

"I thought the Blood Wars were over," Cresenne said under her breath.

Grinsa smiled faintly, his eyes still fixed on the battlements. "It seems people here have long memories. Are you certain you wouldn't rather sail south a bit farther? Maybe cross one of the other sovereignties?"

"Do you think it would make much difference?"

"The captain thought it would."

She looked down at Bryntelle, who cooed in her arms, a toothless grin on her lovely face. This journey had been as hard on Bryntelle as it had been on Cresenne. The baby had eaten poorly for days. This was as happy as she had seemed since they boarded the ship in Rennach.

"I can't, Grinsa," she said at last. "And neither can Bryntelle. Probably we should. But the thought of another day aboard this ship is almost enough to make me weep." She glanced up at him. "I'm sorry."

"It's all right. I'm not certain I could bear to eat another bite of fish. We'll do as we planned, and we'll find a way through to Qirsi lands."

Cresenne nodded, though she still looked apprehensive.

The *Fortune Seeker* continued on her steady course toward the pier, and Grinsa and Cresenne remained on the deck, watching the city draw near, eyeing that hulking fortress as a sea captain might the towering grey clouds of an approaching storm. Before long—too soon, as far as Grinsa was concerned—the vessel had glided to one of the piers. Two of the crew jumped nimbly onto the dock and tied mooring ropes to a pair of heavy iron cleats bolted into the old wood. Other sailors on the dock, who might have spared only a glance for the merchant vessel under other circumstances, stared hard at the Qirsi, most with dark expressions, a few with genuine surprise. Grinsa pretended not to notice, but he moved a bit closer to Cresenne and Bryntelle, and he took hold of his magic, the way a soldier might grip the hilt of a sheathed sword, just in case.

When the ship had been tied fast and the gangway lowered to the dock, Grinsa took Cresenne's hand and made himself smile.

"Ready?"

Before she could answer, Grinsa heard a footstep behind them. Turning, he saw the captain walking toward them.

"Stay here," the man said as he stepped past and made his way to the gangway. "I'll be back shortly."

"Captain?" Grinsa called after him.

He looked back at them, scratching his paunch, the morning sun lighting the silver flecks in his black hair. "Ye shouldn' linger in th' city too long. I'll arrange fer th' horses as I promised ye."

Grinsa approached him, pulling out the small leather pouch that held their gold. "You'll need money."

But the captain held up a broad hand and shook his head. "Ye kin pay 'im after I've arranged matters."

"Can I pay you for your trouble?"

"No." He nodded toward Cresenne. "Th' lady was right. We shoulda warned ye. I'm jest makin' things right atween us."

"You're a good man, Captain."

The man waved the compliment away. "Ye should save yer gold if'n ye can. Or if ye have t' spend it, buy somethin' fer th' little beauty. Later. When ye's away from here."

Grinsa had to smile. "We will. Thank you."

"I won' be long," the man said, and left his ship.

With the captain gone, Pelton Fent took command of the vessel. He stood in the middle of the deck, not far from the Qirsi, his stout legs planted, his arms crossed over his barrel chest, and he watched the men, barking commands occasionally, but mostly letting the crew go about their work, just as the captain had done. He didn't so much as look at Grinsa or Cresenne, and the rest of the men, perhaps following his example, ignored them as well.

"What if he can't find us horses?" Cresenne asked after some time.

Grinsa shrugged. "We'll walk."

Cresenne actually laughed. "Even I'm not that desperate to get off the sea. We'll sail farther."

He glanced at her, grinning. "Do you really need me for this conversation?"

"Who says I was talking to you? Right, Bryntelle?" She kissed the baby's belly, eliciting a loud squeal that drew the stares and smiles of several of the crew.

"We could do worse than to remain on this ship," Grinsa said, lowering his voice.

"I know. But I'd rather it didn't come to that."

A few moments later, Grinsa spied the captain making his way down the main road leading from the city walls to the wharf. He walked briskly, and as he stepped onto the pier, he caught Grinsa's eye and nodded.

"He's done it," the gleaner said.

Cresenne looked at him. "You're certain?"

He took her hand again. "Come on."

They walked to the gangway, meeting the captain just as he stepped onto the ship.

"Well, I've found ye two fine beasts," Rois said. "And at a fair price t' boot."

"Thank you, Captain. We're in your debt."

"Not at all. Th' farrier is a man named Dren Melqen. His shop's just off th' west end o' th' marketplace. Ye shouldn' have any trouble findin' it. I've found ye a bay and a dun—good animals both. Dren wanted eight sovereigns fifty fer each, but he owes me a favor—owed me, that is. I got 'im down t' twelve sovereigns even fer th' pair."

The captain said this last with some pride, and though Grinsa knew as little about Southlands currency as he had about everything else in this strange land, he smiled and nodded.

"Well done, Captain. Thank you." He pulled out his money pouch again. "Will the farrier take Forelands money?"

Rois laughed. "Dren will take any coin ye give 'im. So will any other man or woman in th' markets here. Gold's gold, wherever it be from. Twenty-five o' yer qinde ought t' do it. Tha's a bit on th' generous side, but close enough."

Grinsa nodded. Twenty-five qinde for a pair of horses wasn't a bad price, though in the Forelands it might not have been cause for quite as much satisfaction as he'd seen on the captain's face.

"Tell me, Captain. Will we need different coin when we reach Qirsi land?"

The man shook his head. "They take sovereigns, too. Or qinde. As I say, gold is gold. Th' clans tend t' trade in goods rather than gold, which may be why they's never had much use fer coin. But they'll take gold all right. Th' Talm'Orast and H'Bel seem t' collect it." He laughed, but seeing that Grinsa and Cresenne didn't understand the joke, he quickly grew serious again. "Anyway, yer fine with what ye got."

"Very well." He held out a hand, which the captain gripped. "Again, Captain, you have our thanks. May the *Fortune Seeker* always find helping winds and easy waters."

"I 'preciate that. Ye take care o' these lovelies now, ye hear?" He took Cresenne's hand between both of his own and looked her in the eyes. He was about her height, but so powerfully built that she looked like a child beside him. "I know ye think we done ye wrong, ma'am. But I swears agin, it weren't on purpose."

"I believe you, Captain. And I'm grateful to you for finding us the mounts."

He grinned broadly at the baby and tapped her belly with a fat finger, drawing a giggle.

They left the ship and made their way up the pier toward the city. And almost immediately upon reaching the cobblestone road leading to the gate, Grinsa knew that he was in an alien land. It wasn't just the stares, or the palpable hostility of those they encountered along the way, though they would have been enough to put both him and Cresenne on edge. In the cities of the Forelands, there had been ten Eandi for every one Qirsi. In smaller towns and country villages, the Qirsi had been even less of a presence. But no matter where one went, there were almost always a few Qirsi at least. One could look out across any marketplace and see amid the dark hair and dark eyes one or two pale figures, a shock of bone white hair, or a pair of flame-colored eyes.

But here, in this city, he saw none. Had he not known better he might have assumed, looking at the road and the city gate beyond it, that there were no Qirsi in all the Southlands. On the other hand, he could tell from the glares of the Eandi they encountered that the men and women of Yorl were very familiar with his people, and that this familiarity had bred little but contempt and fear. People actually stopped in their tracks to watch Grinsa and Cresenne walk by. No one said anything to them, but they didn't have to.

"What should we do?" Cresenne asked in a whisper.

"Just keep walking."

"But the gate."

"I know. We'll deal with it when we get there. The captain would have told us if they had laws barring Qirsi from entering the city."

She glanced about nervously. "It's not the laws I'm afraid of."

"Keep looking right in front of you," he told her. "Don't let them see that you're scared."

Cresenne's nod was almost imperceptible. They covered the rest of the distance without a word, stopping before the Eandi guards who blocked the path that led through the heavy stone gate. There were two of them, both dressed in uniforms that matched that purple and gold flag flying above the fortress and that bore the golden insignia of an eagle. They were large men, as tall as Grinsa, and powerfully built. Both wore helms and armor; both were armed with broadswords.

"What's yar business here, white-hair?" one of them asked, in the strange accent of the eastern Southlands. His eyes flicked for an instant to Cresenne and the baby, but then returned to Grinsa.

"We've just arrived on the *Fortune Seeker*—"

"That's no' what I asked. Ya intending t' stay here in Yorl, or are ya passin' through?"

"Passing through." Grinsa kept his voice even, but he didn't shy away from the man's gaze.

"What's yar name?"

"Grinsa jal Arriet."

"That's no' a Southlands name," the man said with a frown, though Grinsa had the sense that he wasn't really surprised.

"No, it's not. As I was trying to tell you a moment ago, we've just arrived on the *Fortune Seeker* from our home in the Forelands. We're new to Aelea, to all the Southlands, really."

"I see. What business d' ya have in th' city?"

"The *Fortune Seeker*'s captain has arranged for us to buy two horses from a farrier here in Yorl. And we need to buy some food as well. After that, we'll be on our way."

The guard nodded, still eyeing him. He gave no indication, though, that he was ready to let them pass. "Ya have th' look of a Weaver, Grinsa."

Grinsa managed with some success to hide his surprise at this, but Cresenne let out a small gasp. In the Forelands, where fear of Weavers ran so deep, most Eandi were remarkably ignorant about what it meant to be a Weaver. Grinsa had never met anyone among Ean's children who was familiar enough with Qirsi magic to identify a Weaver simply by appearance. If he needed any more proof that they were in a land vastly different from his home, here it was.

"You're right," he said. "I am a Weaver. Is that a problem?"

"Tha' depends on you. Weavers have been known t' stir up trouble now an' again. From what I hear, that's even been true in th' Forelands recently. I don't know how my kind deal with yar kind in th' North, but here, we know how to handle Weavers. Ya remember that."

"I will," Grinsa said, still refusing to break eye contact with the man. "Can we go now?"

The guard indicated Cresenne with an open hand. "Is she a Weaver, too?"

"Why don't you ask her?"

His expression soured, but he turned to Cresenne, and said, "Are ya?"

"No, I'm not."

At that, a smile flickered in the man's eyes ever so briefly. "All right," he said. "Ya're free t' go." He and his comrade stepped out of the way, allowing them to enter the city.

Only when they were some distance from the gate did Grinsa realize that his fists were clenched, the skin stretched so tightly over his knuckles that it hurt. He flexed his hands and shook his head slowly.

"For all the foolish Eandi I encountered in the Forelands," Cresenne said, "I've never in my life felt as hated as that man just made me feel."

Grinsa looked around, enduring the stares as best he could. "It can't all be like this."

"No. Only half of it."

They found the farrier's shop and stepped inside. At first they saw no one and Grinsa called out a tentative "Hello." Almost immediately a young man emerged from the back. He was tall and lanky, with red hair and bright blue eyes. Seeing the Qirsi, he stopped, his eyes narrowing.

"What d' ya want?"

"We're here to see Dren Melqen. We were sent by the captain of the *Fortune Seeker*."

"Pa!" the young man called, his eyes never leaving the two of them, as if he expected them to attack him at any moment.

A second man stepped into the shop, and Grinsa knew immediately that this was the young man's father. He was the image of the other—same color hair and eyes, same square handsome face. But where the son was merely tall, this man was positively hulking. He stood even taller than his son, and he was broader in the chest and shoulders than the guards at the gate had been. He kept his shoulders somewhat stooped, as if he feared that he might not fit in the shop if he straightened to his full height. Grinsa had never seen a bigger man.

He looked Grinsa over, then placed a hand on his son's shoulder.

"It's all right," he muttered to the boy. "Ya're th' ones Rois sent?"

"Yes. We're grateful to you for selling us the horses."

"I'm doin' it fer Rois."

"Of course."

The man gestured over his shoulder. "I got 'em out back." With that he turned and stepped out of the shop, trailed closely by his son. Grinsa and Cresenne had little choice but to follow.

They walked through a musty storeroom, and pushed open a door that let them out into a small paddock. The bay and dun were tied at the far end of a plot of wispy grass, but the man and son stood nearer to the door beside a white nag and an old chestnut plow horse.

"Here ya go," the farrier said.

Grinsa shook his head. "Those aren't the horses Captain Dungar described for us."

The man raised an eyebrow, but he didn't look surprised. "No?" He wasn't much of a liar. Probably a man of his size didn't have to be. Who among the Eandi would ever challenge him?

"He said he'd arranged for us to buy the dun and bay over there."

"That right? At what price?"

"I think you know the price, sir."

"Surely no' th' twelve sovereigns we talked about fer these two."

Cresenne glared at him. "You bastard!"

Grinsa put a hand on her back. "How much?" he asked.

The farrier eyed Cresenne briefly, an eyebrow raised and a small smile on his lips. Then he turned to Grinsa. "I'll give 'em t' ya fer twenty."

He felt Cresenne gathering herself to say something more, but he pressed hard against her back and she kept silent.

"No," Grinsa said. "We'll pay twelve, as you agreed. And we'll take the dun and bay. Again, as you agreed."

"I didn' agree t' any such thing."

"Are you saying that Captain Dungar lied to us?"

"No, white-hair. I'm sayin' tha' ya're lyin' now. Rois knows I'd never agree t' sell such fine beasts, at tha' price, t' th' likes o' ya." He grinned. "And so does every man in Yorl."

Grinsa nodded slowly. This much he'd known already. He had no legal recourse. Dren had signed no papers, and no one in this city would take the word of a Qirsi against that of the farrier, even if they knew the man to be a liar and a cheat. The *Fortune Seeker* might still be at the pier, but even the captain might not be able to help him. Yes, he was Eandi, but he was also a Forelander, which probably made him suspect in the eyes of the people of Yorl.

"Come on, Grinsa," Cresenne said, still staring at the man, her eyes blazing like siege fires. "We'll get horses elsewhere."

But Grinsa didn't move. "I'm not leaving without the horses we were promised."

"That's fine," Dren said. "Twenty sovereigns an' they's yars."

"So, you admit that the bay and dun were the ones you discussed with the captain."

It took Dren a moment. Then his face reddened. "I joost knew ya was talkin' 'bout them uns."

"You're a liar, Dren. And what's more, you're a bad one."

The man's face turned to stone, and he picked up a large hammer from the railing beside him. "I've knocked men cold fer less 'an that, white-hair."

He'd meant to provoke him, and had hoped that the farrier would take up a weapon. Reaching for his magic, Grinsa shattered the hammer's head, so that fragments of iron fell to the ground all around the farrier's feet.

"But not a Weaver," Grinsa said evenly.

The farrier stared at the useless piece of wood he still held in his hands.

"I shouldn't have to tell you what other powers I possess," Grinsa said. He drew upon another of his magics, and a moment later the plow horse, which was not tied to anything, began walking toward the farrier's son. At first, not understanding what was happening, the young man ordered the beast to halt. When it didn't, he tried to shove it away. That didn't work either, and slowly, the old horse forced the boy backward toward where the dun and bay were tied.

"Pa?" he said, sounding frightened, his eyes darting back and forth between his father and the advancing plow horse.

"Call him off!" Dren said.

"Tell your boy to untie those horses."

Dren took a menacing step toward Grinsa, but before the Qirsi could do anything, a bright yellow flame burst from the ground just in front of the farrier, stopping him in midstride and forcing him back.

"I'm not a Weaver," Cresenne said evenly. "But I've got a bit of power as well."

"Tell him to untie the horses," Grinsa said again.

The man licked his lips. "This is thiev'ry," he said. "Ya white-hair demons is robbin' me o' what ain' yars."

Grinsa glanced at Cresenne and nodded once. Immediately, her conjured fire died away, and Grinsa grabbed the man's throat in his hand. Dren wrapped his powerful hands around Grinsa's wrists.

"Let go of me," the Qirsi said, "or I'll shatter every bone in your body just the way I did your hammer. Do you understand?"

The farrier glowered at him, but after a moment he nodded and dropped his hands to his side.

"Have you ever heard of mind-bending magic, Dren?"

The man shook his head.

"It may have a different name here. I'm really not sure, nor do I care. It's a power that allows me to make you do whatever I want you to do, say whatever I want you to say. I can force you to tell the truth and admit exactly what you and Rois agreed to earlier today. The problem with mind-bending magic is that it's not that precise. It can hurt if it's used too roughly, and sometimes the damage can't be undone. Now, I'm usually pretty good with my magic, but you've angered me and, well, who knows what might happen if I try it on you when I'm angry?"

While much of what Grinsa told him about mind-bending power was true, this last was not. He had no doubt that he could use his magic on the man precisely enough to avoid hurting him. But he didn't want to use it at all.

"So rather than risking an injury that might leave you permanently addled," he went on, "you might want to consider whether it wouldn't just be better to admit that you're lying, sell us the horses, and be rid of us for good." He let go of the farrier's throat and stepped back.

"Fine then," the man muttered. "Ya can have th' damn horses."

"So your son can hear."

"Ya can have th' horses," he said again, loudly this time.

"The dun and the bay."

"Yeah, th' dun an' th' bay."

"And what was the price?"

Dren exhaled through his teeth and looked away. "Twelve."

"That's the amount you and Captain Dungar agreed to, isn't it?"

"Yeah, we agreed t' twelve."

"But, Pa," the boy called from beside the two beasts, the plow horse positioned in front of him like a sentry. "Ya said—"

"Joost shut up and bring th' beasts here."

The young man did as he was told, leading the two horses to where his father was standing. Grinsa pulled his pouch free and counted out twenty-five qinde. He held out the coins to the boy, who glanced at his father, as if unsure of what to do.

"Take th' money," Dren said sullenly. "An' give 'im th' beasts."

Once he had the reins in hand, Grinsa nodded to the farrier. "Thank you, Dren. I've enjoyed doing business with you."

"Git out," the man said. "An' I wouldn' linger in town too long if I was ya." He bared his teeth in a grin. "It might no' be safe."

Grinsa had started to walk away, but he stopped now, and with no more than a thought, he lit the man's apron on fire. Letting out a cry at the sight of the flames, Dren threw himself to the ground and rolled back and forth until they had been extinguished.

"White-hair bastard!" he growled, looking up at the Qirsi, smoke rising from his clothes.

"I wouldn't set foot outside your shop until we've cleared the city gate," Grinsa told him. "*That* wouldn't be safe."

They led the horses out of the paddock and into a narrow alley behind Dren's shop. From there, they made their way back onto the main avenue and into the city marketplace, where they hoped to buy a pair of saddles.

"How long do you think it will be before he comes after us?" Cresenne asked, as they searched the market for a saddler.

"Not long at all. But we won't stay any longer than it takes to buy some food and find a saddler. As far as I'm concerned we can buy the first saddles we see."

Yorl's marketplace was large, and difficult to navigate, but there were so many peddlers selling their wares that they soon found all that they needed. Before long, the horses were saddled, their travel sack was filled with dried fruits, salted meat, and flat breads, and they were on their way to the city's west gate. Before they reached it, however, they spotted the farrier and his son searching the streets for them, accompanied by four of the city guards.

"Damn," Grinsa muttered.

"We bought the horses as agreed," Cresenne said, as if reassuring herself. "We did nothing wrong."

"Dren won't have said anything about the horses. He doesn't have to. I lit his apron on fire. That's why they're looking for us." He looked at her. "I'm sorry. I shouldn't have done it."

"I'm glad you did. I was ready to; you just beat me to it."

"So what do we do?" he asked.

She thought a moment, and as she did, Bryntelle let out a small cry. A smile crossed Cresenne's face, and then vanished just as quickly as it had appeared. "Leave this to me," she told him.

Grinsa only had time to nod before Dren spotted them, thrusting out an arm with a triumphant smile on his face. He led the guards and his son to where they stood, his long strides carrying him so quickly in their direction that the others had to run every few steps to keep up with him.

"That's 'im!" the farrier said, stopping a few steps from them and looking back at the uniformed men. "That's th' Qirsi who tried t' burn me!"

"Is tha' true?" one of the guards asked, staring hard at Grinsa.

"Actually, it's not," Cresenne said.

"What?" The farrier shook his head and looked at the guards. "She's lyin'!"

"I'm the one who did it. Not Grinsa." She held out her hand, palm up, and an instant later a bright golden flame jumped to life there. "As you see, I have fire magic." The fire died away and she lowered her hand. "I shouldn't have done it, I know, but he threatened us and I . . . I feared for my child." Remarkably, a tear slid down her face. Grinsa nearly laughed out loud at the sight of it. "You have to understand," she went on, her voice trembling slightly. "We're strangers to your land. And you all seem to hate our kind so much. And then this man threatened us that way. I just didn't know what else to do. I'm so sorry."

"I tell ya, she's lyin'! Ya can' believe a word she says, or 'im neither!"

"You didn't threaten us?" Grinsa said. "You didn't tell us that it wouldn't be safe if we chose to linger in the city?"

"Did ya say tha' t' them?" the guard asked.

"No!" the farrier said.

It seemed that the guard knew Dren well enough not to believe him. He just eyed the man for several moments, saying nothing.

"Yeah, all righ'," Dren admitted. "I said it."

"Why?"

"They stole those beasts from me!"

"What?" the guard said. "Why didn't you mention that before?"

"Because it's not true!" Cresenne said, indignant now. "We paid him the equivalent of twelve sovereigns. Twenty-five qinde in Forelands money. He might even have the coins with him now."

Dren's hand strayed to his pants pocket. "It's less 'an they's worth!" he said, before the guard could demand that he produce the money. "They practic'ly stoled 'em from me! They threatened me wit' their magic! Th' boy will tell ya!"

"He'll also tell you, as will the captain of the *Fortune Seeker,* that twelve sovereigns was the price he agreed to."

The guard waved both hands and shook his head. "I don' care 'bout any o' this. It's no' my place t' git ya a better price fer yar beasts, Dren." He looked first at Grinsa, then at Cresenne. "Ya should be on yar way. This is no place fer yar kind." He started away, gesturing for the other guards to follow.

"I oughta kill ya both where ya stand!" the farrier said, his fists clenched.

The guard stopped and took a step back in their direction. "I heard tha', Melqen. Ya're lucky I don' put ya in th' gaol straightaway. Now git back t' yar shop an' leave them be!"

At first the farrier didn't budge, and Grinsa readied his magic, just in case. Finally, though, the man shook his head and started to walk away.

"Come on, then," he called to his son. "They's no' worth th' trouble."

Grinsa and Cresenne didn't move until they'd watched the two of them cross the marketplace and disappear around a bend in the road. Once they were certain that the farrier was no longer a danger, they started toward the gate again, climbing the steep road that led past the fortress.

"How did you do that?" Grinsa asked her as they rode.

The hint of a smile touched Cresenne's lips. "Do what?"

"You know perfectly well what. You actually made yourself cry."

"So? Bryntelle does it all the time."

He laughed. "You mean to say you learned it from her?"

"Not entirely, no." She held up her hand—the one on which she'd balanced the flame when she showed the guards that she possessed fire magic. Her palm was red and had a small blister on it.

"Cresenne!"

"It's all right. I just let my healing magic fade a moment before I extinguished the flame. It hurt enough to bring tears to my eyes, but it's nothing I can't heal."

"You're mad!"

She raised an eyebrow. "It worked, didn't it?"

He could only nod. "Yes, it worked."

"Then stop complaining."

"Yes, my lady."

She smiled, sunshine lighting her face.

Leaving the city proved to be far easier than entering it had been. They dismounted before the west gate, expecting to be questioned again. But though the guards at the city wall eyed them warily as they walked past, the men didn't stop them or ask them any questions.

Grinsa and Cresenne led their mounts through the gate and onto the road outside the city walls. There they simply stopped and stared at the landscape that stretched before them. They were at the top of the rise, on an even level with the outer walls of the fortress. A broad golden plain ran away from them in every direction. No doubt the expanse was dotted with towns and villages, but from just outside the walls of Yorl, Grinsa couldn't see any of them. What he did see, looming in the distance, ringing the plain, were enormous snowcapped mountains, their peaks as jagged as demons' teeth. Grinsa knew from the captain that Eagle's Pass lay due west, and that it afforded fairly easy passage through the mountains. But still he couldn't help but be daunted by the sight of those peaks.

"It's beautiful," Cresenne said.

"It is."

She turned to look at him. "Do you wish we'd stayed on the *Fortune Seeker*?"

"No. You told me yourself that Bryntelle wasn't eating well while we were aboard the ship. And I like your face better without that pale shade of green it always seemed to have when we were on the water."

Cresenne laughed. "Thanks." Her expression sobered. "Do you wish we'd stayed in the Forelands?"

He reached for her hand and held it to his lips. "There's nowhere I'd rather be than here, with the two of you. I swear it." He faced the plain and mountains again. "This is home now. And as you say, it's beautiful."

He took Bryntelle from her and held the child while Cresenne climbed onto her mount. Bryntelle was awake and smiling, her eyes as pale and perfect as candle flames.

"This is home now," he whispered again.

Bryntelle gave a squeal and grabbed at his finger. He kissed her forehead and handed her up to Cresenne. Then he swung himself into his saddle, and together they began the long ride westward toward the Qirsi clans.

Chapter 8

Not far from the lake, along one of the many streams that meandered through the pale, golden fields surrounding their village, stood a tight cluster of low, gnarled trees. It was in a shallow dale, a place sheltered from the cold winds that swept across the highlands during the snowy turns. Yet, during the Growing season, when the sun's heat grew unbearable in the fields, the shade and the cool dampness of the stream and grasses kept it cool. And at this time of year, as the first hint of the Harvest breezes began to touch the crops, whispering softly that their time had almost come, the skies above the dale turned deepest blue, and the leaves of those misshapen old trees shaded to gold and rust.

Jynna couldn't remember when she had discovered this place. She was old enough to understand that she hadn't done so on her own, that perhaps Mama or Papa had brought her here the first time, or maybe one of her older brothers. But it often seemed to her that the others had forgotten about it, that no one else from the village knew it existed. So thoroughly was it hers that she never feared being found there. She went there to cry, to scream her rage at some injustice done her by her parents or brothers or teachers, or just to sit and watch the day float by, like the feathery clouds that drifted above the highlands on these cool Harvest mornings. Often while she was there she saw eagles soaring overhead. Once she saw a mountain lion skulking in the shadows by the trees, and she ran back home, vowing never to go there again. But the lure of the place was too strong. Eventually she returned, bearing an old broken ax handle to use as a club if she needed it. She hadn't seen the lion again, but still she kept the ax handle by the trees, just in case she ever needed it.

On this morning, she had risen early with her father and followed him into the fields to check the grain and feed crops. In another half a turn, when both moons were full again, they would begin the harvest.

Her lessons at the small sanctuary were to begin at midday—their teacher was to be married this morning—and so after she had fed the cows and Papa's plow horses, she had nothing more to do. Of course she went to the dale.

She looked for the lion as she followed the stream toward the trees, but she saw nothing save a plump, brown grouse that watched her approach and flew away on whistling wings as she drew near.

Sometimes she stayed by the stream, just beyond the trees, but the sun was warm today and she made her way toward the shade. As she drew closer to the wood, though, she saw something that made her falter. There was someone hunched over within the copse.

Jynna didn't know what to do. For so long the place had been her secret, her sanctuary. It never even occurred to her that she might find someone else there lurking among the trees. Her first impulse was to run home and tell her father. But she was also tempted to march right into the copse and demand to know what this person was doing in her dale. In the end, she did neither. She did walk to the small wood, but she approached it slowly, peering into the shadows, trying to see if she knew the person who was in her secret place. She moved silently, as she had practiced in this very spot, trying to see how close she could come to the deer that often grazed here late in the day, and so the person hiding there took no notice of her approach.

When at last Jynna had a clear view into the shadows, she saw that it was an old woman, an Eandi by the look of her. The stranger knelt on the ground in a small open area. And arrayed around her in several curving rows, like a rainbow, were woven baskets of all shapes and sizes. The woman was whispering something to herself, but Jynna couldn't make out what it was. Moving a bit closer, she saw that the woman bled from a wound on the back of one hand, and that she held what looked to be dark mud in the palm of the other. Jynna still couldn't hear, so she took another step into the shadows, and doing so, she stepped on a dry twig, which snapped under her weight.

The woman looked up sharply, her dark eyes finding Jynna immediately.

"Who are you?" she demanded.

Jynna took a step back and started to run away.

"Wait!" the woman called. "I'm sorry! You startled me!"

Still the girl ran.

"My name is Licaldi!"

She nearly stumbled on a tussock of grass, but she righted herself, and kept running.

"I can show you magic! That's what I was doing!"

Jynna slowed, then stopped. Magic. She was Y'Qatt. So was everyone in Tivston. But that didn't mean that she didn't know about magic. But she'd been so sure that the woman was Eandi.

She turned and took a tentative step back toward the trees. As she did, the old woman emerged from the shadows. Jynna knew right away that she had been right: The woman was Eandi. So how could she do magic?

She carried a small basket in one hand—the hand that bled. The other hand hung at her side, but when she stepped into the sunlight something glinted there. A knife. Again Jynna backed away.

"It's all right," the woman said. She halted and held up the blade, a smile on her wizened face. "This is for me, not for you."

There was still a good distance between them, and Jynna felt reasonably certain that she could run faster than the old woman if she needed to. "You're Eandi," she said, watching the stranger closely.

"I'm Mettai," the woman told her. "Do you know what that means?"

Of course. She'd heard her father and mother speak of the Mettai. They were Eandi sorcerers who used their blood to do magic. But her parents spoke of them the way they did of the horsemen of Naqbae or the warriors of the T'Saan clan, as if they lived leagues and leagues from Tivston. What was this woman doing here?

"Yes," Jynna answered. "I've heard of the Mettai. Is that why you're bleeding?"

The woman glanced at her hand and after a moment licked away a streak of blood. "Yes, it is. Blood magic." She held up the knife again. "That's why I need this. A Mettai can't conjure without her blade."

"What kind of magic are you doing?"

The woman beckoned to her. "Come here and I'll show you." She smiled again. "I won't hurt you."

Jynna walked back toward where the stranger was waiting for her, but she stopped several paces away, well out of reach of the old woman's blade.

"Good girl," the woman said. "Now watch this."

She dropped to her knees with an ease that seemed to belie her aged appearance and carefully placed the basket on the grass just in front of her. Then she laid the blade on the cut she'd already made on the back of her hand and pulled it slowly across the wound, wincing slightly as she did. Blood began to flow from the cut again, but before it could run away over her skin, the woman caught it on the flat edge of her knife. She carefully switched the blade to her wounded hand, then stooped, ripped away a clod of grass, and pulled out a handful of earth from the hole it left. Mixing the blood from her knife with the earth in her hand, she said, "Blood to earth, life to power, power to thought, flowers to basket."

After a moment, the bloody mixture in her hand began to swirl, as if stirred by some invisible hand. Once, twice, three times it turned in her hand. As it began to go around a fourth time, the old woman, with a light flick of her wrist, cast the mixture at the basket. But rather than merely splattering the lovely weaving, the dark mud appeared to turn to tiny flower petals, or shards of colored glass, or droplets of water shining with the colors of the rainbow.

And suddenly the basket, which had been empty an instant before, was overflowing with blooms. Aster and columbine, larkspur and lupine, snapdragon and pennyroyal, and others Jynna didn't know. Her fear of the woman forgotten, the girl ran forward and knelt opposite her. She started to reach out to touch the petals, but stopped herself.

"Can I touch them?" she asked.

"Of course, my dear. They're quite harmless."

She touched the lupine and the snapdragon. They felt real. Leaning forward, she inhaled, the scents of the blooms filling her lungs. She gently rubbed the leaves of the pennyroyal and then sniffed her fingers. They smelled cool and fresh, like the mint she often found growing beside the stream in her village.

"They're beautiful," she whispered.

"They're yours, if you'd like them," the woman said. "The basket, too."

"Did you make the basket?"

"Yes, I did."

"With magic?"

The woman smiled and shook her head. "No, I wove all my baskets by hand."

"But you were doing magic on them before."

The woman's smile changed, the way adults' smiles did when they were annoyed but didn't want to show it. "What do you mean?" she asked.

"Before, in the trees, before you saw me. You had your baskets out and your hand was bleeding, and you were speaking to yourself, like you did just now when you made the flowers."

"You saw that, did you?"

Jynna nodded. She wanted to get to her feet again and put some distance between herself and the stranger, but she didn't know how to do it without seeming rude.

The woman looked at her bleeding hand and took a breath. After a moment she licked the blood away again, as she had in among the trees. She lifted her gaze, her eyes meeting Jynna's.

"The truth is," she said, "I weave my baskets entirely by hand, and usually I dye them by hand as well. But I've been wandering a long time, making new baskets as I go, and I don't have all my dyes with me. So occasionally, I have to color my baskets using magic. That way I can get gold enough to continue my travels. Do you understand?"

Jynna nodded.

"I usually like to keep this a secret," the woman went on. "We Mettai aren't well liked by the other Eandi. They don't like our magic. But you being Qirsi and all, I didn't think you'd mind too much."

"Actually, we're Y'Qatt."

"Y'Qatt! Really!" the woman said, as if she'd never met one of Jynna's people before. "So then you don't use magic."

"Not at all."

The woman frowned. "Oh, my," she said, looking back toward the trees. "Do you think that means that no one in your village—what village is this, my dear?"

"Tivston."

"Tivston," she repeated. "Do you think this means that no one in Tivston will want to buy my baskets?"

Jynna shrugged. "I don't know. People buy things from Qirsi peddlers when they come through. Not that they come through that often, but when they do."

The woman turned slightly toward the trees and smiled, as if they were sharing a secret. "Would you like to see my baskets?"

"All right," Jynna said, shrugging again.

She followed the stranger back into the shade. The air felt cooler here, and damp.

"What's your name?" the woman asked.

"Jynna."

"That's very pretty. I'm Licaldi."

"I know. You said that before."

"Did I? Oh, yes, I suppose I did."

"Licaldi is a pretty name, too," Jynna said, and not only because she thought it polite to do so.

"Thank you, my dear."

They pushed through the low branches of the trees until they reached the small open area where her baskets were still spread in a small arc.

Jynna had never thought much about baskets. They were what she used to carry dirty clothes to the stream, or where her mother placed a loaf of bread when others joined their family for the evening meal. So she really didn't know much about baskets or weaving. But as far as she could tell, these were the most beautiful baskets she'd ever seen. They had been woven perfectly, and even in the shade of the trees, their colors seemed to glow, as if lit by the sun. Was that the magic Licaldi had mentioned?

"People will buy these," Jynna said.

"You think so?"

She turned to the woman and nodded.

"And you won't tell them that some are colored with magic?"

Jynna looked at the baskets again. She couldn't tell which had been hand-dyed and which hadn't. They all were so lovely.

"No," she said. "I won't tell."

"You're a sweet girl. Just for that, you can choose another one, to take home to your mother."

"Really?"

Licaldi nodded.

Jynna considered them for several moments, chewing her lip. Finally, she chose one that was golden brown and pale blue, like the grain fields that grew beneath the highlands sky. It seemed the perfect choice for this day, and it looked to be just the right size for the loaves her mother usually baked. It was oval in shape and it had a braided handle that twisted in the middle.

"You have a good eye," Licaldi told her. "I think that's one of my best."

The girl smiled.

"It was nice meeting you, Jynna," Licaldi said. "But I have to get to work now. I need to put these back in those big baskets over there." She pointed at a pair of large baskets that were lined with old blankets. "And then I need to carry them to your village so that I can sell them in the marketplace."

"I can help you," Jynna offered. "I can help you put them in the baskets, and I can carry one. They shouldn't be too heavy."

"You'd be surprised. But you're right: You can help me. We'll fill the baskets and then if you'll carry my travel sack, I'll carry the baskets. How does that sound?"

"All right," Jynna said. It wasn't the morning she had in mind—a few quiet hours in her secret place—but she thought it would be fun just the same.

They worked wordlessly for some time, carefully returning the small baskets to the larger ones. By the time they were finished, the baskets were quite heavy, just as Licaldi had said they would be. Jynna was just as happy to be carrying the carry sack, which was pretty light, and the two baskets the woman had given her. As they walked toward the village, Jynna admired the flowers that Licaldi had conjured.

"How old are you, Jynna?" Licaldi asked as they walked.

"I'm eight."

"Only eight? I thought you were at least ten. You seem very mature for eight."

"Thank you," Jynna said, unable to keep from smiling.

"Do you have brothers and sisters?"

"Two brothers, but they're much older than I am. They're practically men. I had a third, but he died a few years ago."

"I'm sorry, my dear. What happened?"

"He got sick—a fever. And the healer couldn't save him. I don't remember it very well. I remember Mama and Papa crying, and lots of people being in our house. But that's all, really."

"I wonder if magic would have saved him."

Jynna looked up at the woman. She was eyeing Jynna closely, as if to see how she reacted to what she had said.

"We're not allowed," Jynna said.

"Not allowed?"

"The god doesn't want us to do magic. Qirsar, that is," she added, realizing that the Mettai probably prayed to a different god.

"But other Qirsi do."

Jynna shrugged. She didn't quite understand it either, but Mama and Papa seemed certain that they were doing the right thing. They had told her about the V'Tol, and she had done her best to listen, both to them and to the prioress. But always in her mind she heard the same words Licaldi had just said. *Other Qirsi do.*

"Well, we don't," she finally said, her voice low. She didn't want to talk about this. It made her feel strange, like there was something wrong with her and with her family, with everybody in Tivston. And the way Licaldi sounded made Jynna afraid that she found the ways of the Y'Qatt odd—so odd, in fact, that she might leave without going to the marketplace.

"I'm sorry, Jynna," the woman said after a long silence. "I didn't mean to make you feel bad."

"It's all right." They were nearing the village now. Already they could see the peddlers' stalls in the marketplace, where the narrow lane they were on ended. "That's the market," Jynna said, pointing. "And that's our house." She pointed eastward, toward the low roof of her home, just visible past Old Menac's farm.

"It looks very nice."

"It is. I have my own room now. I didn't used to. I had to share with my brothers for a long time. But Papa says that I'm becoming a young lady, and that young ladies need to have their own rooms."

"How very nice for you," Licaldi said. But she sounded distracted, the way adults did when they weren't really listening anymore.

Jynna watched the old woman as they drew near to the marketplace. Her dark eyes wandered over the various peddlers' carts and stalls, no doubt seeking out the best place to sell her baskets. That was fine. She'd been nice to Jynna, mostly. But now she had things to do.

As if reading her thoughts, the old woman suddenly halted, and when Jynna did the same, she placed a hand lightly on the girl's shoulder.

"You've been very helpful, Jynna," she said. "But I think I'll be just fine now."

Jynna nodded, feeling a bit disappointed. She loved the marketplace and looked for any excuse to go there. But she also understood that the old woman didn't need a child with her while she tried to sell her wares. Besides, she knew that it would soon be time for her lessons. She pulled off Licaldi's carry sack and handed it to the woman.

"Thank you, my dear. You have your baskets?"

"Yes," Jynna said, holding them up. "Thank you again."

"My pleasure," Licaldi said, shouldering her sack and picking up her baskets again. "I hope you and your family enjoy them."

She was already walking away as she said this last, leaving Jynna to wonder if she had done something to offend the woman. She thought about going after her to ask, but at that moment the sanctuary's bell began to toll, its pealing rolling lazily over the village, beckoning to her and the other children. Reluctantly, Jynna turned her back on Licaldi and the marketplace, and hurried to the sanctuary.

The day's lessons were boring, as they always were for her. She knew her numbers and letters better than did most of the other children, and so Teacher had her help the little ones while he worked with the others. But they didn't learn anything new; they never did. Jynna liked lessons best when Teacher told them stories about the old clans or about the Blood Wars—not the most recent ones, but the ancient wars, fought hundreds of years ago. She often asked for them—she had today—and always the other children echoed her requests. But today Teacher had told her that their lessons were more important than old tales.

Bored as she was, Jynna left the sanctuary without her baskets and was nearly all the way home before she remembered them. She ran back and found both baskets resting on her chair. Teacher was still there at his table, writing out lessons for tomorrow.

"I thought you'd be back," he said, when she ran into the small room they used, panting, sweat running down her temples.

He was about the same age as Delon, her oldest brother, although he seemed much older to her. He wore his white hair long and tied back, and his eyes were an even brighter shade of yellow than her own. The older girls always talked about how handsome he was; many of them had been sad to hear that he was to marry. Once, when Jynna heard them speaking of him, she agreed and they laughed at her, asking what she knew about men and their looks. But even Jynna could tell that Teacher was good-looking. She wasn't stupid.

"I was almost to my house when I remembered them," she said, crossing to her chair and picking up the two baskets. The flowers Licaldi had conjured were already beginning to wilt. She'd need to give them water once she reached home.

"They're lovely," Teacher said. "Where did you get them?"

"A peddler gave them to me, an old woman who was in my—" She stopped, feeling her face redden. Teacher was watching her closely, an odd smile on his lean face. "I met her as she was making her way into the village. I helped her carry her things, and she gave them to me."

"That was nice of her." He paused. Then, "Where did you find those flowers? It's a bit late for columbine and lupine to be blooming."

"I . . . I didn't find the flowers," she said.

"Oh? They were in the basket when she gave it to you?"

She wasn't certain why she didn't want to tell Teacher that the woman was Mettai. Perhaps she feared that she'd get in trouble for merely witnessing magic, even if that magic wasn't done by an Y'Qatt, or even by a Qirsi. And as it happened, the way he asked his question, she could answer honestly and still reveal nothing. "Yes, they were."

He raised an eyebrow and glanced at the blooms. "I wonder where she found them. They look like they opened this morning for the first time."

"Would you like them?" Jynna asked, before she'd even thought about what she was saying.

"What?"

"For you and your new wife." She stepped forward and put the basket on his table. "A wedding gift."

"Thank you, Jynna," he said, smiling broadly. "How kind of you."

She felt herself blushing again. "I should be getting home."

"Yes, of course. I'll see you in the morning, Jynna."

Jynna turned and ran from the room, her cheeks burning. She'd thought the other girls foolish for being sad at the thought of Teacher's wedding, but perhaps she wasn't any less a fool herself.

She didn't stop running until she had passed Menac's farm and could see her house bathed in the late-day sun and casting its long shadow across the grainfield.

Her brothers were outside the barn, putting out hay for the plow horse. Seeing her approach, Delon took off his hat and wiped the sweat from his forehead.

"Where have you been?" he called.

"Lessons."

"This late? Mama's been lookin' for you for an hour at least. She's pretty mad, too."

She had slowed as they talked, but now she started running toward the house again. "I forgot my basket," she shouted over her shoulder. "I had to go back for it."

"I don't care," he shouted back. "Tell Mama."

Jynna could still hear the two of them laughing when she reached the stairs and ran into the house.

Her mother was at the hearth, her hair pulled back from her face in a loose braid. She looked up as Jynna entered and frowned at the girl.

"I expected you long ago." Her eyes fell to the basket in Jynna's hand. "Where did you get that?"

"I got it for you," Jynna said, knowing that she wasn't quite answering the question.

A smile crept slowly across her mother's face. After a moment she pointed toward the table where they ate their meals. Turning to look that way, Jynna saw one of Licaldi's baskets. The colors were different, but it was shaped just the way Jynna's was.

"You bought one," she said, crestfallen.

"Well, of course, silly girl." But then the frown returned. "How did you get that one?"

"I met the old woman who was selling them. She had two big baskets and a carry sack, and I carried the sack for her, and she gave me a basket."

It wasn't quite what had happened, but it was close enough, and it allowed her to skip the whole magic part.

"Is that why you're so late?"

"Sort of," Jynna said. "I left this at the sanctuary and had to go back for it. I'm sorry, Mama."

Her mother smiled. "You see that we picked out the same one?"

Jynna nodded. "I knew you'd like this one."

"Clever girl." Still smiling, she picked up the water bucket and handed it to Jynna. "Now, get to your chores. It's late, and your father and the boys are going to be hungry."

It was nearly dark when her father returned from the fields. Jynna and her mother had just enough time to finish preparing the roast meat, stewed greens, and bread. At first, as they cooked, her mother had asked her questions about her lessons, and also about Licaldi. But as the daylight dimmed, her mother grew quieter and quieter, so that the only sounds in the house were the crackling of the fire and the sizzling of the meat. Jynna heard her father and the boys coming in from the barn long before they reached the door.

They entered the house and Jynna's father gathered her in his arms, lifting her off the ground and kissing her cheek.

"How are you, missy?" he asked.

She giggled. "I'm fine, Papa."

He set her down and leaned toward Jynna's mother to kiss her cheek. But then he stopped, his brow creasing.

"You look flushed," he said. "Are you feeling all right?"

The boys had been laughing about something, but they stopped now and stared at their mother, as did Jynna. She was never sick. And now that Papa mentioned it, she did look flushed, even more than she usually did after working in the kitchen. Her cheeks were bright pink, and a wisp of hair clung to her forehead, which looked damp in the light of the oil lamp.

"I'm fine," she said, forcing a smile. But even her voice sounded weak.

Papa laid the back of his hand against her forehead, then quickly pulled it back. "You've got a fever," he said.

The word "fever" seemed to break her, so suddenly did she double over, clutching her stomach. She stumbled to the doorway and out onto the porch. A moment later they could hear her retching.

"Is it the pestilence, Papa?" asked Blayne, the younger of her two brothers.

"I don't know!" Papa snapped. He shook his head. "Maybe. Qirsar save us all if it is."

Mama staggered back to the doorway, stood there briefly, then whirled away and was sick again.

Papa looked at Delon. "Go get the healer."

Delon nodded once and ran out the door.

For some time Jynna, Blayne, and their father just stood there, the only sound in the house coming from Jynna's mother and the fire.

"You two should eat," Papa said at last.

Jynna and her brother exchanged a look. She was too scared to take even a bite, and judging from the expression on Blayne's face, she guessed that he felt the same way.

"Well?" Papa said, his voice rising again.

"I'm not hungry, Papa."

Blayne shook his head. "Neither am I."

Jynna thought Papa would make them eat anyway, but in the end he just shook his head, and muttered, "I don't blame you. I don't much feel like eating either."

As he said it, Jynna realized that he appeared flushed as well, though she couldn't tell if he was just worried about Mama or if he was starting to get sick also.

Mama appeared in the doorway again. She didn't look flushed anymore. Instead she was deathly pale, her face nearly as white as her hair, and her bright golden eyes sunken and dull. Only the dark purple lines under her eyes gave her face any color at all. She looked like a wraith.

"I need to lie down," she said, the words coming out as a whisper.

Papa hurried to her side, lifted her as if she were a child, and carried her to their bedroom.

He came out again a few moments later, his expression grim, his cheeks nearly as red as Mama's had been a short time before.

"She's already asleep," he said. "And to be honest, I'm starting to feel it, too."

"So it is the pestilence," Blayne said.

At that moment Delon returned.

"The healer says she'll be along when she can," he told them all, looking scared. "But there's lots of people sick."

"Damn," Papa said, sighing the word. He glanced at Blayne. "Well, there's your answer. It's probably too late, but I want the three of you outside. You're not sick yet. Maybe you'll make it through."

"But Papa—"

"I know what you're going to say, Delon. But there's nothing to be done now. Either your mother and I will live or we won't. But you haven't any way to save us, so it's best you save yourselves."

"I have healing magic," her brother said. "Blayne's come into his power, and he has it, too. We *can* save you, if you'll just let us."

Papa glared at him, the muscles in his jaw bunching. For just an instant, Jynna thought he might strike Delon for what he had said. "Never utter such words in this house again. Do you hear me?"

Delon lowered his gaze. "Yes, Papa."

"You're past your fourth four. You're a man now. If your mother and I . . . If the healer can't help us, then it'll fall to you to take care of your brother and sister. You're old enough that you should know better than to speak against the god like that." He started to say more, but then stopped and ran out the door, grabbing at his gut just as Mama had done.

None of them said anything, but Jynna found herself wishing that her brothers would use their magic, just as Delon had suggested. Surely the god would understand this one time.

"So what do we do?" Blayne asked, looking at Delon. Jynna couldn't be sure, but she thought he was probably thinking the same thing.

"We go outside," Delon said. "And we wait for the healer, just as Papa told us to."

The boys held each other's gazes for several moments, but they said nothing, and at last they ushered Jynna out into the darkness. Papa was still on the porch, leaning heavily on the railing. They didn't speak, though all three of them stared back at him as they descended the stairs. Eventually he went back into the house, leaving them alone in the cool night air. The sky was clear and the moons shone overhead, both of them still well short of full.

"What if they die?" Jynna asked, starting to cry.

Blayne shook his head. "They're not going to die." But he wouldn't look at her as he said it, and she knew he was lying.

"They might," Delon said. "Don't lie to her. Not about this." He took her in his arms and kissed the top of her head. She couldn't remember him ever doing such a thing before. His shirt smelled faintly of hay and sweat, as Papa's often did, and she pressed her cheek against it. "The healer's going to come, and maybe he can save them. But if he can't, we'll take care of you. We'll all take care of each other, all right?"

Jynna nodded, but she couldn't stop crying.

They sat down on the grass to wait, and after some time Jynna lay down, her tears still flowing, her stomach hurting, though because she was hungry or sick, she couldn't say. Eventually she woke up again. The boys were standing a short distance away, both of them doubled over.

"Hasn't the healer come yet?" she called to them.

She saw Delon shake his head. "Not yet," he answered, his voice hoarse.

"And now you're both sick." She flung it at them, an accusation. *Who's going to take care of me if you die too?* she wanted to ask, but she couldn't even choke out the words. *I'll be all alone!* Better she should die than face the world without her parents and brothers.

Neither of them said anything, and in the next moment, matters grew far worse. The sky over the village suddenly flared bright yellow, and an arc of fire streaked across the night, as if Eilidh herself had declared war on the people of Tivston. Again the fire flew and a third time.

"What's happening?" Jynna cried. Somehow she was on her feet. She started toward her brothers, but stopped herself after only a step. Who would protect her? "Is it a war?" she asked. She knew how foolish the question sounded, but she couldn't help herself.

She heard a long moan from within the house—the sound she imagined a ghost might make—and an instant later a bolt of flame crashed through the roof of the house. Burning slats of wood spun into the air and fell to earth, smoking, charred at the edges. Again the moan. It was her mother's voice. She had fire magic, Jynna knew, though of course she never used it. Until tonight. Flame burst through the roof again and Jynna heard a scream. Only when the scream kept going, long after this second flame had died away, did she realize that she was the one screaming.

She forced herself to stop, and doing so she realized that others were screaming as well, in the village, in the houses around them. The sky was aglow, orange like a smith's forge. She could hear the rending of wood and the panicked howling of dogs, the neighing of horses and strange, otherworldly cries coming from the cattle and sheep. Flames and smoke began to rise from her house. The boys hurried toward the door, but both of them seemed unsteady on their feet. Before they could reach the top of the stairs, though, the front wall of the house exploded outward, throwing the boys onto their backs, knocking Jynna to the ground, and showering them all with embers and smoking scraps of wood.

When Jynna looked up again, there were her mother and father, leaning on each other, struggling to get free of the wreckage that had once been their home. They managed to descend the stairs to the ground; then both of them collapsed, their chests heaving with every breath. Mama lay on her back, and abruptly she thrust both hands skyward. Flame shot from her palms as if she were a goddess, or a demon from Bian's realm.

Delon gaped at her. "What's happening to you?"

"I can't control it!" Mama said. "I'm trying, but I can't stop!"

Papa rolled himself onto his knees and let out a piercing cry. And then the skin on both his forearms peeled open, like the rind of some pale, evil fruit, and blood began to run over his hands and soak into his clothes.

It took her a moment to understand what was happening to him. Healing magic. Papa had it, too. Except that he could no longer control it, just like Mama couldn't stop using her fire magic. Was this what would happen to Delon and Blayne? Would it happen to her as well?

She crawled backward, away from them all, tears coursing down her face. "No!" she cried. "No. No. No."

"Jynna!" her father gasped, staring at her, the blood on his arms gleaming in the moonlight. "Go! Get away from here! Get help!"

She shook her head so hard that the tears flew from her face. "Where? Where can I go?"

"Anywhere! Away from here!" He stared at the ground for a moment before meeting her gaze again.

Another pulse of fire flew from her mother's hands, but it seemed dimmer this time, weaker.

"Go north!" her father said. "You know which way is north?"

She nodded.

"Go to the lake. Then follow the shore to Lowna. They're Fal'Borna there, not Y'Qatt. They can help you. They can help us."

"You mean with magic?" she asked, her eyes wide.

He hesitated, nodded once. "With magic. Now go! Quickly!"

She stared at him a moment longer. More screams rose from the village. More streaks of flame lit the sky. Not a war, she knew now. A pestilence. A plague. An Y'Qatt plague.

"Go, Jynna!" her father whispered, collapsing onto his side, his blood staining the grass.

She stood and ran.

Chapter 9

The moons were still up as she made her way northward, razor-sharp sickles in the sky, one as pale as death, the other as livid as blood. They were high overhead and gave Jynna no sense of which way was north, but she didn't need them for that. Tivston lay to the south, and though she could no longer see the homes and farms of her village, the occasional flare of fire magic streaking into the night sky told her just where it was. She only needed the moons for their light, and on the treeless plain north of the village, they offered more than enough.

She'd stopped crying, at least for now, made braver than she'd thought possible by the task given to her by her father. Get help, he'd said. And then he'd told her to go to the Qirsi, the Fal'Borna. He was going to let them use their magic to save him, to save Mama and Delon and Blayne. If Papa was willing to go that far, she could hold back her tears for a few hours. She didn't know for certain that they were still alive, but as long as those bursts of fire still lit the sky behind her she had some cause for hope. That's what she told herself again and again. That's how she remained on her feet, how she kept herself moving when all she wanted to do was fall to the grass and cry for her family and her village.

Before long she saw the lake, its placid waters gleaming with moon-glow. Reaching its shores, she realized that she had drifted too far to the east, and she turned westward, following the edge of the water toward Lowna. Toward magic.

She half expected to fall ill herself and succumb to the pestilence before she reached the Fal'Borna. For as long as she could remember, the mere mention of the pestilence had been enough to fill her with terror. The threat of an outbreak hung over her village all the time, a great sword ready to descend, deadly and inescapable. Whenever anyone in

Tivston came down with a fever, every person in the village would learn of it. Parents would keep their children at home, even the most dedicated peddlers would avoid the marketplace, the lanes of the village would remain deserted until word began to spread that the fever had passed. No doubt it was the same in every other village in the Southlands. The pestilence was no trifle; it could wipe out entire cities. The fact that all in her family had been afflicted should have marked her for death as well. But though she couldn't imagine ever being hungry again, she didn't feel sickened or weak with fever. And since she'd yet to come into her power, she felt no surge of magic such as those that had taken hold of her father and mother. Grief, anguish, terror: these threatened constantly to overwhelm her. But thus far she'd managed to stave off the disease.

She had no idea how many leagues lay between Tivston and Lowna. She'd heard it said among the peddlers in the marketplace that the distance could be covered in less than a day, but how much less? How far did her father expect her to go before her strength failed? Already she was weary; on any other night she would have been asleep by now. But she pushed herself on, and as she walked she tried to remember all that she had heard of the Fal'Borna.

Living in an Y'Qatt village, she heard little about the Qirsi clans. Teacher taught them about the Blood Wars, of course. He could hardly have taught the history of the Southlands without mentioning them. But it was one thing to hear tales of the Fal'Borna horsemen and their prowess in battle; it was quite another to know what they were like today. They were said to be shorter than other Qirsi, but more powerfully built. Their men and women wore their hair long and tied back from their faces. Some said that their skin was darker than that of the other clans, that they had lived on the plains for so long, their skin browned by the bright sun, that their babies were even born dark. Jynna wasn't certain that she believed this, but she knew so little else about them that she scoured her mind for anything she had ever heard, no matter how insignificant or foolish.

She did know that all the Qirsi clans rejected the faith of the Y'Qatt. Would they refuse to help her because she came from an Y'Qatt village? She nearly stopped, her resolve failing her for an instant. But no. Father had sent her on this errand. He wouldn't have done so if he thought the

Qirsi of Lowna would turn her away. Her people were dying. How could they not help her?

On she went, her fatigue deepening with every step. As the hour grew later, Jynna began to cast anxious glances westward, toward the moons. They were low in the sky, and it wouldn't be long before they disappeared below the western horizon, leaving her in utter darkness.

As if sensing her fear, a wolf howled in the distance, and was answered by a second on the far side of the lake. Jynna shuddered and began walking faster. A moment later the first wolf called out again, drawing another cry from the second beast. On and on they went, their howls echoing across the lake. Jynna began to cry again, fear gripping her heart. The air had grown cold; she crossed her arms over her chest, trying to keep warm.

And still she walked, her steps growing heavier, the night darkening as the moons dropped lower and lower toward the plain. Mist rose from the lake, chilling her more and giving an unearthly feel to the terrain. When at last the moons did disappear, Jynna started to cry, though she really had no reason. Enough light remained, cast by the stars and reflected in the waters of the lake, for her to see. And even had she been immersed in complete darkness the sound of the water gently lapping at the muddy lakeshore would have enabled her to find her way.

Still, she had never felt so alone, and it occurred to her that it had been some time since last she'd noticed any fire streaking across the southern sky. She tried to tell herself that she'd come too far, that Tivston was so far away by now that she wouldn't have noticed the flames had there been hundreds of them. In her heart, though, she knew better.

But she walked on.

Eventually she must have fallen into a waking dream, some nether realm between sleep and wakefulness, for she abruptly found herself on a dusty lane, with small houses on either side of her. For a moment she merely stood in place, tottering on trembling legs, looking about, trying to remember where she was and why she had come. Then she began to sob and moan and cry out for help, all at the same time.

At first nothing happened. She heard horses neighing and stamping, but she neither heard nor saw any people, and her despair grew unbearable. But then the pale glow of a candle appeared in one window, and a moment later a second. Soon there was light all around her. Doors opened. There were shouts and footsteps. Somehow she had fallen to the ground and was lying on her back. Men and women stood over her, looks of concern on their faces. Qirsi faces, but darker than any she'd seen before. Perhaps the tales were true. That is, if this was indeed Lowna, and these were the Fal'Borna.

A man bent over her and lifted her into his arms, just as her father had done with her mother. Her mother, who was dying of the pestilence. Had that been a dream, or was this? Was it even the same night? Abruptly frightened, she struggled to break free of the man's grasp, but he held her tight, and carried her toward one of the houses, toward that warm glow of candle flame.

She ceased her struggles and gave in to her weariness. The last thing she remembered was someone asking her name.

Jynna awoke to the sound of whispers. Opening her eyes, she saw three men standing over her, all of them Qirsi, all of them with their hair tied back and their faces burned golden brown, the color of dry grasses swaying in the plains wind. The Fal'Borna.

Her eyes flew to the window beside the bed on which she lay. The sun was up, shining brightly into the room. She let out a low moan and covered her face with her hands. By now they were all dead. Mama, Papa, Delon, Blayne. All of them. Quite likely, everyone in Tivston. She should have been crying, but no tears would come. She just felt weary, as if she hadn't slept in days.

"Who are you?" one of the men asked, his voice even, matter-of-fact.

She uncovered her face and looked up at them. They were all watching her, waiting. She had no idea which of them had spoken. For all she could tell, they might have been brothers, so much did they look alike.

"Where are you from? Why did you come here?"

That one. He appeared to be the youngest of the three. He had a handsome, square face, and eyes that were so pale they were almost white.

"I'm from . . . from Tivston."

The three of them glanced at one another.

"You're Y'Qatt," another said. Now that she was looking at them more closely, Jynna realized that their appearances weren't so similar after all. This man was smaller than the other two. His face was rounder, his eyes a deeper shade of yellow. He was older than the first man; quite a bit older it seemed. There were lines around his eyes and mouth.

She nodded.

"Why are you here?" this second man asked.

"Everyone was dying," she said. "My father sent me to get help. He told me to go north, to Lowna." She hesitated. "Is this Lowna?"

They didn't answer.

The young one exhaled through his teeth and looked from one of his companions to the other. "The pestilence?"

The third man held up a hand, silencing the other two. Then he looked down at her, a slight frown on his face. "You're telling us that an Y'Qatt sent his child to get help from the Fal'Borna?"

She nodded.

"And he was willing to let us use magic to help you?"

"Yes."

He shook his head. "I don't believe you. It's a trick," he said to the other two. "I'd wager she's from the J'Balanar, or the A'Vahl."

"She's not J'Balanar," said the young one. "She bears none of the markings."

"She's young to be marked."

"Not true. They start using the pigments at the end of the first four. She's near to her second."

She was just done with her second, but she didn't bother to correct them.

"The A'Vahl then," the third one said.

"To what end, T'Kaar? The J'Balanar may want our land, but the feud with the A'Vahl has been over for nearly ten fours. They've grown weak, complacent. They wouldn't challenge us now."

"So you believe her?" T'Kaar asked. "You really think an Y'Qatt village would send a girl for aid from magic-using Qirsi?"

"That's not what she said," the older man broke in. "She said her father sent her here to get help. That I would believe." He looked down at her again. "What's your name, child?"

"Jynna. And I'm not lying."

The third man glared at her, but the other two smiled.

"Tell us what happened, Jynna."

She shrugged, and finally she was crying, her vision clouding. "They all just got sick," she told them. "First Mama and then Papa, and then Delon and Blayne. They're my brothers."

"Were they fevered?"

"I think so. They were . . . they got sick to their stomachs. All of them."

"The pestilence," the young man said, spitting out the word as if it were a curse.

"Then strange things started happening," Jynna said, the memories coming fast and hard now, forcing the words out through her tears and a sudden wave of panic. *I'm alone! They're all gone!*

"What strange things?" the third man demanded. He still sounded doubtful.

She took a long breath, trying to calm herself. "They started to use magic." She shook her head, knowing that wasn't quite right.

"You mean trying to heal themselves?"

"No, it wasn't like that. They couldn't help it."

They stared at her.

"I don't understand," the older one finally said. "What do you mean, they couldn't help it?"

Jynna still shook her head, slowly now, trying to find the right words. "My mother has fire magic. She never uses it, though. Because we're Y'Qatt. But last night fire was flying from her hands. I don't think she wanted it to, but she couldn't stop herself. And my father. He—" She stopped, gagging on the memory.

"T'Noth," the oldest one said. "Get her some water."

The young one left the room, only to return a moment later with a cup of water. Jynna took it from him with a trembling hand and forced herself to drink. It helped.

"My father has healing magic," she began again, speaking slowly. "But last night it tore his skin open. I think he might have bled to death."

"Could a fever do that, S'Doryn?" T'Noth asked.

The older man shook his head. "I've never heard of it before."

"But they're Y'Qatt," said T'Kaar. "They've hoarded their magic all their lives. Who knows what a fever might do to them? It may be that her mother and father—"

"It wasn't just them," Jynna said, glowering at the man. "It was everyone in the village. There was fire everywhere. I heard houses being destroyed by shaping power. The horses were making horrible noises, and I think it was because people with language of beasts were saying things to them. Things that made no sense."

For a long time, none of them spoke. The oldest of the three men was watching her, his face grim. The other two were eyeing each other.

At last, the older man stood. "All right, Jynna," he said. "You rest here. We'll be back shortly." He smiled at her, though she could tell that it wasn't a real smile. "Are you hungry?"

"No."

The smile faded. He nodded once and patted her leg through the wool blanket that still covered her. "I wouldn't be either."

With that, he stood and led the other two men out of the room. The young one was the last to go, and he glanced back at her. But he didn't smile or say anything, and he made certain to close the door behind him.

Jynna was alone for what seemed a long time. She tried to sleep some more, but couldn't and eventually she climbed out of the bed and began to wander around the room. It reminded her of her parents' room in her old house. *They're all dead! I have no one!* Fear, loss, grief: She felt it all welling up inside her again. This time, though, she pushed the feelings back down. She'd made it to Lowna. She was getting help. What more could she do? It wasn't that she was being brave. She knew that. It was just that she couldn't bear the thought of being so sad again.

So she concentrated on the room and on the wardrobe that stood in the corner near the door. The clothes belonged to a man, someone taller than her father. Maybe they were the young man's; he was the tallest of the three men who had been speaking to her. T'Noth. She thought his name odd. In other ways though, this could easily have been a room in Tivston. The clothes looked similar to those she was accustomed to seeing. So were the blankets and bed cloths. Jynna wasn't certain what she'd expected, but she had thought that the clothes and homes of Qirsi would be different from those in her village. Particularly the Fal'Borna. They were supposed to be nomads, hunters. But this place seemed so much like home.

The door opened and T'Noth poked his head inside. Seeing the empty bed, he frowned. When he spotted Jynna standing near the wardrobe he stepped all the way into the room.

"What are you doing?"

"Nothing!" she said. "Just looking around."

"Why?"

She shrugged. "I don't know. I was bored."

Clearly, he hadn't expected that answer. "Well . . . you shouldn't look through other people's things."

"I'm sorry. Is this your room?"

He frowned again, but after a moment he nodded.

"Do you live here by yourself?"

"Now, what kind of—"

The door opened and S'Doryn walked in. Seeing that Jynna was out of bed, he smiled. "Are you feeling better?"

She shrugged again, her eyes flicking toward the younger man.

He turned to T'Noth. "What's going on?"

"She was . . . she was looking at my things."

The older man raised an eyebrow. "And?"

T'Noth shook his head. "Never mind."

S'Doryn held out his hand to her. "Jynna, I want you to come with me. The leaders of our village have come. They have some questions for you."

"And then will you help me? Will you come back to Tivston with me?"

He faltered, though only briefly. "We'll go back with you. Some of us at least." He started to lead her out of the room, but then stopped and faced her again, placing his hands on her shoulders and looking her in the eye. "I don't know what we're going to find there, Jynna. If this was the pestilence, or something like it . . ." He trailed off, a pained expression on his round face.

She finished the sentence for him. "They'll all be dead."

"It's possible, yes."

"Then can I come here and live with you?" She started to cry again, though she tried hard not to. "I won't have anywhere else."

S'Doryn pulled her to him and held her as she sobbed. "Yes, Jynna. If they're all gone, you can come and live with us. With me and N'Tevva, if you like. All right?"

She was still crying, but she nodded.

He held her for a moment longer, then gently steered her out of the bedroom and into a small common room. There was a hearth in the far wall, though no fire burned there, and beside it a narrow space that must have served as T'Noth's kitchen, though Jynna's mother would have thought it far too small. In the center of the room stood a table and four chairs. Three women and a man were sitting there and three more men stood nearby. Like the men she'd already met, these Qirsi wore their hair tied back from their faces. They also had dark complexions, and they appeared stronger somehow, as if life on the plain had toughened them in ways it hadn't the men and women of Tivston. When Jynna and S'Doryn entered, all of the people turned to look at them, or more precisely, to look at her. Jynna sidled closer to S'Doryn, who placed a reassuring hand on her shoulder.

"This is Jynna," S'Doryn said. "She comes from Tivston. She's Y'Qatt. She tells a most remarkable tale of what seems to be some strain of the pestilence that struck her village yesterday."

"Yesterday?" one of the women asked, her pale eyes widening. "All of this happened yesterday?"

S'Doryn looked down at Jynna, who nodded.

The woman actually stood and stepped toward the door that led outside. "She could still be contagious! How could you have allowed her into the village, much less this house?"

"She's shown no sign of being ill," S'Doryn said evenly. "From all she's told us it seems that the disease came upon them swiftly and with great force. If she were carrying it, she'd be dead by now."

He couldn't have had any idea of how his words struck at Jynna's heart, nor did she let any of them see. Her father had sent her here to get help, and she trusted that some of them—S'Doryn certainly, and perhaps T'Noth as well—would do all they could for her. But she was less certain of T'Kaar and these others. And so she refused to let them see how she ached inside. Standing there, her back straight, her eyes dry, might well have been the most adult thing she'd ever done. In a small part of her mind that remained apart, watching all that was happening to her, Jynna marveled at how she had grown in just this one day.

For several moments more the woman just stared at Jynna, as if the girl were some beast summoned by Bian himself to lay waste to her village. Finally, she returned to her chair, her cheeks coloring somewhat.

"How is it she escaped with her life?" one of the men asked.

"We've wondered the same thing," S'Doryn told him. He smiled for just an instant. "Perhaps if we knew for certain, we'd never again have cause to fear the pestilence." No one else so much as grinned, and he offered a small shrug. "Perhaps she was merely lucky. Perhaps the gods have marked her for some greater purpose. To be honest, I don't know. But she came to us seeking aid, and I for one don't feel that we can refuse her."

An old woman who sat at the table shook her head. "You make it sound easy, S'Doryn. Yet you know it isn't." Before she could say more, she was taken by a fit of coughing that racked her body. No one said anything, although T'Noth did offer her some water, which she waved away even as her paroxysm went on. Eventually her coughing subsided and she pulled a white rag from the folds of her dress and wiped her mouth. "Forgive me." She glanced at Jynna. "I've been sick a long time. Sooner or later it will get the best of me, though I daresay I have some time left."

She grinned, and Jynna decided that she liked the woman, regardless of what she meant to say.

"It's not that easy," she began again, shifting her gaze back to S'Doryn. "You and I are old for Qirsi, even for Fal'Borna. But others here have young families to care for, children to protect. Jynna may want our help, but our safest course is to let whatever disease has struck her village run its course, and then burn to the ground what's left."

"The disease might well have taken care of that for us already."

"What do you mean?"

S'Doryn looked down at Jynna and nodded. And for the second time that morning, she told of the strange and horrible effect the pestilence had on her people. The reaction was much the same this time: silence, followed by speculation that the Y'Qatt had brought this on themselves by refusing to use their magic.

"For all we know," one man said, as T'Kaar looked on and nodded, "the pestilence has always done this to the Y'Qatt. Their faith is old, but it's only recently that so many have subscribed to it."

"I've never heard of this happening before," S'Doryn said. "But even if you're right, what does it have to do with Jynna and her plea for help?"

"The risk is too great," the old woman said. She looked at Jynna. "Forgive me, child. I can't begin to imagine how you've suffered in these past few hours. I'm sorry for you. Truly I am. But surely you can see that

I have to protect my people, to keep them from suffering as you and yours have."

Jynna met the woman's gaze, but she neither nodded nor shook her head. Eventually the old Qirsi looked away.

"Jynna and her people are Qirsi," T'Noth said. "Haven't the Fal'Borna sworn an oath to protect all Qirsi, even those of enemy clans?"

T'Kaar and the other man who'd spoken of the Y'Qatt faith shook their heads. "Her kind stopped being Qirsi the moment they stopped using magic," the man said.

The old woman frowned at them. "Nonsense. That's the coward's way out. If you fear going to Tivston, as I do, then just say so. But don't pretend that she's not Qirsi simply because of her faith."

T'Kaar looked genuinely abashed. "Yes, A'Laq. Forgive me."

Jynna stared at the woman. A'Laq? Was she the leader of the village then? If so, then her word would be final, and there would be no help for Tivston.

The woman appeared to notice Jynna's gaze. "Yes," she said. "A'Laq. I lead the clan council in Lowna. My name is U'Selle."

Jynna bowed to the woman, drawing smiles from nearly everyone in the room. "Forgive me, A'Laq. I didn't know."

"There's nothing to forgive, child. You're not Fal'Borna. You owe me no obeisance."

It came to Jynna so quickly that she barely had time to think it through. She just spoke, and hoped it would work.

"But I am Fal'Borna. At least I am now. S'Doryn has said that if my family is gone, I can live here in Lowna with him. Doesn't that make me one of you now?"

The woman narrowed her eyes, a sly smile on her wizened face. "Perhaps."

"In which case, I wouldn't be an outsider asking for help. I'd be one of your own. Doesn't that change things?"

"Now, see here—!" T'Kaar broke in.

But U'Selle raised a hand, silencing him, her eyes fixed on Jynna. "The Fal'Borna are warriors. True, it's the men who ride to war, but all of us would gladly die to keep our people free; men and women, adults and children alike. Will you die for us as well?"

"Yes, A'Laq."

"An easy promise to make," T'Kaar said. "But keeping it—"

"Silence!" U'Selle said, casting a dark look his way. She faced Jynna again. "We use our magic every day, in violation of your faith and all that you've been taught since the day you were born. Will you use your magic when the need arises? Will you heal an injured comrade if Qirsar gives you the gift of healing magic? Will you raise a wind to stop a fire if it threatens the homes of your neighbors?"

"Yes, A'Laq."

"She'd say anything—"

"Be silent, T'Kaar! Or leave! I will not tolerate another interruption!"

T'Kaar glared at Jynna for an instant and then stormed out of the house.

"He may be right, you know," the a'laq said, eyeing Jynna. "You would say anything to get us to help you. I know you would. I've been desperate before. Perhaps not as desperate as you are now, but desperate enough. A person in your circumstance will tell all sorts of lies, promise all sorts of things to get her way. That's why T'Kaar doesn't trust you. Can you give me one reason why I should?"

The words were hard, but Jynna sensed that U'Selle wanted her to give a good reason, that in the end, the a'laq wanted to help her. She wasn't certain what the right answer was, but a response came to her, and with nothing more to offer, she gave it voice.

"Because I have no one else, A'Laq. Because you're right, I am desperate. I'm alone. And if my family is dead, if my village is gone, I have only the Fal'Borna. Why would I risk lying to the only family left for me?"

For several moments the woman just looked at her, and even when she began to nod, she didn't smile. "A good answer, Jynna. Good enough at least." She turned her gaze to S'Doryn, and Jynna exhaled. U'Selle might have been old, but there was power in her eyes. "You'll take her back to Tivston. You and T'Noth. Normally I'd send four of you, for luck. But I fear there isn't enough good fortune to help in this endeavor, and I'm reluctant to risk more lives."

"Can we take horses?" S'Doryn asked.

"Yes. Take several, in case there are other survivors. Don't tarry there. Look around. Learn what you can. Then leave. But I don't want you to return here for eight days. If you're all still well after that, you can come back. Do you understand?"

"Yes, A'Laq," S'Doryn said, bowing to her.

U'Selle and the rest of the clan council rose and filed out of the small house, leaving Jynna with T'Noth and S'Doryn. When U'Selle and the others were gone, the two men looked at each other.

"I didn't mean to get you into this," S'Doryn said.

T'Noth shrugged. "I was in it when I brought her into my house."

"Your brother won't be happy."

"He rarely is."

"Your brother?" Jynna said. "You mean T'Kaar?"

"Yes."

"I thought you looked alike." She turned to S'Doryn. "And are you their father?"

As soon as T'Noth began to laugh, she knew she'd said the wrong thing. She felt her color rising.

"No," S'Doryn said with a grin. "I'm just a friend. An older friend."

"Much older, it would seem," T'Noth said, and laughed again.

"I'm sorry," Jynna said.

But S'Doryn shook his head. "It's nothing, child. He's just a foolish, small-minded man. If it wasn't this, he'd find some other way to make my life miserable." He said it all with a smile, giving Jynna the sense that T'Noth was far closer to S'Doryn than he was to his brother. "Pack some food," he said to the younger man, growing serious once more. "I need to speak with N'Tevva. She should know that I'm going away." He glanced at Jynna. "She should also know that I've offered to let Jynna live with us. I'll get the horses, too. I'd like to be on our way before midday."

T'Noth nodded once. "Right."

S'Doryn put his hand on Jynna's shoulder and looked her in the eye. "I'm going to leave you here for a time. Do what you can to help T'Noth. We'll be on our way to your village before long."

She nodded and made herself smile, though it took a good deal of effort. Strange. Until yesterday, she'd always thought of herself as being quick to smile. Not anymore. Not ever again.

S'Doryn opened the door to leave and nearly collided with T'Kaar. S'Doryn stood in the doorway, eyeing the man. Then he stepped aside and let him into the house before leaving. The two of them didn't exchange so much as a nod.

"You heard?" T'Noth asked, as he began to pile food on the table—dried fruits and bread, salted meat and a block of cheese.

"You're fools, both of you," T'Kaar said. But he didn't sound angry. Rather, he seemed resigned to their decision. "This undertaking would be folly, if it weren't so dangerous." His eyes flicked toward Jynna. "Forgive me," he said, surprising her. "Despite what you must think of me, I am sorry for all that's happened to you. You're awfully young to have seen such things."

"So you believe me now?" Jynna demanded. She could hear the bitterness in her voice, but she didn't care. She liked T'Noth and S'Doryn quite a lot. But this man she already hated. "I thought I was just a liar who'd say anything to get what she wants."

A faint smile flitted across his features. He wasn't as handsome as T'Noth—his face wasn't as square, his cheeks were a bit too fat—but he would have been nice-looking if he smiled more.

"I suppose I deserved that."

Jynna looked away. She'd been sure that he did deserve it, but now she wasn't quite so certain.

"I should come with you," T'Kaar said, turning back to his brother.

T'Noth frowned. "Why?"

"Because neither you nor S'Doryn has healing magic. You might need it."

Jynna hoped T'Noth would tell T'Kaar that he couldn't come, but he didn't. He stared at the floor for several moments before nodding. "You're right. If you want to come, we'd welcome the help. But we're not to return here for eight days. Are you sure you want to leave A'Vinya and the baby alone for so long?"

"No, I'm sure I don't. But I think I should."

"Fine, then," T'Noth said. "We'll need more food, and S'Doryn wants to be on our way before midday."

T'Kaar took a breath. "All right. I'll be back soon." He let himself out of the house.

T'Noth continued to stare at the floor, as if lost in thought. At last, he shook himself and looked up at Jynna. He gave her a small smile, but he said nothing. She thought it best to do the same.

It wasn't long before S'Doryn returned with several horses, all of them far too large for Jynna to ride. He must have noticed how she eyed the beasts, standing on the stairs outside T'Noth's door, because he walked over to her and said quietly, "Don't worry. You're going to ride with me."

"Good," she said, still watching the animals. She'd seen horses before, of course, but never the mounts of the Fal'Borna. They were not only the finest horses she'd ever seen, but also the largest. Though she thought them beautiful, Jynna was also frightened by them.

"T'Kaar is coming with us," T'Noth said, tying the satchel of food to one of the saddles.

S'Doryn looked at the younger man, saying nothing for a long time. "That right?" he said at last.

"He says we may need a healer."

"What about A'Vinya?"

T'Noth shrugged. "He's willing to make the journey, and he knows that we have to wait before returning."

"All right." S'Doryn looked like he might say more, but at that moment T'Kaar came into view, carrying two travel sacks.

I don't like him, Jynna wanted to say. *Tell him he can't come.* But she kept these thoughts to herself, and within a few moments they were on their way, T'Noth riding in front, followed by S'Doryn and Jynna, and then T'Kaar.

Jynna rode just in front of S'Doryn, who kept an arm around her and occasionally let her hold the reins. It was a bit scary being so far off the ground, but the horse responded with alacrity to S'Doryn's commands and she never once feared that she might be thrown. It was a glorious day, clear and warm, and a soft, cool breeze blew across the lake, rippling its waters.

The distance between Tivston and Lowna had seemed impossibly great the night before, but on this day, carried by the great Fal'Borna mounts, they came within sight of Jynna's village in only a couple of hours. Actually they saw the smoke first, well before even the largest buildings—the silo and the sanctuary—came into view. But aside from the shifting cloud of black smoke that hung over what was left of the village, and the large flock of crows and kites that circled low over the houses, they saw no movement at all.

"Jynna, maybe you should wait here," S'Doryn said, his voice low.

She stared at the village, trying to spot her house, searching desperately for someone—anyone—who might have survived the night. "No" was all she said.

They rode on, advancing on the village, all of them silent now. Jynna wondered if the three men were as frightened as she of what they would find.

It was the birds—the carrion eaters—that first drew her eyes to the bodies. The first one made her stomach heave, and she clenched her teeth to keep from being ill. Then she spotted another, and a third. By the time they steered the horses onto the lane leading through the marketplace, she could see so many that she lost count. Already they had started to grow rank, and flies buzzed everywhere. As they rode among the buildings the kites flew off and began to circle overhead, complaining loudly. The crows, though, weren't so easily driven off. They'd flutter away as the mounts stepped past, but would quickly return to their feast.

Jynna tried not to look at the corpses. She kept her eyes moving, scanning for survivors, occasionally glancing in the direction of her house, hoping against hope that she'd see her parents or her brothers walking toward them. But all was terribly still. Occasionally she'd point in the direction she wanted them to go, and always S'Doryn steered them as she commanded. For the moment at least, he seemed content to let her lead the way.

When at last they came to what was left of her home, Jynna let out a stifled cry and buried her face in her hands. Every one of them was there. Mama, Papa, Delon, Blayne. All of them dead, the three men horribly disfigured by their healing magic. How could something as good as healing power do such damage?

"Your family?" S'Doryn asked.

She merely nodded.

"I'm sorry, Jynna."

They stayed there for some time, until at last S'Doryn must have given a signal for them to ride on, because the horse she was on started to turn.

"No!" Jynna cried, opening her eyes and struggling to break out of S'Doryn's grasp.

"Jynna!"

But she fought her way free and fell from the saddle, landing hard

on the dirt just beside her mother's body. She scrambled to her feet and
ran toward the house.

"Stay out of there!" T'Kaar shouted after her.

She didn't stop. Instead she climbed the stairs and made her way to
her room. Most of the house was in shambles. But her room remained
relatively undamaged and she dove onto her bed and began to sob,
clutching her blanket to her face. After several minutes she heard a footstep at her door. S'Doryn. She expected him to tell her that she had to
leave. Instead, he tossed an empty carry sack onto the bed next to her.

"Anything you want to keep you should put in there. I don't expect
you'll want to come back again."

"Thank you."

"T'Noth and T'Kaar are going to have a look around the rest of the
village. I can stay with you if you like."

"No, it's all right."

"Then, we'll come back for you soon." He glanced around briefly.
"This is a nice room. We'll have to make certain that your room in
Lowna is just as nice."

He left her, and Jynna began to look around her room for things she
wanted to keep. In truth, there wasn't much: her blanket, her clothes, a
doll her parents had given her a few years back, a small wood carving of
a deer that Delon made for her. She went to her brothers' room and
found a shirt of Blayne's that she'd always liked. It didn't fit her, but she
wanted something of his. And she found a wooden hair comb that had
been her mother's. She took that as well. While in her parents' room she
spotted the basket that the old Mettai woman had given her the day
before—was it really only a day?—and she nearly took that, too. But in
the end she decided not to. She wanted no reminders of yesterday.

When the men returned, they had five survivors with them. All of
them were children—boys and girls she knew and had played with at the
sanctuary, in between lessons. Two of them were badly burned and one
had lost a hand. But they were alive, just like her.

Of the two who were unhurt, one was a boy her age, named Etan,
and the other was a younger girl whose name Jynna couldn't remember,
and who refused to say anything to any of them.

Etan sat on one of the Fal'Borna horses, looking terribly small, and
he watched as Jynna tied her carry sack to the saddle of S'Doryn's horse.

"How did you find them?" the boy asked suddenly. "The Fal'Borna, I mean."

She paused and looked up at him, shielding her eyes against the sun. "My father sent me for help. He told me to follow the lake north to Lowna."

He looked over at S'Doryn and T'Noth, who were speaking quietly. "And now we're going to live with them."

"Yes."

"Do you think they'll let us be Y'Qatt?"

She shrugged. "I don't know. Do you want to be Y'Qatt?"

He didn't answer and a moment later S'Doryn called Jynna over and helped her back into the saddle.

"It's only children who survived," she said, as he climbed up behind her. "Why is that?"

"I don't know, Jynna. Maybe it has something to do with magic. One of the girls who was burned is older than you are, but not old enough to have come into her power yet. That's the only thing I can think of that makes any sense."

"But does that mean it wasn't the pestilence?"

"I'm not certain what it means."

They started riding out of the village. From what she had overheard of S'Doryn's conversation with the brothers, it seemed that they were going to stay in the low hills west of the lake until they were allowed to return to the Fal'Borna village.

"Is there anything else you can tell me about what happened yesterday, Jynna?" S'Doryn asked after they had ridden for some time. "Anything at all unusual?"

"Well, there was the old woman."

He looked down at her. "What old woman?"

"I saw her . . ." She was reluctant to mention her secret spot, until she realized with a pang of regret that she probably wouldn't ever be going back to it. "I met her in a dale near the village. She was working on some baskets to trade in the marketplace."

"And did she seem at all ill?"

"No, she was fine."

He frowned and faced forward again. "Still, she might have gotten sick later. She was Qirsi, right?"

"No. She was Mettai."

"Mettai?" He sighed and shook his head. "That's blood magic. If this is a strain of the pestilence that strikes at Qirsi magic, it probably wouldn't have come from her."

Again they fell silent, until Jynna said, "Her baskets were pretty. She gave me one."

"Did you bring it with you?"

She shook her head. "No. I was afraid it would remind me of yesterday. But now I wish I had."

Chapter 10

Dreaming Moon, second day of the waxing, 1147.

It's been more than half a turn since Licaldi appeared in our village, and I despair of knowing little more about her today than I did that first sunny morning. I was encouraged in those first few days, satisfied that I was learning more about the girl with each day that passed, but I realize now that all that I gleaned then were trifles: the mere fact that she could speak, her name, the fact that she was Mettai, even the knowledge that some terrible tragedy has befallen her and those she loves. Aside from her name, these details, while certainly of some value, tell me little that I couldn't tell simply by looking at her, by recalling how she appeared that day she arrived—emaciated and filthy and haunted.

She seems contented to follow me around day after day, as I attend to my duties as eldest and do all that I must to keep my house—our house—clean and the garden growing. I remain concerned for her, and I try to remind myself each day that she has another home, perhaps a family who are searching desperately for her as I write this. Still, I have to admit that I enjoy having her with me. I've become quite fond of her, for though she doesn't speak of anything that happened to her before she came to Kirayde—and in fact seems to take great care in avoiding any mention of her past—she speaks at length of other matters, offering her observations on the workings of our marketplace, on the ease with which I use magic (she has expressed admiration for my skill as a sorceress, and I have to admit that I'm flattered), and on the various people she's encountered in my company. Through all of this, she's shown herself to be quite clever and possessed of a sharp wit. She laughs freely and at times strikes me as being a fine, normal young girl.

But then a shadow falls over her eyes, or a remark slips out that seems to hint at her former life, and the light I see in her is extinguished as swiftly as a candle in a sudden wind. If I pursue these matters with questions, she withdraws, grows silent, even sullen, as if by asking I have committed some breach of trust. At these times it doesn't matter what tone of voice I use, gentle or hard: Licaldi remains reticent. And my frustration grows.

I sense that she is aware of my feelings. And here I mean far more than the obvious. Of course she knows how eager I am to know more about her— my questions, which I've repeated probably dozens of times, can leave little doubt as to that. But I think she knows as well that I've grown attached to her, that in many ways she has rescued me from a life that was a good deal emptier than I ever realized. For too long I've lived without companionship, without love. I was starved for it, though I never knew it. Licaldi did, though. I'm just as certain of that as I am of the fact that she has seen horrors beyond my imagining. I'm not so foolish as to think that she chose this village for that reason, or even that she contrived in some way to end up with me. That was the will of the gods, who may well have marked us for one another long ago.

But I do believe that she uses my need against me. Perhaps if I had a husband and a family, I wouldn't be so frightened that I might drive her away with more persistent questioning. Perhaps if I hadn't grown so accustomed to her presence here in the short time we've had together, I would be more eager to find the truth and return the poor girl to her rightful home. I don't know how much of what she does is meant to bend me to her will, and how much merely has that effect inadvertently, but I have seen her haggle with peddlers on my behalf, and I have seen her turn others to her purposes and I recognize some of the devices she has used on them as being the same she has used to good effect with me.

Just a few days ago, for the first time, she played with some of the other village children, and in no time at all she had made herself their leader, though she was neither the oldest nor the biggest. She convinced them to play a game of find the wraith by rules I had never seen before. She didn't bully them, though I believe some of the other children are afraid of her. She merely got her way, as she so often does.

I don't mean this to sound as mean-spirited as it probably does. It's late and I'm weary and I should be sleeping. She's a good girl, and I've come to love her very much. But she is someone who makes the world as she wants it, and woe to those who would stand in her way.

Except that isn't right either, for I can't imagine that her world is anything like what she imagined or hoped it would be just a few turns ago.

Dreaming Moon, sixth day of the waxing, 1147

At last, a spar of light in the shadows. Some of the mystery surrounding the poor girl was lifted today, though learning what I have I am more convinced than ever that she has been through a terrible ordeal, one she was fortunate to survive. And I'm equally certain that those she loved were not as fortunate as her.

We were in the marketplace, as we often are in the mornings these days after breaking our fast and walking in the garden to see how the crops are coming along and what damage one determined and cunning rabbit had done over the course of the previous night. We've never seen the creature, though he leaves ample evidence of his visits. Licaldi has named him Terki, after the trickster of Mettai lore. I think it a fine name and have resolved not to leave snares for him, though only a turn ago I would have done so without hesitation. Didn't I say that she almost always gets her way?

But I am avoiding that which is so unpleasant to write.

We were in the marketplace, looking at bolts of cloth that were being sold by a Qirsi merchant from the Talm'Orast. She'd been with me long enough, and had become so much a part of my home, that I wanted to make a cover for her bed, which now stands in the corner of my own bedroom. She had chosen a fabric we both liked and the merchant and I had agreed to a price of one gold and two silvers.

It was a good price for such fine material, but I'd known this merchant, a woman named K'Malai, for many years and she often does well by me when it's clear that I want something. She's wise enough to want to stay in the good graces of the village's eldest.

As I was pulling out the coins, she remarked that she hadn't seen Licaldi before and she asked the girl how she'd come to be living in Kirayde. I paused, interested to hear Licaldi's answer.

The girl looked at me, and I knew that she wanted me to help her, to make up some story that would answer K'Malai's question without forcing her to delve into the truth. This one time, I refused her, simply by doing nothing.

I saw anger flash in her emerald eyes and an instant later she spun away and fled the marketplace.

I called after her once, drawing the stares of others nearby, but Licaldi didn't stop.

"I'm sorry," K'Malai said. "I didn't mean to upset her."

"It's not your fault. She came to us just before the full of the previous moon, and we still don't know where she's from or what drove her from her home."

"You know nothing about her?"

"She's Mettai. Her name is Licaldi. She came to us half starved and wretched from having wandered in the wilderness for who knows how long. I believe that something terrible has happened to her, but I'm only guessing. We know nothing for certain."

The merchant appeared to consider this for some time, her hands on her hips, and her lips pursed. "You say she's Mettai?" she asked at length.

"She says she is. She's too young to show any signs of knowing blade craft."

"Still, she looks it."

"If you suspect something, you'd best tell me. Even the hint of a rumor would be better than the nothing we know now."

"It's more than a rumor, though it's far from certain that it has anything to do with the girl. But there's a Mettai town south of here, one I used to stop in when I came up this way." She winced. "I say there is a town; I should say was. It was struck by the pestilence not long ago. As far as I know, no one survived."

"No one?"

She shook her head, a haunted look in her pale yellow eyes. Even for the Qirsi, whose power to heal the sick runs far deeper than any magic of ours, the pestilence is cause for terror. "As I say, this might have nothing to do with her."

But I knew better. "You said not long ago. Can you be more exact?"

She shrugged, narrowing her eyes. "About a turn, I'd say. Maybe a bit more."

It seemed to me that a turn would be about right. "What was the name of the village?" I asked.

"Sentaya."

I repeated the name and nodded. "Thank you, K'Malai." I gave her the coins and took my cloth.

"I hope this has nothing to do with the girl," she called after me, as I started to walk away.

"So do I," I answered. "But it does. It has everything to do with her."

I took the cloth home, hoping that I'd find Licaldi there. When she wasn't I began to grow concerned. She hadn't strayed far from my side since the day she arrived in Kirayde, and I didn't know if she could find her way back to the house without me. Clever as she is, though, I should have known better. I found her in the garden, sitting among the bean poles, her knees drawn up to her chest, and her long hair hanging over her face.

I sat down near her, but I said nothing. I wanted her to start this conversa-tion. For a long time, she remained silent, and I had the sense that she was just as determined that I be the first one to speak. I've heard parents speaking of engaging their children in a contest of wills. This was my first experience with such a thing. Does this mean that I'm a parent now? I feel that I become more of one with each day that passes.

Eventually I decided that this was a contest I didn't necessarily need to win.

"Her question frightened you," I said quietly.

Silence.

"Eventually, you're going to have to tell me what happened."

That of all things drew a response.

"Why?" she demanded, tears on her face. "Why do you need to know? Isn't it enough that I'm here? Can't we just pretend that it's been like this all along?"

"This isn't play, Licaldi. And it hasn't been this way all along. Something happened to you, and if I'm going to take care of you, I need to know what it was."

She sat there a moment longer, and then she started to climb to her feet. I grabbed her arm and, not gently, forced her to remain where she was. I'd never done anything of the sort before, and she gaped at me as if I had slapped her across the face.

"I'm not done speaking with you," I said sternly. "And until I am, you'll stay right where you are."

She looked frightened, though of me, or what she thought I might ask her, I'm still not certain.

"You're from Sentaya, aren't you?"

All the color drained from her cheeks and tears spilled down her face. But she didn't answer me.

"The pestilence came, and everyone got sick but you. Isn't that so?" I took her hand, and though she didn't grip my fingers in return, she didn't pull it back either. "Your mother and father died."

A sob escaped her.

"Perhaps a brother or a sister, as well?"

"Two sisters," she whispered.

At that moment it seemed that my heart split in two. Part of me grieved for her and all that she had lost, while another rejoiced at hearing her voice, at having her trust me enough to offer even this simple answer. It was a fleeting sensation, for in the next moment she frightened me terribly.

"Please don't make me say more!" she said, throwing herself on me, clinging to me as she sobbed and sobbed.

More! How could there possibly be more? Wasn't this enough? Hadn't the gods heaped enough anguish on this child? Already they had taken too much from her; already they had forced her to endure horrors that would have overwhelmed people twice her age. I tried to tell myself that she referred only to the ordeal of watching them succumb to the disease. Surely she would have shrunk from reliving that. But I believe there really is more, something that remains trapped within her, like some terrible beast fighting to break free.

I didn't push her any further and she volunteered nothing else. We remained in the garden for more than an hour, and she cried for a good deal of that time until at last she fell asleep, her head in my lap, my fingers stroking her hair. I let her remain that way another hour before shaking her gently.

When she awoke, her spirits seemed greatly improved, almost as if she had forgotten the events of the morning. I couldn't be certain whether this was genuine, or if she was acting this way for my benefit, but I decided that she had been forced to reveal enough of herself for the day, and I didn't broach the matter again.

That, then, is how matters stand tonight. She is sleeping soundly at present, though it wouldn't surprise me if the day's revelations trigger another spate of dark dreams. I'm prepared, of course, to help her in any way I can, but I have to admit that I have fears of my own. I've yet to learn all there is to know about Licaldi's past. What I've gleaned thus far is dark enough. I dread what I might learn next.

Besh laid the daybook aside and rubbed his eyes with his thumb and forefinger. Glancing out the window of the old hut, he saw that the sun had sunk low in the western sky, its light shading toward gold and shimmering on the waters of the small rill that ran by the village. Another day gone, and he found himself feeling much as Sylpa did: frustrated by how little he had learned, afraid of the revelations still to come.

The fact was that these days he often thought as Sylpa did. Perhaps it was inevitable, delving into her private writings each day, but he had discovered that his mind and hers worked in similar ways. She would have been younger than he when she wrote all this about Lici, but not so much younger that he couldn't find much in common with her.

When he first mentioned to his daughter that he had become consumed with learning the truth about Lici and her disappearance, Elica had asked if he loved the old woman. Of course he didn't. She terrified him.

Oddly, though, he now believed that he had come to love Sylpa.

Never mind that she had been dead for more than eleven fours, or that even had she been alive, she would have been fifty years older than he. For the past half turn, he had been reading her journal, glimpsing the workings of her keen mind, sounding the depths of her compassion for the poor girl whom fate had thrust upon her. Aside from Ema, he had never known any woman so intimately. At first he had sworn to himself that he would only read those portions of the journal that touched upon Lici and her past, but in recent days he had spent as much time reading about Sylpa's life as he had trying to learn what he could about the girl.

As Besh anticipated, he had found references to his parents in the journal. He hadn't expected, however, that Sylpa would have unkind things to say about his mother, about her pettiness and her tendency to hold a grudge. Nor had it occurred to him that, upon seeing his mother through this woman's discerning eye, he would agree with most of her criticisms. It struck him as odd that he should place so much faith in the judgments of someone he'd hardly known, and yet it also felt perfectly natural. At times, as he walked through the village, or even as he sat at Elica's supper table, listening to the prattle of his grandchildren, he would have private conversations with Sylpa, sharing his own observations and imagining things she might say.

Up until recently, it was something he had only done with his beloved Ema, and he couldn't help feeling that he had somehow betrayed her. If he had fallen in love with a living woman and allowed her to share his heart with his dead wife, he wouldn't have felt nearly as guilty as he did daydreaming about this other woman, dead so many years. He never mentioned Sylpa to Elica, unless it was in the context of something he had learned about Lici, and then he rarely uttered Sylpa's name. It was as if he were having a secret love affair with a wraith. A part of him knew how ridiculous it was—Elica herself might have found it humorous. But he could never work up the courage to tell her.

The only person who had any idea was Pyav, with whom he shared all that he learned of Lici's childhood. And if the blacksmith had noticed anything unusual in the way Besh spoke of Sylpa, he had the courtesy to keep his observations to himself.

Besh pushed himself out of the chair and stretched his back. Then he returned the journal to the old wooden box in the back room of the house, taking care to place Lici's bag of coins on top of it, so that all was just as he had found it that first day when he and Pyav searched the hut. He wasn't certain why he bothered doing this every day. He was the only person who ever entered the house, and he was starting to doubt that Lici would come back, though he'd yet to say as much to anyone. Still, he left everything just as it had been, even going so far as to return the chair he'd been sitting in to its original place by the hearth. Only then did he make his way to Pyav's shop.

Besh had gone to speak with the village eldest each day after reading the journal. By now Pyav expected him; he was sitting out front when Besh arrived.

"You look tired, my friend," the blacksmith said as Besh sat on the bench beside him.

Besh smiled wanly. "It's all the reading. Sylpa's hand isn't the easiest." It almost seemed that she was there at his shoulder, listening. And he added, as if for her benefit, "Though it's a good deal better than mine."

"Anything today?" Pyav asked. He already sounded bored, and not for the first time Besh wondered if the man thought him foolish for going to all of this trouble.

"Actually, yes." He was pleased to see the surprise on Pyav's broad face. "It seems that Lici's village was ravaged by the pestilence. That was how she happened to be wandering alone in the wilderness."

"Her family?"

"All of them died. Her parents and two sisters."

The eldest exhaled through his teeth. "Well, such a thing is bound to lie heavily on anyone, particularly on a child of that age."

"I agree."

"Still," Pyav said, raising his eyebrows. "I'm not certain that it explains all that we know of Lici. Such a thing might leave a person scarred, even bitter. But Lici goes far beyond this. There's a darkness in her that I can barely fathom."

"Sylpa thinks there's more to this tale than we've heard thus far," Besh said. He regretted the words immediately.

"Sylpa thinks?" Pyav repeated. He laughed, though he seemed uncomfortable. "You do realize that the woman is dead."

"Of course," Besh said, making himself smile. He felt his face coloring, and once more he had the sense that Sylpa was there, waiting to hear how he would handle this. "Forgive me. I've spent so many hours with the daybook that I forget sometimes whether I'm living in Sylpa's time or ours."

Pyav frowned. "I'm concerned for you, Besh. I shouldn't have to remind you that you're not a young man. You're pushing yourself awfully hard, and I'm not certain that it's worth the effort. Even if there is more to Lici's story than this tragedy you read about today, what difference does it make? Do you honestly still believe that Lici left here because of something that happened during Sylpa's lifetime? Do you even still believe that Lici's alive?" He passed a hand over his face, wincing slightly. "I'm sorry to say this to you, Besh. Truly I am. But I think you're wasting your time. At first, when you started reading the daybook, I thought maybe there was some point to it. We know so little about Lici, and I felt that anything we might learn about her would be helpful. So this is my fault as much as it is yours. Probably more. But I think it's time we admitted to ourselves, and to everyone else in the village, that she's gone, that she's not coming back, and that we have no idea why she left." He placed his hand on Besh's shoulder. "I think it's also time we admitted that we're relieved to be rid of her."

At first, Besh didn't say anything. He wanted to ask if this meant that he no longer had the eldest's permission to read Sylpa's daybook, but he realized that he was afraid to hear Pyav's answer. His friend, though, mistook the cause of his silence.

"If you're worried about her gold, don't be. You mentioned some time ago that you thought the gold should be used to build a new well for the village. I think that's a fine idea."

"Actually, that was Sirj's idea," he said, his voice low.

"Then when the time comes, Sirj can lay the first stone. The point is, no one will be getting rich off of Lici's misfortune, and all of us will benefit from the coins she left behind. That's what you were worried about, isn't it? Isn't that how all of this began?"

He knew that Pyav was trying his best to make him feel better, and he should have been grateful. But all he could say was "Are you telling me I can't go back and read the daybook anymore?"

"I'm telling you that I don't think you should, that it's a waste of your time."

Besh didn't respond and after another moment Pyav shook his head and looked away.

"If you want to go back, you can, Besh. It's not in my power to order you away from Lici's house. But I wish that the word of a friend was enough to make you see how foolish this is."

"I appreciate your concern, Eldest."

"But you're going back."

"I still think there's something to be learned from that journal. And I still believe that Lici is alive."

Pyav's mouth twisted sourly. "Very well. Do as you will. If you learn anything of value, I'll want to hear about it."

Besh nodded, understanding that this was the last of their daily conversations. "Thank you, Pyav." He stood and started to walk away.

"Why are you doing this?" the blacksmith called after him.

Besh halted, sighed, and turned. "She left sixty-four years to the day after her arrival. Doesn't that strike you as odd?"

"Of course it does, but everything Lici has ever done strikes me as odd. She's the strangest person any of us has ever known."

"This is strange even for her, and I think it means something."

"Isn't it possible that she chose that day to go off and die? Couldn't it be that simple?"

"Maybe," Besh said. "But I'm a good deal closer to the day of my death than you are to yours, and I can tell you that if I was going off to die, I wouldn't leave my home as she left hers."

Pyav smiled kindly. "Of course you wouldn't, my friend. But you would be leaving behind people you love. That would be a terrible burden to leave for Elica and Sirj. Lici had no such concerns. She was alone and I believe she hated the rest of us. I can easily imagine her doing this to the people of Kirayde. Actually, it would have surprised me if she'd shown us any more consideration than she did."

Besh knew that Pyav was making a great deal of sense, probably more than he himself was. But he could hear Sylpa's voice inside his head, insistent and no less convincing. "You're probably right," was all he said.

Pyav gave him a sly look. "Now you're humoring me."

He had to smile. "Yes."

"Go, then," the eldest said, smiling as well. "And tomorrow, after you've read, come and tell me what you've learned."

"You're certain?"

"I'm eldest of this village. I should know its history." He shrugged again. "To be honest, I find all that you've told me about Sylpa rather interesting."

"All right, then. Tomorrow."

Besh raised a hand in farewell and started toward home. The sky overhead was darkening and the air had grown cool. Another day gone. He couldn't remember the last time he had taken Mihas with him to the garden or found the time to play with Annze and Cam. No doubt Elica had noticed how consumed he was with Lici's disappearance and Sylpa's journal. She hadn't commented on it recently, but he knew she wouldn't remain silent for long. It wasn't her way.

"You're going to have to tell me what you know, Sylpa," he whispered in the twilight. "I can't keep on this way forever."

If you're so eager to know, find the passage and read it. Not Ema's voice, though the words could well have been hers. This was Sylpa, speaking to him as his dear wife so often did.

"I wouldn't know where to look. I could just as easily skip past it as find it."

That's an excuse and nothing more. You read at this pace because you wish to, because you like having my voice in your head.

"Am I wasting my time then? Is this just the folly of a lonely old man?"

No, the voice said. So certain, so forceful, that he almost looked around to see who had spoken. *The answer is there, in the book.*

"But is the question worth asking?"

He didn't need to hear her response. He knew already; he had all along.

Before he reached the house, he saw Mihas running toward him and heard him calling, "Grandfather! Grandfather!"

Besh smiled to see the boy and held out his hand for Mihas to take.

"Where have you been?" he asked breathlessly, taking Besh's hand and turning to walk back home.

"I was speaking with Pyav. And before that I was at Lici's house."

"Did you find what you were looking for?"

"Not yet," Besh said. "But I think I'm getting closer."

"Does that mean you know where Lici is?"

"No, I'm afraid not."

They reached the house and went inside. Annze was placing food on the table and Elica stood at the hearth stirring a pot of stew. She cast a dark look Besh's way, but didn't say anything. Sirj and Cam were playing on the floor and Cam managed to say hello between giggles.

They sat down to eat a few moments later. Elica's stew was quite good, but Besh could tell that she was angry with him, and neither of them said much. The children asked him question after question about Lici's house, as they always did. They'd heard so many tales about the woman that it seemed they thought Besh spent his days in the company of wraiths. As soon as he formed the thought, he grinned. Hadn't he been thinking much the same thing earlier that day, as he pondered the feelings he harbored for Sylpa?

"What are you smiling at?" Elica demanded.

He regarded her placidly. "My own foolishness."

She didn't know how to respond to that and so fell back into her sullen silence.

Sirj chuckled appreciatively. "A good answer. I'd do well to remember it." He winked at Besh.

Elica said something cutting to her husband, but Besh didn't hear it.

Once more, the old man found himself wondering why he'd been so dismissive of Sirj for so many years. No man who could laugh at himself and help raise such fine children deserved to be treated so. Had Besh simply allowed himself to become one of those fathers who thought no man was good enough for his daughter?

Would it surprise you to learn that you were so thickheaded?

There could be no mistaking that voice. Ema. Why was his mind so filled with the thoughts of the dead?

The rest of the meal passed in relative silence and before long, Elica and Sirj shooed the children off to bed and began to clear the table. Besh would have liked to go outside, light his pipe, and think some more about what he'd read today. But after spending so much time away from the house, he felt that he should remain with his daughter, at least for a time.

He stood and wrapped what remained of the bread in a cloth. After that, there was little left for him to do, but he lingered in the kitchen, watching Elica as she cleaned.

"How many more days will you be going there?" she asked at last, refusing even to look at him.

"I don't know. As many as necessary."

"You're wasting your time."

"Pyav told me the same thing."

She looked at him. "Then why do you go back? What is it about that woman?"

It took him a moment to realize that she meant Lici and not Sylpa.

"I've told you before: I'm troubled by her disappearance. Everyone assumes that she's dead by now, but I don't believe she is. She's out there somewhere, and I won't be able to rest easy until I know where she is and what she's up to."

"But if there was something in her house that could tell you those things, don't you think that you'd have found it by now? People are talking, Father. They think . . . they think your mind is slipping. They think you're so consumed with Lici that you're becoming more and more like her every day."

He laughed. "Is that what they're saying?"

She nodded, looking utterly unamused.

"Well then, perhaps I am. As to your question, I have found something that may tell me what's become of her. Sylpa's journal. I'm making my way through it as quickly as I can. I'm not as good with my letters as you are, but I'm getting better. And I'm learning things about Lici as I go. Did you know that she came here because she lost her family to the pestilence?"

Elica turned pale. "Did you learn that today?"

"Yes. Why?"

She shook her head. "It's probably nothing."

"Tell me."

She shrugged, as if trying to make light of what she was about to tell him, but her expression belied the gesture. "It was just something I heard in the marketplace today. Apparently there have been outbreaks of the pestilence north of here, and on the other side of the wash."

"Ravens Wash?"

"No, Silverwater. It's been striking Qirsi villages."

Something I heard in the marketplace . . . Just as Sylpa learned of Sentaya's fate among the stalls and peddlers' carts. His mouth had gone dry, and he felt light-headed.

"Are you all right, Father?"

"What else did you hear?"

"That was all. Not a lot, but enough to make me fearful for all of us."

It had to be a coincidence, this echo of the past. What else could it be? And yet that voice within him, the one he had come to trust, even love, over the past half turn, was telling him otherwise.

The pestilence strikes and a turn later she arrives in Kirayde. Sixteen fours pass. She leaves Kirayde and a turn later the pestilence strikes. This is more than mere chance or the random act of the gods. It's her.

He turned and walked out of the house.

"Father?" Elica called to him. "Where are you going?"

"Back to Sylpa's journal," he said. "Don't wait up for me. I'll be late."

Chapter 11

Standing outside the walls of Yorl, gazing westward at the imposing peaks of the Aelind Range, Grinsa and Cresenne had felt daunted nearly to the point of despair. Already they had endured the bitter hostility of the Eandi living in the coastal city, and if the captain of the *Fortune Seeker* was to be believed, every man and woman they encountered in western Aelea and Stelpana would be filled with just as much hate for all Qirsi, if not more. Even knowing that Eagle's Pass lay due west of the city gate, they had wondered how they would ever manage to make their way through those mountains. Yes, they had food and they had horses. But they were strangers in a land that felt both unfamiliar and malevolent. Had there been any true alternative to crossing the plain that stretched out before them that first day, they would have taken it and counted themselves fortunate to have the choice.

But there were no alternatives, and, they soon realized, all was not nearly as bad as they had feared. While the plain had appeared to have few forests in which to find shelter, and fewer towns in which to find additional stores, they soon discovered that it was not nearly so barren. As they crossed the expanse they found several small woodlands, tucked away in shallow dales through which flowed rills and creeks. They also realized that the mountains had looked so formidable from the city walls because the distance to them was not nearly as great as they had assumed. As it turned out, Aelea was a small realm, at least when compared with the kingdoms of the Forelands. The distance between Yorl and the first line of mountains was but twenty-five leagues. Without pushing their mounts too hard, they were able to cross the plain in five days. And because they managed to complete the crossing so quickly, they were never in danger of running out of food and so had no reason to risk entering an Eandi settlement.

Grinsa had worried that they might have trouble finding Eagle's Pass, but once they reached the foothills, they spied a well-worn path that wound up into the peaks. When they found the path late in that fifth day a storm hung low over the mountains, and so they made camp in the shadow of the range and hoped the weather would improve by morning. It didn't, and once more he felt his apprehension mounting. Their swift crossing of the plain would be worth nothing if they were forced to remain in the foothills, eating what was left of their supplies and making no progress.

But late that night a storm passed over their small camp, soaking their sleeping rolls and clothes, and chilling them with a hard, steady wind. When morning broke, they were cold and wet, but the skies over the range had cleared and they were able to begin their climb into the pass.

To this point, Bryntelle had borne what few hardships they encountered without complaint. But the wind only increased as they rode farther into the mountains, and they had no dry blankets with which to keep her warm. She fussed loudly throughout the day, and by nightfall Cresenne feared that she had taken ill with a fever.

Once again, however, it seemed that the gods were smiling upon them. The wind died down overnight, and when Bryntelle awoke the next morning, her fever had vanished and, aside from being famished, she showed no ill effects from the day before.

There was a reason why Eagle's Pass was so well traveled. While the surrounding peaks towered above them, stark against an azure sky and gleaming with a fresh blanket of snow, the pass was broad and low enough to be lined on either side with forests of spruce and hemlock. Rainwater from the storms cascaded off the mountains, ribbons of silver against the stone cliff faces. The roar of rushing water overwhelmed all other sound and echoed through the pass. The track was muddy from all the rain—pools of standing water reflected the sunlight—but no snow blocked their way. Before long, they were steering their mounts down the far side of the pass. Enormous mountains still loomed in front of them, but Grinsa could see a clear path through.

Still, it took them another full day of riding before they emerged from the mountains into the dry foothills west of the range. Reaching a small clearing, they dismounted and allowed the horses to graze. Grinsa and Cresenne stepped to the end of a stone ledge and once again found themselves staring out at a broad plain. This time, however, there were no mountains in sight. Just pale heath and farmland, and in the distance, a pair of broad rivers, carving through the grasses and pastures, as dark as sapphires and running to the horizon in both directions.

"Maifor's Wash and Ravens Wash," Cresenne said softly.

Grinsa glanced at her. "Thank you. I'd forgotten the name of the first one."

"There's a third, beyond these two. Silverwater, I think it's called. We'll have to cross all three of them to reach Qirsi land."

"I know."

She shifted Bryntelle so that the child's weight rested mostly on her hip. "And we're going to need to find food in the next day or two. We're almost out."

He took her free hand. "I know that, too. It'll be all right."

She smiled at him, though as she faced the plain again her expression sobered. "I've never seen a land so beautiful. And I've never been anywhere that scared me more."

"We'll find a town along the river, someplace that isn't too small, someplace that will have seen Qirsi before. There have to be Qirsi peddlers who trade in these lands."

"How do you know?"

"I don't really," Grinsa admitted. "But it makes sense. Back in the Forelands there was always trade among all the realms, even between the most bitter enemies. What was the old saying? 'Kings must have their wars, and merchants must have their gold'? I'd wager the same is true here."

"And how does that help us?"

"If we can find a town that sees some Qirsi traffic, even if it's just the occasional peddler, we'll stand out less. That's got to be better than winding up in a village that a Qirsi hasn't passed through since the last Blood War."

"I suppose," Cresenne said. She didn't sound convinced.

They made camp that night in the foothills before descending to the plain the following morning. Once on level terrain, they were able to make better time once more, and late in the day they reached the banks of Maifor's Wash.

It was a broad river, which had looked placid and slow from a distance. But as Grinsa and Cresenne drew nearer, they could see that in fact it ran so swift and deep as to make a crossing too dangerous. The waters of the wash swirled in tight eddies and looked turbid with silt and mud.

They followed the riverbank northward, hoping to find a spot where they might cross safely. Finding none before nightfall, they made camp and ate what was left of their food. In the morning, they resumed their search, still riding north.

Before midday they came within view of a large settlement set just beside the river. Farmhouses and barns dotted the land around the village, and broad lanes led into it from the south and east. More important, Grinsa spotted a broad stone bridge spanning the river from near the marketplace in the middle of the town.

"We have no choice, do we?" Cresenne said, eyeing the village grimly.

It was a pleasant-looking place. The houses looked clean and cheerful, the crops appeared to be doing well, and there were quite a few peddlers crossing the river into the village marketplace. Had they still been in the Forelands, or even the western half of this land, they wouldn't have hesitated to ride into town. But their experience in Yorl remained fresh in Grinsa's mind. He was no more eager than Cresenne to enter the village.

"I don't think we do," he said, his eyes meeting hers. "This may be our only chance all day to find more food. And who knows where else we'll be able to cross the river?"

She nodded, taking a deep breath. "All right. Lead the way."

He kicked his mount into motion and started up the lane again, with Cresenne just behind him.

"We'll get some food and be on our way," he said, glancing back at her. "Who knows? Maybe we'll find a Qirsi peddler."

She offered no response and they rode in silence the rest of the way to the village. Along the lane they passed an Eandi merchant who rode atop an old wooden cart, pulled by a grey nag. He glared at them as if he thought they had used their magic to pilfer his wares, but he said nothing, and they deemed it best to do the same.

Unlike the city of Yorl, this village, whatever its name, was not fortified. There was no city wall, no guarded gate through which they had to pass. But in other ways, it was all too similar to the coastal city. Once again, it seemed that every person they saw was Eandi, that every gaze that fell upon them was filled with hatred and fear. Grinsa slowed his mount slightly, allowing Cresenne and Bryntelle to pull abreast of him. He scanned the lane as they rode, his gaze never resting, his magic ready, lest they be attacked.

But while the people in the lane didn't offer so much as a nod of greeting, neither did they give any sign that they intended to hurt them, or even demand that they leave. Grinsa wasn't certain if this was because they didn't dare challenge a Qirsi of unknown power, or if they were forbidden from doing so by the laws of the land. Really, he didn't care. He watched them; they watched him. That was the extent of their interaction.

Upon reaching the marketplace, Grinsa began to relax. There, among the Eandi peddlers with their carts and stalls, he spotted a few Qirsi traders. They were vastly outnumbered, to be sure. All told, there couldn't have been more than five or six. But they were there, and Grinsa steered his mount toward the nearest of them.

"It seems you were right," Cresenne said.

"Fortunately. I had my doubts when we first rode into the village."

They stopped and dismounted in front of the cart of the first Qirsi peddler, a young man who was just completing a transaction with an Eandi woman and her daughter. He wore his hair loose and long, and he had elaborate black markings etched into the skin around his right eye. Grinsa and Cresenne waited until the Eandi had moved off before stepping up to the cart.

"Good day, cousin," Grinsa said, grinning at the man and offering a hand.

The man stared at him a moment, then glanced down at his proffered hand and sneered. "You're no cousin of mine."

Realizing that he had erred, Grinsa felt his smile melt away. Qirsi often called each other cousin in the Forelands, even if they were strangers. Most of the sorcerers there were descended from the invading army that had gone to the Forelands from these realms nine centuries ago, and so most assumed that they were related to one another. In addition, the fact that the Qirsi of the Forelands were so vastly outnumbered by the Eandi fostered a certain camaraderie; calling one another cousin came naturally.

But it occurred to Grinsa there were far more Qirsi in the Southlands, and nearly all of them probably belonged to one of the great clans. Here, calling a strange Qirsi "cousin" might well have been seen as presumptuous, maybe even insulting.

"Forgive me," Grinsa said. "Where I'm from, Qirsi often address each other so. I meant no offense."

"What is it you want, white-hair?"

Grinsa glanced at Cresenne, who raised an eyebrow.

"Quickly!" the man said. "Do you want to kill off all my business?"

"You think that by standing here, we're keeping Eandi customers away."

The man glared at him as if he were simple. "Of course, fool! Now either buy something or move on!"

Grinsa glanced down at the man's wares, which consisted mostly of trinkets and extravagances—gems, ivory combs, blades with jeweled hilts, multicolored blankets. He had nothing Grinsa wanted to buy, at least nothing tangible.

"I need information."

The man frowned. "What information? I'm a peddler, nothing more."

"What's the name of this town?"

The man regarded them both through narrowed eyes, as if seeing them for the first time. "Your speech is strange. Where are you from?"

"We've just come from the Forelands. We took a ship south to Yorl, then crossed Aelea, made our way through Eagle's Pass, and came here."

"I'm not certain I believe you," the man said.

"It's true. We're still learning about your land. We know that we're in Stelpana, on Maifor's Wash, but we don't know the name of this village."

He eyed them a moment longer, then said, "Greysford."

"Greysford. Thank you. And your name?"

He hesitated. "M'Than."

"What clan are you from, M'Than?"

The man chuckled. "You are strangers to this land, aren't you?" He pointed to the markings on his face. "You see this? This means that I'm J'Balanar. Do you know of the J'Balanar?"

Grinsa shook his head.

"You will if you're in the Southlands for long. Our people are the swiftest horsemen of the uplands and the finest seamen on the Ofirean."

"And which are you?"

He grinned. "Both. I grew up riding in the downs. When I reached the end of my fourth four, I left the uplands and made my way to Sir-aam, where I learned to sail."

His fourth four. While on the *Fortune Seeker* Grinsa had heard some of the men speak of fours, meaning four years. It seemed that this was common among both Eandi and Qirsi.

"How long have you been trading?" Grinsa asked the man.

"Two years now, actually almost three."

"And do you sell your wares in both Eandi and Qirsi lands?"

"Of course. Most peddlers do. There's a saying here: 'Commerce cares nothing for the color of a man's eyes.'"

Grinsa glanced at Cresenne, who nodded, a small smile on her lips. Facing M'Than again, he asked, "Does that mean that there are Eandi peddlers here who'll sell us food?"

"You have gold?"

"Forelands gold, yes."

"Gold is gold," M'Than said, much as had Captain Dungar. "They'll sell it to you if they've got it to sell. You won't get a good price, but there's little to be done about that. You might have a better chance in one of the middle nations—Qosantia or Tordjanne. But not in Stelpana." He grinned again, his teeth yellow and crooked. "When I'm here, I take as much gold as I can from a dark-eye. It's just the way of things."

Grinsa nodded. "Thank you, M'Than. You've been most helpful."

The peddler shrugged. "You can thank me better than that." He indicated his goods with an open hand. "Something for the lady? Or maybe the little one?"

Grinsa smiled and after a moment's consideration, chose a blanket of blue and green. "How much?"

"Ten of your qinde ought to do it."

He laughed. "I'll give you six."

"Eight."

"Six, or I walk away with the information and nothing else."

"Fine then," the peddler said. Grinsa got the impression that he was trying to sound cross, but there was a slight grin on the man's face. They both knew that the blanket was barely worth six.

"How far are we from Ravens Wash?" Grinsa asked, as he placed the blanket in his travel sack.

"No more than fifteen leagues, heading due west. You're going to the Fal'Borna?"

"I don't really know," Grinsa said, glancing at Cresenne once more. "We just want to reach Qirsi land as quickly as possible."

"It'll be the Fal'Borna, then. Not particularly friendly to strangers, but a fair bit better than the Eandi, I'd wager. Cut southward after you cross Ravens Wash. You want to get across the Silverwater, and that turns eastward as it heads south. You'll reach it quicker if you turn south."

"Again, M'Than, you have our thanks."

"Well, move on then. I'm wanting to get some dark-eye gold before the morning's done." He smiled again as if to soften the words, but Grinsa had no doubt that he did want them far away from his cart.

He nodded to the man once more, and he and Cresenne walked on to the next Qirsi peddler. He, too, was selling fabrics and jewels.

"They all will be," he muttered to himself, as they wandered away from the man's cart.

"What?"

He looked at Cresenne. "I'm just realizing now that we're not going to find any Qirsi peddler selling food."

"Of course not," she said. "They're too far from home to have brought it with them, and they'd have to spend too much buying it here from Eandi merchants."

"You'd already figured that out?"

She grinned, raising an eyebrow. "You hadn't?"

He shook his head, smiling ruefully. "I'm still thinking as a Forelander."

"Really? I would have thought the Qirsi with markings on his face would put an end to that."

Grinsa laughed, and Bryntelle let out a loud squeal.

"So, if we want food, we have to buy it from an Eandi," she said a moment later.

"I'm afraid so."

"Then let's get it over with and leave this place. I prefer the plain."

They circled the marketplace until they found a peddler who was selling food—cheeses, smoked meat, hard breads. Grinsa had steeled himself for an unpleasant encounter, but the Eandi peddler, an older man with white hair and a lopsided, ruddy face, proved easier to deal with than he had expected. He offered little in the way of pleasantries or conversation, and he tried to charge them far too much for what they wanted, but he wasn't openly hostile. When Grinsa refused to pay the four sovereigns the man demanded for all they were buying, he came down to three and a half.

"That's still too much," Grinsa told him. "That's seven qinde, and I won't pay it."

The man shook his head, his brow furrowed and his lower lip pushed out, as if he were considering the matter. "You won't find a better price in this marketplace."

Grinsa started to lead his mount away, and Cresenne followed. "Maybe not," he said over his shoulder. "But it won't be for lack of trying."

The man let him go five paces, perhaps to see if he'd stop on his own accord. Then he called out, "Two and a half!"

"Sovereigns?" Grinsa asked, turning to look at him.

"Yes. And not a silver less."

"Done." He led his horse back to the cart, paid the man, and began to pack the food in his travel sack.

"Where you from, white-hair?"

Grinsa glanced up at him. The man had asked the question mildly enough, and M'Than had called him white-hair as well. It was an aspersion in the Forelands; apparently in the Southlands it wasn't.

"The Forelands," he said.

"I figured that much. Where?"

"Eardley, on the eastern shore. You know it?"

"I used to sail those waters," he answered. "As a younger man. I know it."

He said nothing more, and Grinsa didn't pursue the matter. Clearly that was as much courtesy as the man was willing to show him. He finished packing the food, tied the sack to his saddle, and walked out of the marketplace with Cresenne and Bryntelle at his side.

They followed a lane west toward the wash, and soon found the bridge. A few more Eandi stared at them, and one old man went so far as to pull a dagger free, as if expecting them to assault him right there in the middle of the path. But as before, no one said anything to them, and in just a few moments they had crossed the bridge and were out of Greysford and back on the plain.

"That could have been far worse," Grinsa said, as they climbed onto their horses once more.

Cresenne kissed Bryntelle's forehead and nodded, but she didn't look relieved. "We're not out of Stelpana, yet."

They rode for much of what remained of that day, and spent the next two days riding as well. They maintained a course due west, and, on the third morning out from Greysford, came within sight of Ravens Wash. The weather had held for the first few days, but this one had dawned grey and windy. By the time they reached the water's edge, a steady rain was falling, chilling them and darkening their moods.

Once again, they found that the river was too deep and swift to cross. Had it been just the two of them, Grinsa and Cresenne might have made the attempt this time. Ravens Wash did not appear quite as daunting as had Maifor's Wash. But with Bryntelle in Cresenne's arms, they didn't dare. Remembering the advice given to them by the Qirsi peddler, they followed the wash southward. The rainfall increased throughout the day, and when the grey skies finally began to darken, they still had not found any shallows. But as the light failed, they caught sight of a village in the distance. It looked to be another league from where they were—they wouldn't reach it before dark, and if they couldn't find lodging in the town, they'd be forced to make camp in the dark and rain.

"At this point I'd pay ten qinde for a dry room," Cresenne said, looking miserable and pale as she sat huddled on her mount, a grey woolen blanket wrapped around her shoulders and covering her head. Bryntelle fussed within her blankets, as if agreeing with her mother.

Grinsa felt much the same way. They rode on, reaching the town an hour or so after nightfall. It was located on the western bank of the wash, but just north of the village a narrow stone bridge spanned the water.

They crossed the bridge and made their way through the deserted lanes and marketplace of the village, looking for an inn. It was a far smaller settlement than Greysford, and Grinsa began to wonder if a town of this size would even have an inn. But near the southern end of the village, along a lane that led back onto the plain, they found a small tavern that seemed to have rooms for lease. A weathered sign hanging out front read THE THISTLE PATCH.

They tied the horses outside and stepped into the tavern. It was warm inside, and the air smelled of musty wine and some kind of spiced stew that made Grinsa's mouth water. A fire blazed in a large hearth near the back of the room. About half the tables in the tavern were taken, and several men stood at the bar, drinking ale and laughing loudly. The barkeep was in the middle of filling a cup, a smile on his round face, when he saw Grinsa and Cresenne standing near the door. Immediately, his expression hardened. Others noticed this and turned to look. Conversations stopped; silence spread through the tavern, until the only sounds were the drip of the rain and the high squeak of the sign swaying in the wind outside the door.

"You lost?" the barkeep finally demanded, his voice like stone grating on iron. He had red hair, a thick beard, and dark eyes that shone with the light of the oil lamps.

Grinsa met and held his gaze. "No. We'd like a room for the night, and some of that stew, if there's any left." He pulled out his money pouch and jangled it. "We have gold."

"We're full up," the man said. "An' the stew's gone."

"You're certain?" Grinsa said. He nodded toward Bryntelle, who clung to Cresenne, her large, pale eyes scanning the room. "It's not a night for a child to be sleeping out on the plain."

The man's mouth twitched. One of the others standing at the bar caught his eye and gave a small shake of his head. The barkeep shifted his ample weight to his other foot, his mouth twitching a second time.

"We're full up," he said again.

Grinsa held his gaze a moment longer before glancing around the tavern. All conversations had stopped and all the patrons were watching them, many of them looking fearful, as if they expected the Qirsi to tear the tavern to its foundations with their magic.

But after a moment, he merely shook his head and said to Cresenne, "Come on. Let's get out of here."

She continued to stare at the barkeep until at last he averted his eyes. "You should be ashamed of yourselves," she said. "Putting a family out on such a night, simply because of the color of their eyes."

"We didn' tell you t' leave your clan, missy," said the man sitting at the bar. "It's not our fault."

"We're not from a clan," she told him. "We're new to your land. And this is a fine way to treat strangers."

With that, they left the tavern. They untied the horses and began to lead them out of the village. At least they had managed to cross the river. The night wasn't a total loss.

Before they had gotten far, they heard shouts coming from behind them, and turning they saw the barkeep hurrying after them.

"Wait!" he was calling. "Wait!" When at last he caught up with them, he was breathless. His soaked hair clung to his brow and water ran down his face. "I can rent you a room," he said. "I thought you was clan Qirsi. I didn' know you was from another land. Th' Forelands is it? I've always wanted t' see th' Forelands."

He looked at one of them and then the other, making himself smile.

"So, you'll rent a room to Qirsi from the Forelands, but not from your own land?" Cresenne demanded.

He rubbed the rain from his face, looking confused.

She looked back at Grinsa and gave a shake of her head. "No," she said. Then, facing the barkeep she said it more forcefully. "No. I won't give you gold. I don't care how cold and wet it is. I don't want my daughter sleeping even one night under your roof."

The man stared at them. "You're fools."

"And you're small-minded."

She turned and started leading her mount away, leaving Grinsa alone with the man.

"You can all rot for all I care," the barkeep said. "She's right. All you white-hairs are the same."

"Maybe," Grinsa said. "Fortunately I know plenty of Eandi who are nothing like you."

He followed Cresenne out onto the plain. After a time she stopped to fix Bryntelle's blankets and Grinsa caught up with her. She was crying.

"I'm sorry," she said, without looking at him. "We should have just taken the room and gotten ourselves warm. But I couldn't do it. I just couldn't."

"It's all right." He kissed her cheek, then took Bryntelle from her. "I didn't want to give him our gold either, but I wouldn't have had the courage to refuse him if you didn't."

A small smile touched her lips. "Is that a polite way of saying it's my fault that we're getting soaked?"

"Yes, I suppose it is."

She climbed onto her horse and Grinsa handed Bryntelle up to her. Then he mounted as well, and they steered their horses away from the river.

They hadn't gone far before they spotted a fire burning in the middle of the plain. After a brief discussion they decided to ride toward it rather than around it. The blaze looked inviting, and given Grinsa's formidable powers, they knew that they wouldn't be in too much danger.

What they found as they drew near to the fire both surprised and delighted them. There must have been a dozen men and women gathered in the darkness, all of them Qirsi, all of them peddlers it seemed. Arrayed around them were carts and wagons filled with all sorts of goods. Several broad tarpaulins had been raised around the perimeter of the fire, so that every person was protected from the rain. One man had a lute in his lap and was strumming it softly, singing a song Grinsa didn't recognize. A few of the others were singing along. Others were listening. And still others were ignoring the music, carrying on conversations of their own. But all of them looked happy and warm.

Not wishing to unnerve them with their arrival, Grinsa called out and, raising a hand above his head, summoned a small flame so that the men and women could see them and know them for Qirsi.

"Come on, then," one of the men called. "Into the light with you. Let us see who's come."

They rode to the edge of their circle, dismounted, and walked into the firelight.

Grinsa started to say something, but the man cut him off.

"Not a word!" he said. "I don't want to hear your accent. I can tell your clan just from the look of you." The stranger was tall and thin, with long limbs that gave him the look of a child's puppet. His white hair was cut short, and he had a pale, wispy beard that made his face look even longer than it was. His face was lined, and Grinsa had the sense that he was old for a Qirsi, though his bright yellow eyes were clear and his smile revealed straight, strong teeth.

"Give up already, R'Shev," a woman shouted at him, laughing. "You haven't gotten one right in two turns."

The man spun toward her, looking aggrieved. "That's not true." He pointed at a woman with long white hair and intricate markings around her eye that were similar to those Grinsa and Cresenne had seen on the peddler in Greysford. "I knew G'Trayna here was J'Balanar the moment I saw her."

Everyone laughed uproariously, and the man turned back to them, narrowing his eyes as he looked first at Grinsa and then at Cresenne.

"Difficult," he said. "Very difficult. Your clothing is odd. The mounts could be those of the Fal'Borna, but your skin is too pale." He stared at them a moment longer before nodding once. "You're H'Bel, aren't you?"

Grinsa smiled. "I'm afraid not."

"Must be A'Vahl then. Had to be one or the other. I thought Talm'Orast for a moment, but neither of you is fat. All the Talm'Orast have gotten fat."

The others laughed at this as well, though Grinsa had no idea why.

"No, I'm afraid we're not A'Vahl either." The man opened his mouth to speak again, so Grinsa held up a hand to forestall another guess. "Actually, we're not from this land at all. We're Forelanders, and we've only recently arrived here."

This was met with stares and silence, and for a moment Grinsa feared that he and his family would be as unwelcome among these Qirsi peddlers as they had been among the Eandi. But a moment later, R'Shev grinned.

"Well, wherever you're from, you're here now. Come and sit. You look cold and hungry."

"We are that," Grinsa said, smiling in return. "Though we have our own food."

"All the better then!"

Several people shifted their positions, making room near the fire for the three of them. A skin of wine somehow found its way into Grinsa's hands and after only a moment's hesitation he drank a bit and handed it to Cresenne.

"So, what are your names?" R'Shev asked.

"I'm Grinsa jal Arriet, and this is Cresenne ja Terba."

"And the little one?"

"Bryntelle ja Grinsa."

"She's a beauty," R'Shev said. "Just like her mother." He winked at Cresenne, drawing a smile.

"You'll have to forgive R'Shev," said the J'Balanar woman. She looked to be older as well, the lines around her eyes blending with her markings to make her look like some strange demon in the firelight. She wore a smile, however, and her eyes flicked toward R'Shev as she spoke. "He sometimes forgets how old he is, and he starts to act like a rutting drel."

The others laughed.

"Unfair!" R'Shev said, shaking his head. "Unfair! Even a rutting drel tends to stay with only one ewe. I have no such scruples."

More laughter.

"Well, allow me to introduce this rabble," R'Shev said. He went around the circle, pointing at each person in turn, and saying their names and clans far too quickly for Grinsa to keep any of them in his mind. Turning back to Grinsa and seeing the frown on his face, the man waved his hand, as if dismissing all he'd just said. "Don't worry about it. You'll learn them eventually. Or you won't, and no one will hold it against you." He regarded the two of them briefly, his eyes narrowing. "What brings you to our circle?"

Grinsa shrugged. "We tried to find a place in the Eandi village back along the wash. I don't even know what it's called. The inn was the Thistle Patch. In any case, the barkeep refused to let us stay there, so we rode on, and happened upon you."

R'Shev nodded slowly. "Actually, I meant 'What brings you to the Southlands,' but we'll start with the village. It's called Bred's Landing, and I'm afraid it's all too typical of Eandi villages in Stelpana. I take it things are quite different in the Forelands."

Grinsa had to smile. "Yes," he said. "Very different. Qirsi and Eandi don't keep themselves separate the way they do here. They live side by side in villages and cities. Eandi nobles are served by Qirsi ministers."

"But you've had trouble with that," said the man with the lute, looking over at them even as he continued to pluck at the strings of his instrument. "Forgive me for interrupting, but we know you have. We heard about it down here."

"Yes," Grinsa admitted, his eyes flicking toward Cresenne. "We had some trouble, but that's over now."

"And yet you're here," R'Shev said, drawing Grinsa's gaze once more. "You left the Forelands. Why?"

"That's a long, difficult tale," Grinsa said.

Cresenne had been chatting with G'Trayna, while the older woman held Bryntelle on her lap. But she was looking at Grinsa now, appearing pale and wary. R'Shev seemed to notice her expression, because he smiled and patted Grinsa lightly on the shoulder.

"Perhaps it's best saved for another time, then," he said. "You should eat something." He handed Grinsa the wineskin, which had made its way around the circle to them once more. "And have some more of this."

"Thank you, R'Shev."

He started to pull food from his travel sack, but the man put his hand on Grinsa's arm, stopping him.

"Have something warm. I get the feeling you've got some distance yet to go, and that food needs to last. We've plenty here."

"Again, my thanks."

"Where are you headed?"

"Not north, I hope," said the man with the lute.

"If you want to join our conversation, D'Chul, I'd suggest you move over here. At least that way I'll know you're listening, and I won't say anything unkind about the way you play that lute of yours."

D'Chul grinned, looking ghoulish in the dim light, and made his way over to where they were sitting. He was a younger man, also thin, though not as tall as R'Shev. He wore his hair long, and tied back from his face, which was round and so fine-featured as to look feminine.

As he sat, Grinsa noticed that his lute was as beautiful as any instrument of its kind he'd ever seen. Its neck was inlaid with pale woods, and its rounded back was so finely smoothed that it shone in the firelight.

"Your lute is magnificent," Grinsa said.

"Thank you," D'Chul said, grinning again. "I made it."

"You made it?"

"D'Chul is M'Saaren," R'Shev said, as if that explained the man's obvious talent. "Woodland people. Their woodwork is the finest in the land."

"The A'Vahl would argue," said the younger man.

"Of course they would. And as usual, they'd be wrong." R'Shev glanced at Grinsa. "I'm glad you didn't turn out to be A'Vahl. As a rule, I can't stand them. Arrogant. Not nearly as skilled as they think they are. Or as smart."

"You said you hoped we weren't headed north," Grinsa said to the young man. "Why?"

"There's talk of the pestilence to the north." He cocked his head to the side. "You have the pestilence up in the Forelands?"

Grinsa nodded. His blood had run cold at the mention of it, fear for Cresenne and Bryntelle making him shudder. He'd lost Pheba, his first wife, to the pestilence. She was Eandi, and she might have survived, if only the other Qirsi in their village had been willing to heal her. But she was the Eandi wife of a Qirsi man, and the healers, seeing their marriage as an abomination, had let her die. He didn't mention this to the men sitting with him, but it did make him wonder if he'd been too quick to point out the differences between the Forelands and Southlands. Perhaps they weren't so dissimilar after all.

"I'd hoped we wouldn't have to worry about that here," Cresenne said quietly, staring at the fire.

Grinsa reached out and took Cresenne's hand. Her fingers were icy. "We'll be all right. We're headed south anyway. And both of us have healing magic, if it comes to that."

"You're trying to get across the Silverwater," R'Shev said. "Into Qirsi land."

"That's what we had in mind."

"That's a wise course. The Fal'Borna are hard as clans go, harder than most. But you'll be a good deal safer there than in Eandi land. And," the older man added, smiling kindly at Cresenne, "you'll be far from where the pestilence has struck."

"What about all of you?" Grinsa asked. "Where are you going next?"

"Oh, different places. Each of us goes his own way. I tend to move back and forth between the Silverwater and Ravens Wash, visiting the towns along both. I'll probably be in Bred's Landing tomorrow. I'm heading north, as it happens, though with the pestilence up that way, I'll turn back well before I get near the Companion Lakes. Others here are going in the opposite direction. At least a few of us find each other most nights. Sometimes we're only three or four. Other times we number as many as thirty."

"It sounds like a nice life," Cresenne said.

"We're Qirsi peddlers trading in Eandi lands. It's the only way to stay sane."

The wine came around again, and D'Chul began to play and sing. His voice was only ordinary, but he played wonderfully and the others sang along. Grinsa and Cresenne didn't know any of the songs, but they were happy just to listen. Bryntelle, who should have been asleep hours before, was wide awake, and seemed delighted by the music and laughter.

Eventually, people began to wander off to sleep. Many of them had small beds in their carts, and others had fashioned crude shelters from cloth and rope and wood. R'Shev told Grinsa and Cresenne that they could place their sleeping rolls under the tarpaulins by the fire, and after some time, Cresenne did.

Grinsa stayed up a while longer, speaking in low tones with R'Shev, learning what he could about the various clans, and the Eandi villages that lay between Bred's Landing and Fal'Borna land.

After a time, they fell silent. But just when Grinsa was ready to bid the man good night, R'Shev surprised him.

"You're a Weaver, aren't you, Grinsa?"

The Eandi guard he and Cresenne encountered in Yorl had divined this as well, so Grinsa wasn't completely unprepared. He did wonder, though, why the man was asking.

"I am."

"Is Cresenne?"

The guard had asked this, too.

"No, she's not. Why?"

"Forgive me," he said. "I don't mean to pry, but are the two of you joined, formally I mean?"

"As it happens, we're not." There hadn't really been time for a formal joining ceremony before they left the Forelands, and in truth, neither of them had seen a need for one. In all ways that mattered, they were husband and wife, their lives bound together not only by their love, but also by Bryntelle. In the Forelands, at least, formal joinings were usually reserved for nobility. But maybe that wasn't the case here. "What is it you're getting at, R'Shev?"

The man rubbed a hand over his narrow face. "It may not come to much. It will depend on which clan you settle with. But among some, Weavers are expected to marry other Weavers. It's a way of ensuring that more Weavers are born, and to some clans that's very important. There haven't been many wars fought among the clans in the last hundred years, but some of the rivalries remain, and, rightly or wrongly, Weavers are equated with power. The more a clan has, the better their prospects in battle with other Qirsi. And if ever the Blood Wars start up again, a clan with many Weavers will have the best chance of taking Eandi land. That's the thinking anyway."

"But I don't belong to any clan."

R'Shev smiled, though if anything, it made him look sad. "The clan you settle with may well see it differently." His brow furrowed. "Perhaps I shouldn't have said anything. I hope I'm wrong. I hope it doesn't matter at all. But you should be prepared, just in case it does."

"Yes, of course," Grinsa said absently.

"I've troubled you."

He met the man's gaze. "As you said, I should be prepared."

R'Shev nodded. Standing, he stretched his back and began to walk off. "Good night, Grinsa."

"Good night, R'Shev. Thank you for everything. This could have been a miserable night for us. Instead it was the best we've had in the Southlands."

"I'm glad."

The man walked off, leaving Grinsa to brood on what the peddler had told him. After some time, he untied his sleeping roll, placed it beside Cresenne, and lay down. She stirred. He kissed her lightly on the lips and she smiled.

"What were you and R'Shev talking about?" she asked sleepily.

He hesitated, but only briefly. "Nothing we need to worry about right now," he said. He kissed her again. "You should sleep."

Chapter 12

◆━╋━◆

By the time they awoke the next morning the rain had eased, but clouds still hung low over the plain, and the air remained chill. The peddlers rose early, some of them with first light, and in mere moments had taken down the tarpaulins and packed up their carts. R'Shev apologized to Grinsa and Cresenne for waking them and taking down the shelter he'd built around the fire ring, but he, too, worked quickly and efficiently. Grinsa offered to help, but the peddler shook his head and smiled.

"I've done this just about every morning for the past fourteen years. I'm better off working alone."

True to his word, the man had his cloths and poles packed away in no time at all and soon was bidding them farewell.

"I wish I was headed west," he said, taking Cresenne's hand in his own and looking from her to Grinsa. "And not only because I enjoy the company of a lovely woman."

Cresenne smiled, though she was surprised by how sad she felt to have to leave the old peddler. She and Grinsa had known him and the other peddlers for less than a day, but already they were their friends, the only ones they had in the Southlands.

"Thank you for everything," she said, stepping forward and kissing his cheek.

"Well, I don't think I did anything at all. But I'd gladly do nothing again if it earned me another kiss."

She grinned.

He glanced at Bryntelle, who was still asleep in Cresenne's arms. "Take care of the little one," he said. "You have enough food? I can sell you some if need be. At cost," he added.

One of the older women was walking by as he said this, and she paused. "Take him up on it, just for our sake. We've never seen the old goat sell anything at cost."

"Get away, nag!" he said, shooing her away as she laughed.

"I think we have enough," Grinsa said. "Thank you, though."

R'Shev's expression sobered. "Be certain. The Eandi of Stelpana grow more hostile to our kind as one moves west. There are some villages near the wash that even I won't venture into."

Grinsa and Cresenne exchanged a look, and after a moment she nodded.

"All right," Grinsa said. "It probably can't hurt to have a bit extra."

R'Shev nodded. "That's right."

They bought more cheese and smoked meat from the man, and paid far less than they would have in any marketplace. After that, there was nothing to do but bid him farewell.

"I hope we meet again," Cresenne told him, knowing of course that they wouldn't.

"That's kind of you, my dear, but I hope we don't. My life's on these plains, and this is no place for a family like yours."

He climbed onto his cart, clicked his tongue at his old horse, and started rattling eastward toward Bred's Landing.

Grinsa and Cresenne were soon ready to continue on their way as well. As it happened, D'Chul, the young lutenist, was also headed west toward Silverwater Wash. Cresenne was delighted to ride in the company of another Qirsi, and she expected that Grinsa would be as well. But for the first several hours of the day, he said little, and he appeared to be occupied with dark thoughts. He rode with his shoulders hunched, his eyes trained on the ground before him, his brow creased so that he seemed to be scowling. Cresenne wondered if he was brooding on something he'd heard the night before, or if he was concerned about what they would do if the skies opened up again, or if he simply didn't like D'Chul.

At one point during the morning, Cresenne steered her mount next to his and reached out to take his hand. His face brightened immediately and he smiled at her.

"Are you all right?" she asked quietly.

"Yes, of course."

"You seem troubled."

He shook his head. "Really, I'm fine."

Cresenne had nodded, taking him at his word. And why shouldn't she? Usually he kept nothing from her. But when she looked at him again only a few moments later, he looked just as he had before: tense, even apprehensive, which was not like him at all. She knew how strong he was, though, and she trusted that no matter what it was that had him worried, he'd find a way to overcome it.

For her part, she hadn't been this happy since the day they left the Forelands, more than two turns before. She liked D'Chul and she enjoyed hearing him speak of the clans and of life on the plain. He'd been born in a small settlement in the Berylline Forest along the western bank of the A'Vahl River. Listening to him speak of his home, Cresenne had to remind herself again and again that all of his neighbors, all the people who lived with him in the village, were Qirsi. She knew this to be true—she'd been in the Southlands long enough to understand that this was not at all unusual in the western half of the land—but every time she pictured the marketplace he described, or the sanctuary where he worshiped, or any other part of the village, she pictured Eandi faces as well as Qirsi, indeed, more of the former than the latter. She couldn't help herself.

Yet, at the same time, she thrilled to the thought that this was the world in which she would soon find herself. In just a few more days, she and Grinsa would cross into Qirsi land and, she hoped, quickly find a settlement in which to build a new life. Bryntelle, awake now, her eyes wide as she watched D'Chul, would grow up thinking it normal to live among only Qirsi, without the hostility and mistrust of the Eandi. No doubt she would take such a life for granted. Cresenne could think of no greater gift for her child.

Yes, she had Eandi friends, though not many of them. Once, when she had allied herself with Dusaan jal Kania, the Weaver who had sought to overthrow the Eandi courts in the Forelands and create a new Qirsi empire, she had believed that she hated all Eandi. She knew now that she didn't. Some among Ean's children had been kind to her in the days leading up to the Weaver's war, kinder than she'd had any right to ask or expect, given her role in the Qirsi conspiracy. But she had to admit that she longed to live the rest of her days free from prejudice and the constant tension that seemed to pervade the cities of the Forelands. And though she would have had trouble admitting as much to Grinsa, who counted an Eandi noble among his closest friends and who once even loved an Eandi woman, she believed that the only way to find such peace was to live apart from all Eandi.

D'Chul proved to be a fine companion for such a grey day. After he'd talked about his home for some time, he began to sing for them, or more precisely for Bryntelle, who laughed and squealed each time he began a new song. Eventually, the young man's singing even drew Grinsa out of his dark mood. As was the case with the songs he had played the night before, Cresenne didn't know any of the ones he sang. They sounded like children's songs, and she had the sense that they would have been as familiar to a Qirsi child in the Southlands as "Four Tired Lambs" or "Moons and Stars" had been to her when she was a girl.

One song in particular delighted Bryntelle and caught Cresenne's ear, though probably not for the same reason. She couldn't follow the verses, which made little sense, but after a few rounds, she was able to piece together the refrain:

Little Dark-Eye, Little Dark-Eye,
Run away back home;
Little Dark-Eye, Little Dark-Eye,
'Tis not your land to roam;
Little Dark-Eye, Little Dark-Eye,
Run away and hide;
Little Dark-Eye, Little Dark-Eye,
No one's on your side.

It seemed that Grinsa also was struck by the lyric. When D'Chul finished singing, he asked, "What was that one called?"

" 'Little Dark-Eye,' " the man answered, grinning. "It's a grim song, eh?"

"I couldn't make out most of it," Grinsa said.

"That's because most of it's been changed. It was a Qirsi war song; dates back to the first of the Blood Wars. You can probably guess what it's about."

"The last line of the refrain was changed, too, wasn't it?"

D'Chul looked at Cresenne. "You could tell that, could you?"

She nodded.

"It was originally 'All your friends have died,' but that was changed long ago. Better for the little ones this way."

"How did you know?" Grinsa asked her, smiling slightly, but also looking annoyed, as if angry with himself for not figuring this out as well.

She shrugged. "It just didn't sound right. 'Died' is the natural rhyme there."

"You've got an ear for music," D'Chul said.

Cresenne laughed at that. She was just about the least musical person she knew. She couldn't even sing in tune. "No," she said. "I think I just have a dark humor."

"There's no escaping it, is there?" Grinsa asked, still looking troubled, his voice grim.

D'Chul frowned. "What do you mean?"

"This feud between Eandi and Qirsi. The Blood Wars. These songs you sing. The Eandi villages that won't give a room to Qirsi travelers. It's everywhere."

Cresenne feared that the lutenist might take offense, but instead, he regarded Grinsa for several moments and then began to nod slowly.

"It must seem that way to you," he said. "I don't think we give much thought to how our land might be perceived by strangers." He seemed to consider this for several moments. At last he nodded again. "Yes, I guess it is everywhere. The wars have been over for some time now, but the fighting didn't end because we suddenly stopped hating one another. I'm not sure people can do that."

"Then why did the wars end?"

He shook his head. "Neither side had the stomach for them anymore. The clans decided that the wars were costing too many lives, even as they continued to take land from the dark-eyes. Already there are more Eandi in the Southlands than there are Qirsi. Not by a lot—not the way we hear Qirsi are outnumbered in the Forelands. But enough to scare our leaders. And the Eandi sovereignties made no effort to continue the fighting. Every time a war was fought they lost land. It's not really surprising that they'd welcome a truce."

"So the two sides never really forged a peace," Grinsa said. "They just stopped killing each other."

D'Chul raised an eyebrow. "I suppose that's one way of putting it. I don't think there's much danger of the wars starting up again, if that's what concerns you."

"No," Grinsa said. "It's not that."

"Then what?" Cresenne asked.

He looked at her, their eyes meeting. "I don't know, really. I just find it all . . . unsettling."

She should have understood. In a way she did, though only vaguely. But mostly, Cresenne felt herself growing impatient with him. Of course the Southlands weren't perfect. What place was? Everyone they'd talked to had said the same thing: The wars had been over for more than a century. The various realms of the Forelands had battled one another as recently as that, and he wouldn't have thought anything of living there, had that been a choice.

He appeared to read the annoyance in her glance, because he forced a smile and shook his head.

"I'm just being foolish," he said. "I suppose it'll take me some time to grow accustomed to this place." He turned to D'Chul. "Forgive me."

The young man shrugged and grinned again. "There's nothing to forgive."

Cresenne thought he was being more generous than she would have been.

They rode with D'Chul for the rest of that day and for two more before finally coming within sight of the Silverwater Wash. By the third morning, the skies had cleared, though the air remained cold.

"This feels like the Harvest," D'Chul said as they rode that third day, turning his face up to the sky and closing his eyes, as if savoring the touch of the sun on his ghostly skin. "I expect we've seen the last of the warmer days until next year's Planting."

Fine, lacy clouds drifted above them, pure white against the deep blue sky, reminding Cresenne of Harvest days in the Forelands. Some things, it seemed, were the same everywhere.

Late that day, D'Chul guided them to a shallow part of the river where they were able to cross into Qirsi land without first entering an Eandi village. They made camp together one last time, joined this time by several other Qirsi peddlers who were on their way into Stelpana. D'Chul played his lute for them again, and by now Cresenne had learned enough of the songs to join in the singing, which she did without hesitation, despite her poor voice.

Grinsa, as usual, had moved off a short distance with one of the older merchants, with whom he spoke in low tones, looking intent and smiling only occasionally. No doubt he was learning all he could about the Fal'Borna—the man with whom he was sitting had darker skin than any Qirsi Cresenne had ever seen, and she recalled hearing R'-Shev say something about the Fal'Borna being a dark-skinned clan. This was one of the things she had come to love about Grinsa: his sense of duty, the determination with which he took care of those he loved.

But she wished that he'd allow himself to have fun, just this once. They were in Qirsi land now, and though she wasn't foolish enough to believe that this simple fact was the answer to all their worries, she couldn't help but feel that the most difficult part of their journey was over. Surely that was cause for celebrating, for taking this one night to be at ease and enjoy their new friends.

Then again, she knew that Grinsa would only rest easy when he had convinced himself that he could keep her and Bryntelle safe. That was his way. Cresenne forced herself to ignore him and trust that he was enjoying himself in his own manner.

The following morning, D'Chul left them. He intended to follow the river southward toward the inland sea, stopping at villages along the way. He recommended that they continue toward the west.

"You're better off now that you're in Qirsi land," he told them, solemnly. "But R'Shev was right when he said that the Fal'Borna are hard. You'll be better off among the J'Balanar. You'll stand out a bit." He grinned. "Unless you have yourselves marked as they do. But they're more likely to welcome you into their settlements. Better still, you could go on to the forest and join the A'Vahl or my people."

"I thought R'Shev said the A'Vahl were arrogant," Grinsa said, smiling.

"They're not as bad as he made out. He did that mostly for my benefit. There's a belief among the other clans that the M'Saaren and the A'Vahl are rivals, probably because we share the woodland, and we fought a couple of wars several centuries ago. The truth is we get along well enough now. The A'Vahl are good people; most of them at least. You could do far worse."

Grinsa stepped forward and embraced the man. "Thank you, D'Chul. You've been a fine guide and a good friend."

"Good luck to you," the lutenist said, smiling broadly.

Cresenne kissed his cheek, surprised once more by how sad she felt to be leaving someone who had been a stranger only days before.

"I'll remember your playing for the rest of my days," she said. "And I'll sing the songs you taught us to Bryntelle. She'll know the words at least, even if I give her only a poor sense of the tune."

D'Chul climbed back onto his cart and picked up the reins. "Farewell," he said. "May there always be open roads before you and kin at your back." He grinned at them one last time. "That's an old Qirsi blessing."

He clicked his tongue at his horse and started away, turning one last time to wave good-bye.

Grinsa and Cresenne watched him go for several moments. Then they climbed onto their horses and began to ride westward. During the time they'd been with D'Chul they'd spoken little to each other. Now that they were alone together, except of course for Bryntelle, Cresenne found that she wasn't certain what to say. She hadn't felt this way around him in a long time, and it made her uneasy. For his part, Grinsa seemed no more inclined to start up a conversation than she was.

Eventually, however, he glanced her way, his expression revealing little. "You've been angry with me," he said.

A faint smile touched her lips and was gone. He knew her so well; better, she sometimes believed, than she knew him.

"I wouldn't say angry," she answered, an admission in the words.

"Then what?"

She considered this. "Frustrated," she finally said.

He didn't look at her, and his expression didn't change, but he nodded once, acknowledging what she'd said. She would have preferred it if he'd gotten angry with her. That's probably what she would have done had their roles been reversed. But he always found a way to control his emotions. It was something else that she admired in him, and that she also occasionally found . . . well, frustrating.

"Are you going to tell me why?" he asked at length.

"I want this to work, Grinsa. I want us to find a home here, somewhere we can be happy, where Bryntelle can grow up proud of who and what she is."

He looked at her. "I want that, too."

She exhaled and ran a hand through her hair. "I know that. But it seems like you're always looking for the next thing that's going to go wrong."

"That's not true."

"Isn't it? D'Chul sings us a song, and all you can think about is how the Blood Wars haven't really ended. Last night all of us were laughing and singing songs, but you spent the entire night huddled with that old Fal'Borna peddler talking about who knows what." She shook her head. "It seems to me that you refuse to be happy."

He smiled sadly. "I'm happy with you and Bryntelle."

Cresenne smiled in return. "I know that. I love you, Grinsa. You know I do. But I'm tired of carrying the weight of the world on our shoulders. We did that in the Forelands, and I've had enough of it. I just want to live a quiet life here. Can't we do that?"

"I want to," he said. "But it's not quite that simple. There are matters here that you and I need to discuss, things we have to be ready for."

"See?" she said. "This is what I mean. Maybe you and I are just different in this way. I know there are going to be problems, but we can deal with them as they arise. We don't have to let them occupy every waking thought."

He frowned. "I think some problems can be handled that way, but I'm not certain this is one of them."

"Are our lives at stake?"

Grinsa's eyebrows went up. "Our lives? No, I don't suppose they are."

Cresenne shrugged. "Then, it can wait."

Again, she expected him to get angry. Instead he laughed. "All right," he said. "But don't forget that I warned you."

"Fair enough."

They rode on, once more saying little. Every now and then, however, Grinsa would chuckle to himself, until at last Cresenne demanded to know what he found so funny.

He merely shook his head. "You don't want to know," he said, sounding as close to coy as she'd ever heard him.

Darkness fell before they reached a settlement. They passed another night under the stars and resumed their travels with first light of morning. By midday, they were several leagues into Fal'Borna land, and had yet to see any villages or towns.

"I'm beginning to think there aren't any villages here at all," Cresenne said at last, raising herself up out of her saddle and scanning the horizon.

"There aren't," Grinsa said mildly.

"What?"

He looked at her, smiling slightly. "The Fal'Borna have established towns along the Silverwater and the other rivers in their territory—the Threades and the K'Sahd—and also on the shores of the Ofirean Sea. But away from the water, they're nomads. They follow wild herds of what they call 'rilda,' which I gather are like the highland antelope of the Forelands."

"So, we're not looking for a settlement. You've known this all along."

"It didn't seem like the type of thing you'd want to hear about."

She gave him a sour look, though it was all she could do not to laugh. "Is there anything else I should know?" Before he could say anything she raised a hand and shook her head. "No, don't answer. I said that I didn't want to hear."

Perhaps two hours later, they came within sight of what looked to Cresenne to be a settlement of some sort. As they drew nearer, though, she realized that all the structures she saw were temporary, fashioned from animal skins, cloth, and wooden poles. Still, she could see a good many people—as many as she would have expected to see in a country village in the Forelands. A narrow stream wound past the shelters, and then by a large paddock in which grazed at least two hundred horses of various colors. Smoke rose from a dozen small fires and near the paddock children ran and laughed.

Cresenne and Grinsa had halted upon seeing the structures. Now Grinsa glanced at her.

"Are you ready to meet the Fal'Borna?"

For several days, she'd been looking forward to doing just that, but faced with the prospect of riding into this odd-looking village that stretched out before her, Cresenne realized that she was more than a bit intimidated.

"I think so," she said. "Are you?"

"As ready as I'm likely to be."

They looked toward the village again, and saw four riders coming toward them, their hair gleaming white in the sun, spears held ready.

"Seems we'd better be ready," Cresenne said. "If there's anything I really need to know, you should tell me right now."

She glanced at him. He was sitting straight-backed and tall atop his mount, his eyes alert, the muscles in his jaw bunched.

"No time now," he said, his voice low and tight. "Let me do the talking. They're a patriarchal clan—more so than most, at least here on the plain. Only speak to them if they ask you a question."

She nodded, feeling foolish for ever having been impatient with his precautions.

The Fal'Borna rode swiftly, and as they came closer Cresenne noted that all four of the riders were men, and all of them rode without saddles.

They stopped a short distance from where Cresenne and Grinsa waited. Cresenne wondered if they should dismount, or bow, or show in some other way that they meant the men and their people no harm. But Grinsa remained motionless in his saddle, and she thought it best to follow his example.

"You're on Fal'Borna land," one of the men said, his voice sharp. He was a young man, powerfully built, with a square face and skin that was almost golden, like the color of freshly baked bread. Cresenne couldn't help noting that he was remarkably handsome. Indeed, so were his companions. They were dressed in loose-fitting pants and shirts that appeared to have been made from animal skins. Their shoes were of dark leather. The man who had spoken wore a thin black necklace from which hung a single white stone. Otherwise the men were unadorned. "Who are you?" the man asked. "What clan?"

"My name is Grinsa jal Arriet. This is Cresenne ja Terba and our daughter, Bryntelle ja Grinsa. We're not from any clan of the Southlands. We've come from the Forelands."

The man showed no surprise at this last bit of information, but merely asked, "Why are you on Fal'Borna land, Forelander?"

"Our ship made land in Aelea. We had no choice but to cross Eandi land as quickly and directly as possible. That brought us here."

This seemed to satisfy the man, at least for the moment. "You ride proud animals," he said. "You got them from the Eandi?"

"Yes, we did."

He nodded, regarding the horses for another moment before looking at Grinsa again. "Are you bound to a clan, Forelander?"

"Not yet, no."

"But you intend to be?"

"Perhaps."

"You're a Weaver."

The guard in Yorl also had known that Grinsa was a Weaver, and though Cresenne understood that Weavers were far more common here than in the Forelands, it still took her by surprise to hear people speak of them so openly. Weavers were feared in the Forelands. Here it seemed they were openly revered.

"That's right."

He glanced at Cresenne. "And is she as well?"

Something in the way he asked this told Cresenne that he knew the answer already, but felt the need to ask, not for her sake, but for Grinsa's. An instant later she remembered the Eandi guard asking the same thing. Were Weavers here expected to be joined to each other?

"No, she's not."

Again, the man nodded. "The Qirsi of rival clans are not permitted to cross Fal'Borna land without leave from the Tesserate."

"I've already told you: We belong to no clan."

"But you also say that you might bind yourself to one."

"We might bind ourselves to the Fal'Borna," Grinsa said.

The man grinned, though not kindly. "That's not a decision for you to make. The Fal'Borna choose who we will and will not accept into our clan."

"Fine then," Grinsa said coldly. "Where will I find this Tesserate of whom you speak?"

"Thamia, on the north shore of the Ofirean. And the Tesserate isn't a person. It's a council. It could take several turns to gather all its members and the clanlord so that they can render a decision."

"What is it you want?" Grinsa asked.

"What makes you think I want anything?"

Grinsa didn't answer, at least not directly. But an instant later Cresenne heard the splintering of wood, four times in rapid succession. And as she watched, the heads of the men's spears fell to the ground. It wasn't what she would have done in his position, and she could only hope that he hadn't provoked the men.

Grinsa didn't appear concerned. He grinned, just as the Fal'Borna had done moments before. "As you say, friend: I'm a Weaver. And as such, I'm not someone to be trifled with."

The man's grin had vanished, but he didn't look particularly troubled by what Grinsa had done. He nodded once more. "Good, Forelander. Very good. A Fal'Borna Weaver would have gotten to it faster, but you're a stranger here, and I'll assume that you were trying to show some patience."

"He was testing you?" Cresenne asked, looking at Grinsa.

"He's a Weaver, too," Grinsa said, his eyes never leaving the man's face.

Another Weaver. At least she'd been right in assuming he knew without asking that she wasn't a Weaver. A Weaver could sense without asking what magics another Qirsi wielded.

"My name is Q'Daer."

He dismounted and stooped to pick up the head of his spear, which looked to be made of bone. His companions did the same, and a moment later Grinsa dismounted as well. He cast a quick look Cresenne's way, indicating that she should, too. He took Bryntelle from her, and she climbed off of her mount. Only then, facing the four Fal'Borna, did she realize how short they were. They looked formidable on their mounts, but even this Weaver, Q'Daer, was nearly half a head shorter than Grinsa.

Q'Daer brushed the dirt and grass off his spear tip and slipped it into a small pocket on the side of his pants.

"A Fal'Borna wastes nothing," he said. He extended both hands to Grinsa. When Grinsa put his hands out, the man gripped Grinsa's wrists in such a way that Grinsa could do the same. "That is a proper Fal'Borna greeting."

"You honor us," Grinsa said.

"You're a Weaver," the man said, as if that explained everything. "A Weaver with no clan—" He stopped himself and smiled thinly. "I'm getting ahead of myself. The a'laq will want to see you. We can talk after."

"The a'laq?"

"Every sept has an a'laq, a leader. Ours is named E'Menua, though you're to call him A'Laq."

Q'Daer returned to his horse and swung himself onto the animal's back. "Follow," he said.

The other Fal'Borna remounted and rode after the man, leaving Grinsa and Cresenne little choice but to do the same.

"That went better than I thought it would," Cresenne said, as she got back onto her mount. "Particularly after you broke their spears."

He nodded, handing Bryntelle up to her. "We're not safe yet. If this E'Menua doesn't like us we'll be lucky to get away. From what I hear, the Fal'Borna aren't gentle with those they consider their enemies."

They rode after the four men, following them to the middle of the settlement. Once again, people stared at them—it seemed to Cresenne that since reaching the Southlands, they had been the objects of endless curiosity. But at least here, she sensed none of the hostility that she had felt in Yorl and the other Eandi villages. Men and women, young and old—they all stared at them, but for the most part their expressions were mild, and even those who looked at them warily did so seemingly without hatred.

And in truth, Cresenne couldn't help staring back at them. She had never seen so many Qirsi in one place—there were hundreds of them, and not an Eandi face to be seen. Just white hair and pairs of pale eyes in more shades of yellow than she had ever known existed. Like the men who rode out to greet them, all of these Qirsi had light golden skin. *They're beautiful*, she thought to herself. *They're the most beautiful people I've ever seen.*

Grinsa seemed to notice as well. "In all my years of living with the Eandi," he said to her in a whisper, "I never felt as conscious of how white my skin is as I do right now."

She just nodded, and they rode on.

Q'Daer dismounted before a large circular structure. It was made of wood, and it had animal skins pulled taut all around it. Cresenne saw Grinsa look the building up and down, admiration in his eyes. At last, he nodded.

"Sturdy, secure against wind and rain, but light, and probably very easy to take down and carry."

"All our z'kals are made so," Q'Daer told him. "We move with the herds. We can't spare time to build heavier homes and dismantle them. And as I told you, the Fal'Borna waste nothing."

"Don't you get cold during the Snows?"

"Each z'kal has a fire circle within, and a vent at the top for smoke." He grinned. "And if it grows too cold, well, that's why Qirsar gave us women, isn't it?"

Grinsa smiled halfheartedly and glanced at Cresenne, who wasn't smiling at all.

"I'll tell the a'laq that you're here," the man said. He entered the shelter through a flap that was held in place by a series of hooks, also made of bone.

"What are we going to say to this a'laq?" Cresenne asked in a low voice, surveying the settlement. "I'm not ready to cast my lot with these people, but I'm not sure that we can tell him we'd like to speak with the other clans before deciding who we want to live with."

"I don't know. We don't even know for certain that we'll be asked to join their clan. Let's just wait and see."

Cresenne nodded, but she could feel her apprehension growing by the moment.

Before long, Q'Daer emerged from the shelter and nodded to Grinsa. "He'll see you now."

Both of them started forward, but the man held up a hand and shook his head. "Your concubine can wait out here."

Cresenne gaped at him. *His what?*" she demanded, her voice rising so that others in the settlement turned to look at her.

Q'Daer glanced at her, his expression infuriatingly placid. Then he faced Grinsa again. "It would be best if she remained out here."

But Grinsa shook his head. "I'm sorry, Q'Daer. If the a'laq wants to see us together, so be it. But I won't go in alone."

"The a'laq doesn't give audiences to concubines."

"I'm not his concubine!"

"She's not my concubine!"

They said these simultaneously, shared a brief look, then faced the Fal'Borna again.

"She's not a Weaver."

"No, she's not. But in the Forelands, that doesn't matter."

Q'Daer shook his head, clearly unnerved by all of this. Cresenne wasn't certain whether he was merely offended, or if he actually feared delivering these tidings to the a'laq. "It's not wise to defy an a'laq, Fore-lander," he said at last. "Particularly a man like E'Menua."

"Then perhaps it's best that we move on, without meeting him."

"No," the man said. He looked at them both, his lips pressed thin. Then he went back into the shelter.

"You knew about this concubine thing, didn't you?" Cresenne said quietly.

A small smile crept across Grinsa's face. "You said you didn't want to hear."

"Yes, I did. But I think you enjoyed that just a bit too much."

He laughed.

Q'Daer emerged again just seconds later, appearing relieved. "He'll see you both," he said. He watched them expectantly, no doubt wondering why they weren't more pleased.

Wordlessly, they stepped past him and into the shelter.

It was warm within, and it smelled strongly of smoke and cooked meat and sweat. A fire burned low within a ring of stones in the center of the space, and on the far side of the fire, directly opposite the entrance, sat an old Qirsi man. He was dressed much as Q'Daer had been, down to the thin necklace and white stone. Like the other men they had seen, he wore his long white hair tied back from his face. Even sitting, he appeared powerful, with a broad chest and thick neck. His eyes were large and round, like those of a cat, and his face tapered to a thin, sharp chin, giving him the look of some preternaturally intelligent beast.

Cresenne and Grinsa stood just inside the entryway for several moments as the a'laq regarded them. The fire popped loudly and Bryntelle chattered as she stared at the flames, but otherwise no one made a sound. At last, the man motioned for them to sit.

"I don't usually allow the concubines of other men into my z'kal," he said in a gravelly voice, once they had settled themselves beside the stone circle.

Cresenne fully intended to fire back that she didn't usually tolerate being called a concubine, but Grinsa laid a hand on her arm and she managed to keep silent.

"Cresenne isn't my concubine, A'Laq. She's my wife."

"She isn't a Weaver. She can't be your wife."

"Those are your customs, not ours."

He grinned at that, his face harsh in the dim glow of the fire. "You're in the Southlands now, Forelander. Our customs are your customs. Have the two of you been formally joined?"

Grinsa only hesitated for an instant, but it was enough. "In all ways that matter, Cresenne is my wife."

"Ah," the a'laq said, nodding slowly. "I see. There is room, then, for discussion."

"No," Grinsa said. "There's not."

"Are you bound to a clan yet, Forelander?" the a'laq asked, as if the previous matter had been settled.

"We've only been on the Qirsi side of the Silverwater for a few days. The Fal'Borna are the first clanfolk we've encountered."

"How fortunate for you," the man said, seemingly without irony.

"We look forward to exploring other parts of the land as well, and perhaps meeting other folk from other clans."

The a'laq's smile faded slowly. "Why would you want to do that?"

"We're new to the Southlands. We're curious."

For a long time, the man said nothing. He held two fingers to his lips, tapping them absently. At last, he reached for a small log and threw it onto the fire, sending a flurry of bright orange sparks into the air.

"I have some idea of how Weavers are treated in the Forelands. I know they're feared, even hated. I know that many have been put to death over the centuries. Isn't that so?"

Grinsa nodded.

"Perhaps you've noticed that their status here among the clans is somewhat different."

"I've gathered as much, yes."

"A Weaver who comes among us unbound to any clan is rare indeed. Weavers are something of a commodity, not like drel, mind you. They're not common chattel. They're gold. They're gems. They are prized by all. This is why we insist that Weavers join with other Weavers, so that they might beget yet more Weavers." His eyes flicked toward Cresenne. "Your . . . your *wife* is very beautiful."

He said the word "wife" with such condescension that Cresenne almost wished he'd go back to calling her a concubine.

"I can see why you chose her," he went on. "But she is far less likely to give birth to Weavers than another Weaver would be."

"I understand the reasoning behind your custom, A'Laq."

"I'm sure you do. But this is not my point. Unbound Weavers are rare, and to have one appear in our sept as you have is a great boon. You wish to leave, to explore other parts of the Southlands. But we're determined that you should stay."

Cresenne felt icy fingers closing around her heart, and she clutched Bryntelle closer to her breast, drawing a low cry from the child. Grinsa's eyes, shining in the brightened glow of the fire, were fixed on the man, but his expression hadn't changed.

"Are we to be your captives, then?" he demanded.

The a'laq eyed him briefly. "What happened to your shoulder, Forelander?"

Grinsa's good hand reached up to his deformed shoulder and rubbed it gently, as if he could feel the pain again. Cresenne knew what had happened, of course. It was shattered by the Weaver who led the conspiracy against the Eandi courts of the Forelands. Grinsa managed to destroy the Weaver despite his injury, but the shoulder, which had been broken once before by a servant of the Weaver, never healed properly.

"I hurt it battling a Weaver," Grinsa answered, his voice barely more than a whisper.

The a'laq nodded. "I thought as much. I sensed that the injury had been caused by magic. And who else other than another Weaver could do such a thing to you?" He gestured toward the entrance to his shelter. "There are three Weavers out there. And of course I'm one, too. We have four in our sept. Four Weavers. There are other Fal'Borna septs larger than ours, but few have so many. I have three children, and all of them may prove to be Weavers. And still I find myself wanting more. I'm an old man, with only a few years left. There should be Weavers to take my place."

"You didn't answer my question," Grinsa said. "Are we captives?"

But Cresenne had the sense that the man had answered. There were four Weavers here. How was Grinsa supposed to fight their way free past four Weavers?

"You're our guests," the a'laq said.

"Guests are free to leave whenever they wish."

The a'laq's eyes flashed. "Captives are treated poorly. You won't be. We'll have a z'kal built for you by nightfall. You'll eat as the rest of us do. Have you tasted rilda?"

"No," Grinsa said thickly.

"Then this will be a night to remember. For both of you," he added, with a quick glance at Cresenne.

For some time the two men sat staring at one another, neither of their gazes wavering.

"Cresenne is to be accepted as my wife," Grinsa said at last.

E'Menua seemed to consider this briefly. Then he nodded. "At least for the time being."

Grinsa shook his head. "For as long as we're here. Or else I'll try to leave right now. The other Weavers may stop me, but you won't. And then your sept will only have three, rather than five."

Cresenne expected the a'laq to rage at him. She wouldn't have been surprised if they'd started to do battle right there in the shelter.

Instead, the old man began to laugh. "Very well then," he said. "You'll make a fine Fal'Borna, Forelander." He laughed again, gesturing at his crotch. "You have the stones for it." He waved a hand at the entryway. "Now, go. We'll speak again later."

Cresenne and Grinsa looked at each other, then stood and left the shelter. Outside, the sun seemed overly bright and the air felt cold. A gust of wind made Cresenne shiver.

"Now what?" she said.

"Now we find something to eat."

She looked at him sharply.

"There's nothing else we can do, Cresenne. Not today. For better or worse, we're Fal'Borna now."

"Which I suppose makes me your concubine."

He raised an eyebrow. "True. Maybe there's an upside to this."

She punched his arm, hard.

Chapter 13

The skies above her had turned grey days ago, blotting out stars and sun, the red and white of the moons and the blue Harvest mornings. Occasionally it rained on her. Most times it was merely cold and windy. And grey. Color had vanished from her world, or so it sometimes seemed. But no, there was color still. The primrose yellow and fiery oranges, the lavenders and larkspur purple, the berry-stain reds and that startling indigo she'd found the previous year. And so many shades of brown—earth, straw, pale gold like the sunbaked grasses of the plain, warm brown like Mettai skin, flax and bay and chestnut and dead leaves and all browns in between.

Yes, there was still color in her world. Not in the sky or in the villages or in the people she encountered. But there, in her baskets. A world of color, a lifetime of color, in the weaving she had done, in the spells she had cast, in the damage she had done thus far and would do again.

She had gone farther west, beyond the Companion Lakes, deeper into Qirsi land. Always she remained to the north, though, because this was where the Y'Qatt had settled. It was hard land. Uncompromising cold during the Snows, stubborn winds that swept down off the mountains during the Harvest and the early Planting, and during the Growing a relentlessly hot sun that sucked moisture from the earth, just as the Y'Qatt believed magic sucked life from their bodies. The storms, when they came, their rain like mercy, were fierce, violent affairs. There was no sympathy in this land, no respite from its cruelty. How well she knew. This was the land that was left to outcasts. Of course the Y'Qatt would settle here. Their white-hair brothers and sisters to the south would think nothing of ceding this land to them. Just as the Eandi had ceded the land near the eastern Companion Lakes to the Mettai.

It should have occurred to her long ago, as she prepared for this last great undertaking of her life. But only after leaving Kirayde had she started to understand what should have been so obvious. She'd seen only the differences—Y'Qatt and Mettai were to each other as wraiths of the night were to creatures of day, as death was to life, as bone and dust were to blood and flesh. But as she spoke to the man in Runnelwick, the one who'd called her "Mettai" the way he might have called another woman "whore," it had come to her like lightning on a steamy day. Y'Qatt and Mettai—opposites yes, but as two edges of the same sword. Both were outcasts from their own races, but also they were bridges to the other race: Eandi sorcerers, Qirsi who rejected magic.

There were days in the darkness of the Snows when it seemed that Morna was offering a glimpse of the Planting to come: warm breezes and sunshine that melted the ice on the lakes and began to coax buds from trees that yearned for the Growing turns. Sometimes there would be several of them in succession and Sylpa would call it a false Planting, as if the winds and the sun were trying to trick them into putting in their crops too soon. There were similar days late in the Harvest, when the warmth would return briefly, like a memory of the Growing. Sylpa had a name for these as well: the shadow Growing.

False Planting and shadow Growing. They were separated by more than half the year, and yet the days were the same. They didn't belong— warmth when there was supposed to be cold, clear skies when there should have been grey and wind and snow. So it was with the Y'Qatt and the Mettai. They didn't belong, they had been cast out of societies that had little in common other than their rigidity, and so they were much alike.

Her realization changed nothing, of course. If anything, it made worse all that had happened before, and thus made her even more determined to see this through to the end, despite how tired she had grown in recent days.

It was more dangerous now that she was so far beyond Silverwater Wash. The white-hairs who shared this land with the Y'Qatt had no particular cause to dislike the Mettai, or to shun her for being one, but they were Fal'Borna, and no Qirsi hated the Eandi more. She'd learned, though. She wouldn't be caught unaware again, as she had been by that fool of a girl near Tivston. And she was ready to take on something greater, something more than just these tiny villages she'd visited thus far.

C'Bijor's Neck. She'd passed it by heading north, because she hadn't been ready yet. The others had been preparing her for this. Now, though . . .

C'Bijor's Neck was one of the largest Y'Qatt settlements in the north, nearly as large as the great white-hair cities on the Ofirean. She'd been there once before, many years back, as she'd started preparing in earnest for this day. She'd heard of the place from peddlers she met while trading her baskets. The Neck, they called it, because it sat on a spur of land that jutted out into the Silverwater, just below Turtle Lake. They'd encouraged her then to sell her baskets in the marketplace there—they told her it was huge, the largest market along the northern half of the river. But she'd known then that she should wait, that to show herself and her wares in C'Bijor's Neck too soon would be a mistake. So she nodded, and she listened, and she tucked away every bit of information she could glean from them, like a beggar hoarding coins.

They liked deep baskets in the Neck, or at least those were the ones that sold best. Deep, with high handles, usually braided, because they felt best against the hand when the baskets were laden with fruit or grain. They liked bright dyes, or else earth colors—nothing in between. And they had little use for small baskets, ornamental ones with no practical use. The Y'Qatt of C'Bijor's Neck were a sturdy, sensible people, well adapted to the harsh life afforded them on the northern plain.

So early that morning, in the cold, dim grey that precedes a cloudy dawn, as Lici prepared to make her way into the village, she gathered all her small baskets and hid them in her cart. She left her horse and wagon within the shadows of the small copse in which she'd bedded down the night before. Then she dragged the blade across her hand, as she had so many times before, and cast her spell on the baskets that remained with her. These she packed up and carried to the city, arriving in the marketplace with the first of the peddlers. Without her cart she was left to spread out her blankets on the ground. She arranged the baskets in neat rows; sturdy, sensible rows. She almost laughed aloud at the thought.

Before she'd finished, there were people standing before her wares, silently admiring them, no doubt trying to decide what to offer her, so that they might go away with a bargain, as well as a fine basket. They didn't know just how eager she was to sell them. They didn't know that if she'd had to give them away in order to get these ensorcelled baskets into their hands and their homes, she would have. Nor could she give them any reason to guess at this. She'd drive a hard bargain. She'd leave the Neck with gold heavy in her purse, and the need for vengeance resting just a bit lighter on her shoulders.

Yellow eyes. White hair. Narrow, bony, pale faces. Did they really think they were so different from the Qirsi who lived south of here? Did they really believe that there was virtue to be found in denying who and what they were?

"You made these yourself?" one man asked, eyeing her shrewdly.

"Yes, sir, I did."

"Where do you come from?" he asked.

"East of here. A small village near the lakes. I'm sure you wouldn't know it."

"You're Mettai, aren't you?"

"Yes, I am."

"And the colors in these baskets?"

She knew what he was getting at. She'd have to answer the same question throughout the morning, as buyers tried to determine the value of her work. Dyed baskets were worth far more than those colored with magic.

"Dyed by hand, sir. I assure you. Pick one up. Examine each osier if you must. Each strand of grass." *Hold it close. Breathe deeply of its scent. Rub your hands over it, as if in a caress. And die well.* "I do good work, but you'll see that the color isn't uniform."

He stooped and picked up one of the more colorful baskets. He eyed it closely for several moments before returning it to the blanket.

"That can be feigned. You can use magic to make it look like that."

She smiled, hating him. "Yes, I can. But I didn't. You don't have to believe me, of course. An eye as discerning as yours should have no trouble seeing the truth. And if you think there are better baskets here in this marketplace, you should buy them." Lici looked past him to another man, who'd also paused to admire her weaving. "Can I help you, good sir?"

"Wait now," the first man said, glancing over his shoulder before facing Lici again. "I didn't say I was going to look elsewhere. I just wanted to be certain that you weren't trying to sell ensorcelled baskets in an Y'Qatt city."

"I'd never do such a thing, sir. I'm quite aware of where I am and what sort of people live in your fine city."

He stared down at the basket for several moments, his eyes narrowed. He was tall and lean, like so many Qirsi, with eyes the color of pinewood, and short-cropped hair. Eventually he met her gaze again.

"How much?"

"Three sovereigns."

He laughed and shook his head. "Too much." But he didn't walk away. She'd get two. She could get more, but she didn't want the price going too high.

"I'd go as high as one sovereign, two silvers."

"The price is three."

"Come now, madame," he said. "You can't expect to get three sovereigns for a single basket."

"It's early," she said. "Look how your friends gather around my wares." There were at least ten people standing in front of her blankets now. Seeing this, the man frowned.

She was tempted now to get two and a half sovereigns, not only because she didn't like this man, but also because with so many watching, this first sale would set the price for the rest. Some baskets would go for more, of course. Others would sell for less. But all would be measured against this first one. She had to remind herself that she wanted them to sell quickly, that before the day was through, she wanted her baskets spread throughout the city. And she herself wished to be on her way out of the Neck by midday.

"Two then," he said.

She couldn't appear to give in too easily. "Two is low," she said. "But I'll let this one go for two if you'll buy a second at the same price."

"I have no need of two."

"None?" she asked coyly. "Your wife wouldn't find a use for a second basket of this quality?"

He frowned again and rubbed a hand over his face. "Four for the pair."

Lici nodded.

"Very well." He quickly chose a second and paid her the four sover-eigns, before hurrying away, as if afraid that she might enchant him into buying more.

After that, she did a brisk trade, selling nearly a dozen baskets in the first hour of the morning. As the day progressed, however, business slowed, so that as midday approached she'd only sold two more, and still had ten left. She'd watched from afar as the other villages succumbed to her curse, but she had no desire to be anywhere near C'Bijor's Neck when her magic began to take effect. The city was too large; too many people would be sickened. Not that she didn't want to see, but she feared the outpouring of so much magic. Magic, the likes of which would bleed a Mettai to death. Magic that would leave this entire city in ruins.

"Slow day."

She turned at the sound of the man's voice. He was Qirsi, his white hair tied back from his face, his skin nearly as dark as her own. Fal'Borna. He was an old man for one of their kind. His hair had grown thin, so that she could see his golden scalp between strands of white, and he wore a fine, pale beard that made him appear gaunt as a mountain goat.

"Yes," she said.

"I thought you'd sell everything you brought in the first hour."

"I'd hoped to."

"You did all right. Better than most of us."

"I suppose." She eyed him, an idea blossoming in her mind, like a small flame. "Is it usually like this?"

He shook his head. "Usually better. Most days it's as busy as this morning all the way through to dusk. But this weather has people scared. They think it'll be a hard winter, so they're saving their coin, in case the crops aren't enough to see them through."

"You live here," she said. Fal'Borna by birth, but now Y'Qatt.

He nodded and stepped over to her, extending a hand. "Y'Farl. You are?"

"Licaldi."

"Nice to meet you, Licaldi. I'm surprised we haven't met before. Baskets that fine would have attracted the notice of every peddler be-tween here and the Ofirean."

"I'd stopped selling them long ago. I only began again recently."

"Why would you have stopped?"

She shrugged, looking away. This had to be done carefully. "My husband died, and it was all I could do to keep our crops going. But they're mostly in now, and my boys are doing the rest."

"So he died recently?"

She nodded, but said nothing.

"I'm sorry."

Lici shrugged and made herself smile, knowing it would look forced. He'd expect that. Then she knelt and began to pack up her baskets, gathering them together, and placing them slowly and carefully into the larger baskets she used to carry the others.

"You're leaving?" Y'Farl asked.

"I haven't any choice. I have to sell these, but I also need to get back before nightfall, and it's a walk of several hours."

"There are inns here. You could sell the rest tomorrow. You've made enough gold this morning. . . ." Seeing her shake her head, he trailed off.

"No," she said. "I need to get home, and I can't spare even a bit of the gold I have, particularly if the rest of these baskets don't sell."

He watched her pack away the baskets for a few moments longer before walking back to his cart. He said nothing, and for just an instant Lici feared that she had miscalculated. Still, she continued to gather her baskets, and soon he had wandered back her way.

"How much for the lot?" he asked.

She looked up at him and frowned, as if not understanding. "I'm sorry?"

"How much would you sell them for? All the baskets?"

"They all sell for different amounts. How should I know—?"

He shook his head impatiently. "If I were to buy them all, how much would you want me to pay for them?"

"You . . . ? But why?"

"To sell again," he said, surprising her with his candor. "Baskets that fine don't usually find their way to the Neck. They may not all sell today, but they'll sell eventually."

Still she frowned, regarding her wares now, as if uncertain as to whether to part with them. "I don't know."

"It would be gold in your pocket, Licaldi. Perhaps not as much as you would have gotten had you sold all of them yourself." He smiled. "I'd need to make some profit, after all. But it would be more gold than you have now."

"I could have sold them for twenty sovereigns."

"I'm sure you could have. But I won't pay that much. I'll give you ten."

"Ten? For the lot?" She shook her head and went back to packing. "That's ridiculous."

"That's what I'm prepared to pay."

For a long time she refused even to look at the man, though she knew he was watching her. Finally, she sat back on her heels and sighed. "Fifteen."

"Twelve. That's as high as I'll go."

She glared at him. "You're taking advantage of me."

"Yes. I'm a merchant. It's what I do."

Lici had to laugh. "Very well, then, merchant. Twelve sovereigns for the lot."

She pulled the baskets out once more and began to hand them to him. He placed them on the table from which he'd been selling his goods—blankets mostly, though also some clothes, blades, and tools. When he had rearranged his table to fit her baskets, he returned and counted out twelve sovereigns into her slender hand.

"If you come back this way with more of these baskets, I'll be interested in them as well," he told her.

"I won't be in such a hurry then," she said. "And I'll expect more gold."

He found that amusing. The fool was still laughing as Lici walked away, her two large baskets tucked under her arms, empty save for the blankets. It was only midday. She had time to retrieve her cart and start making her way to the next Y'Qatt village. She wasn't even certain which one she'd go to next. There were so many. And she intended to find all of them.

Torgan Plye had been a merchant for the better part of ten fours. He'd traded in every part of the Southlands, from Eagles Inlet in Aelea to the Lost Bay of Senkora Island, from Briny Point, at the southern tip of Naqbae, to these cold, isolated villages near the Companion Lakes. In the course of his travels, he'd done business with Eandi and

Qirsi alike. He'd sold wine and delicacies to the Eandi of Tordjanne and Qosantia, as well as to the Talm'Orast and H'Bel; he'd sold weapons to the warriors of Stelpana, and also to the Fal'Borna and T'Saan; and he'd traded horses from the plains of the J'Balanar for fish from the waters off the Aelean coast.

He'd seen fat times and lean, and everything imaginable between the two. Early on, when he was still trying to establish himself as a merchant of some renown, he made the mistake of borrowing gold from a coinmonger in Medqasse, in central Tordjanne, near where he grew up. An older man, another merchant, had promised to sell him a shipment of red wine that he swore was coming from a place called Sanbira in the Forelands. But he needed some gold to help secure the shipment. One hundred sovereigns would do it, he'd said, and one hundred more on delivery. It would sell for three times that amount. The man swore it on the memory of his poor mother. And Torgan, ass that he was, believed him.

He never saw the man again, nor the one hundred sovereigns he'd paid up front. He paid the coinmonger the one hundred he had left, plus another thirty that he'd managed to put away for himself. But by then, with the daily fees accruing, he owed nearly three hundred, and when he couldn't pay, the coinmonger's cutthroats took out his left eye. That was the lowest of the lows.

But he survived. Better one-eyed than dead, he decided. He never borrowed again, nor did he ever pay up front for anything he couldn't see with his own eye. He left Medqasse, and spent a few years on the sea, earning gold as a merchant sailor and learning his profession. Less than five years after losing his eye, he had enough gold to quit the sea and try once more to make it as a land merchant. This time it took. He worked hard, he wandered more leagues than he cared to count, he trusted no one but himself. And he scraped by. Until at last, ten or twelve years back, he was rewarded for his perseverance.

He was in R'Troth land, in the foothills to the Djindsamme range, a lone Eandi merchant in the mining country of the white-hairs, when he stumbled upon a cache of raw gemstones. They were in an old canvas bag that had been tucked away in a shallow cave near the headwaters of the Iejony. They'd been there for years, it seemed. The bag had moldered and was covered with bat droppings. As best he could tell, they had been stolen years before, hidden in the cave, and forgotten. Perhaps the thieves had been unable to find the cave a second time. Maybe they were dead. Torgan didn't care. He sold them for over seven hundred sovereigns.

He could have quit then. He could have settled down along the Qosantian coast or in the Aelean Highlands near Lake Naaf. But he would have gotten bored. He hadn't many friends, and even before he lost his eye, he'd never had women flocking to his side, or more to the point, to his bed. And he'd never been a man to put down roots.

Torgan couldn't remember the last time he had spent more than three nights in the same city or town. Even three seemed long. After two, his feet began to itch, he began to feel hemmed in, the way a wild horse would feel in a paddock. He had no knack for words or music or swordplay, or any of the other pursuits to which wealthy men of his age were drawn. He was happiest in the marketplace. His single talent was making the sale. Some men collected blades or horses. Some collected women. He collected gold.

After he found the gems, his good fortune continued. A year later, he bought twelve carved bowls from one of the finest wood turners among the A'Vahl. Three days later, the man was killed in a sudden flood. Torgan sold the bowls for three times what he paid for them. Suddenly it seemed that every deal he made turned out well. It was as if the gods had finally decided to smile upon him. Or maybe they were merely compensating him at last for the loss of his eye. Truth be told, he didn't care why it was happening; he merely resolved to enjoy himself for as long as he and the gold lasted.

That wasn't to say that he made no concessions to his new wealth. He no longer had any need to work as hard as the other merchants did, particularly the younger ones. They kept to regular schedules, making their way from city to city, keeping to those places where they knew they could turn a quick profit. Torgan liked to wander, and so he allowed himself to range far and wide across the land. Most merchants traded with the A'Vahl and the M'Saaren, the Talm'Orast and the H'Bel, the Nid'Qir and B'Qahr. Fewer bothered with the seafaring folk of the D'Krad, though their smoked fish was the best in the land, or with the miners of the I'Prael, though their mines produced the finest grade of silver and copper. These clans were on the fringe of Qirsi land. There was less profit in roaming so far, so most merchants traded in inferior products. It made perfect sense.

But Torgan could afford to take the time to go all the way to the Nahraidan Peninsula or to cross the A'Vahl into D'Krad land. He was willing to venture north into Y'Qatt territory in search of something— anything—that another merchant might miss. He had the time and the gold, and he enjoyed seeing so much of the land. He knew that most other merchants hated him. They resented his wealth. They thought him unreasonable and hard and arrogant, and he was all those things. Again, he could afford to be. No deal was so important to him that he had to make it, which meant that he could walk away from any sale if the terms weren't to his liking. The willingness to walk away: a merchant had no greater weapon. But though few traders liked him, all knew that he sold the finest products. If a lesser merchant needed fine wine for a wealthy client, or the best blade for a discriminating swordsman, they always came to Torgan Plye. Put quite simply, he had the best goods.

Perhaps this was why the baskets of the Mettai woman caught his eye. Torgan knew quality when he saw it. He also knew a skilled trader when he watched one at work. And however well Y'Farl thought he had done in buying the woman's remaining wares—and from the smug look on the Y'Qatt's face as he watched the woman leave the marketplace, it seemed clear that he thought he had done very well indeed—Torgan knew better.

He liked the clarity of the marketplace, the simplicity of the game. Everyone there was interested in the same thing: gaining the most from the exchange of goods and gold. Whether buying or selling, a person wanted to feel that they had done well. A buyer wanted to get the best product for the least amount of money; the seller wanted to turn the greatest profit possible. So simple. And yet, there were so many ways to achieve those ends. That was what fascinated him, what made the marketplace more than just his place of business. It was also his source of entertainment. He had been known to spend an entire day just watching others buy and sell. For Torgan it was much like watching a battle tournament, a contest between combatants of various skill levels. Actually it was better than a battle tournament, since he found watching swordplay dreadfully boring.

Y'Farl had always struck him as a competent merchant. Not the best by any means, but skilled enough to have made a living at it for several years. On this day, however, he'd met his match, and then some, in the old woman. Whatever terms they had come to had pleased Y'Farl. That much was clear. Yet, the woman had been delighted as well. Torgan was sure of it. He'd watched too many merchants and peddlers at work for too many years to be mistaken about such a thing. She'd gotten what she wanted and had managed to convince Y'Farl that he had done well. Only a skilled trader could do that. Yet, with all the different places he had visited in the Southlands, he couldn't recall ever seeing this woman before. Nor had he seen baskets of this quality, at least not for many years. It was all too curious for him to ignore.

He sauntered over to Y'Farl's table. The Y'Qatt was moving his new baskets around, trying to arrange them to best effect. Hearing Torgan's approach, he looked up. His expression darkened.

"Torgan Plye."

"Good day, Y'Farl. Feeling pleased with yourself?"

"If you must know, I am." He gestured at the baskets. "I got all these for twelve sovereigns—I'll sell them for at least twice that much."

"You seem quite sure of yourself."

"Look at them. Finest baskets I've seen here in the Neck. Ever. Even you'd be proud to sell them."

Torgan picked one up and turned it over in his hands. He'd looked at them earlier, during the morning, when so many had pressed around her blankets, eager for a look at the wares of this newcomer to the C'Bijor's Neck marketplace. He'd been struck then by how fine they were—the coloring was even and vivid, but clearly done with dyes rather than magic. The weaving was meticulous and neat, the osiers and grasses strong and free from any fraying. But now that he knew how little the woman had gotten for them he wanted to see them again. Perhaps he'd missed something before.

Even on second examination, though, they looked to be as finely made as any baskets he'd found in this part of the Southlands. The Qirsi of B'Qahr were excellent weavers as well, and their work might have been somewhat better than this. But not much.

"Well?" Y'Farl asked, sounding just a bit too smug.

Torgan returned the basket to the Y'Qatt's table. "You're right. She makes lovely baskets."

"Perhaps you'd like to buy them."

"Perhaps I would."

"Thirty sovereigns."

Torgan laughed. "Thirty? Just a moment ago you were talking about doubling your money. Now you want to nearly triple it."

"That's not nearly triple."

"It's too much."

Y'Farl sniffed. "I don't think so."

"She sold them for two each."

"She didn't know what she was doing."

Again Torgan laughed. "She knew better than you did."

"What's that supposed to mean?"

"Never mind, Y'Farl." He started to walk away. "Good luck selling your baskets."

"Wait a moment, Torgan," the Y'Qatt said, hurrying after him and grabbing his arm. "I want to know what you meant."

Torgan looked down at the man's hand and then at his face.

Y'Farl colored and let go of him. Torgan was a big man. At this point in his life some might have called him fat, though not to his face. And they might have been right. But he was broad as well, and still strong. Strong enough, certainly, to take on a Qirsi, particularly one who didn't use magic.

"Please," the Y'Qatt added, rather meekly. "You seem to think that she got the better of me. I'd like to know how. You see these baskets. You know their worth, and what I paid. How can she have bested me?"

"To be honest, Y'Farl, I don't know. I'm wondering that myself. Maybe she was more foolish than I believed, and didn't know what her baskets were worth. Maybe she's mad—an old woman like that, anything is possible. But she walked away from here feeling pleased with herself, every bit as pleased as you were."

"How can you know that?"

He opened his hands and smiled. "It's my business to know. It's why I've done so well over the years."

"Then she must have been mad. I know quality when I see it, and those baskets are worth every sovereign I paid for them, and then some."

Torgan said nothing. He didn't have to. Y'Farl was doing his work for him. *Worth every sovereign I paid for them* . . . . A moment before he'd been asking for thirty. Now he was trying to justify the twelve he'd spent.

The Y'Qatt wandered back to his table and picked up one of the baskets, no doubt seeking reassurance.

"Look at this weaving," he said. "Look at these colors. Of course she was mad."

"You're probably right," Torgan said with an easy smile. He returned to his cart and began to neaten his piles of cloth, and straighten the rows of M'Saaren wood planes and Naqbae leather.

Y'Farl managed to wait at least a few minutes before strolling over. He tried to look unconcerned as he stood there glancing at the cloth, but Torgan wasn't fooled.

"So, are you interested?" the man finally asked.

"In what?" Torgan asked. He knew he was being cruel, but he couldn't help himself.

"In the baskets, of course!"

"Oh, right." He frowned and shook his head. "Not really. Not at thirty."

"I was kidding about that. They're not worth thirty."

Torgan eyed him. "Oh? What are they worth?"

Y'Farl's face fell. Clearly, he knew that he had placed himself in a weak position. Now he had to name a price that was high enough to leave some room for negotiation. But he'd already admitted that thirty was too high.

"I . . . I don't know," he said. "What do you think they're worth?"

"You paid twelve."

The Y'Qatt scowled at him. "You can't expect me to let them go for the same price. I'll do far better than that selling them here."

"You're still sure of that."

"Yes, of course. Twenty-five. They're worth twenty-five."

"Fifteen."

"You want them for twenty," Y'Farl said.

"I want them for fifteen."

"Yes, yes. That's what you say. But you want me to split the difference. I won't. Twenty-two. That's final."

Torgan shrugged. "That's too high." He turned his back, pulled a few more bolts of cloth from the back of his cart, and laid them out for display. Y'Farl hadn't moved. "Was there something else you wanted?"

Y'Farl blinked. "Aren't you going to make another offer?"

"I offered fifteen."

"But surely that's not—"

"You think they're worth twenty-two, Y'Farl. At least you do now. But the woman couldn't sell them at two apiece, though she tried for the entire morning. I think that's why she was so pleased. Because she knew she couldn't sell any more of them here, but you didn't. Now you're stuck with ten of them. You want me to save you from your own misjudgment, but I won't do it. You bought them. You sell them." He walked around to the other side of the cart, ostensibly to check on his horse. Mostly, he wanted Y'Farl to think that he was done with their bargaining.

It worked.

"All right, twenty then," the Y'Qatt said, coming around from the other side.

"I thought twenty-two was your final offer."

Y'Farl opened his mouth, closed it again.

Torgan laughed and shook his head. "You're not very good at this, are you, Y'Farl?"

"I beg your pardon?"

"This. Trading. I never thought you were great at it, but I always assumed you were better than this."

"I've been doing this for more than half my life!"

"Well, all that experience hasn't imparted any real wisdom, has it? You were right about one thing—I'll give you credit for that. I did want them for twenty. But now I want them for eighteen. And I know I'll get them for that, because I know now how weak you are."

"You arrogant son of a bitch! What if I won't sell them for eighteen?"

"But you will. Because you're no longer certain that you can get rid of them. You're starting to wonder if maybe you'll be stuck with these baskets for a turn or two. Maybe longer. But mostly you'll let me have them for eighteen because you're just not brave enough not to. You don't have the stones for it."

There was hatred in the man's pale eyes. But there was frustration as well, and a certain amount of resignation. Because he knew Torgan was right.

At that moment, a woman, another Y'Qatt, stopped in front of Y'Farl's table and picked up one of the baskets.

"Those are fine baskets, madame," the peddler called to her, eyeing Torgan as he did. "I just found those today, and they won't last long. Only two sovereigns."

She smiled at him and nodded. But a moment later she put the basket back down and wandered off.

"Fine then, you bastard," Y'Farl said. "Eighteen. Take them and get away from me."

"There's no need to be nasty about it, Y'Farl. You've turned a profit today, and I've got baskets to sell in other towns, places that haven't seen the old woman's work yet. We've both done well."

"Then why do I feel like I've just come through an encounter with road brigands?"

Torgan smiled. "I really couldn't say."

"This is why no one likes you, Torgan. This is why you have no friends."

"Perhaps. But this is also why every peddler in this marketplace—including you, Y'Farl—would gladly trade places with me."

Torgan pulled out eighteen sovereigns and gave them to the man, and together they returned to Y'Farl's table to gather the baskets. It took Torgan two trips to get all of them to his cart, and the Y'Qatt refused to help him.

As he started away with his second load, he noticed that Y'Farl's cheeks had turned red.

"You look a bit flushed, my friend," Torgan said. "Are you all right?"

Y'Farl barely even looked at him. "I'm well enough. At least I will be once you've gone."

"You may be right. It's a fair distance between here and the nearest settlement. Maybe I should set out now."

"Good riddance, then. I hope this is the last I see of you."

Torgan grinned. "Come now, Y'Farl. You're taking this far too hard."

Y'Farl glared at him. "Am I? You call me weak and a coward, and then you pretend to be my friend, as if I should just forget all that."

"We're merchants. This is what we do. We both wanted the same thing. I just happened to win this time around."

"Well, it may all be a game to you," the Y'Qatt said, smiling thinly, his cheeks ruddy, a faint sheen of sweat on his brow, "but it's my livelihood. Now go. And next time you're in the Neck, stay away from me."

Torgan eyed him a moment longer, then shrugged and walked away. He thought the man was overreacting, but he also thought it best simply to pack up these baskets and be on his way. That was something else he'd learned over his many years of travel and trade: Part of being a successful merchant was knowing when to move on.

Chapter 14

FAL'BORNA LAND, WEST OF THE COMPANION LAKES

Torgan saw it as a measure of his success and comfort that he no longer raced across the land from town to town as he once had, as other merchants still did. He could afford to move at a more leisurely pace, to enjoy the journey as well as each arrival. So though he set out from C'Bijor's Neck not long after midday, he was barely two leagues west of the city by the time he stopped for the night.

The skies had begun to clear near dusk, after so many days of rain and cloud, and as he sat near his small fire, eating a modest meal of salted meat, fruit, and nuts, and sipping Qosantian wine, he could even see a few stars overhead. He was surprised, then, to see flickers of lightning to the east, back toward the Neck. Even earlier in the day, it hadn't rained on him; it certainly hadn't stormed. He heard no thunder in response to the flashes, and at last he walked a short distance from his blaze and peered into the darkness, trying to see if something else might be causing the night sky to glimmer so.

To the merchant's surprise, he soon realized that the flashes were being caused by narrow beams of fire that darted up from the plain, licking at the sky, as fine and quick as lizard tongues. It had to be Qirsi fire—what else could it be?—but the bolts of flame seemed to be coming from C'Bijor's Neck itself. It made no sense. Why would the Y'Qatt suddenly resort to using fire magic?

Unless they were under attack.

Torgan had never frightened easily. He'd heard talk of the pestilence up here in the north, but he hadn't let that keep him from coming. And he had been rewarded with the fine baskets he'd bought from Y'Farl. Even as a younger man, when he had known that the coinmonger in Medqasse had his cutthroats out looking for him, he hadn't allowed himself to be driven from the city by fear. Like so many young men, he'd confused foolishness for bravery and so had lost an eye.

But seeing that Qirsi fire rise from the city, Torgan was afraid. Was he watching the start of a new clan war? And if so, who would bother attacking the Y'Qatt, and why? Were there Qirsi raiders abroad in the land again, as there had been centuries before? He'd heard tales of their attacks on small settlements throughout the land, Eandi and Qirsi alike. But even back then, the white-hair brigands had confined themselves to the southern lands, not daring to pit themselves against the Fal'Borna or J'Balanar.

After watching for several moments, Torgan laughed at himself for allowing his fears to overmaster his judgment. Those bolts of fire were flying into the sky. Either the brigands had terrible aim, or he'd imagined a threat where none existed. It had to be a ritual of sorts, something the Y'Qatt did, something of which he'd never heard. What else could it be, really? No one had cause to attack an Y'Qatt city. And even if someone did, they wouldn't send their fire magic into the sky like that. It made no sense. And yet, as he continued to gaze eastward, he thought he could make out the glow of flames consuming the city, and great billows of smoke rising from the earth.

As the night went on, the bursts of fire didn't abate. If anything, they grew more frequent. Torgan stood transfixed, unable to look away. Dark thoughts chased one another through his mind, but none of them made any sense; none of them truly explained what he was seeing, for in truth, Torgan didn't even know what that was. A ritual? An attack? A battle? Or something worse? A civil war among the Y'Qatt? The collective madness of a city? Every option horrified him. None made any sense.

At last, seeing no change, no end to the flame and smoke, he returned to his cart and the small fire he had built. It was little more than embers now, baleful orange, a thin line of smoke drifting into the cool air. He climbed into his cart and lay down, hoping to sleep. For a long time, though, sleep wouldn't come. Each time he closed his eyes, he saw the flames again, the bursts of light, the smoke. And when at last he did drift into a fitful slumber, he was plagued by strange, dark dreams. In one, from which he awoke to darkness and the distant, mournful howls of wolves, he was in the C'Bijor's Neck marketplace, surrounded by dead and dying white-hairs. His cart was burning, and with it all his wares, including the baskets he had purchased that day from Y'Farl. The flames were as brilliantly colored as the baskets themselves, and in his dream Torgan was so captivated by the dancing fire, that he reached his hand into it, searing his flesh.

He lay awake for hours after that, and when he finally closed his eyes again, odd, disturbing visions continued to haunt his sleep. Upon awaking to a cold clear dawn, Torgan scrambled out of his cart and stared back toward the city, hoping that he'd see nothing unusual. Better to wonder if he had been deceived by his eyes, and made fearful by imagined horrors, than to see that any of it had been real. But there could be no mistaking the columns of black smoke that rose from the eastern horizon. C'Bijor's Neck had burned.

He thought briefly about going back to see what had happened. Perhaps there were wounded in need of aid. Perhaps, though, the city was still under siege, or at war with itself. Perhaps there were raiders behind him on the plain making their way westward. He packed up his belongings, not bothering with breakfast, and drove his cart northwest, keeping the smoke and the sun at his back. He didn't spare the whip either. Trili, the old horse pulling his cart, wasn't capable of much anymore, but on this day Torgan determined that the beast would give her all. He rested only occasionally, ate little, for he wasn't hungry, and tried to put as much distance as possible between himself and the Neck.

There were said to be Fal'Borna settlements throughout the north. This was where the rilda spent the warmer months, and though the Harvest had begun, they might still be up this way. The Fal'Borna were a difficult people, even as Qirsi went, and because Torgan was Eandi, they had shown him little friendship over the years. But he enjoyed a reputation among the various septs as a merchant who sold quality goods, and who could be trusted. It wasn't much, but it was all he had, and if there were brigands on the plain, he wanted to be under the protection of the Fal'Borna.

When evening fell, however, he was still alone. He stopped for the night in a small ravine and, despite the cold, didn't make a fire, for fear of attracting the notice of anyone else on the plain. Climbing out of the ravine and keeping low to the ground, he looked back toward the Neck. He saw nothing. No orange glow. No bolts of light. This meant little, though. He'd covered at least five leagues on this day; even if there had been something to see, Torgan wasn't certain that he was still close enough to see it.

The night passed without incident, as did the following two days and nights. He found no septs, but neither did he encounter any brigands. And as the memory of that first night grew more distant, he began to question what he had seen. Perhaps there was another explanation for the fire and smoke, one that didn't involve warriors or raiders. Maybe, alone in the darkness, he had allowed his fears to get the better of him. By the time he fell asleep on that third night, he had convinced himself that this was so. But once again, he didn't build a fire.

For two more days he searched the northern reaches of the plains, until at last he decided to turn southward and seek the Fal'Borna there. He could have gone farther west, but he didn't wish to cross the mighty Thraedes so late in the year, lest he find himself forced to cross it on the way back after the weather had turned wetter and colder. As his frustration at finding no septs grew, his fears continued to fade. On those fourth and fifth nights he allowed himself a fire, and though he jumped at every unexpected noise and loud pop from the flames, his blaze attracted no brigands.

At last, late in the morning of the sixth day, he spied a sept in the distance and drove his cart toward it. It was a large settlement—larger than most of the Fal'Borna villages he had encountered in the past—and as he drew near he saw that several other merchants had set up their carts on its fringe. Seeing his approach, several Fal'Borna children ran toward his cart calling out for him to show them what he had to sell and asking if he sold sweets or toys or anything else that they could think of that was more interesting than cloth or fruit or baskets. Of course he had sweets, he told them. For he did. Selling sweets to children often made it easier to sell more substantial goods to their parents.

The men and women of the sept eyed him with a combination of suspicion and challenge and curiosity that he'd come to realize was unique to the Fal'Borna. They were a violent, difficult clan. But they were also uncommonly acquisitive, far more so than the other warrior clans, the J'Balanar and the T'Saan.

Torgan climbed off of his cart and pulled out the sweets first, distributing them one by one to all the children who had gathered around him. He didn't bother to keep track of faces or names. The cost of the treats was minimal; the goodwill he could engender by giving them away couldn't be fixed with a price. After the children wandered off, their mouths full, he began to bring out the rest of his wares. Slowly, a crowd of older Fal'Borna wandered toward his cart. Many of them recognized him, nodding when he caught their eye. Others stubbornly refused to look at him at all, staring intently at his goods instead. This, too, he had experienced before. Even a few of the other peddlers strolled over, no doubt to see what he had and what prices he was asking. Torgan Plye's arrival in a marketplace rarely went unnoticed.

As he had expected, the baskets he'd bought from Y'Farl drew a good deal of attention.

"How much for these, Torgan?" one of the peddlers asked, lifting one and examining it closely. He didn't know the man's name, though clearly the stranger knew his. He was a younger man. Eandi. "Mettai work, isn't it?"

"Yes, Mettai," Torgan said. "And they're three sovereigns."

The man's eyebrows went up. "Three?"

"Firm price," Torgan added. "No bargaining on those."

"But three," the man said.

"Look at them. If you can show me any baskets that are finer, I'll let you have it for two."

"I thought you said the price was firm."

He grinned. "I did. That's my point."

The other merchants laughed. He even drew grins from a few of the Fal'Borna.

"Where did you find them?"

"Back in the Neck."

"What?" the man said.

"C'Bijor's Neck."

Everyone stared at him, their expressions turning his innards to water.

"Is that supposed to be funny, dark-eye?" one of the Qirsi asked, his voice hard.

"Not at all," Torgan managed to say, though abruptly his mouth was so dry that he could barely move his tongue. "What's happened?"

"You truly don't know?" another peddler asked.

How could he answer? He had seen fire and smoke. But what did he know? What *had* he seen that night?

"Please, tell me."

"Pestilence," the Fal'Borna said. "Worst I've ever heard of."

"Pestilence?" Torgan repeated. Of all the things they might have said, he least expected that.

But the Qirsi nodded. "According to some, the fever drove them mad. Houses and shops were burnt to the ground or shattered. There's talk some were even blown over by winds, though I doubt that."

"But how—?"

"Magic," another peddler told him. "Y'Qatt magic. The pestilence drove them to use their magic."

"Demons and fire," he whispered.

"Indeed."

"How long ago did you leave there, dark-eye?" the Fal'Borna man demanded.

"Days," he said, too stunned to think clearly. "Five days, maybe six."

The Qirsi shook his head. "If it had gotten in your blood you'd be dead by now. You were fortunate."

Fortunate. To say the least. The Fal'Borna had no idea just how close Torgan had come to dying. Hours. Maybe less. Suddenly he remembered how flushed Y'Farl had looked when they concluded their trade. Torgan had assumed at the time that the man was merely angry. But maybe he'd already been feeling the effects of the disease, in which case Torgan should have been dead.

"I trust you're not feeling ill," the man said, eyeing him closely.

Torgan shook his head. "I wasn't until now. But hearing this . . ."

The Fal'Borna nodded. "Yes, I know. This isn't the first we've heard of the pestilence in this part of the plain. The cold turns could be long and hard this year."

Torgan said nothing. He really did feel ill, as if the fever were upon him. His stomach felt hollow and sour; his body ached. One of the peddlers asked him something else about the baskets, but he barely heard and he offered no response. At that moment, all he wanted was to leave, to get as far away from the Fal'Borna and the north as he could.

"Come on, Torgan," one of the peddlers said, picking up a basket. "Two and a half. Three is just too high."

"Yes, all right," he said absently.

The other traders gaped at him. One might have thought he had told them they could have his entire cart for that amount, so surprised did they look.

"What did you say?" the peddler asked.

Torgan turned to look at him, making up his mind. Two and a half per basket would make him a small profit, and then he'd leave. The truth was he felt fine. At the first mention of the pestilence he'd imagined himself growing ill, but he knew better. Somehow he had managed to avoid the disease. It was nothing short of miraculous, a gift of the gods. And having been given such a gift, he now resolved to do what he should have done in the first place. He'd been warned about going north, about the dangers of the pestilence, and he'd gone anyway. He'd been reckless, and had nearly paid with his life. It was time to head south.

"You can have the basket for two and a half. In fact, I'll sell all of them at that price."

"But you said—"

"I know what I said. But this once, I'll make an exception, as a way of honoring my friend in C'Bijor's Neck who sold them to me, and who's now dead, for all I know." He shuddered, but forced himself to smile.

The peddlers crowded around his cart, each trying to find the best ones, and in just a few moments Torgan had sold all of them.

He made a show of remaining in the marketplace and chatting with the Fal'Borna and the other peddlers for an hour or so. He even sold a few more items, mostly cloth, and also a few ornate blades. But with the sun still high above the plain, he began to pack up his goods. The peddlers watched him, some of them frowning slightly, others speaking in low tones as their eyes wandered in his direction. One of the Fal'Borna approached him.

"You're leaving already, dark-eye?"

"Yes," Torgan said. "To be honest, I'm unsettled by the news from C'Bijor's Neck. I'd just as soon be gone from this place."

"The Neck is a long way east of here."

"I know it is. But it's time I was headed south."

The Fal'Borna nodded once, but his tone remained grim. "The a'laq usually expects that peddlers will sup with him the night of their arrival here. He also expects a small tribute from those who sell in his sept."

Torgan should have expected as much; he'd done business with the Fal'Borna before. But with all that had occupied his thoughts on this day, he'd forgotten. He reached into his purse and pulled out four sovereigns.

"Who is a'laq of this sept?" he asked.

"S'Plaed, son of I'Baln."

He handed his coins to the man. "Please give this to him with my respects, and my deepest apologies for having to leave so soon."

"He won't be happy."

Torgan shrugged. "I'm sorry. But I'm leaving just the same."

The Qirsi frowned at him, but then he pocketed the money and walked away without saying more.

"Where will you go, Torgan?" asked the young peddler, the one whose name Torgan didn't know.

"To the Ofirean, I think," he answered, making up his mind in that moment. He resumed his packing. "I'm sure I'll find a few septs between here and there, but I think I'm done with the plains for a while."

"Well, good luck to you," the man said, sticking out his hand.

Torgan had to smile. Had he once been this eager? "What's your name, friend?"

The peddler grinned, pumping Torgan's hand. "Jasha Ziffel. I'm a big admirer of yours."

"Have we met before, Jasha?"

He shook his head, still grinning. He was a small man, a good deal shorter and thinner than Torgan. He spoke with a Tordjanni accent, and his hair was yellow, like that of so many from the Tordjanne coast. The bridge of his nose was generously freckled and his eyes, widely spaced in an open round face, were pale blue.

"I've seen you," the young man said. "We've been in the same marketplace a few times. But we haven't been introduced, at least not so's you'd remember."

"Well, it's good to meet you," Torgan said, giving his hand one last shake before turning his attention back to his cart.

"Is it true what they say about your eye?"

Torgan glanced at him. "What is it they say?"

"That you lost it in a fight with a coinmonger. That you lost your eye, but he lost his life."

He briefly considered telling Jasha the truth. He quickly decided, though, that it might be convenient to have such a reputation, just in case there were brigands on the plain. Besides, anyone foolish enough to believe such a tale didn't deserve the truth.

"That's close enough," he said at last. "There were actually two of them: the coinmonger and one of his men. But the rest is true."

Jasha stared at him, just drinking it all in. Torgan could have told him that he'd bested five men, and the man would have believed him. He *wanted* to believe him. Fine, then.

In another few moments, Torgan had finished packing up his wares and was climbing onto his cart.

"Good-bye, Torgan," Jasha said, waving. "May gold find you wherever you go."

It was an old merchants' saying, one that he hadn't heard anyone use in years. The boy was trying far too hard.

"You, too" was all he said before clicking his tongue at Trili and steering his cart away from the sept.

He didn't push the beast hard on this day. She had labored enough recently—the last thing Torgan needed was for the old nag to fail him now, when he was this far north. When he halted for the night and made his camp, he was no more than a league south of S'Plaed's sept.

So when the first burst of fire arced into the night sky, Torgan saw it clearly. He was holding a half-eaten piece of dried meat, which he promptly dropped.

Coincidence. That was the word that came to him. It had to be a coincidence, a random act of magic that had nothing to do with what had happened in the Neck.

Then a second burst of flame lit the night, and a third. Torgan thought he heard cries coming from the settlement, though surely he was too far away for that to be possible. He stood, as if to go somewhere, but he didn't take a step. He just watched as the night came alive. Streaks of yellow fire stabbed up into the darkness like blades. Smoke began to rise from the plain. And yes, those were cries he heard. And screams. And the whinnying of horses.

He still had a mouthful of meat that he'd been chewing, and he spit that out now, though he didn't look away.

Pestilence, the Fal'Borna had said. Worst he'd ever heard of. Men and women driven mad, Y'Qatt destroying their own homes with magic. And now it was happening again.

Coincidence.

Surely, that's what it had to be.

He felt his stomach heave, and he bit back the bile rising in his throat. He'd been fine a moment before. But seeing what was happening at the sept, knowing with the certainty of a condemned man that this was the pestilence come again, he knew that he should have been sick. He'd escaped the disease once; how could he possibly expect to do so again? His stomach heaved again and he gagged. But that was all.

I'm not sick.

"I'm not sick." Saying it aloud calmed him, and he said it again. "I'm not sick."

Trili looked at him and stamped.

More shafts of flame carved through the night. Smoke rose into the sky, obscuring the stars. He could smell it now: burning wood and grass, the bitter smell of charred flesh.

"That's the shelters burning," he told himself, reassured by the clarity of his thinking, the solid sound of his voice. "The z'kals," he added, remembering the Fal'Borna word for them, as if he were conversing with someone.

Why was the pestilence here? As the Fal'Borna said, if he'd been infected, he would have been dead days ago. He couldn't have brought it with him. It had to be one of the others. But they hadn't seemed sick either. Someone else then.

Worst he'd ever heard of.

"I'm not sick."

He sat down slowly, his eyes fixed on the northern sky. What were the chances of the pestilence striking two towns that were so far apart, on the very days he had visited them? Not just the pestilence, but a strain of the disease that was so severe, it drove people mad and caused Qirsi to lose control over their magic. That was what was happening. That was what had happened in C'Bijor's Neck.

Coincidence.

He wanted to believe it, but he couldn't.

It's me.

This he didn't say aloud.

How could it be him if he wasn't sick? It had to be something else. What else did this sept and C'Bijor's Neck have in common?

He dismissed the thought as soon as it came to him. How could an object—or even ten—sicken people? More to the point, how could they infect entire towns and yet leave him unaffected? No, it couldn't be the baskets any more than it could be Torgan himself.

But the thought continued to echo in his mind. What did the two settlements have in common? Torgan, and the old woman's baskets. Yes, he had other items in his cart, but he'd had them for far longer, and as far as he knew, none of the villages or cities he'd visited prior to the Neck had been struck by the pestilence. If it was anything he carried— and really, how could it be?—but if it was, it had to be the baskets.

Still the streaks of fire darted up into the night. Still the smoke drifted over him, thicker now and acrid. The cries sounded closer, but he saw no riders approaching, no sick Qirsi converging on his small camp.

Why had that woman been so eager to be rid of her baskets?

He'd thought of Y'Farl several times in the past few days, wondering if the old peddler would still be angry with him the next time they met. He could only assume now that they wouldn't meet again in this world, and while he hadn't considered the Y'Qatt a close friend, he was sad-dened nevertheless.

Since leaving the Neck, however, he'd not given a thought to the old Mettai woman. It all came back to him now, though. The way she'd looked as she left the city. The satisfaction she seemed to feel at having gotten so little for baskets that appeared to be worth so much.

Had she known that there was something wrong with them? Not merely that they weren't as fine as they looked, but something truly wrong. Something . . . *evil.*

"This is nonsense," he whispered to the night.

It had to be a coincidence. Dark, even tragic, to be certain. But a co-incidence, and nothing more.

Yet, now that the old woman had entered his mind, he couldn't drive her out. Nor could he help thinking that he was glad to be rid of those baskets. He knew that he wouldn't sleep—not this night. So once again, he started to pack up his belongings, intending to drive his cart farther south. The skies were clear, and this late in the waxing the moons were close to full and would be out for most of the night. He could put another two or three leagues between himself and the sept if he pushed himself.

Before he could finish loading his cart, however, he heard a horse approaching. An instant later he recognized the rattle of cart wheels. A peddler then.

He knew before the cart reached him that it was Jasha, and he stepped out into the open so that the lad would see him in the moonlight. Jasha steered his cart directly toward him, stopping when his horse was only a few fourspans from where Torgan was standing.

"Why did you do it?" the peddler demanded. His face looked white in Panya's glow.

"I don't know what you're talking about."

The man leaped down from his cart and strode toward Torgan, his fists clenched. "I don't believe you! You brought this here! You did to the Fal'Borna exactly what you did to C'Bijor's Neck!" He halted just in front of Torgan. "Tell me why!"

"I didn't do anything."

"You're lying!" Jasha said, shoving him as he spoke. He stood a full head shorter than Torgan, and even pushing with what seemed to be all his might, he barely moved the merchant at all.

"Don't touch me again, Jasha."

"Or what? You'll make me sick, too?"

He shoved Torgan again, and this time the merchant hit him back, his fist catching the young man square in the jaw. Jasha staggered back a step, then fell onto his rear. For a moment he sat there in the firelight, looking dazed. Then he began to sob.

"It was awful," he said, tears glistening on his cheeks. "Everyone around me was getting sick—all the Qirsi at least. The pestilence. It had to be. The fever, and the . . . the . . ." He clamped his teeth shut and shook his head. "But then the magic started to come out of them," he went on a moment later. "They couldn't help themselves. They couldn't stop. Fire and winds and shaping." He shook his head again, swiping at his tears, though more slid down his face. "There was a healer, and his skin just opened, like he'd taken a knife to himself."

"You say it was only the Qirsi who got sick?"

Jasha lifted his gaze, looking as if he'd forgotten Torgan was even there. After a moment he nodded. "Only the Qirsi. But you knew this would happen, didn't you?" he said, his voice hardening again. "That's why you left so early."

"It's not true. I swear it."

"You saw it happen in the Neck, and you brought it here."

"No."

"That's what the Fal'Borna think."

He'd been frightened already. How could he not be, watching a second village succumb to this strange, terrible illness? But at Jasha's mention of the Fal'Borna, Torgan felt himself go cold.

"They think I did this to them?" he asked, his voice falling to a whisper.

Jasha's tears had ceased, at least for the moment. "You came to them from the Neck, and then you refused to remain in the village for more than a few hours. What are they supposed to think?"

"But I did nothing!"

"Didn't you?"

"No! It was . . ." He shook his head, uncertain of what he was going to say.

"It was what?"

"I think perhaps it was the baskets."

Jasha let out a harsh laugh. "The baskets? Do you think I'm a fool?"

Saying it out loud, Torgan could hear how crazed he sounded. He briefly considered trying to explain it all—the woman, and Y'Farl, and the odd bargain they struck. But he knew that Jasha wouldn't believe him, and if he truly had made himself an enemy of the Fal'Borna, he needed to get away from here as quickly as possible.

"No, Jasha, you're not a fool."

He extended his hand to the young man. Jasha eyed it a moment as if it were a dagger. But then he grasped it and allowed Torgan to pull him to his feet.

Torgan turned away and began to climb onto his cart. After a moment, though, he stopped and faced the peddler again.

"I didn't do this. I swear it to you." He wasn't certain why he cared, but when Jasha finally nodded, he knew a brief moment of relief.

He climbed into his seat and took up the reins. Jasha stood watching him. Beyond the young man, the sky was alive with fire and smoke.

"Where will you go?"

Torgan smiled grimly. "Are you asking for yourself, or for the Fal'Borna?"

"What did you mean when you said it was the baskets?"

The merchant shook his head. "It doesn't matter. Even if I could make you understand, you wouldn't believe me."

"You don't know that."

He hadn't the time for this, and yet someone should know, in case the Fal'Borna managed to hunt him down.

"I bought the baskets from a friend. Y'Farl. He lives . . ." He paused, staring at the sky above S'Plaed's sept. "He lived in C'Bijor's Neck. He had gotten them just moments before from a Mettai woman who sold them to him for far less than she should have. Y'Farl thought he'd made a fine deal for himself, but I watched the whole thing, and it seemed to me that she was anxious to be rid of them, and that she let him have them, knowing full well that he would have paid more."

Jasha just stared at him, as if waiting for more. When at last he realized there was no more, he scowled. "That's it? A Mettai woman makes a poor deal for herself, and you think that explains all this?" He gestured back toward the settlement.

He hadn't the time to explain further, and even if he had, it wouldn't have done any good.

"You're right," Torgan said. "It makes no sense. The baskets probably had nothing to do with this. But in that case, I don't have any other explanations. It wasn't my doing. Other than that, I know nothing." He flicked the reins, and his horse started forward. "Good-bye, Jasha," he called, without bothering to look back. "Gods keep you safe."

Torgan had gone a fair distance before he realized that Jasha was following him in his cart. He slowed, allowing the younger man to catch up.

"What do you think you're doing?" he demanded.

Jasha didn't answer at first, and when he finally said something, it wasn't at all what Torgan had expected.

"Do you think she used magic of some sort?"

Torgan narrowed his eyes. "You mean the Mettai woman?"

"Yes. Do you think she did something to the baskets? Put a spell on them or something?"

"I suppose that's possible. I hadn't really thought it through. Until tonight, I'd simply assumed that the pestilence had come to the Neck, and that I was lucky to be alive. Now . . ." He shrugged. Torgan had never been one to crave company as he steered his cart throughout the land. But on this of all nights, he was glad to have someone with whom he could speak of what had happened, of what was still happening.

He glanced back and saw narrow beams of yellow fire reaching to the sky.

"Why would she?" Jasha asked.

Torgan shook his head. "I know nothing about her, save that she makes fine baskets." He looked sharply at the younger man. "You bought one from me. Do you still have it?"

Jasha tried to smile, failed, then shook his head. "I sold it to a Fal'Borna woman. I got three sovereigns for it."

"You should be glad to be rid of it. Even if they had nothing to do with this, I'd be just as happy never to see the woman or her baskets again."

The younger man's eyes widened. "No," he said.

"No, what?"

"We have to find her."

"You can't be serious."

"Of course I am," Jasha said. And indeed, he did look to be in earnest. "We have to find her and demand to know what she did to the baskets."

"What are you talking about? I'm not searching for some Mettai woman who might have done nothing wrong except take too little money for her wares. I'm heading to the Ofirean. I'm going to roll my cart into the marketplace in Thamia, or better still, Siraam, and I'm going to stay there until the Snows have ended in the north."

"Do you really think there's something wrong with those baskets?"

Torgan hesitated.

"Right. In that case we have no choice. We have to find her."

"You're welcome to try," the merchant said. "But I'm going to the sea."

"You'll be stopping in villages along the way, won't you?"

"What of it?"

"We can look in those marketplaces."

Torgan found himself growing less and less pleased with his new traveling companion.

"I'm not doing this."

Jasha said nothing.

The merchant looked at him. "Did you hear me?"

"Yes, I heard you."

"If you want to follow me to the Ofirean that's fine, though if the Fal'Borna are after me, you probably ought to go your own way. But as for the rest, you can just forget about it."

Silence.

"Are you listening?"

"Yes, Torgan. I hear everything you're saying. You're going to the Ofirean, and you're not looking for the Mettai woman."

"That's right."

Torgan started to say more, but he realized that he'd just be repeating himself, and clearly the young peddler had heard him. He sensed, though, that Jasha was just as determined that they should search the plain for the woman.

"We should go our own ways," Torgan said, after a long silence. "You don't want to be with me—not if the Fal'Borna are hunting me. And I don't want you following me around, selling your cheap wares next to mine, taking gold out of my pocket."

"All right," Jasha said.

But he didn't stop, nor did he change directions. He kept his cart just beside Torgan's and together they drove southward, with the moons above them, and the fires of the Fal'Borna sept at their backs.

Chapter 15

KIRAYDE

ow many villages is it now?"

Pyav's expression was grim as he regarded Tashya, as if he didn't wish even to answer her question. "At least three," he said at last. "We know of outbreaks in Runnelwick, Greenrill, and Tivston. There's no telling where else it's struck."

"And these are all Qirsi villages?"

"Runnelwick and Greenrill are Y'Qatt," Marivasse said. "As for Tivston . . ." She trailed off into a fit of coughing, and it seemed to Besh that the other elders leaned back in their chairs, afraid to breathe in the same air as the old woman. After a time, her spasm subsided and she wiped at her mouth with an old cloth. "I know nothing about Tivston," she said hoarsely.

For the fourth or fifth time this day, the eight of them lapsed into silence. Most of them watched Pyav, waiting for him to tell them what was to be done. Besh could hear voices in the marketplace. A baby cried. One of the dogs that sometimes wandered through the village began to bark, only to be hushed by a sharp word from someone in the lane outside the sanctuary. But inside, no one spoke.

Besh had been up much of the previous night, reading through Sylpa's daybook. He stifled a yawn now and shivered. The sun shone outside, but it had been a clear, cold night and chill air still lingered in the chamber.

He'd found nothing new for all the reading he'd done by candlelight in Lici's abandoned hut. After learning the previous day that Lici first came to Kirayde because her home village of Sentaya had been devastated by the pestilence, he'd hoped that Sylpa's journal would quickly reveal the remaining secrets of Lici's past. Instead, much to Besh's frustration, Sylpa had stopped pushing the girl for more information. It almost seemed that she was as reluctant to hear more about those dark events as the young girl was to speak of them.

And now that the pestilence had come to the plains, Besh could no longer afford the luxury of simply enjoying Sylpa's narrative. For more than half a turn, he had been living in two times: his own, and Sylpa's. Now, though, the exigencies of his own life were forcing him to step out of hers. He needed to know things that she had yet to learn.

"It may be that we have nothing to fear," said Korr, another of the elders. "Each of those villages is to the west of the wash."

Tashya shook her head. "That means nothing. The pestilence can't be held back by rivers or mountains or city walls. We may be safe now, but all it takes is a single stranger—a peddler, a bard, even a soldier."

"So, what would you have us do?" Pyav asked, drawing the woman's gaze.

"Close the village to all outsiders."

Several of the elders voiced their disapproval, but Tashya didn't pause. She merely raised her voice so that she could still be heard.

"Shut down the marketplace and have every peddler who doesn't live here escorted out of the village. And then post guards on all the roads leading into Kirayde. The only way to keep the pestilence out is to make an island of our home."

"Even that might not work," Besh said. "I don't necessarily disagree with what you're proposing, but you should know that it might not do any good."

"I know that," Tashya said. "That's a risk I'm willing to take."

"People have crops they want to sell," Korr said. He was one of the older members of the council, nearly as old as Marivasse, though like her, he remained spry and sharp of mind. He'd made his living as a miller before passing his business on to his son, Ojan. He was nearly bald, with a narrow band of white hair on the back of his head. He stood a full head taller than Besh, though with his stooped back and rounded shoulders, he didn't look nearly as imposing as he had as a younger man. "Ojan has flour to sell. What is he supposed to do? Where's their gold supposed to come from?"

Tashya shrugged. "They'll have to make do for a while. Not forever, perhaps not even for a full turn. Just until this outbreak has run its course."

"But this is the Harvest," Korr said. "In another turn, the weather will have turned too cold. Some will lose their crops. And who's to say that when we're ready to open our village to trade again, the peddlers will want to come back?" He shook his head. "We can't do this. Too many will suffer."

"Better to lose their gold than their children!" Tashya said, anger flashing in her bright green eyes.

Besh had seen Tashya's hard stare cow men far more certain of themselves than the old miller. Korr was overmatched, and he appeared to know it. He eyed her a moment longer, then looked away without saying anything more.

"What about the rest of you?" Pyav said, looking around the chamber. "Are there any other suggestions short of shutting down the marketplace?"

"Not just the marketplace," Tashya said. "If we merely keep out peddlers while letting others in, we accomplish nothing."

A wry smile touched the eldest's lips. "My pardon. Any other suggestions aside from closing the lanes into the village?"

Tashya nodded her approval.

"What about you, Marivasse?" Pyav asked. "You're our herbmistress. Surely you have some ideas."

But the old woman shook her head. "I've yet to find a tonic that could contend with the pestilence, and I've yet to meet a Mettai sorcerer powerful enough to stave off the disease with blood and blade." She glanced Tashya's way. "I don't particularly like Tashya's solution, but I don't see that we have any choice."

Pyav looked at Besh, who gave a slight shake of his head. The eldest frowned.

"I'll consider this," Pyav said, turning back to Tashya.

"What's to consider?" she demanded. "We know that the pestilence is killing people only a few leagues from here. We have to do something immediately."

"It's more than a few leagues, Tashya."

She started to say more, but Pyav raised a hand and she fell silent. Korr might have been afraid of her, but the eldest was not.

"You may be right. It may come to this. But Korr makes a good point as well. The Snows are coming, and people in this village need gold to get through. Closing Kirayde to peddlers is a last resort. But the first we hear of outbreaks on this side of the Silverwater, we'll do it."

"And what if we're the first?"

"I'm hoping we won't be."

There was nothing she could say to that, and a few moments later the council adjourned.

A few of the elders continued their discussion outside, gathering in a small knot near the door to the sanctuary. But Besh started away immediately, intending to return to Lici's house and Sylpa's journal.

"Besh, wait a moment."

He stopped and turned. Tashya was striding toward him, her black hair shimmering in the morning sunlight. Despite the ghosts who hovered at each shoulder—Sylpa and his beloved Ema—he couldn't help but think that Tashya was the most beautiful woman he'd ever met. Even now, well past her tenth four, she remained as lovely as she'd been in her youth.

Besh expected her to speak to him of their discussion in the council, but she surprised him.

"You're on your way to Lici's," she said, a statement, not a question.

"Yes."

She nodded once. "Pyav has told me what you're looking for."

"He thinks I'm wasting my time."

"I don't," she said. "And while the eldest may think there's little of use to be found in Sylpa's daybook, he admires you for making the effort. He told me so."

It was rare for Tashya to show so much kindness. Not that she was a bad person, but she didn't often take the time to speak so to anyone. Besh wondered where all of this was leading.

As was her way, she wasted no time in making her point. Once again, though, she surprised him, this time by suddenly growing uncomfortable, even shy.

"I'm wondering," she said, her gaze dropping. "Have you found any mention of my father in Sylpa's journal?"

"Your father?"

"His name was Menfyn."

"Yes, I remember him," Besh said.

She looked up at that, her eyes sparkling like emeralds. Lovely indeed. "You do?"

"Of course. He was an elder. And more to the point, his was the finest garden in the village year after year, much to my father's annoyance."

She laughed, but quickly grew serious again. "He was also . . . well, there was talk. After my mother died. Talk about Sylpa and him."

Understanding at last, Besh shook his head. "I've found nothing like that."

"You're certain?"

"Yes. I promise."

She nodded, looking both relieved and disappointed, if that was possible.

"When I was younger, I didn't want to believe it was true. But later, after I lost my husband, I started to realize how selfish I'd been. I almost wish . . ." She looked away again, and laughed, but it sounded forced. "I don't know what I wish."

"If I find anything, I'll tell you. You have my word."

She met his gaze once more. "Thank you, Besh." She smiled briefly and walked away, leaving Besh alone in the lane thinking what a powerful thing memory could be. When Lici first disappeared, everyone in the village had been so concerned about her gold. But Besh was no longer certain that her bag of coins was the greatest treasure the old woman had left behind.

Smiling at the thought, he returned to the house, pulled out the old daybook, and began to thumb through it. He quickly skimmed over several entries that followed those he'd read the previous night and saw little of interest. Then there was a bit of a gap during which Sylpa wrote nothing at all. But the opening lines of the entry following this gap caught his eye.

Hunter's Moon, first day of the waxing, 1147.

I've been remiss about writing recently. The Harvest is always a busy time, and this year's Harvest brought storms that flooded the rill and destroyed several homes. But something interesting happened today, and it may shed more light on all that's befallen Licaldi.

It was a cold day, the coldest we've had since last year's Snows. But the sun was shining, and with the garden plot all but empty, Licaldi and I had little that we needed to do. I've been promising her new clothes for the colder turns that are soon to come, and so we took this day to return to the marketplace.

She loves the market. Given the chance I believe she would spend her entire day wandering among the peddlers' carts, simply looking at their wares and seeing how far she can get them to lower their prices. She likes cloth and often encourages me to buy a bolt of something with bright colors and intricate patterns that we might use to make pillows for chairs or covers for what little furniture we have in our house. She likes baubles, as well—shiny blades, too small and ornate to have any practical use, or wood boxes carved by the clans of the western woodlands. If she had her way, the house would be filled with these, and we'd barely have room to sit, much less cook and sleep.

The other thing she loves to do is weave. I've taught her a bit about basketry, and she's taken to it so quickly that I find myself wondering if she'd already learned the craft from someone in Sentaya. I haven't asked her, nor have I noticed her becoming sad or withdrawn when we weave. It may just be that she has a penchant for the work.

Today we took some baskets to the market—mostly mine, but one that she made, simple in design, but tightly woven. She was quite proud of it and wanted to see how much we could get for it.

The marketplace was particularly crowded today. With the Snows approaching, and the storms finally over, it seems that peddlers are flocking to the villages of the northern plains, hoping to line their pockets with our gold before the weather drives them to the shores of the Ofirean.

We found a Qirsi merchant with whom I'd done business before, and tried to trade our baskets for a bolt of blue and red cloth. He refused, and when Licaldi asked him why, he pulled several baskets from his cart. They were of very good quality—some of the finest I've seen—and I asked him where he'd found them.

"West of here," he said. "I traded for them in an Y'Qatt village in Fal'Borna land."

Licaldi actually dropped the box she was looking at. Fortunately it landed on a bolt of cloth, but she didn't appear to notice or care. "What did you say?"

"Licaldi, what is it?" I asked.

But she ignored me, keeping her green eyes fixed on the Qirsi trader.

"I got them from the Y'Qatt," he said again.

"What does that mean?" she asked, her voice rising. "That word: Y'Qatt. What does it mean?"

"Surely you've heard of the Y'Qatt," I said.

But she shook her head, looking my way at last. Her eyes were wide and the color had drained from her cheeks—signs I'd learned to understand over these past few turns. This had something to do with the tragedy that brought her to me.

"They're Qirsi," the merchant said, looking from me to the girl. "Sorcerers who refuse to use magic."

"Why?"

He shrugged. "I'm not sure I can explain. Most of the rest of us think they're fools. I think they believe that Qirsar never intended for us Qirsi to use our magic. They think that's why magic shortens our lives."

"So they never use it for anything?"

He shook his head. "Nothing that I know of."

"Licaldi, what's this about?"

But she wouldn't answer me. For another several moments she stared at the box she had dropped, saying nothing. Then she simply turned and walked out of the marketplace. I could see that she was headed back to our house, and having learned that I couldn't force her to reveal anything she wanted to keep secret, I didn't bother to follow.

Later, when I returned to the house, I found her chopping ramsroot for supper. She seemed in a fine mood, and when I asked about her conversation with the Qirsi merchant, she acted as though she couldn't remember what they had discussed. I know better, of course. She remembers everything. But I didn't push her.

It is another mystery—one among so many. Yet, I'm certain that we're getting closer. Soon, very soon, I'll hear the rest of her dark tale. And no doubt, upon hearing it, I'll wonder why I was ever so eager for the truth.

Another gap followed: more than twenty days to Sylpa's next entry. That one told Besh nothing, nor did the next two. But at last, in the third after this second gap, he found what he'd been seeking.

Memory Moon, fourth day of the waxing, 1147.

It snowed again today, small, sharp flakes that stung like blown sand when the wind raged. I can hear the storm still. The snow scratches like claws at my door and walls, and the wind howls like some wild beast loosed upon Elined's earth by Bian himself.

But we've plenty of wood piled by the hearth, and the house is warm enough. I had to venture out briefly to see the herbmistress, and even after I'd returned and been inside for an hour or two, I still felt that I'd never be warm again. But blankets, and a fire and a warm cup of tea have warmed me once more.

Licaldi is asleep now, though she lay awake for a long time, and her sleep has been fitful. Her fever has yet to break and her face looks pale and thin. Three days she's been ill and I have to admit that I fear for her. The healer says she'll be fine, that if it was something truly dangerous she would have grown far worse by now, but still I worry. And why shouldn't I? I know now beyond doubt that she is alone in the world except for me. More, I know that I would be lost without her. We are bound to one another for as long as I shall live. And at last, after today, I know how this came to be.

Throughout the day, the poor girl had convinced herself that she was dying, that this fever was kin to the one that struck her village, and would be the end of her. I tried to tell her that this wasn't so and that she'd soon be well and running around the house as she usually did. But the scars from her past run deep, and she was inconsolable. And in the midst of her despair, she decided that the time had come to tell me all that she had been keeping from me. Though I tried to reassure her about her prospects for recovery, I did nothing to dissuade her in this regard, and so at last I have heard her story.

It is as dark a tale as I imagined it would be, and it explains so much that has come before. Licaldi swore me to secrecy, though I tried to tell her that she need not be ashamed or feel guilty. But I write it all down here—in her own words as best as I can remember them—lest she wish to share her secret with another someday without having to endure the pain of relating it again herself.

"I was at the river most of that day," she began, staring up at our ceiling, tears flowing from the corners of her eyes and wetting the pillow on which her head rested. "I'd done my chores early, and was at the river, fishing with my friend Sosli. Even after she went home, because she was hungry, I stayed at the river. It was such a nice day, and I had no other chores to do." She looked at me then. "So, I didn't know. I swear it. I didn't know."

"It's all right, child," I told her, smoothing her hair, which was damp with sweat. "I believe you."

"After a while I got hungry," she went on, crying still. "And it seemed late, and I was wondering why Mama hadn't called for me yet. So, I walked home, carrying my fish. I'd caught three, and I was so proud. I wanted to show Papa, 'cause he'd taught me." She smiled faintly through her tears, but then appeared to catch herself, and grew serious once more. "That's when I found out they were sick."

"Your family?"

She nodded. "Mama, Papa, Kytha, Baetri. And others as well. Nearly everyone in the village. I even think Sosli got sick."

"Were they . . . ? How bad off were they?"

"They weren't dead yet, if that's what you mean. I only saw Mama. She was outside in front of the house . . . I think she'd just thrown up. And I could hear Kytha and Baet crying in the house.

"I started running to Mama, but she yelled at me to stop. She said I couldn't come in the house, or even get near it, or else I'd get sick, too. She asked me if I felt all right, and I said I did. I asked her what it was—what was wrong with her. I think I knew already, but I was hoping that I was wrong. But then she said it was the pestilence, and I knew that all of us were going to die.

"Except I didn't get sick. I sat outside the house, listening to my sisters crying, and waiting for the pestilence to get me, too, but it didn't. Papa came out at one point and talked to me. I think he was trying to pretend that everything was fine. He asked me about the fishing, and said nice things about the ones I'd caught. But he didn't come near me and he didn't look good. He was sweating, and his face looked grey, and there was sick on the front of his shirt.

"I asked him if I could come in the house and help them, but he said that Mama was right, that I had to stay outside. I asked him where the healers were, and he said that he'd sent for a healer, but with so many people sick it would take time for her to get there. He said that Mettai magic wasn't strong enough to help us, but they'd sent someone south to one of the Fal'Borna settlements along the wash, hoping that the Qirsi would send healers. Qirsi magic might work, even against the pestilence.

"So I waited some more. It started to get dark, and still no one came. And then I started to hear thunder and the sky started to cloud over, and I got scared. I don't like thunder, and I wanted to go inside. But Mama still said that I couldn't. I couldn't hear my sisters anymore, and I was afraid they were dead already, but Mama promised me that they weren't, that they were just sleeping, which was good for them. But she was getting worse, and so was Papa. I could tell. And no healers were coming, and it started getting windy and colder.

"So finally, Mama said that I should go south to the Qirsi and bring back healers. She told me that probably whoever had been sent before hadn't made it there. Probably he'd gotten sick like the rest and hadn't been able to go on.

But I wasn't getting sick, and she didn't think that I would. So, I should go. I could save the village, she said. I could be everyone's hero. Papa came out and made me a torch. He took care not to touch the part I'd be holding, and he lit it for me, so that I wouldn't have to go inside to the fire. They told me to run to the marketplace and shout to everyone what I was going to do, so they'd know that someone was getting help for them. And then they said I should go as quickly as I could because storms were coming, and people in the village were getting worse.

"I was crying, 'cause I didn't want to leave them. But I did what they told me to do. I ran to the marketplace and shouted, and then I left Sentaya and walked to the Fal'Borna settlements. I had my torch, but it was starting to rain. The wind was blowing hard, and I was cold and the lightning and thunder scared me. And it was so dark."

She started to cry again, great sobs escaping her until she could barely breathe, and I tried to comfort her, telling her that it was all right, and that anyone would have been scared. But she shook her head. She even pushed me away, which she almost never does.

"You don't understand," she said. "I went to the bridge—there's an old stone bridge near Sentaya. It crosses the Silverwater into Qirsi land."

"N'Kiel's Span?" I said.

She looked at me with wonder. "Yes! That's what it's called! You've heard of it?"

Any other night and I would have laughed at such a question. If she had known more of the history of the Blood Wars, she would have realized that many people in the land knew of it. In the final years of the wars, as the Fal'Borna continued their push eastward, battles were fought for control of the span. Men and women died trying to destroy it, or capture it, or keep others from using it. It was probably the most famous—or infamous—bridge in all the Southlands. With the wars over, the span has lost much of its importance. It's used occasionally by peddlers, but there are few important towns anywhere near it, and I don't think it's even guarded anymore. But at least now I knew where Sentaya was.

"Yes," I said. "I've heard of it."

"That's right near my—" She broke off, looking stricken, and for a long time she said nothing at all. When at last she began again, it was in a low voice. "That was how I got across the Silverwater. And then I started going toward the nearest of the Fal'Borna settlements."

Her cheeks colored and she turned away from me. "Or I thought I did."

I could barely hear her. "You mean you didn't?"

She started crying again. "I walked a long way before I realized it. There's lots of trees there. It's mostly forest along the wash. And the storm was coming on me, and I didn't know for such a long time. But finally . . ." She broke off again, unable to speak for her sobbing.

I said nothing, though I took her hand, which she suffered me to hold, and I waited.

"Finally, I realized that the wash was on my right, not my left. That's how it had been before I crossed the bridge, so I didn't think anything of it at first. But then I realized it, and I knew. I'd gone north instead of south."

She cried and cried, but eventually she managed to go on. "I probably should have turned back, but it seemed like I'd gone such a long way, and I didn't know if maybe there was another Fal'Borna settlement to the north. There might have been. I've heard that they move around a lot, so it was possible. And I didn't know if maybe it was close by, and by turning around I was just going to make things worse than they already were. So, I kept going. I still didn't find anything, but then I was even more certain that I didn't want to turn around. I didn't know what to do. I just wanted to sit down and cry.

"My torch was starting to die, and I didn't know what to do. And then the path went up a big hill, and just as I reached the top there was a flash of lightning, and I saw that I'd found a village after all. I was so happy, I just ran toward the houses, shouting as loudly as I could and waving the torch over my head. I didn't know what town it was, but I didn't really care. I just shouted and shouted until people started opening their doors and looking out at me.

"I told them that I needed help. I said that the pestilence had come to our village and everyone was sick and we needed Qirsi healers. I remembered it all, everything Mama and Papa told me to say.

"But instead of saying they'd help me, they told me to leave their village. I said it all again, or at least I tried to, but they cut me off and said I had to leave right away, that they were Y'Qatt and they couldn't help me." She looked at me, her eyes brimming yet again. "I didn't know what that meant. They kept on saying that they were Y'Qatt and that they wouldn't do anything to help me. And I didn't understand. I kept on asking them, begging them. I told them my mama and papa were dying. But they wouldn't do anything.

" 'We're Y'Qatt. You've brought the pestilence to an Y'Qatt village.' That's what they said, again and again."

"It's not their way to use magic," I said, trying to explain, though I'm not certain why I bothered.

Licaldi glared at me, as if I were the one denying her pleas for help.

"They threatened to kill me," she said.

"What?"

"When I wouldn't leave, they said they'd kill me. They said they had to, to protect themselves."

I just stared at her, unable to believe that even the Y'Qatt would go to such lengths to avoid using their magic.

She scowled at me, looking so hurt that I still shudder to think of it. "You don't believe me. I can remember exactly what the man said. 'The pestilence is just as deadly for us as it is for you. More so, because we're Qirsi. Now if you don't leave us immediately, we'll have no choice but to kill you and burn your body. We have bowmen here; men who can kill you from a distance if necessary.' Then he called to a man named Fikar, who stepped out of his house holding a bow. He'd already nocked an arrow in it."

She eyed me again, that same pained look on her face. "You still don't believe me."

"Yes, I do," I said. And I did. Horrible as it was, I believed every word of it. "What did you do then?"

Licaldi shook her head and closed her eyes. "There was nothing to do. I said something terrible to them and I left." She opened her eyes again, though she wouldn't look directly at me. She seemed spent now, tired beyond tears. "My torch died on the way home, but I managed to find my way without it. I think it was raining still. I don't know for certain. I remember there was more lightning and thunder, but the rest . . ." She shrugged.

"And when you reached the village?" I asked.

She stared up at the ceiling. She shed no tears now, and when she spoke again her voice was flat. "It was too late. Mama was at the river. Papa, Kytha, and Baet were in the house. But they were . . . they were all dead. I think everyone in the village died that night. All because I went the wrong way. And all because the Y'Qatt wouldn't help me."

"Anyone could have made that mistake, Licaldi. On a night like that, with your family sick and a storm blowing, anyone could have gone north instead of south."

"They were depending on me, and I failed. And because of that, they're all dead."

"You're just a girl!" I said, feeling tears on my own face. "You're eight years old. You're too young to bear such burdens. You need to find a way to forgive yourself."

She met my gaze then, looking too sad and too wise for her years. "If it was you, could you forgive yourself?"

I had no answer, and for a long time neither of us spoke. Finally, I asked her, "What was it you said to the Y'Qatt?"

Licaldi closed her eyes again. "Do I have to tell you?"

"Of course not, child. I was just asking." I leaned forward and kissed her forehead, which still felt hot. "I think you'll be better in the morning," I said, wanting it to be true. "You should rest now."

She nodded.

I got up, crossed to my bed, and picked up this journal, intending to write down all she'd told me. But as I sat, she spoke my name. Looking at her, I saw that her eyes were open again, shining with the light of candles.

"I told the Y'Qatt that I hoped the pestilence would come to their village," *she said. "I told them I wanted them all to die."*

Perhaps I should have scolded her. It was an evil thought, even for a child who must have been so angry and desperate and forlorn. But I merely nodded, thinking to myself that I probably would have said much the same thing.

So, now she sleeps, and I write, having learned at last all there is to know of her tragic tale. I am hopeful that as her fever fades and she grows strong again, she will be better off for having unburdened herself. But it is only a hope. She is so young to have seen and lived such horrors. It is said among our people that where a healer's touch fails, time works its own magic. Some wounds, though, can never heal. Instead they fester.

It remains to be seen which kind of wound fate has dealt this child.

Besh sat back and laid the daybook aside. Any doubt that had crept into his mind over the past turn was gone now. Lici was alive. He was certain of it. And more, she was wreaking vengeance across the land. *Sixty-four years to the day after she appears in the village, the old woman vanishes. And within a turn of her disappearance the pestilence strikes at three Qirsi villages, at least two of them Y'Qatt.* He stood and strode out the door into the midday sun. Walking quickly to the marketplace, he found a Qirsi trader, a young woman who was selling wines from the Nid'Qir.

"Buy a skin today, good sir?" she asked, smiling at him.

"No, thank you. Tell me, though: Have you ever heard of a town called Tivston?"

"Tivston?" she repeated, frowning. She shook her head and made the warding sign against evil, as if she were Mettai instead of Qirsi. "I know Tivston. It's very bad there now."

"Yes, I've heard. Is it a Qirsi village?"

"In a sense, yes," she said.

And he knew. Even before she could say anything more, he felt the hairs on his neck and arms standing on end.

"They're Y'Qatt in Tivston; Qirsi who use no magic."

Besh nodded. "Thank you." He started to walk away.

"Of course, good sir. Perhaps now you'd like to buy some wine."

He knew he should have, out of courtesy if nothing else. She'd answered his questions, and so had told him the last thing he needed to know before speaking of this with Pyav. But the thought of taking even a sip of wine just then made his stomach turn. He merely shook his head and walked to the eldest's smithy.

Pyav was resting when Besh got there, his face ruddy as always and covered with a fine sheen of sweat.

"You're early today," the smith said, grinning as Besh approached. But then he seemed to notice the old man's expression. His smile vanished and he stood. "What is it?"

"I know where Lici is. Or at least where she's been."

Pyav's brow creased. "What do you mean?"

"I told you that her village was ravaged by the pestilence. It killed her family. It killed everyone she knew."

"Yes, I remember."

"It seems there was more to the story," Besh said. "She went for help. She was looking for Qirsi healers, but instead she found an Y'Qatt village."

The eldest winced. "And they wouldn't help her."

"That's right."

"But what does that—?"

"Runnelwick and Greenrill—they're near N'Kiel's Span, aren't they?"

"I believe so." Comprehension hit him like a fist. "Blood and bone," he whispered.

"I just spoke with a Qirsi peddler. Tivston is an Y'Qatt village, as well. At least it was."

"A conjuring?"

"Perhaps. Probably. Would it surprise you to learn that she could use her magic that way?"

"I suppose not." The eldest stared at the ground for a few moments, shaking his head slowly. "I wouldn't know how to do it. Would you?"

"I couldn't even begin to conceive such a thing."

Pyav glanced at him, a sad smile on his lips. "And yet you figured it out. At least you think you have. Perhaps the workings of your mind are darker than you think."

Besh nodded, though he didn't smile in return. "Perhaps. They'll have to be if I'm to find a way to stop her."

Chapter 16

✦✦✦

Pyav stared at him, as if wondering whether he had heard correctly. "You?" the eldest said at last, sounding simple. "You're going after her?"

"Someone must."

That faint smile touched Pyav's face again and was gone. "You're a good man, Besh. I've said as much quite often over the past turn, and yet I'm not certain I knew how right I was until just now. You're honorable and clever, and you're even braver than I would have credited." He shook his head. "But you can't do this."

"Can't I?"

"How old are you, Besh?"

Besh might have been a good man, as the eldest said, but he knew as well as anyone that he wasn't without his faults, pride chief among them. Ema had told him so more often than he could count, and so had Elica. He felt himself bristling at the eldest's question, and he struggled to keep his temper in check.

"I'm old enough to know that Lici is our responsibility. No one else knows what she's done, and so no one else will think to stop her."

"That may be, but—"

"Will you go after her, Eldest?"

The blacksmith straightened, his expression hardening just a bit. "If need be."

"You have a family. Your children may be grown, but they need you still. You have a shop to maintain. You're eldest of our village. You're needed here."

"So are you, Besh."

"Not in the same way." The eldest opened his mouth, no doubt to argue the point, but Besh held up a hand, stopping him. "This isn't the self-pity of an old man, nor is it a last grasp at some sort of heroism. El-ica has her husband and her children. Ema is gone. Aside from my gar-den, no one will miss me."

Pyav smiled again, the kind smile this time, the one Besh had come to know so well in recent days. "I know that's not true. I'm not certain what Mihas would do without you. Or Annze and Cam, for that matter."

Besh felt his throat tighten at the mention of Mihas and the little ones, but he knew he was right about this. "There are plenty of children in this village who get along without their grandfathers. They'll be fine."

"I can't let you do this, my friend."

"With all respect, Eldest, you haven't any choice. You can't keep me here against my will, and we both know that there's no one else you can send."

Pyav opened his arms wide. "Why send anyone at all?" he de-manded, his voice rising. "What is it you think you can do? I admit that what you've told me is compelling, but we don't know for certain that Lici is to blame for what's happened in Greenrill and Runnelwick and . . . and . . . wherever else—"

"Tivston."

"Yes, right," he said impatiently. "My point is, this is all just conjec-ture on our part."

Besh frowned. "A moment ago you believed me. Now you don't?"

Pyav rubbed his forehead, his eyes squeezed shut. "I don't know what to believe. You've been convinced all along that Lici is alive still, that she had some purpose in leaving the way she did. And I allowed you to act on your suspicions. Perhaps that was a mistake."

"It wasn't. Don't you see? I was right all along. Sylpa's daybook proves that!"

"Sylpa is dead! Her daybook is a relic! Nothing more! Now, this nonsense has to end!"

The eldest appeared to wince at what he heard in his own voice, and for several moments neither of them spoke.

"I shouldn't have said that, Besh. Forgive me."

"Of course, Eldest," Besh said, his voice tight.

"I'm out of my depth. You have to understand. You're so sure of yourself in this matter. You're so certain about Lici, and I don't know her at all. How am I to make the kind of decisions you're asking of me?"

"By trusting me," the old man said, surprising himself with his passion and surety. "You're right: I am certain about Lici. I understand the way her mind works, whether because I know her, or merely because I know what it means to grow old. She's out there killing entire villages, spreading some sort of plague among the Y'Qatt. And she has to be stopped."

"And you can stop her?" Pyav asked. "Don't get me wrong; it's not merely your age that makes me ask. I could send a man half your age and twice your size, and I wouldn't know how to tell him to stop her. If all you say is true, she's mad or evil, or both. And she commands magic the like of which I've never encountered among the Mettai."

"So are we simply to remain here then, and let her have her vengeance?"

The eldest's expression darkened. "You're trying to goad me."

"Not at all. I don't believe you need goading. You know as well as I that we have to do something. If there's even a chance that Lici is causing so many to die, we have to stop her, or at the very least warn the other Y'Qatt villages that lie in her path."

"Is that what you plan to do? Will you merely warn the Y'Qatt? And what will you tell them? 'An insane Mettai woman is on her way here, spreading disease wherever she goes.' Or do you have it in mind to do more? Do you intend to kill her?"

"Now who's doing the goading?"

"It's a fair question, Besh. You speak of stopping her. But how? If she's capable of killing so many, do you truly believe you can reason with her, convince her to stop? Because I don't think you can. If all this is true—if she's really out there killing the Y'Qatt—there will be no reasoning with her. You'll have to use force. You'll have to take her life to spare the lives of others. And I'm asking you, friend to friend, if you're prepared to do that."

Besh looked away and took a long breath. He'd thought of this already, and had come to the startling realization that he was ready to kill the woman if the need arose. Reading Sylpa's journal, he had come to understand Lici, perhaps even to pity her. Though he didn't care for her as he did for Sylpa, he couldn't bring himself to hate her. But she had become something darker and more dangerous than a young girl whose heart had been twisted by a cruel fate, or an old woman desperate to avenge old wounds before she died. Pyav had called her evil a moment before, and that seemed the right word. Whatever the cause of her pain, however just her rage and grief, she had become a demon, murdering indiscriminately, destroying the lives of people who had done her no harm at all. He couldn't allow that to continue.

He met the eldest's gaze once more, and nodded slowly.

"Yes, Pyav," he said. "If need be, I'll kill her."

The blacksmith's eyes widened, but Besh didn't give him a chance to speak.

"You think me old, kindly, a good man. And I may be all of those things. But I've been a husband and a father and now a grandfather. I would have killed to protect Ema and Elica. I'd kill today to keep Mihas safe. Lici is a threat not only to the Y'Qatt, but also to the Mettai. Our people are hated enough without some madwoman menacing the land using blood magic to destroy villages." He pulled his knife free and dragged the blade across the back of his hand. Blood began to flow from the wound, spreading into the fine lines that time had etched into his brown skin. Making a fist, he held up his hand for the eldest to see. "I swear this oath to you, Pyav—Mettai to Mettai, friend to friend, elder to eldest—if Lici can be stopped, I'll stop her. I won't return to our village until I've made good my oath." He lowered his hand, never taking his eyes off the eldest, and licked away the blood before returning his knife to its sheath.

Pyav shook his head slowly. "I fear you're nearly as mad as she is, making an oath like that."

Besh grinned, feeling his face color. He'd offered the blood oath on impulse—it wasn't at all something he would usually have done. But according to Mettai law, once made, such an oath could only be broken on pain of death. And that was all right, because when Elica heard of what he had done, she'd probably kill him.

"Is it madness wanting to protect my family and my people?"

"In this case, yes."

"Why? Because I'm old?"

Pyav nodded. "Because you're old. Because Lici is quite likely insane. Because you don't know where she is, or where she might go next. Blood and bone, Besh! This is mad in so many different ways I hardly know where to begin!" He rubbed a hand over his face. "And now I have no choice but to let you go."

"You could kill me and save Elica the trouble."

The eldest stared at him for a moment, then burst out laughing. "I'd forgotten about Elica. And here I thought that Lici was the dangerous one."

Besh shook his head. "After facing my daughter, going after Lici will be like paddling downstream."

Pyav's smile faded slowly. "I should go with you," he said after some time.

"No. I'm going precisely so that no one else will have to. I'll go alone."

"You have a better chance of succeeding if someone is with you. If this is as important as you say it is, you'll let me accompany you."

Besh could hear the frustration in the blacksmith's voice. The blood oath, he realized, had changed everything. It was up to Besh now to decide how he was to fulfill his vow; just as Besh would be put to death if he failed, another Mettai was subject to the same punishment if he or she did anything to interfere. Though Pyav was eldest, he was powerless in this matter.

"As I've already said, you're needed here."

"And you're a stubborn fool." Pyav shook his head again. "Will you at least allow me to give you some food to take along? The village owes you that much."

"Gladly. Thank you, Eldest."

"You won't like this idea, but you may need some gold as well. I'd suggest you take it from Lici's house."

Besh considered this. He'd fought long and hard to keep anyone from taking the old woman's coins. But knowing what he did now about all she had done, he felt justified in making an exception. He nodded once. "I'll do that," he said. "Tonight, after dark."

"Good." Abruptly, it seemed that Pyav didn't know what to say. "When will you go?" he finally asked.

"Tomorrow, with first light."

"What would you have me tell the others?"

"The other elders, you mean?"

"The elders, the rest of the villagers. Whoever asks."

Besh shrugged. "Tell them whatever you think is best. The truth is fine as far as I'm concerned, but I'll leave that to you."

"Very well." They fell into another awkward silence until at last the eldest extended a meaty hand. Besh took it, and Pyav placed his other hand over Besh's, which looked tiny by comparison. "Gods keep you safe, Besh, and return you to us."

"Thank you, Eldest."

"I'll have the food brought to your home before dark."

"Not too much," Besh said. "I'll have only the one carry sack." He grinned. "And after all, I'm an old man."

Pyav grinned in return. "I'll try to keep that in mind." He released Besh's hand. "'Til we meet again, Besh."

"Be well, Eldest. May the gods smile on you and your family and keep our village safe."

He turned away and started toward his home, wondering if this would be the last time he made this walk.

Cam was playing out front when he came within sight of the house. It was early still for Mihas and Annze to be back from their lessons.

"Grandfather!" the boy cried out, running to him. Besh found himself blinking back tears. Somehow he'd managed to convince himself that he wasn't needed, but what about his own needs? Perhaps it wasn't Elica who was going to kill him; perhaps it was the simple act of walking away from this house and this family.

"Where have you been, Grandfather?" the boy asked, as Besh lifted him into his arms. "Were you at Lici's house again?"

"I was," he said, making himself smile. "And then I went to speak with the eldest."

"Father helped me make a fishing stick. Do you wanna see?"

"Yes, of course."

The boy smiled. "Maybe you can take me fishing later."

His eyes stung. "We'll have to see about that, all right?"

"All right."

He put the boy down and followed him to where the fishing pole rested in the grass. It was a simple pole, much like those Besh himself had made for Elica when she was a girl, and for Mihas when he was Cam's age.

"That's a fine fishing pole," he said.

"It's a fishing stick," Cam said, looking up at him.

"What's the difference?"

"Everybody has fishing poles. Mine's a fishing stick. That's what I call it."

Besh laughed.

Elica came out of the house and glanced in their direction. "I see you've found the fishing stick," she said, walking to the woodpile and gathering kindling for the cooking fire.

"Yes, I have." He looked down at Cam, who was holding the pole, pretending to fish. "I need to speak with your mother," he said, tousling the boy's dark hair. It was as soft as corn silk and as black as raven feathers. *Will I ever touch this head again?*

Cam nodded without even looking up. "All right."

Besh joined Elica by the woodpile and began gathering branches, all the while ignoring his daughter, who was staring at him.

"So?" she said at last. "You have something to say to me?"

"Inside," he said, turning away, climbing the stairs, and stepping into the house.

Elica was just behind him. "Is it the pestilence?" she asked, upon closing the door behind her. The house was dark with the door shut, and her eyes shone with the faint gleam from the single window opposite the hearth. "Everyone's talking about it in the marketplace. It is, isn't it?"

"No," Besh said. "It's not the pestilence. It's Lici."

She scowled at him. "Not this again."

"Listen to me. When Lici was a young girl the pestilence ravaged her village, killing her family and nearly everyone else she knew. She managed to survive and she went for help. She wound up finding an Y'Qatt village, and they refused to help her."

"Father, I don't—"

"Keep quiet and listen!" he said sharply.

She glared at him, but held her tongue.

"This talk of the pestilence in the north isn't groundless—there is something. It began not long after Lici left here, and as far as we can tell, the disease has only struck at Y'Qatt villages, all of them close to Sentaya, the village in which she was born."

She sat down slowly, staring at him still, an appalled look on her fine features. "You think she's doing this?"

"I think it's possible."

"But how?"

"Magic," Sirj said, emerging from the back room.

"What do you know about it?" Elica asked.

Her husband shook his head. Dark hair fell in his eyes and he brushed it away. "Not a lot. When I was a child my grandmother used to speak to us of dark conjurings. I think she did it to scare us, because she thought it was fun, for us as well as for her. She refused to actually do any of the magic she described, but she said she'd seen some of it done right here in Kirayde. At the time she refused to tell us who it was that did it. But later—when I was older—she told me it was Lici."

"What kind of conjurings?" Besh asked.

Sirj shrugged. "This comes from my grandmother, you understand. But she said that Lici had a dispute with a friend of hers and put a spell on the friend's dog. That night it was ill, and by the next morning it was dead."

"A dog?" Elica demanded. "You think killing a dog and killing off a village are the same thing?"

"Of course they're not," Besh said before Sirj could answer. "But they're not as far apart as you might think."

"You're serious about this," she said.

"Serious enough to have made a blood oath to the eldest."

Her eyes narrowed. "What kind of blood oath?"

Besh held her gaze. "There's only one kind."

"What is it you swore to do?" She appeared to be trembling, though she sounded more angry than frightened. Then, that was her way, just as it had been her mother's.

"I swore that I'd find Lici, and keep her from doing any more harm."

Elica closed her eyes. "Oh, Father."

"Do you even know where she is?" Sirj asked.

"We know where she's been. That's a start at least."

"Pyav will let you do this?" his daughter asked, eyeing him again, looking as if she'd half a mind to find the eldest and thrash him.

"It was a blood oath, Elica," Besh said. "He had no choice."

"Why would you do this, Father? What is it about that woman that moves you so?"

He probably could have explained it again. Certainly Elica had asked him this plenty of times, as had the eldest. But in truth, Besh was no longer certain. Did he do this for his family, for his friends, for the entire village? Did he do it for Sylpa, or perhaps for Lici herself—not the twisted old woman, but the sad, scared little girl he'd read about these past few days? Or was it more complicated than that?

Offering that oath had been foolish, impetuous. It had been the act of a far younger man. He'd told Pyav that this wasn't the sad attempt of an old man to make himself a hero, but now he wasn't so certain. A part of him hungered to see the world one last time, to wage a battle against something or someone more formidable than the grasses invading his garden.

Could it be that this had nothing to do with Sylpa or Lici or Elica? Probably it was a question that should have frightened him, made him question the oath he'd sworn, perhaps even the soundness of his mind. Instead, it made him want to laugh. He was tired of being wise old Besh, who sat in council with the other elders and tended to his goldroot. He wanted more from these last years of his life, even if it meant an early, violent end.

He couldn't tell his daughter all of this, of course. She'd never understand. She'd simply think him a fool, and in a way she'd be right.

So he gave her another answer, one that also was true. "I do this because if I don't, no one else will. And I believe it must be done."

"And you go alone?" Sirj asked.

"There's no one else to go," Besh told him. "Others have children to care for or trades that would keep them from leaving. Pyav offered to come with me, but this village needs its eldest."

"And you're not needed?" Elica said. "Is that it?"

Besh started to say something clever, but then stopped himself, seeing that there were tears on her cheeks. He crossed to where she sat and knelt before her, taking her hands in his. "I'm not needed as you are, or as Pyav is. This isn't to say that I'm not loved. I know better. But as it is I haven't many years left. If something should happen to me, the rest of you will be fine."

She didn't rail at him, nor did she argue the point. She merely stared into his eyes, and, after several moments, nodded once. He could see how scared she was, but he sensed as well that she was trying to mask her fear, for his sake, as well as for her own. It was as much as she could do just then.

"All right," she said at last. "I suppose we have no choice but to do our best."

He lifted her hands to his lips and kissed them. "Thank you," he whispered.

She smiled, though there were still tears coursing down her cheeks. Like her mother before her, she was wise and strong. He truly believed what he had told her a moment ago: she and her family would be fine.

"I'll go with you."

They both looked up at Sirj, whose expression hadn't changed at all. It almost seemed that someone else had spoken.

"What did you say?" Besh asked.

"You heard me," the man said. "I'll go with you. Elica's right: You shouldn't do this alone."

"No," Besh said, standing. In the past few turns he'd come to accept that he had been wrong about Sirj, that the man had a better mind and a stouter heart than Besh had believed. But still, Besh had no desire to spend so much time in the man's company, nor did he want to put the father of his grandchildren in danger. At that moment, he couldn't have said for certain which was the stronger impulse.

"You need to stay here," he said. "With me gone, Elica and the children will need you more than ever."

Sirj kept still.

Besh turned to his daughter. "Tell him," he said. "Surely you don't want him wandering off like this, leaving the rest of you behind."

"I don't want either of you to."

"But what of the children? You need him here."

"Yes, she does," Sirj said. "But you'll need me more."

Sirj crossed to Elica and took both her hands in his. Besh expected her to fight him on this, but once again she surprised him. They merely stood there for several moments, their eyes locked. It was something Besh and Ema would have done and after a moment Besh looked away, feeling that he was intruding on their privacy simply by watching.

"He's right," Elica said at last.

Looking at her, Besh saw that there were fresh tears on her face.

"I can manage," she went on. "You need him with you."

"This isn't what I want," Besh said. He looked from one of them to the other. "I'm going because I can—I don't want this burden falling on anyone else."

"If by this burden you mean Lici," Sirj said, "I think everyone in this village shares it already. You can no more claim it as your own than you can the rill or the marketplace."

"You need to take care of your family."

Sirj grinned. "You are my family. You may not like to admit it, but it's true."

Besh blinked, opened his mouth, then closed it again.

"You've silenced him," Elica said, smiling, though she was crying still. "I've been trying to do that since I was six years old."

Sirj's grin lingered, but he didn't answer. He just watched Besh, as if waiting for him to admit defeat.

"Father?"

He should have known what to say. Probably Sirj deserved an apology for the way Besh had treated him all these years. Certainly he should have thanked the man for making this sacrifice. But at that moment his pride wouldn't allow any of it.

"Fine then," he said at last, turning away from them both and starting toward the small room where he slept. "If you're going to insist on coming along, you'd better gather your things. That's what I intend to do."

"You'll need food," Elica said.

"Pyav is seeing to that. It'll be here before nightfall."

He didn't wait for them to say more. Once in his room, Besh pulled out his travel sack and began to fill it. A change of clothes, a woolen overshirt, a waterskin, an extra blade, and his fire flint. After a few moments he sat on his pallet, realizing that his hands were trembling.

"Damn," he muttered, not quite certain what it was that had put him in such a state.

"Father?"

He turned and saw Elica standing in the doorway, her brow creased with concern.

"You should be helping him pack his things."

"He sent me to help you."

Besh looked away, twisting his mouth sourly.

She came and sat beside him on the bed. "He's a good man, you know; better than you've ever been willing to admit." She paused, and then, "Why is that?"

"I don't want to talk about this right now."

"Well, I don't know if I'm ever going to see you again," she said, suddenly angry again, "so you're damn well going to talk about it!"

He faced her once more.

"Tell me, Father! What did Sirj do to deserve your contempt? I have a right to know! He's in the next room preparing to follow you on this mad errand of yours! He's ready to get himself killed trying to keep you safe! So if you're going to steal my husband from me—if you're going to leave my children fatherless—I have a right to know why you've treated him like a cur all these years!"

"I don't know," he said softly.

She shook her head. "That's not an answer."

"It's the truth. I've been asking myself the same question, and I simply don't know. I decided long ago that I didn't like him. Maybe it was the same thing that made your grandfather hate me so."

Her eyes widened in surprise. "Grandfather hated you? Why?"

Besh shrugged and smiled. "I loved his daughter. I wasn't the strongest or the smartest or the best, and I had the audacity to love his daughter. And what was worse, she loved me."

Elica sat for some time, staring at the floor, her forehead creased. At last she lifted her gaze, meeting his. "Why are fathers such fools?"

Besh laughed. "I wish I knew." He looked away briefly, but quickly made himself face her again. "I was wrong about him. Sirj is a good man, and a fine father. And for what it's worth, I'll do my best to keep him safe. I may be an old man, but I've been wielding my blade for a long time, and I know something about magic."

She kissed his cheek. "That's worth a good deal, Father. To Sirj and to me." She stood and surveyed his small room. "Do you need any help getting ready?"

"No. I can do it on my own."

Elica nodded and left him.

For several moments after she was gone Besh didn't move. He felt too weary to stand, much less venture into Y'Qatt lands and do battle with a crazed Mettai witch. Despite all that he'd said to Elica he still didn't relish the notion of having Sirj with him as he searched for Lici. He and Sirj had nothing to say to each other; at least they hadn't for the past dozen years. Better to be alone than with a man he didn't understand. But somehow it seemed that choice had been taken from him, as if his being old gave others the right to make decisions on his behalf.

At least you'll have someone to carry all the food Pyav has promised you. Ema's voice. Besh grinned. Had she still been alive, she would have taken his hand to soften the remark. He could almost feel her fingers touching his. He tried to force himself into motion once more. He still had a few more things to pack, and he should have helped Elica prepare the evening meal this last time. But he couldn't bring himself to move. He just sat on the bed, staring at the scars on the back of his hand. At one point he heard voices he didn't recognize out in the kitchen and he expected that Elica would come and get him. But she didn't, and still he sat.

The light began to fade and the house filled with the aromas of roasted fowl and boiled greens.

"Grandfather?"

Besh looked up. Mihas stood in the doorway, peering at him with wide eyes, as if he feared what Besh might say to him.

The old man smiled. "Come here, boy."

Mihas walked to the bed and sat beside him.

"Your mother told you?"

"My father."

"You have questions for me?"

He hesitated, but only briefly. "Are you going to fight her? Lici, I mean. Are you and Lici going to fight?"

"I don't know, Mihas. I hope it won't come to that, but she's hurting people right now, and we can't let her do that."

"What if she . . . what if she hurts you? Or Papa?"

Hurts. Kills. The word didn't really matter; Besh knew what the boy was asking.

"She's not going to kill your father," he said. "I promise you that. Your father is coming with me to make certain that I make it back to all of you safely. I'm not a young man anymore." He smiled; Mihas didn't. "Anyway, I won't let anything happen to him. And when the time comes, I'll face Lici alone."

"But that's—" He broke off, shaking his head. "What about you?"

Besh shrugged. "I can't make any promises about me. I'm in no hurry to die, and I certainly don't want Lici to be the one to send me to Bian's realm. But I don't know what's going to happen. My magic doesn't flow that strong."

"Then don't go," Mihas said, staring at the floor.

Besh bent lower and looked at the boy, forcing Mihas to meet his gaze. "Do you really mean that? Do you really think that I should stay here and let all those people die? Is that the kind of man you think I am? Is that the kind of man you want to be?"

"No," the boy said grudgingly.

"Of course it's not. And that leaves us with no choice. I have to go, and you have to help your mother care for your sister and brother." Besh made himself stand. "I imagine it's time for us to eat," he said, forcing a smile. "It must be, because I'm pretty hungry."

"Do you remember what I told you about Nissa's father?" Mihas asked.

"Nissa's father?"

"He said that wherever Old Lici walks, four ravens circle above her. And you said that he might be right."

Besh nodded, the conversation coming back to him. "Seems he was even more right than we knew."

"But the ravens—"

"The death omen. That doesn't mean me, Mihas, at least not necessarily. Lici has already done plenty to fulfill a thousand death omens. Maybe . . ." He faltered, unsure as to whether to put the thought into words. After a moment he decided the boy was old enough to hear him say it. "Maybe the next death will be her own." He held out a hand. "Now come with me to supper."

The boy stood and took Besh's hand, and together they walked out into the common room, where the others were already eating. Elica and Sirj looked up as the two of them sat, but neither of them said anything, and the meal passed in almost complete silence.

After, as Elica bathed the little ones, Besh left the house and made his way to Lici's. The sky still glowed faintly in the west, but a few pale stars had emerged overhead and the lanes of the village were dark and quiet. A turn before, Besh would have needed a torch to find his way through Lici's house, but not anymore. It was almost as familiar to him as his own home.

He quickly found the pouch of coins in the back room, carried it to the window at the front of the house, and in the dim light that remained, counted out twenty sovereigns. He returned the sack of money to its place in the wooden box, though not before taking out Sylpa's daybook. He started to leave with it, thought better of it, and put it back in the box beneath the coins. He almost made it to the door, but then returned to the back room and pulled it out again. This time, he didn't change his mind, though once outside he hesitated again, and had to remind himself of all that Lici had wrought with her magic.

"I might need it," he said aloud, as if Sylpa were listening. "Who knows what else I might learn from what's in here?"

The breeze freshened briefly, rustling the leaves of the trees above him.

"If Lici and I both survive, I'll give it back to her. I swear it."

He expected no response, of course, but it almost seemed that someone was watching him, listening to his oath and making note of it. Besh hurried home.

Sirj was waiting for him in front of their house, sitting on the tree stump and gazing up at the stars. A single candle burned in one of the windows, casting a faint yellow light, but Besh could barely see the man.

"Elica wanted me to tell you that someone came from the village with a sack of food earlier, while you were still in your room. We forgot to mention it while we were eating."

Besh nodded. "Thank you. That's good to know."

"I've put most of it in my travel sack, but I couldn't fit it all."

"That's fine. I can carry my share."

Sirj nodded, and they both fell silent.

After several moments, the man nodded at the journal in Besh's hand. "What's that?"

Besh felt his face color and was glad to be standing in the shadows. "It's Sylpa's daybook," he said. "I thought it might be helpful as we search for Lici."

Sirj nodded.

"I took a bit of her money as well. The eldest suggested it."

"I'm sure we'll be glad to have it."

Another silence. Besh wondered how he would endure the man day after day.

"You don't have to do this, you know," he said. "I was prepared to go alone. I still am."

"I'm not doing it because I have to."

"Then why?"

"I told you: You're my family. Besides, Elica won't rest a single night while you're gone. You think I want to stay here for that?"

Besh laughed in spite of himself.

Sirj stood and patted Besh's shoulder before starting toward the front door. "You'll see," he said. "It won't be so bad."

Besh said nothing, and long after Sirj had disappeared into the house, he remained where he was, grappling with the realization that he didn't want Sirj with him for one simple reason. He'd never be able to face his daughter or grandchildren if something happened to the man.

Chapter 17

Jynna sat with Etan atop the tallest of the low grassy hills that over-
looked the plain and lakelands, gazing back eastward to where the ruins
of Tivston still darkened the landscape. There was no smoke anymore,
and the great flocks of crows and kites had moved on, leaving the bones
of her family and friends and neighbors to dry and whiten in the harsh
sunlight. Birds still circled over what remained of her home, but only a
few, the sad unfortunates who had arrived too late for the feast.

Etan hadn't said much since that first day when T'Noth, T'Kaar, and
S'Doryn found him with the others. None of the children had. Even
Jynna spoke only occasionally, though she had been the first to meet the
Fal'Borna, and had come to trust all three of the men who were caring
for them now, even T'Kaar. She simply had little to say. Her thoughts
were consumed with memories of her family, grief at the loss of all she
had known and loved. When the men asked questions of her, she answered. When they asked her to speak on their behalf to the other children, she did as they requested. The rest of the time she kept to herself,
or sat with Etan, saying nothing, but taking comfort from the mere fact
that he was there, feeling the same things she was.

Vettala sat a short distance from them, also saying nothing, also looking to the east. She was three years younger than Jynna and Etan, and like
them, she had come through that horrible night of disease and wanton
magic without injury. She was a pretty girl, fine-featured with long sil-
very hair and deep golden eyes. Jynna remembered her having a nice
smile and a loud bubbling laugh, but she had to trust all to her recollections, for Vettala hadn't made a sound in these eight days. She avoided all
of them. Aside from those times when the children were forced to ride,
sharing mounts with the Fal'Borna men, she didn't allow anyone to come
near her. She ran away from the wounded children—Hev, the older boy

who lost his hand to his father's shaping magic; Pelda and Sebbi, sisters burned on their faces and hands and chests by the fire that consumed their home. She refused even to look at the Fal'Borna.

But it seemed that she drew some comfort from having Jynna and Etan nearby. She followed them everywhere, keeping her distance, but also keeping them in sight. Under any other circumstance Jynna would have been annoyed by this; probably she would have tried to run away from the girl. In an odd way, though, she understood. Etan did, too. They made no effort to include her in their conversations or tell her where they were headed each time she started to follow them. But they let her follow, and they kept an eye on her, making certain that she came to no harm.

Jynna wasn't certain what the girl would do once they returned to Lowna and she found herself surrounded by the Fal'Borna. She wasn't even sure that Vettala understood that they would be headed to the city before this day was out. S'Doryn had tried to explain this much to all of them over the past several days, as they awaited the end of their isolation. Vettala, however, had given no indication that she cared or even understood.

Jynna was ashamed to admit it, but she had avoided the injured children as well. She didn't run from them, and when forced to be near them, she tried to be as kind as she could be. But she never chose to be with them. The truth was she felt sorry for them and guilty for having escaped injury. Had her father not sent her away, she might well have been burned or killed herself. None of the other children said anything of the sort to her, but they didn't have to. She knew it was true. So she kept her distance. She avoided T'Kaar as well. Though she trusted that he meant her no harm, she hadn't liked him from the beginning. While others in Lowna had been willing to believe her tale and accept her as one of their own when it became clear that she had lost her family, he continued to doubt her. She liked his younger brother, T'Noth, and S'Doryn, though she even tried to keep away from them at times. Both of them asked her questions constantly. Do you recall seeing anyone unusual in the market that day? Is there more you can tell us about the sickness that took your parents? What else do you remember?

I remember everything! she wanted to scream at them. *I remember it all, and I just want to forget!*

That was why she stayed with Etan. He didn't ask her anything. He didn't bear any scars from that night, at least none that she could see. He was just like her: sad and scared and desperate to think about anything other than their last day in Tivston.

If only they would let her.

"Here he comes again," Etan said softly, nodding toward the bottom of the hill.

S'Doryn was trudging up the slope, the morning sun at his back so that his shadow reached up the hill, darkening the golden grasses. She'd spotted him several moments before, and she merely nodded.

"He'll ask you more questions," Etan told her.

Jynna nodded at this as well.

"They have to let us live with them, right?" he said. "Even if we can't tell them anything?"

"They don't have to, but they will."

She was mostly certain of this. S'Doryn and T'Noth were too nice to leave them out here alone after all they'd been through. But she wasn't totally sure, which was why she tried to answer the questions as well as she could. Her father and brothers had spoken of the Fal'Borna; of how fierce they were in battle, and of how wary they remained of outsiders. She saw how T'Kaar looked at her still, and she knew this last was true. She remembered U'Selle, the a'laq from Lowna, and she wondered if the woman would welcome the Y'Qatt back to the village if Jynna didn't tell these men what they needed to know. U'Selle had seemed fair-minded, but as a'laq she could do nothing that might endanger her people. What if that included letting Jynna and the others stay with them?

"Try to remember, Jynna," Etan whispered as S'Doryn drew nearer. "It'll be better if you remember."

"I *am* trying," she shot back in a low voice.

They didn't have time for more.

"We've been looking for you," the Fal'Borna said, as he reached the top of the hill. He was slightly out of breath, and tiny beads of sweat covered his brow. His bright yellow eyes flicked toward Vettala. "For all three of you, actually. We'll be leaving soon, returning to Lowna."

"So you are taking us with you," Etan said.

S'Doryn frowned, though there was a bit of a smile on his lips. "Of course we are. You thought we'd leave you here?"

Etan shrugged and wouldn't look at him again. After several moments, the Fal'Borna glanced at Jynna, a question in his eyes.

"I haven't been able to answer your questions," she said. "We were afraid you were angry with us."

He shook his head and smiled, the kind smile she remembered from the first morning she met him. An instant later, though, his brow creased again. "No," he said. "We're not angry. If we thought you were keeping things from us on purpose, then maybe we'd be angry. But I don't think you're doing that."

"We're not."

"Tell me about the woman again," he said. "The Mettai." They'd been through this before. Then again, they'd been through everything at least two or three times, and the old woman was the only odd thing that Jynna could recall from that last day in Tivston.

"What do you want to know?" Jynna asked, her voice flat.

"When you found her, she was doing magic. Isn't that right?"

"Yes. She was in a thicket of trees, with her baskets spread out around her."

"And do you know what she was doing to them?"

"I've told you. I know, but I can't say. I promised her."

"Jynna, there's a good chance that this woman is dead by now, killed by the same pestilence that took your family."

"What if she's not?"

"What if she's responsible for what happened to your village?" S'Doryn answered.

"She isn't."

"What if she lied to you, Jynna? What if none of what she told you about the magic she was doing was true?"

Jynna shook her head and opened her mouth to deny it, but then she stopped herself. Maybe S'Doryn was right. How much did she really know about the woman? Hadn't she been afraid of her at first? Hadn't she tried to run away?

"She was coloring her baskets," she finally said, her voice low.

"Coloring them?"

"Mettai baskets are supposed to be made by hand and dyed by hand, too. They're less valuable if they're colored by magic. But she had some new ones that she needed to color, and she hadn't brought her dyes with her."

"And that's what she was doing when you found her."

She nodded. "She made me swear that I wouldn't tell. And when I promised, she gave me another basket."

S'Doryn nodded slowly, but he was frowning still, as if deep in thought. "So she only had out a few of her baskets."

Jynna stared at him. "What?"

"Well, you make it sound as though she only needed to color a small number of baskets. The new ones, right? So if that's the case, she would have had out only those that needed coloring."

Jynna shook her head slowly. "She had all of them out." Her stomach felt queasy and her mouth had gone dry.

"You're certain?"

She nodded, feeling more ill by the moment. Had the woman lied to her? If she wasn't coloring the baskets, what was she really doing to them? "I helped her pack them up and carry them to the marketplace. She had all of them out, spread in a half circle."

"And you're certain she was really using magic on them."

"She'd cut herself. That's how they do it, right? They use their blood?"

"Yes."

"She was doing magic, then." A tear rolled down her cheek and then another.

"Jynna—"

"It's my fault," she sobbed. "I should have run and found my father as soon as I saw her. That's what I started to do, but she called me back and I listened to her."

"We don't know anything for certain, not yet."

"But she lied to me!"

S'Doryn hesitated. "She may have, yes."

"She must have been doing something to those baskets. Why else would she lie? She put a curse on them or something. She made everyone sick."

"Not you," he said. "You say you handled the baskets?"

Jynna nodded, took a long breath, nodded again. Perhaps it wasn't her fault after all. "Yes, I helped her pack them, and she gave me two. One I gave to my teacher, the other I took home to my mother."

S'Doryn opened his hands and smiled. "Well, then it probably wasn't the baskets, right?"

"Right." She actually managed a smile, though it faded quickly. "But then why would she lie to me?"

"Most likely she colored all her baskets with magic, and didn't want you to know. You're right: They are more valuable when they're dyed by hand. She probably was afraid they'd fetch a lower price in the market-place if you knew the truth."

Jynna nodded, feeling better. "Probably."

The smile remained on S'Doryn's face, although it began to seem forced. Jynna could tell that he had more questions for her, but after a few moments, he merely turned and started back down the hill.

"We'll be leaving soon," he said. "You should come down and make sure that you have all your things packed and ready to go. I want to be back in Lowna well before nightfall."

"All right," Jynna said. "We'll be down in a moment."

He nodded and continued down the slope.

She looked at Etan, only to find that he was watching her, a guarded look in his pale eyes.

"What?" she said.

"Do you really think it was your fault?"

"No. You heard S'Doryn. If it was the baskets I would have gotten sick."

"Maybe it wasn't the baskets. Maybe she did something else. My f—" He looked away. "People say that the Mettai are evil. That's why they do blood magic."

"It wasn't her!" Jynna said. But she had her doubts. The Mettai witch had been odd; Jynna had continued to think so even after the woman gave her the baskets and the beautiful flowers.

"It might have been."

"No! It wasn't!"

"Don't fight!"

They both looked behind them at the same time. Vettala was stand-ing a short distance off, her fists clenched, her face looking pale in the sunlight.

Etan and Jynna exchanged glances.

"It's all right, Vettala," Jynna said.

"No, it's not! You can't fight!"

"Why not?" Etan asked.

"You'll make them mad, and they'll send us away, maybe back to the village. They won't take care of us and we'll be all alone again."

"No, they—"

Jynna laid a hand on Etan's arm to stop him.

"It's all right," she said. "We won't fight."

"Promise?"

She nodded. "Promise."

The little girl eyed them both a moment longer. Then she nodded once and started down the hill, following S'Doryn's footsteps. "Come on then," she said, without looking back. "We shouldn't keep them waiting, either."

S'Doryn was still pondering what he'd learned from the girl when he found T'Noth and T'Kaar.

"You look like you've lost something," T'Kaar said, as S'Doryn drew near to where they were sitting.

T'Noth laughed. "That happens as you get old. You'll have to be careful, brother," he added, with a sly look at T'Kaar. "It won't be long before you're misplacing things as well."

"What's wrong?" the older brother asked, ignoring the gibe.

S'Doryn shook his head. "I'm not certain. It's probably nothing."

"Probably," T'Kaar repeated.

"The girl told me a bit more about that old Mettai woman she saw in Tivston the day the pestilence struck."

T'Noth's expression sobered. "What about her?"

"Apparently she was using magic on all of her baskets."

"Didn't we know that already?"

"Yes."

The younger man raised an eyebrow.

"As I say, it's probably nothing. She told Jynna that she was using her magic to color just a few of the baskets. But she had all of them spread out around her."

"So she was coloring all of them. You've done enough trading in your day, S'Doryn. You know how much more a Mettai can get for baskets that are colored by hand."

"That's what Jynna and I decided."

The brothers shared a look.

"So, then there's more?" T'Noth asked.

"No. That's it. I know it makes no sense, but something about that woman bothers me. I can't help thinking that she did something else to those people, aside from whatever it was that she did to those baskets."

"But if Jynna—"

"I know. She spent more time with the woman than anyone. She should have gotten sick, too. But then again, all our survivors are children. Maybe whatever the woman did had no effect on Jynna because she was too young."

The two brothers appeared to consider this for several moments.

Finally, T'Kaar stood. "I'm going to check on the others," he said, walking away. "I'll make certain they're ready for the ride back."

S'Doryn nodded and watched him walk away. T'Kaar could be difficult at times, but he was a good man. He'd spent hours with the wounded children, healing their injuries and comforting them in their grief. S'Doryn had been reluctant to let the man accompany them on this journey, but he was glad now that T'Kaar had come along.

"Why would she do it?"

He looked over at T'Noth. "What?"

"Assuming for a moment that the Mettai woman was somehow responsible for what happened, why would she have done it? Do the Mettai hate Qirsi that much? Do they hate the Y'Qatt?"

"Truly, my friend, I don't know. I've never heard of any feud between Qirsi and Mettai. More to the point, I don't know how she might have done it. I know little about blood magic and Mettai spells."

"S'Doryn!"

He turned. T'Kaar was already walking back in their direction, his strides long and purposeful.

"What is it?"

"All three children recall seeing baskets in their homes the day their families fell ill. And two of them remember seeing at least one of their parents speaking with the woman in the marketplace."

S'Doryn felt himself grow cold. "Demons and fire."

"It could mean nothing," T'Noth said, though judging from the young man's expression, it seemed he didn't believe this any more than S'Doryn did.

"What do we do?" T'Kaar asked.

S'Doryn started toward the horses. "We ride home, speak to U'Selle and the clan council of what we've learned."

The brothers said nothing, but when S'Doryn glanced back, T'Noth was just behind him, and T'Kaar was on his way to the injured children. S'Doryn called for Jynna, Etan, and Vettala, and in less than an hour, everything was packed and tied to the horses, and all of them were ready to go.

The ride back to Lowna took less than half a day, and upon reaching the village, S'Doryn and the two brothers carried the wounded children to the healers for further care. N'Tevva was there to greet them, as was T'Kaar's wife and child. S'Doryn would have liked to take N'Tevva home and to bed—eight days was too long to be away from her. But it was a measure of how concerned he was about this Mettai witch wandering the land that he merely kissed her and asked her to follow as he led Jynna, Etan, and their little shadow to the a'laq's home. U'Selle was waiting for them in an old weathered chair outside her house. She was taken by a fit of coughing as they approached, and for some time after they stopped before her, she was unable to speak. Eventually, though, the paroxysm ran its course, and the a'laq managed a wan smile.

"You survived, I see."

S'Doryn grinned. "Yes, A'Laq."

"That's nearly more than I can say for myself." She turned to Jynna. "It seems you're one of us now."

The girl bowed. "Yes, A'Laq."

"You're welcome here, but I am sorry. I had hoped that you might find that your family had survived." She eyed the other two children before meeting S'Doryn's gaze again. "You did find survivors."

"Not many—not nearly enough—and all were children."

She pressed her lips thin for just a moment, but then made herself smile again. "And fine children they appear to be. What's your name, boy?"

"Etan, A'Laq."

"Welcome, Etan. Are you prepared to become one of us, to be a Fal'Borna warrior when you grow to manhood?"

The boy dropped his gaze. "I think so."

"Etan!" Jynna said.

But U'Selle smiled. "It's all right, Jynna. That's a good enough answer for now." She looked at Vettala, who shrank away from her gaze, hiding behind Jynna. "What's your name, girl?"

The little one said nothing.

"She's Vettala," Jynna said at last.

U'Selle raised an eyebrow. "She can't answer for herself?"

"She hasn't spoken since . . . since the outbreak," S'Doryn said quietly.

"She said something today," Etan said.

Everyone looked at him.

The boy's cheeks shaded to crimson. "It's true! She told Jynna and me not to fight."

The a'laq appeared to stifle a grin. "Sage counsel from one so young. Very well, Jynna. You may speak on Vettala's behalf until she's ready to speak for herself."

"Thank you, A'Laq."

U'Selle looked at S'Doryn again. "We didn't know that you'd bring others back, so we haven't made any arrangements for them yet. You can take Jynna?"

He looked at N'Tevva.

"Of course we can," she said, smiling. "Gladly."

They'd never had children of their own, and S'Doryn had given up hoping for them long ago. He knew that N'Tevva had as well. But the gods worked in strange and wondrous ways. It seemed they were to be parents after all.

He placed a hand on Jynna's shoulder. "Is that all right with you?" he asked her.

She nodded, though there were tears in her eyes. He could only imagine how hard this must be for her, for all the children.

"I believe that Etan might be happy with T'Noth," he said after a moment, "at least for the time being."

The a'laq smiled. "Is that all right with you, Etan?"

"Yes, A'Laq."

"Good. And perhaps Vettala can stay with me." The woman smiled kindly, but Vettala gave a small cry and buried her face into Jynna's dress. U'Selle's smile gave way to a grimace and she looked at S'Doryn once more. "Perhaps it would be best if you took them both for now," she said. "We can see how matters stand after a few days."

"Of course, A'Laq."

"She doesn't mean anything by it, A'Laq," Jynna said, concern on her pale features. "She's just scared still."

"It's all right, Jynna. I understand. And I think she's very fortunate to have such a good friend."

"With your permission, A'Laq," S'Doryn said, "we've ridden a long way. I'm sure the children are even hungrier than I am."

"Of course, S'Doryn. We'll speak again later."

S'Doryn bowed to her, and he and N'Tevva led the children away from the a'laq's cottage. They walked Etan to T'Noth's house before continuing on to their own. Along the way, S'Doryn wondered how they were going to fit them both. They hadn't a lot of space and while finding a bed for Jynna wasn't a problem, he didn't know where they'd put Vettala. In the end, however, it seemed less of a problem than he had feared it might be. Vettala never strayed from Jynna's side, and when Jynna asked the younger child if she wanted to share a bed for the first few nights, Vettala nodded enthusiastically.

T'Noth and Etan joined them for the evening meal. N'Tevva had made plenty, no doubt anticipating that he would be hungry. She might have even known that T'Noth would join them; he often did. After they'd eaten their fill of stew and greens and dark bread, the children went outside, leaving the adults alone. S'Doryn wasn't sure if they intended to play or merely to speak where they couldn't be heard. It seemed to him that Jynna and Etan had every bit as much to discuss as did he and N'Tevva. His wife, though, appeared concerned as she watched them leave the house.

"They've traveled a long way today," she said, frowning. "And they've been through so much. Shouldn't we put them to bed?"

"We will soon," he told her. "But not quite yet. I imagine they need some time to themselves, without us around. The sooner they begin to feel comfortable here, the better for all of us."

She nodded, though she continued to glance anxiously toward the door. It had only been a few hours, but already she was trying to protect them as might their natural mother.

Before long, S'Doryn, N'Tevva, and T'Noth were joined by

U'Selle. N'Tevva offered her some food, but the a'laq refused, and was taken by another coughing fit.

When she could speak again, she asked about the eight days they'd spent in the hills with the children.

"Did you learn anything from them?" she asked.

S'Doryn briefly described Jynna's encounter with the Mettai woman.

For several moments after he finished, the a'laq merely stared at the floor. "It does all sound a bit odd," she finally muttered, "but really that's all. I don't see how this woman could have anything to do with an outbreak of the pestilence."

"Couldn't she use magic to put a curse on the people she met?" T'Noth asked.

She actually smiled. "A curse? I think you've listened to too many tales of Mettai blood magic." She shook her head. "As far as I understand it, Mettai magic is not all that different from our own. Yes, it comes from blood and earth, but their powers run no deeper than our own."

"They wouldn't have to run deeper," S'Doryn said. "They'd just need to be . . . different. We have healers who can mend wounds and tame fevers. Couldn't they just as easily cause illness as cure it?"

She frowned, but a moment later she conceded the point with a shrug. "I suppose. But you're assuming that she did far more than that. For any of this to make sense, she would have had to make herself immune."

"Or," T'Noth said, "she would have had to create a disease that strikes only at Qirsi."

"At Qirsi adults," S'Doryn corrected.

"Or at Qirsi magic."

All of them looked at N'Tevva.

"That makes more sense than directing it at adults," she said. "Doesn't it?"

S'Doryn shuddered, knowing that she was right. "Yes, it does."

"I asked this of S'Doryn in the hills," T'Noth said. "And now I'll ask you, A'Laq. What do we do about this?"

"About what?" U'Selle answered, sounding frustrated. "We have only a tale told to us by a child." She raised a hand, seeming to anticipate S'Doryn's objection. "I know she's clever, and I believe her to be honest, but I also know that she's been through a terrible ordeal. Her life these past nine days has been a waking nightmare. How do we separate what she truly saw from those things that haunted her sleep or grew from her imagination? None of us has seen this woman. Did you even see her baskets?"

"I didn't," S'Doryn said. "But according to T'Kaar, the other children remember seeing baskets in their homes that day."

She nodded. "Well, that's something at least. But do they confirm the rest?"

He shook his head. "No. That comes from Jynna alone."

"I see."

"I believe her," S'Doryn said.

T'Noth nodded. "I do, too."

A small smile crossed U'Selle's lips. "To tell you the truth, I'd be inclined to as well. But I'm not certain what we can do about it. Even if we take as true everything that Jynna told you, we wouldn't know where to begin searching for this woman."

T'Noth shook his head. "So we do nothing," he said, his voice flat.

"For now. Keep talking to the children. Learn as much as you can from them. And in the meantime, I'll speak with the a'laqs on the plain and along the wash. Perhaps they'll know something about this woman."

"Thank you, A'Laq."

She smiled and stood, patting T'Noth on the shoulder as she stepped past him. "You both did well," she said, pausing in the doorway. "I hadn't foreseen the coming of these children into our village, but now that they're here, I think each will be a blessing to us in his or her own way. Good night, N'Tevva. I believe those girls will be very happy to have you around, after spending so many nights with nothing but Fal'Borna men and their horses."

The two women laughed, as did S'Doryn. T'Noth smiled as well, though he looked a bit confused.

Once U'Selle was gone their mirth faded, leaving them all silent and pensive. It was growing dark outside, and after a time N'Tevva went in search of the children. Left alone, S'Doryn and T'Noth continued to sit there, saying nothing, S'Doryn staring out the door at the deepening shadows around his home, T'Noth toying with his empty cup of wine.

"This could start a war," the younger man finally said.

S'Doryn looked at him and shook his head. "The Mettai are weak. They have no armies, no warriors. It wouldn't be much of a war."

"If the Mettai are attacked by a Qirsi army, Eandi warriors will come to their defense."

"It's just one woman, T'Noth, if it's even that. There's no reason for our people to do anything to the Mettai."

"You say that now, but what if this woman is responsible, and what if she takes her plague to other Fal'Borna villages, or to the J'Balanar? What then?"

S'Doryn had to admit that it was a sobering question. "Let's hope someone finds her soon," he finally said.

"Let's hope."

A moment later, N'Tevva returned with the children. All three of them were flushed and laughing, even the little one, which gladdened S'Doryn's heart.

T'Noth and Etan said their farewells, and walked off to T'Noth's home. N'Tevva began preparing the girls for bed in the bedroom that she and S'Doryn usually shared. For the time being, at least, that would be their room, and the adults would sleep in the common room. After a time, she came out again.

"They want you to say good night to them," she said.

He nodded and walked back to their bedroom. Now it was the girls' room. Was that how they'd speak of it from this night on? Was he really a father now?

They were tucked into the single bed, Vettala by the wall, her pale eyes shining in the light of the single candle that burned by the door.

S'Doryn crossed to the bed and sat beside Jynna. "Good night," he said.

Jynna smiled. "Good night."

"You're comfortable?"

She nodded.

He looked at the younger girl. "And you?"

She hid her face in the pillow.

It seemed that smiling with the other children was one thing. Accepting him as a friend, much less as a new father, was quite another. He stood, walked to the door, and bent to blow out the candle. Before he could, Vettala let out a small cry.

"I think she wants it lit," Jynna said.

"All right then." He straightened and stepped out of the room.

"Thank you," Jynna called to him. "From both of us."

He grinned. "You're welcome." He pulled the door until it was nearly all the way closed, and went out to the common room. N'Tevva was sitting at the table.

"Did the younger one say anything to you?" she asked, looking concerned.

"Not a word," he said, sitting beside her.

She shook her head. A pale wisp of hair fell over her brow and she brushed it away. She still looked much as she had when they first were joined. Her skin remained smooth, save for a few lines around her eyes and mouth, and she still wore her white hair tied back loosely. Her eyes were the color of the winter sun on a hazy day.

"She wouldn't even look at me," she said. "I tried everything, but you would have thought that I was a demon from the Underrealm itself the way she shied away from me."

"It'll take some time. But Jynna will help her through it."

"I know," she said. She smiled, though the look in her eyes remained sad. "There are children sleeping in our home."

"I've been thinking about that. It's not quite how we always hoped it would happen."

"No, but that's all right. They need us."

"We're a bit old to be starting out as parents."

"I don't know what you're talking about," she said airily. "Oh, I suppose you're getting on in years, but I'm certainly not."

He laughed, then leaned over and kissed her. "I missed you."

"I missed you, too." She took his hand, but he could see that she was troubled. "All this talk of a Mettai witch frightens me. It's going to frighten a lot of people as it gets around the village."

"It should," he said. "If she's really out there, doing to other villages what we think she did to Tivston, we should all be terrified."

Over the next several days, the girls began to settle into the rhythms of Fal'Borna life. They accompanied N'Tevva into the fields and they fished the waters of the lake with S'Doryn. They even went to the sanctuary for lessons with other children their ages, though N'Tevva was concerned about Vettala, who had yet to say a word to either her or S'Doryn, and who seemed unwilling to leave Jynna's side.

According to the older girl, however, Vettala willingly went off with children her own age once they reached the sanctuary. Even there, she spoke to no one, but she played some of the games that the younger children played, and she appeared to listen attentively to her lessons.

U'Selle had said that she would speak with other a'laqs, using her powers to walk in their dreams, as all Weavers could. But S'Doryn heard nothing from the a'laq, and he didn't presume to ask her, knowing that if she had anything of importance to tell him, she would do so.

The full of the two moons came and went, marking the beginning of the Harvest waning, and still the a'laq told him nothing.

"You should ask her," T'Noth urged one evening, as S'Doryn and T'Kaar walked the fields with him.

"Don't you think she'd tell us if she knew anything?" T'Kaar asked.

"Perhaps she hasn't even reached for them yet," the younger man said. "She's not been well, you know. It might have slipped her mind."

"And what if it hasn't?" S'Doryn asked. "What if she takes the question as an affront?"

T'Noth offered a small shrug. "You could . . ." He shrugged a second time. "She'd probably understand. She knows how anxious we are for any word of the woman."

"Perhaps it slipped her mind," T'Kaar said, grinning now.

"Yes," S'Doryn said. "I think you should remind her, T'Noth. Old as I am, it might slip my mind as well."

T'Kaar laughed.

"Fine," the younger man said, walking away from them both. "We'll wait."

They didn't have to wait long. Three days into the waning, at mid-morning, as he worked his crops, S'Doryn received word that the a'laq wished to speak with him. He hurried to her house, arriving there just as the brothers did. It seemed they had been summoned as well.

"Do you know what this is about?" T'Noth asked.

He sounded eager, as only a young man could under such circumstances. For his part, S'Doryn had started to hope that Jynna had been wrong about the Mettai woman, that her tale really was just the product

296 DAVID B. COE

of fear and grief and a young girl's imagination. He dreaded hearing whatever it was the a'laq had learned.

Stepping into the a'laq's cottage, they saw that the other members of the clan council were there as well, some of them seated around her table, others standing. Far more surprising, Jynna, who was supposed to be at the sanctuary, sat at the table beside U'Selle, looking pale and young and very scared. Every person in the room looked up as the three men entered.

"At last," the a'laq said brusquely. "Come in, please. There isn't much room, but I hadn't the strength to make my way to the sanctuary."

"Not good," T'Kaar muttered, his voice tight.

S'Doryn had to agree.

Jynna looked as though she wanted to be near him, but was afraid to offend the a'laq. U'Selle appeared to notice this as well, for she whispered something to the girl, and immediately Jynna was on her feet. She ran to him, threw her arms around him, and pressed her face to his shirt.

"What's going on?" she asked, the words muffled. "Why did they bring me here?"

"I don't know, Jynna," he said, stroking her hair. "But we'll find out. Sit with me."

She nodded, and followed him to the table. T'Noth and T'Kaar sat with them and the rest of those who had been standing came to the table as well.

"When Jynna first came to our village with her story of the pestilence and its odd effect on her people," the a'laq began, "we didn't quite know what to make of it. Some wondered if this were some new form of the disease that struck only Qirsi victims. Others thought it might be unique to the Y'Qatt, a product of their forswearing of magic. And still others thought it might be the work of the Mettai, a spell directed at Qirsi magic.

"I've considered all of these possibilities and at the same time have been in contact with a'laqs throughout Fal'Borna lands to see if there are other villages or septs that have suffered as Jynna's people did, dreading the day I would find them."

She took a breath and was taken with a fit of coughing. When it finally passed, she dabbed at her mouth with a small cloth.

"I found them this morning. Or rather, they found me. Another a'laq, a man named S'Plaed, spoke to me as I slept, Weaver to Weaver."

Jynna turned to S'Doryn, looking puzzled.

"Weavers can walk in the dreams of other Qirsi," he whispered to her. "Even from afar. It allows us to communicate with other septs, even other Qirsi clans if need be."

U'Selle had paused in her tale, allowing him to explain. Now she went on. "S'Plaed leads a sept on the northern edge of the plain. Not long ago they numbered five thousand strong. Then they were visited by an Eandi merchant. Within hours of this man's appearance, the pestilence struck, sickening thousands—at least half of S'Plaed's sept. As with Jynna's people, this strain of the disease took hold of their magic so that fire and shaping and healing raged out of control. Hundreds more died in the destruction the afflicted did to their families and neighbors. The a'laq usually meets with all merchants who visit his village, but in this case the man was in too great a hurry to leave. His haste is all that saved S'Plaed's life.

"According to S'Plaed, the merchant's name is Torgan Plye and among the wares he was selling that day were Mettai baskets of uncommon quality. This man has been named an enemy of all Fal'Borna people, and is to be killed on sight."

"Did you ask about the woman?" Jynna asked, drawing stares from all around the table. "There was a Mettai woman! She made the baskets!"

S'Doryn feared that U'Selle might be angered by the interruption, but the a'laq just shook her head.

"He said nothing about a woman, or about any Mettai for that matter."

Jynna started to say more, but U'Selle silenced her with a raised hand.

"The baskets are enough, child. I believe what you told us about the woman, and as soon as I heard that he was selling Mettai baskets, it occurred to me that she and the merchant are partners in some dark scheme. I don't know how or why she came to be working with this Torgan Plye, but clearly there are Eandi abroad on the plain who seek to destroy all Qirsi people, be they Fal'Borna or Y'Qatt."

"How long ago did this happen, A'Laq?" T'Noth asked.

"Not long. A matter of days. You should also know," she said, "that most of those who survived were children, just as with the outbreak in Tivston."

"It has to be the magic," S'Doryn said. "That's the only way to explain it."

"The only way?" asked one of the council members.

"I believe so. This is a disease that kills Qirsi adults but spares their children, and the Eandi who spread it. How else could that be possible?"

"Then it must be the Mettai," said another member of the council. "A curse of some sort. The Eandi couldn't do such a thing on their own."

"I told you this would lead to war."

S'Doryn looked at T'Noth, who was eyeing him closely, his expression grim.

"I told S'Plaed about Jynna," U'Selle was saying to them all, quieting the rising din in the room. "I also told him about the Mettai woman. It seems our people are under attack, though in a way that none of us has seen before, or even considered. Well, fine then. Our foes will find that the strength of the Fal'Borna hasn't slackened at all in the years since the last Blood Wars. Others will be watching now for the Mettai witch who struck at our friends in Tivston, just as we are, just as we will also be watching for this demon merchant, this Torgan Plye. If they're on the plain, they won't live long." A dark smile touched her face and was gone. "Enemies of the Fal'Borna never do."

Chapter 18

✦✝✦

Grinsa and Cresenne's first days among the Fal'Borna weren't quite as difficult as Grinsa had feared they might be. Yes, they were captives; there could be no denying that. Had their welcome from E'Menua, the sept's a'laq, been friendlier, had they been given the option of staying with the sept or moving on as they saw fit, Grinsa and Cresenne might very well have chosen to remain, at least for a time. From all they had heard from R'Shev, D'Chul, and the other merchants, it seemed the Fal'Borna were a hard, uncompromising people, and certainly their captivity seemed further evidence of this. But the Fal'Borna could also be friendly, open, and generous.

As the a'laq had promised, their shelter was up and ready for them before nightfall on that first day they reached the sept. They were given food and wine, including roasted rilda, which might have been the most delicious meat Grinsa had ever tasted. And over the course of those first few days family after family came to welcome them to the village. The women cooed at Bryntelle and spoke to Cresenne of their own children and all they had learned over their years of caring for infants. The men ignored both Cresenne and Bryntelle, instead vying with one another for Grinsa's attention. There could be little doubt that all the attention they received, perhaps even the kindnesses shown to Cresenne, whom all thought of as merely Grinsa's concubine, was due to the fact that he was a Weaver. It was unclear whether the Fal'Borna hoped to convince him to remain with the sept of his own accord, or merely assumed that he would remain and were seeking to curry favor with their newest Weaver.

In the end, the Fal'Borna's motivations mattered little. Knowing that they were not permitted to leave made Grinsa and Cresenne think of leaving nearly all the time. The courtesies shown them by the men and women of the sept were particularly hollow for Cresenne, who knew that had Grinsa not been a Weaver, they would have ignored her completely. Indeed, even as they complimented her on how beautiful Bryntelle was, and how healthy the babe appeared to be, some of the younger women also cast looks at Grinsa, as if hoping that they might find a way into his bed as well. This at least is what she told him their second night in the village, as they lay alone in their shelter, listening to Bryntelle's steady breathing and the distant howling of a wolf.

Under other circumstances, he might have thought that she was imagining this. But one of the men who had been speaking to him earlier in the night had as much as offered Grinsa his daughter.

"Many of our Weavers have taken two, even three concubines," the man told him, explaining the offer as he might have explained the Harvest weather or the rising and falling of the price of grain in the marketplace. "A Fal'Borna Weaver spreads his seed as he pleases. For the good of our people, of course."

"Of course," Grinsa had said, smiling pleasantly. "But Cresenne isn't my concubine. She's my wife."

The man's eyes widened. "Oh! Forgive me! I didn't know she was a Weaver as well. I thought . . . Well, I was mistaken."

Grinsa should have let it go at that, but regardless of whether they were to remain, he didn't want to have any of them thinking him a liar.

"She's not a Weaver," he told the man. "Where we come from, Weavers are free to be joined to whomever they choose."

"Well," the man said, smiling in return, "you're here now."

It was much the same thing E'Menua had said to them the day before.

"I have you," Grinsa told Cresenne that night, kissing her brow. "Why would I need another concubine?"

She laughed, though she also kicked him under the blanket.

"You're finding all of this far too amusing," she said, and while she was still smiling, he could hear the tightness in her voice.

"I'm sorry. Really. This can't be easy for you."

"Half the time, it's like I'm not even here. They talk about finding a wife for you from one of the other septs, about how your arrival here means so much to them all."

"It seems that some of the women have been kind to you."

She nodded. "Some of them have. But I'm starting to suspect that the ones who are nicest are the ones who have been concubines themselves. And they're kind to me right up until I insist that I'm not just your concubine. As soon as I say anything to that effect, they grow cold, distant." A bitter smile touched her lips. "It seems like I'm better off playing along. Maybe I should help them find you a wife."

"I have a wife."

She looked at him. "No, Grinsa, you don't. I know that you love me, and I love you, too. But the fact is we were never joined. With all that happened in the turns before we left the Forelands, we never found the time. And even if we had, I'm not certain that it would count for much here."

He felt a tightness in his throat. "What are you saying?" he asked.

She smiled at what she saw on his face, and kissed him softly on the lips. "Nothing terrible. I may not be a Weaver, but I'll fight with every bit of strength and magic I have if they try to take you away from me. I'm just saying that we're going to have to tread carefully here. We might even have to play along for a time, let them think that you're open to being joined."

"Cresenne—"

She held a finger to his lips, then kissed him again. "It's all right. We can do this. Just for a little while, just long enough for us to figure out how to get away. It might be the only hope we have."

"That all sounds fine for me," he said. "But what about you? Can you bear being treated as a concubine for that long?"

"I'll manage it." She shrugged, a small grin lighting her face. "I may have to convince some other Weaver that I'd be willing to become his concubine. Just to keep up appearances, of course. Although the men here *are* very handsome."

Grinsa smiled. "Is that so?"

She nodded, giggling as he started to kiss her neck.

"If you ask me," he said, "they're just short."

Her eyes sparkled in the candlelight. "They're tall enough."

He kissed her again, and this time she held him, kissing him back deeply.

"We'll get out of here," he whispered, as she nestled against him and closed her eyes. "I'm not sure how yet, but we will."

"I know," she said, sounding sleepy. "I just hope we can find a way to leave without making the Fal'Borna our enemies. I have a feeling that would be dangerous."

The next few days were much like their first among the Fal'Borna. As time went on, and they were accepted into the community, they came to feel less like curiosities. Several of the women made clear to Cresenne that she was expected to work with the rest of them at various tasks, be it tanning rilda skins, or grinding wild grain into meal for breads, or gathering roots and greens from the small copses that covered the nearby hills. Other women with young children, even those with babes younger than Bryntelle, left them in the care of some of the girls who were not yet old enough for such work, and they told Cresenne to do the same. At first, she later told Grinsa, she was reluctant, but seeing how happy all the children appeared to be, she eventually relented.

For his part, Grinsa was not expected to do any labor. Instead, the other Weavers expected him to sit with them outside the a'laq's shelter, smoking pipeweed and watching as the other men and women of the sept went about their daily tasks. The idea of it troubled him and at first he demurred, offering to help some of the other men, who were stretching finished skins over wooden poles for a new shelter. He quickly realized, though, that he was merely making these men uncomfortable and actually hindering their efforts. After just a short time, he returned to where the other two Weavers sat.

Neither of them said anything to him as he sat back down, and that suited him fine. He didn't much feel like talking. He could only think how eager he was to get away from this sept, indeed, from all of the Fal'Borna. More to the point, he had nothing to say to the two young Weavers. Though others in the sept had attempted to win his friendship, these two, Q'Daer and L'Norr, had not. Instead, they'd been hostile, as if Grinsa had given offense in some way and they had yet to forgive him. It hadn't taken Grinsa long to realize that they were jealous of him. While others in the sept were eager to welcome another Weaver into their community, seeing his arrival as a boon, Q'Daer and L'Norr saw only a new rival who, because he was older, and perhaps because he came from a distant land, might eventually form a close bond with the a'laq. On the one hand he would have liked to assure them that he had no interest in remaining here long enough to pose a threat to their standing. But it had also occurred to him that having the a'laq's closest advisors eager for him to leave might help him do just that.

As he returned to the a'laq's shelter, the Weavers were speaking of nothing in particular, at least nothing that interested him. They seemed to be reminiscing about a previous hunt. After a time, though, they fell silent. For several moments, they just sat there. Then Q'Daer, the first Fal'Borna Grinsa and Cresenne had encountered, turned to him, a puzzled look on his tanned, chiseled face.

"Why do you do that, Forelander?"

Grinsa didn't even look at him. "Do what?"

"Deny what you are. We tell you that Weavers do not labor with the others; that your place is here by the a'laq's z'kal. But you don't listen. You go off and try to do common work anyway, and I'd imagine that all you did was get in the way of the others. I doubt they even spoke to you."

"They spoke to me," he said, which was true, though in fact, the men had said precious little. They'd been courteous to a fault, but beyond that, they hadn't spoken at all, not to him, not to each other.

"You had an actual conversation with them?" Q'Daer asked.

"What's your point?"

"Simply this. You are a Weaver. Whatever that meant in the Forelands, it means here that you are one of the select, chosen by Qirsar to be a leader among the Fal'Borna." He raised a hand, as if anticipating an argument. "And before you object, this is by no means unique to our clan. The J'Balanar, the Talm'Orast, the T'Saan, the M'Saaren and A'Vahl—nearly every clan in the Southlands treats its Weavers so."

"Nearly every one?"

He shrugged. "The B'Qahr may not. To be honest I don't know. They're a strange people—even if the a'laq consents to let you leave us, I'd suggest you avoid them. Unless you're hopelessly wedded to the sea and its ways."

The brief hope Grinsa had felt at the mention of this clan faded, leaving him discouraged. Joining a clan of sailors would be just about the last thing Cresenne would want.

L'Norr was watching them, listening to their exchange, but saying nothing. He and Q'Daer could have been brothers, so much did they resemble one another. They had the same rugged good looks, bronzed skin, long hair, and clear eyes that all the Fal'Borna men seemed to have.

But as Grinsa sat with the two men now, it occurred to him that there should have been women here as well.

"I thought Fal'Borna Weavers were only joined to other Weavers."

Q'Daer nodded. "That's right."

"So neither of you is joined yet."

The man straightened. "Not yet. But L'Norr here has a concubine already, and . . . and U'Vara, the a'laq's eldest child, who is just coming into her power, shows signs of being a Weaver. Before long, she'll be wed to one of us." He offered this last as if a challenge. *She's ours*, he seemed to be saying, though Grinsa sensed that it had yet to be decided which of the two men would be joined to her. He gathered as well that this last question was a matter of great import, certainly to Q'Daer, and most likely to L'Norr, too.

"But the a'laq told me that his sept has four Weavers."

"It does," L'Norr said. "E'Menua is joined to the fourth, of course. Her name is D'Pera."

"So does she labor with the other women?"

"No," Q'Daer told him, as if he were simple. "She oversees the work of the others, but she doesn't labor."

"It sounds, though, as if your sept will soon have five Weavers."

L'Norr nodded, but Q'Daer merely laughed, though not kindly.

"We already have five Weavers, Forelander. Soon it will be six."

Grinsa didn't argue the point.

A moment later, the flap of animal skin covering the shelter entrance was pushed aside, and E'Menua stepped into the sunlight. Immediately, Q'Daer and L'Norr were on their feet. After a moment, Grinsa stood as well.

"Well met, A'Laq," Q'Daer said. "How may we serve you?"

Grinsa had spoken with E'Menua only one time since their initial conversation, but then, as the first time, the a'laq had seemed a genial man, quick to smile, despite his willingness to use threats to get his way. On this morning, however, he looked grim and deadly serious. He was shorter than the younger Weavers, but broader as well, which somehow gave him the appearance of being larger than they were.

"I see you're finding your place, Forelander," he said. "I'll trust Q'Daer and L'Norr to show you what it means to be a Weaver in a Fal'Borna sept."

"Yes, they already have been. It seems I'm not allowed to work *or* leave. Do all your Weavers enjoy such . . . freedom?"

The a'laq shook his head. "I haven't time for this today."

Q'Daer cast a dark look at Grinsa. "What's happened, A'Laq?"

"I've had word from the north," he said, eyeing the two younger men.

"More talk of the pestilence?"

"In a sense." The a'laq glanced at Grinsa, as if deciding whether he wanted him to be party to this discussion. "They have the pestilence in the Forelands, don't they?" he finally asked.

It wasn't the first time he'd been asked this since arriving in the Southlands, and once more he thought of Pheba, whom he'd lost to the disease many years ago. He didn't think it wise to mention her, though. He wasn't certain how the Fal'Borna would react to learning that he had once been joined to an Eandi woman. "Yes, of course" was all he said.

"Have you ever heard of it afflicting Qirsi . . . differently?"

Grinsa frowned. "I'm not sure I understand what you mean."

The a'laq exhaled slowly. "To be honest, I'm not entirely certain myself. It seems that this pestilence is striking at Qirsi magic, making our people so sick that they can't control their power. It pours out of them, destroying all in its path and exhausting them until they die."

"Demons and fire! I've never heard of such a thing."

"None of us has," E'Menua said. "And there may be a reason for that. It seems that this is a disease contrived for us by the Mettai."

"What?" Q'Daer said, his pale eyes widening.

Grinsa was nearly as amazed as the young Weaver, though for a different reason. "The Mettai?"

"You've heard of them?" the a'laq asked.

"Yes, in legend. But I thought the Mettai died out centuries ago."

"Oh, no. They're still very much alive. There are small Mettai settlements throughout the northern reaches of Stelpana and Aelea. They live apart from other Eandi—it seems the dark-eyes don't like magic, even when it comes from the blood of their own kind."

"So, they really use blood magic?"

E'Menua nodded again. "To great effect, it seems. According to some of the other a'laqs, a Mettai woman has cursed us, and with help from an Eandi merchant is spreading the disease throughout Qirsi lands."

"A merchant?" Q'Daer repeated.

"Not just any merchant. Torgan Plye."

Q'Daer's mouth dropped open.

L'Norr just shook his head. "Torgan? Are you certain?"

"S'Plaed was certain."

"But Torgan wouldn't do anything to destroy his profits. You know that. He cares about gold and nothing else."

"It seems something has changed, L'Norr," the a'laq said, a hint of annoyance in his tone. "Unless you think the other a'laqs are lying to us."

"No, of course not, A'Laq!"

"I don't understand," Grinsa said. "How could one Mettai and one merchant spread a disease throughout Qirsi lands?"

The a'laq eyed him briefly, as if he thought Grinsa was questioning their strength or their intelligence. "We don't know," he said after a moment. "But clearly it has something to do with our magic. The only survivors have been children too young to have come into their power."

"So the merchant is Mettai as well?"

E'Menua looked at the other men, who both shook their heads.

"I didn't think he was," the a'laq answered. "Now I'm not certain."

"So it's possible that the merchant had nothing to do with it."

"He refused to meet with S'Plaed," E'Menua told him. "He spent only a few hours in the sept, long enough to make his share of gold and spread this venom the Mettai have contrived. Then he left. The pestilence struck later that day. He knew what he was doing."

"You don't know that for certain," Grinsa said.

It meant nothing to him. Of course, the notion of a pestilence outbreak frightened him. He feared for Cresenne and Bryntelle, as well as for himself. But the rest of it he barely understood. Certainly, he didn't care a whit for this merchant of whom they spoke. So then why did he continue to argue? Was it just in his nature? Back in the Forelands he had argued similarly on behalf of a young lord falsely accused of killing the daughter of a rival house. He had risked his life to save the boy, though at first he'd thought him nothing more than a spoiled noble. Later, the boy proved himself a true friend and valuable ally in the fight against the dark conspiracy that almost consumed the Forelands. But Grinsa had hardly glimpsed the lad's potential when he fought for his release. What was it, then, that drew him to fight every injustice, no matter the cost to himself? He couldn't answer, nor could he explain why he risked angering the a'laq.

"You know more about this than I do?"

"I know only what I've heard you say just now," Grinsa said, holding the a'laq's gaze. "But from that, I've learned that this Torgan Plye is a merchant who cares for little beyond his own wealth and the selling of his wares. Since you know him by name and reputation, it seems that he must do a fair amount of trading with Fal'Borna septs, which makes me wonder why he would suddenly decide to kill you off."

E'Menua narrowed his eyes. After a moment he began to chuckle. "You don't hesitate to speak your mind, do you, Forelander? I like that." He turned to the other two men, as did Grinsa.

Q'Daer didn't look at all pleased, and Grinsa thought he knew why. A moment before it seemed that Grinsa had angered the a'laq. Now the sept's leader appeared even more impressed with him than he had been before. This could only serve to fuel the younger Weaver's jealousy.

"Word is Torgan is headed south, toward the Ofirean," E'Menua said. "That might bring him near us. Find him." He glanced at Grinsa before adding, "But don't kill him. Bring him to me."

"What if the Mettai woman is with him?"

The a'laq looked at Grinsa again and raised an eyebrow. "Well?"

"I know little about Mettai power, but if they need blood to wield it then I'd assume that they carry a blade of some sort."

The a'laq nodded. "They do."

"Then tell them to surrender their blades," Grinsa told the two young Weavers. "Tell them that if they refuse you'll kill them where they stand. And, if necessary, use mind-bending magic to keep them from defying you."

Q'Daer and L'Norr eyed Grinsa sullenly, clearly unhappy about having to take orders from him. Q'Daer looked particularly resentful; Grinsa couldn't help wondering if he regretted their initial encounter on the plain and wished he had turned Grinsa and Cresenne away from the sept. But E'Menua nodded and laughed. "Who would have thought that a Forelander would have such stones? Go," he said to the two men. "Take forty warriors with you. Let Torgan see that we don't mean to play games."

"Yes, A'Laq," Q'Daer said.

Both men bowed, then turned and strode toward the paddock of horses west of the village.

"They're both shocked that I allow you to speak to me so."

"I wasn't aware that I was speaking disrespectfully."

E'Menua looked at him. "You do not address me as A'Laq. You challenge me and argue with me without hesitation. Few men who are not a'laqs themselves would dare do the same."

"My apologies," Grinsa said, but again, he didn't call the man A'Laq. Was he purposefully goading E'Menua?

"Is it because you were used to leading Qirsi in the Forelands? Do you miss having such authority yourself?"

"No, I was never a leader like you are. I was a simple gleaner in a traveling festival. And then I served an Eandi king in his war against renegade Qirsi."

E'Menua regarded him briefly. After a few moments he turned his gaze to the hills beyond his sept. "I'd heard some talk of this war, and of the Qirsi who fought with the dark-eyes, but I never understood. Why didn't you join with our people?"

"Our people fought on both sides," Grinsa said pointedly. "The man—the Weaver—who led the renegades would have been a despot. He was cruel and arbitrary and would have ruled through fear and violence. I would have opposed him no matter the color of his eyes."

"He was defeated. You had a role in that?"

"I killed him," Grinsa said.

"But not before he shattered your shoulder," the a'laq said.

"That's right."

"And today you risked my ire by arguing for the innocence of an Eandi merchant. Some would say that your blood runs more Eandi than it does Qirsi."

"They'd be wrong. But they'd also be wrong to assume that I'll always side with a Qirsi against an Eandi, no matter the circumstances."

"That's a dangerous attitude in this land," E'Menua said. Though he'd been living among the Fal'Borna only a short time, Grinsa knew that at times the a'laq spoke in veiled threats. He didn't seem to be doing that now. He was just offering an observation, Weaver to Weaver. "I'm not saying it's wrong," he went on, sounding thoughtful, "but it is dangerous."

"I understand."

"Be sure that you do, Grinsa." The a'laq turned to face him. "You wish to leave us, to move on and perhaps find another clan to live with. We wish for you to stay, and it remains to be seen which of us will get his way. But no matter where you and your family settle, you'll need to keep such thoughts to yourself, at least until you're better known and more fully trusted. The Blood Wars have been over for more than a century, but they're not forgotten. Our grandfathers' grandfathers made peace with an enemy they hated. To this day, that peace has endured, and so has the hatred. Make no mistake, my friend: Weaver or not, if the Qirsi with whom you settle believe you to be a traitor to our people, they'll kill you, and your family as well."

Grinsa searched his mind for some appropriate response, something brave, something that would show the a'laq that he wasn't afraid. But nothing came to him, nothing at all.

Q'Daer seethed as he and L'Norr went to gather riders. Who did this Forelander think he was, giving them orders as if he had already moved into E'Menua's z'kal? And for that matter, why was the a'laq already placing so much faith in this man, who seemed so eager to reject Fal'Borna ways and challenge E'Menua's every word?

Q'Daer had served the sept faithfully for nearly six years now, ever since coming into his power. L'Norr had done the same for nearly as long. They followed custom; they obeyed the a'laq's commands. Fairness demanded that someday one of them would assume leadership of the sept. Yes, they were rivals, despite their friendship, which was as old as memory. But Q'Daer never questioned L'Norr's worth. If eventually E'Menua chose the younger man to succeed him, so be it; Q'Daer would accept that. He'd do all in his power to win the a'laq's favor, but at least in L'Norr, the sept would have a Fal'Borna leader, a man who understood his own people.

This Forelander, though, was a different matter. Q'Daer had been, quite literally, the first to welcome Grinsa into their community. He could see the value of adding another Weaver to the sept, of strengthening themselves against their foes and enhancing their prestige among the other Fal'Borna on the plain. But what good to them was a man who remained so wedded to the ways of the Forelands? What benefit could come to the sept if Grinsa refused to be joined properly to another Weaver? How could E'Menua even consider allowing such a man to become one of his trusted advisors?

And he was considering it. Q'Daer could tell as much. When was the last time the a'laq praised him the way he did Grinsa? When had E'Menua ever tolerated any display of disrespect from either Q'Daer or L'Norr? Yet E'Menua allowed this Forelander, who had been living among them for but a matter of days, to say whatever he pleased.

"We should take H'Shem and his horsemen," L'Norr said, as they walked among the z'kals toward the paddock.

Q'Daer nodded absently. "Fine," he said.

"You disagree?"

He looked at the man, pulling himself out of his musings. Or trying. "Not at all. H'Shem is a good choice."

Q'Daer meant it. Like most a'laqs, E'Menua had chosen his best riders and made them a'jei, leaders of smaller hunting parties. Each party consisted of eight men, plus the a'jei. Some septs might have as many as three dozen such leaders. E'Menua had twenty-six. H'Shem was the most competent of them, and the one Q'Daer liked best. It bothered him just a bit that L'Norr had thought of H'Shem for this undertaking. An a'laq might choose his successor based in part on the recommendations of his a'jei, and for some time now Q'Daer had assumed that H'Shem would support him. But if L'Norr and the a'jei were building a rapport . . .

"He's a very good choice," Q'Daer said, unable to keep a hint of bitterness from creeping into his voice.

"What's the matter with you?" L'Norr asked.

"Nothing."

L'Norr just kept watching him, waiting. They were as close as brothers; their fathers had been as well. That both of them turned out to be Weavers had seemed at first too good to be true. And perhaps it was. They spent much of their time together, but they were constantly vying against each other for E'Menua's esteem. How could they help it? Both of them wanted to be a'laq. Both of them wanted to be the first to be joined to another Weaver, for how many opportunities would there be for either of them to marry? As the older of the two, Q'Daer had the natural advantage. Simply by dint of Fal'Borna custom, he was to be given command of most hunting parties and raids against rival septs.

Even this tradition, though, had proved to be a blade that cut both ways. He'd had his share of successful hunts, and one glorious skirmish against a small J'Balanar raiding party, during which he himself had killed the leader of the invaders. But there had also been the one disaster, and he knew for certain that E'Menua hadn't forgotten.

It happened less than a year ago, early in the Planting. Too early, the a'laq had warned. But the Snows had been harsh and their stores of food were depleted. Q'Daer pushed hard and finally persuaded E'Menua to let him take a small hunting party—just one a'jei and his men—south to find a herd of rilda. Their hunt was successful: sixteen bucks killed. Before they could return to the sept, however, a storm swept down over the plain, bringing fierce winds and blinding snow. The riders searched for a sheltered spot where they might wait out the squall. Small clusters of trees grew along the banks of the streams flowing out of the Fallow Downs, and they tried to find these. But Q'Daer lost his bearings in the blizzard and led the riders away from the hills rather than toward them. By the time he realized his mistake, night had fallen and the riders had little choice but to lay low in their rilda skins and blankets, exposed on the plain. Five men died that night, including G'Fen, the hunting party's a'jei.

It was no one's fault, of course. Morna's moods, it is said among the people of the plains, are as fickle as her winds. Only the goddess herself could have foreseen that storm. E'Menua told him as much upon the survivors' return to the sept. But it seemed to Q'Daer that the a'laq held him responsible nevertheless. The hunt had been his idea in the first place. More to the point, it was the way of the Fal'Borna. No matter the circumstances, a leader—be he an a'laq, a Weaver, or an a'jei—was always judged according to the fates of those under his command. Q'Daer had gloried in his previous triumphs; it was only just that this failure should bring him shame.

It was no coincidence that L'Norr now had a concubine and he did not. The girl's father, S'Qel, had offered her to the younger Weaver after the storm and Q'Daer's failure on the plain. Had she come into her power only a few turns before, she might well have been his. It shouldn't have mattered to him—she was a warm body; nothing more—but still it rankled. It made him wonder if E'Menua might make a similar choice when U'Vara, the a'laq's daughter, came into her power. She was the one Q'Daer wanted, the one who all in the sept believed would be their next Weaver. Though young still, she showed all the signs. Already she had given indications of possessing fire magic, mists and winds, shaping, and language of beasts. So many magics, and she'd yet to complete her fourth four. Surely she would be a Weaver, and a beautiful one at that.

As the older unjoined Weaver, Q'Daer should have been the clear choice to be her husband. Now, though, after the storm, with L'Norr already having a concubine, nothing was certain. Grinsa's arrival in the sept only served to complicate matters. Had he been properly joined to a Weaver, Q'Daer might not have minded so much. But in just these past few days Q'Daer had begun to hear talk of U'Vara being a perfect match for the Forelander, one whose beauty and youth might lure the man away from his concubine and convince him to make E'Menua's sept his home.

Neither Q'Daer nor L'Norr could allow that to happen, though his friend seemed oblivious of the danger. E'Menua's other two children were both boys. In all likelihood, they would be Weavers, too, and when they came of age, they would need to find wives. How many female Weavers could one expect to find in a single sept? How many fathers would choose Q'Daer or L'Norr for their daughters rather than the son of the a'laq? It seemed likely that U'Vara would be the last Weaver from this sept to whom either Q'Daer or L'Norr could hope to be joined. Sometimes Weavers from separate septs were married as a way of forging new alliances or strengthening old ones, but this was rare.

U'Vara had to be his. He wanted sons; sons who would someday be Weavers. He wanted to rule the sept. And by Fal'Borna custom, only a joined Weaver could be named a'laq.

"Who else, then?" L'Norr asked him, as they continued to make their way through the sept. "Aside from H'Shem?"

"I don't know," he muttered.

This time L'Norr halted, grabbing Q'Daer's arm to make him stop, too. They were about the same height, and they stood watching each other, their eyes locked. "Something's bothering you," L'Norr said. "I want to know what it is."

Q'Daer took a breath. "It's the Forelander; I don't like him. You shouldn't, either. None of us should."

L'Norr shrugged. "I'm not sure I do like him. We've only known him for a few days. I haven't made up my mind about him one way or another."

"Well, I have," Q'Daer said, looking away. "He cares nothing for our customs. He argues with E'Menua at every turn and mocks us with his disrespect. We should send him away, and his whore and bastard with him. They have no business living in our sept."

"You've decided all this already?"

"Haven't you heard the others talking about him, about what a fine husband he'd make for U'Vara?"

L'Norr shook his head slowly. "I don't think Grinsa has any intention of marrying anyone. His woman might not be a Weaver, but I have no doubt that he loves her as he would a wife."

Q'Daer dismissed the remark with a wave of his hand. "That's not the point."

"Isn't it? You dislike him because he doesn't respect our ways. But in this instance, that's a good thing, right? He won't live by Fal'Borna customs, so he won't see any need to marry a Weaver. He's happy with the woman he has."

Just as Q'Daer had thought: His friend didn't understand the danger. And for now at least, perhaps that was all right. Q'Daer would take care of the problem himself, and so would reap the rewards that would come of getting rid of the man. Eventually, E'Menua would tire of the Forelander's disrespect. And when that happened, Q'Daer would be ready.

"You're probably right," he said, nodding and forcing a thin smile.

"I think you're humoring me."

Q'Daer grinned and placed a hand on the younger man's shoulder. L'Norr might have been too trusting of strangers, but he certainly understood his friends well enough.

"I am," he admitted. "But still, I see the sense in what you're saying. And anyway, there isn't much I can do about Grinsa right now. Let's gather the men, and go hunting for those dark-eye merchants." He looked to the west and then up at the sun. It seemed a fair day, but Q'Daer knew that a storm was coming. He could feel it in the wind. "I want to be back before nightfall," he said. "It'll be raining by then."

L'Norr said nothing. Perhaps he thought that Q'Daer had become too cautious when it came to storms, but he had the good sense to keep this to himself. He merely nodded, and they started off again in search of H'Shem and the other horsemen.

Cresenne could not have been more surprised. She'd told Grinsa that they'd have to play along with the Fal'Borna for a time; that they'd need to do everything possible to become part of the sept. So when the women of the village made it clear to her that they expected her to join them in their daily labors, she could hardly object. True, she'd been resistant at first, particularly when it became clear that they expected her to leave Bryntelle in the care of several girls who couldn't have been much past their Determining age. But the other mothers trusted these girls, seemingly without hesitation, so Cresenne forced herself to do the same. And at the end of that first day Bryntelle had been just fine. Better than fine, Cresenne had to admit. She'd never seen her child in such a good mood, and it occurred to her that Bryntelle had spent precious little time in the company of children her own age, or of any other age for that matter. No wonder she seemed so happy.

But it was Cresenne's own experience that came as such a shock to her. On this, her fifth day as a Fal'Borna laborer, she had come to the undeniable conclusion that she was a skilled tanner of rilda skins. It wasn't just her opinion, either. Several of the women commented on her work, on the grace and ease with which she spread the tanning agent—a foul mixture of animal fat and ground organs—over the skins as she prepared them for smoking, on the evenness of the color she drew from the hide, and on the suppleness of her first few finished pieces. For the first time since their arrival in E'Menua's sept, Cresenne felt that she had been noticed for something other than being Grinsa's concubine or wife, or whatever she was.

What made all of this even more surprising was that she enjoyed the work. She'd spent her early days with her mother, roaming the kingdom of Wethyrn in the Forelands with the Crown Fair. Her mother had been a gleaner with the fair, following it from town to town, telling children of Determining and Fating ages what their futures would bring. Eventually, when she came into her power, Cresenne began to glean as well. Later, when the Weaver found her and drew her into his conspiracy, she continued to glean, though with a dark purpose. And after she turned against the Weaver's movement, she occupied herself day and night simply with staying alive, with keeping the Weaver from entering her dreams so that he might kill her as she slept, and fighting off the assassins he sent for her. But never before had she worked with her hands in this way. It was ironic, really. In the Forelands, where Qirsi magic was poorly understood and even feared, she had been almost solely a creature of magic. Only now, living in a land where Qirsi power was accepted to the point of being taken for granted, was she learning to make her way in the world without magic.

She had also, quite unexpectedly, made a friend of her own. The woman's name was F'Solya, and she was the mother of twin boys just a few turns older than Bryntelle. Like the other Fal'Borna women Cresenne had met, F'Solya seemed sturdy, and not merely in appearance. Yes, she had the short stout legs and powerful upper body that the others had. The beauty of the Fal'Borna was nothing like the soft grace and willowy frailty of so many Foreland Qirsi. Rather, these people were as strong and wild as the rilda they hunted. They even looked a bit like the rilda, with their light brown skin and the pale manes of fine hair that cascaded over their shoulders and backs.

But quite beyond her powerful build, beautiful round face, and widely spaced golden eyes, F'Solya struck Cresenne as . . . well, solid. There was nothing shy about her. Her questions were direct and honest. When she spoke to Cresenne, she looked her in the eye, and her earthy humor seemed always to lurk just below all that she said. In some ways, she reminded Cresenne of her mother, or rather, her mother as she might have been as a young woman. They met the first morning Cresenne started tanning, and by the end of that day she felt that she had known F'Solya for years.

On Cresenne's second day, and in the days since, F'Solya had sought her out, and made a point of sitting beside her. On this morning, the woman was in high spirits, a broad smile exposing large, straight teeth.

"Here early, eh?" she asked as she sat. "If I didn't know better I'd say that you actually like tanning."

Cresenne grinned. "I do."

"You'll tire of it after a time. Everyone does. I certainly did."

"Why don't you do something else then? It seems there are plenty of other chores to be done. They told me I could grind grain into meal, or gather roots, or . . ."

F'Solya was nodding. "Tired of those, too." She smiled, and started working on a hide. She might have claimed to dislike the labor, but the woman was a skilled tanner—Cresenne had learned much in five days, just from watching F'Solya work. "How's your little one today?" she asked after a time, as she went on with her work.

"She's well, thank you. How are your boys?"

"They're trouble, as boys always are. One of them would have been plenty, but two?" She shook her head. "The gods are testing me. No doubt about it."

They fell into another silence, until at last F'Solya looked up from her work, a small frown on her face.

"They're saying things about you. You and your man both."

Cresenne felt her stomach knotting. She thought of F'Solya as her friend, but really they'd known each other for only a few days. It wouldn't take much to drive the woman away. "What things?" she said, her eyes fixed on the hide she was holding.

"Things I don't understand. Things I'm not certain I believe."

"And what if it turns out that they're true?"

"Then I'll look forward to having you explain them to me, so I can understand."

Cresenne looked up at that and smiled at the woman.

F'Solya smiled back.

"Tell me what you've heard."

"Well," she began, "they say there was a Qirsi civil war, with both sides led by Weavers. And they say that one of the Weavers was Grinsa."

"And what do they say of the other?"

"That he's dead now, but that when he lived, you were his lover as well."

A bitter smile touched Cresenne's face and left her just as suddenly, leaving her trembling and angry. His lover!

"No," she said, "I wasn't his lover." She lifted a finger to her face and traced the pale, thin scars that ran along her jaw and cheek and brow. "You see these scars?"

F'Solya nodded.

"He gave these to me. I was part of his movement once. He claimed that he wanted to lead the Qirsi of the Forelands to a new, better life—I believed that he was speaking of something like what you have here. I wanted to believe that. I wanted to think that if Bryntelle grew up to be a Weaver that she could live without fearing the persecution that Weavers have endured for centuries in my land. But after a time I realized that all he wanted was power. He was an evil man, and when I turned my back on his movement, he entered my dreams and did this to me. Later, he attacked me again and . . . and did far worse." She shuddered, remembering it all. The wounds he inflicted upon her body and her mind, the terror of waiting for his next attack, or the next assault by one of his servants. There were times when she wondered how she had survived those long, terrifying turns. "If it wasn't for Grinsa, I'd be dead now," she said at last. "And all the Forelands would be ruled by a demon."

"The two of you fought on the side of the Eandi?"

In the Forelands, it had made perfect sense to do so. The nobles of her homeland—all of them Eandi—were flawed, to be sure, some of them deeply so. But all of those who joined the alliance against the Weaver were honorable and peace-loving. The same couldn't be said for their Qirsi enemy. Here, though, even this argument might not be enough to convince her friend that she had been right to oppose the Weaver's movement. Could a Southlands Qirsi ever justify siding with an Eandi against one of her own?

"Yes," she said at last, "we fought to preserve the Eandi courts. Many Qirsi did."

F'Solya looked troubled. "Most Qirsi here would find that hard to understand."

"I know."

The woman nodded vaguely, but for a long time she said nothing more. Cresenne half expected her to take her skins and tannin and sit elsewhere. She didn't.

"Things here are easier," Cresenne said at length. Immediately she regretted the words. "That didn't come out right."

"I think I know what you mean. We remain apart here—Qirsi and Eandi, I mean. We come together in trade and in warfare, and in little else."

"Yes! Precisely. In the Forelands, it's different. We all live and work together."

"Do you miss that?"

Something in the way the woman asked the question made Cresenne hesitate. It seemed that they had reached the boundary of their friendship and that F'Solya was waiting to hear Cresenne's answer before deciding whether they would continue to build upon what they had already. Really, it should have been an easy question to answer. For days Cresenne had been relishing being part of a completely Qirsi community; after their terrible experiences in Aelea and Stelpana, she had convinced herself that she never wanted to spend another day among the Eandi. But there were Eandi in the Forelands who had shown her unexpected kindnesses, even after she revealed to them that she had once cast her lot with the renegades.

She looked down at her hands, making her decision.

"I know what it is you want me to say," Cresenne told her. "But I left lies and false friendships in the Forelands." She met the woman's gaze. "The truth is I do miss it a bit. Living among Qirsi, without any Eandi at all, is new to me, and it's wondrous. But I can't tell you that there are no Eandi who I miss from my life in the Forelands."

F'Solya stared at her for several moments. "You're very brave," she said at last. "I know many Qirsi—many Fal'Borna even—who would have lied had they been in your position. Thank you for telling me the truth."

Cresenne could hear in the woman's voice that she wasn't telling her everything. "But?"

"You might think carefully about being so honest with others."

"I've offended you."

"No, you've honored me. But others may not feel the same way."

Grinsa had warned her about this. He'd been trying to tell her since they set foot in the Southlands that life here would be complicated and difficult in ways she couldn't even anticipate. And of course he'd been right. No surprise there.

"I say this to caution you," F'Solya said. "I didn't mean to anger you."

"I'm not angry."

"I didn't mean to sadden you, either."

She didn't deny it.

F'Solya put down her work. "You were honest with me, and I'm grateful. I'm only trying to be as honest with you. I believe I understand what you were telling me about the Eandi. It's very different from anything I've ever felt toward the dark-eyes, but I understand. But other Fal'Borna won't. Some will think it strange. Others will be offended, and still others will tell you that you're a traitor to our people."

A traitor to our people. How many times had the Weaver called her that, and worse? Perhaps these two lands were more similar than she had imagined. Maybe these same problems could be found in any land shared by Eandi and Qirsi.

"I suppose I should thank you in turn, not only for being so honest with me, but also for offering the warning."

F'Solya smiled sadly. "I probably shouldn't have told you any of this."

"No, it's all right. If we're to remain here, I should know what people are saying about me."

"If I hear others saying it, I'll tell them they're wrong."

Cresenne almost told her not to. The thought of so many people speaking of her past unnerved her, perhaps because she remained uneasy with so much of what she had done, and of what had been done to her. But she and Grinsa were new here, and no matter what she or Grinsa or F'Solya said to anyone, they would continue for some time to be a topic of conversation. Best to let the stories run their course. F'Solya was offering a kindness, and an apology of sorts. She could hardly refuse.

"Thank you" was all she said.

Before they could say more, Cresenne heard voices behind her and then the hoofbeats of what sounded like a herd of horses. A frown crossed F'Solya's features.

"Now where are they off to?"

Turning to look as well, Cresenne saw several dozen riders heading northward away from the sept. Two men rode ahead of them, and all of them bore weapons.

"Who were they?" she asked.

F'Solya was still staring after them. "Warriors. My I'Joled was with them. The two at the head of the column are called Q'Daer and L'Norr. They're both Weavers."

She remembered Q'Daer from the first day they reached the sept, though she hadn't recognized him.

"Maybe they're hunting?" she offered.

A tight smile crossed her lips. "They're hunting all right, but not as you mean it. That was a war party."

Cresenne stared after the men, her stomach tightening again. She'd had too much of war in the last year. "Does that mean there are Eandi warriors nearby?"

"More likely the J'Balanar or maybe the Talm'Orast. Don't worry," she added, seeing the look on Cresenne's face. "That was a small party— E'Menua has hundreds of warriors in his sept. If we were in danger, he would have sent out a larger force."

She nodded, knowing that she should have been grateful for the woman's reassurances. But looking to the north again, watching as the riders vanished in a haze of brown dust, she couldn't help but wonder what new peril was about to enter her life.

Chapter 19

✦┼✦

They were cutting southwestward, because that was really their only
choice. Torgan would have given a good deal of gold to get to
Stelpana and the safety of Eandi land. But the Fal'Borna and the Y'Qatt
had settlements all along the Silverwater, and he would have had to venture dangerously close to them in order to find a bridge across the wash.
He also sensed that the Qirsi were watching the riverbank, knowing that
the Eandi lands beyond its banks offered Torgan his best chance of escape. He knew enough of Qirsi magic and the power of Weavers to understand that their communication could be as instantaneous as thought.
Torgan's only hope at this point lay to the west, and a small hope it was.
He had the rivers to cross: the Thraedes and the K'Sahd. And even if he
managed to get across those, he'd still have to face the J'Balanar. There
had been bad blood between the two Qirsi clans for centuries, but always, when faced with a common Eandi enemy, they had put aside their
disputes and fought as allies. If the Fal'Borna were hunting him, and had
alerted the other clans to what they believed him to have done, he was a
dead man.

Jasha was with him still, his cart rattling alongside Torgan's own. The
two men said little to one another, which was just how Torgan wanted it.
In fact, he would have preferred that the young merchant simply leave
him, abandon him to his fate, no matter what it might be. But Jasha remained convinced that they had to find the Mettai woman who had sold
those cursed baskets to Y'Farl in C'Bijor's Neck, and though Torgan had
tried to convince him of the futility of this search, the lad refused to be
dissuaded. That was the other reason they were still in Fal'Borna land.
Jasha wouldn't let them leave, and perhaps in some small way his argu-
ments were beginning to sway Torgan. It was foolishness, he knew. And

yet, how could he allow her to do to another village what she had done to the Neck, what he had helped her do to S'Plaed's sept?

Finding her wasn't worth his life, which was why they continued to head south and west, away from where they were most likely to find her. But given the chance to hand the woman over to the Fal'Borna he would have done so gladly, and not merely because it might well keep the Qirsi from killing him.

When they happened upon a sept, the two merchants kept their distance, at least long enough to find someplace where Torgan could wait, out of view, while Jasha returned to the settlement to trade his wares and, more to the point, to search for the Mettai woman. So far they had been fortunate—they had spotted the septs before they themselves had been seen. Their luck couldn't hold forever.

Torgan wondered at how quickly his life had been transformed. Only days ago, it seemed, he had been crossing the northern plains, smug in his certainty that no other merchant in the Southlands could be as comfortable as he. He could walk away from any sale; he didn't have to hurry from settlement to settlement as others did. He was known throughout the land for the quality of his goods. His was a life of ease. He would have laughed out loud had the irony not tasted so bitter. Ease? He could hardly sleep at night. Every sound in the darkness set his heart racing like a Naqbae stallion. A hundred times each day he thought he saw Fal'Borna riders in the shimmering heat, or heard war cries in the plaintive calls of a circling hawk. Yes, he was known and recognized. How many merchants of his size and race were missing their left eye? The Fal'Borna would know him—all the Qirsi would. It would make killing him that much easier. Never before had he known such fear, even in the days leading up to the loss of his eye, when he knew he was being hunted by the coinmonger's cutthroats.

"I see smoke ahead."

Torgan reined his horse to a halt, scanning the horizon. There, due south. He wouldn't have spotted the thin ribbons of smoke had he not been searching for them. The lad had keen eyes.

Jasha halted as well, stood up in the seat atop his cart, and looked around, no doubt searching for somewhere Torgan could hide while he investigated the sept. After a moment he frowned.

"There isn't much here," he said.

"Then we'll skirt the sept and continue on our way."

The young merchant's frown deepened. "What if she's there?"

"She's not, Jasha! She's probably forty leagues from here!"

Jasha continued to survey the plain, as if he might will a hollow or copse to form in that moment.

"Look," Torgan said, "she's an old woman. She can't have come this far as quickly as we have. If you're determined to find her, you should head north again. I can't, obviously. I need to get out of Fal'Borna land. But you're right to want to stop her."

Jasha regarded him coolly. "You've been trying to rid yourself of my company for days now, Torgan. What makes you think I'm going to leave you now if I haven't already?"

"Why do you stay?" Torgan demanded, flinging his arms wide. "If you think this woman is responsible—"

Comprehension struck him dumb, and for several moments he just stared at the young merchant. "You don't think it was her, do you?" he finally said, his voice low. "You probably don't even believe that she exists. You've thought it was me all along. You're not trying to find that woman; you're just unwilling to let me out of your sight."

Jasha pressed his lips thin and said nothing.

"What is it you really do when you go into these villages?"

"Just what I tell you I do," the lad said. "I look for the woman."

"On the off chance that I was telling the truth?" he asked, acid in his voice.

"Put yourself in my place for a moment, Torgan. Would you have believed the story you told me? Or would you have come to the same conclusion I did, the same one the Fal'Borna have come to?"

Torgan glared at him a moment longer, then looked away and rubbed a hand over his face. Jasha was right. Of course he was telling the truth about the Mettai woman, but the tale sounded far-fetched even to him. Why should anyone else believe it?

"She's real," he said weakly. "I don't care that you don't believe me. She's real, and she's the one who did this, not me."

"In the time we've been together," Jasha said, choosing his words carefully, "I've seen nothing to suggest that you wanted to harm the Fal'Borna, or even that you have the ability to."

"But you also haven't seen anything to convince you that the woman exists."

The young merchant shrugged, conceding the point.

"So you intend to keep following me?"

"I'd think that you'd want me to," Jasha said, the hint of a smile on his youthful face. "If for no other reason than because I usually spot the septs well before you do."

Torgan gave him a sour look. "Come along then. We're going around this one."

He snapped his reins and Trili started forward. After only a few seconds, however, he realized that Jasha wasn't following. He turned to look at the merchant and saw that he was staring southward, his face ashen in the bright sunlight. He swiveled in his seat, following the direction of Jasha's gaze. What he saw made his breath catch in his throat.

From this distance it appeared to be no more than a cloud of dust, a wisp of brown against the golden grasses and blue sky. It could have been kicked up by a sudden gust of wind, or a small herd of rilda. But even without Jasha's keen sight, even without asking the lad what he saw, Torgan knew that it was neither the breeze nor the wild beasts.

Riders. Fal'Borna riders.

"Have they seen us yet?" he managed to ask, his mouth abruptly so dry he could barely make himself understood.

"I don't think so."

Torgan looked around, much as Jasha had done moments before, and with much the same result. There was nowhere to hide out here. He snapped the reins again, fiercely this time, and he yelled at Trili to run. To the beast's credit, she leaped forward, straining against the harness, yanking the wagon into motion. Torgan was nearly thrown to the ground, and the cart shuddered and bounced mercilessly as they rushed over the grasses and rocky soil. But at least for a few precious moments he could fool himself into believing that they were getting away.

Then Jasha shouted to him to stop. At first Torgan ignored him, but within moments the lad had caught up to him with his cart.

"Torgan, stop!" he said again. "This is folly! We can't outrun Fal'Borna riders!"

"We can try!" he shot back, though he knew Jasha was right.

"If they see you running, they'll kill you! You know they will! Your one chance is to confront them, convince them that you've done nothing wrong!"

"I've been with you for days and I haven't managed that! How am I supposed to convince the white-hairs?"

"I don't know!"

Strangely, it was this candid answer that reached Torgan and made him slow his horse.

"I don't know," the lad said a second time, slowing as well. "But you can't escape them, and if they see you making the attempt, they'll never believe anything you say."

"So you're saying I should just surrender to them."

"What choice do you really have?"

"They'll kill me."

"Chances are they'll kill both of us."

Torgan hadn't even considered the idea that Jasha might be in danger, too. But of course he was. "Do you really believe that?"

"I'm an Eandi merchant riding with another Eandi whom they consider an enemy. I'd be surprised if they didn't."

"Then why don't you run? Your horse is faster than mine." He glanced to the south again. The dust cloud had grown, and he could make out a lengthy column of riders headed in their general direction. He couldn't tell if the Fal'Borna had spotted them yet. "You can unhitch her from your cart. You might be able to outrun them. It's me they want." He'd never been one for heroism, and he wasn't quite certain why he was choosing this moment to start. Jasha had been nothing but a bother since they started traveling together, and knowing now that the lad thought him a liar and murderer, Torgan should have damned him to whatever doom the Qirsi had in mind for them.

He couldn't do it, though. He'd had nothing to do with Y'Farl's death or the tragedy that befell the people of the Neck, and whatever harm he'd brought to S'Plaed's sept had been unintentional. Still, he'd been carrying the weight of those deaths for days now. Perhaps one more shouldn't have bothered him, but it did.

"Maybe we have time to hitch your wagon to the back of mine. The Fal'Borna need never know that we were together."

Jasha actually smiled, looking older and wiser than Torgan had seen him. "They'd know, Torgan. They can track a single rilda over rock and water. They can track me on this plain. No," he said, shaking his head and facing south again. "We'll face them together. It's really all we can do."

So they sat atop their carts, watching the horsemen approach, noting the slight shift in their direction as they finally spotted the two merchants. Torgan had never been any braver than he was heroic, and as he waited for the Fal'Borna to reach him, he felt himself succumbing to a debilitating fear. He grew sweaty, his hands trembled, and his teeth chattered as if they were in the midst of the Snows rather than the Harvest. His innards turned to water, so that long before the Qirsi got there, he had to climb off of his cart, walk behind it, and relieve himself. Even after he was back on his wagon again, the stink clung to him, hanging in the air around them. Jasha, who could not help but notice, was kind enough not to say anything.

The Fal'Borna continued their advance. Torgan could make out their white hair now, tied back in tails that streamed behind them like battle flags.

"I'd be grateful if you didn't tell them that you think I've been lying," he said. "If they choose not to believe that the woman is real, so be it. But they don't need any prodding from you in that regard."

Jasha smirked, his eyes never leaving that approaching column. "I won't say a thing."

"They may ask you."

"I'll tell them that I never saw the woman, but I did see her baskets. Will that do?"

Torgan exhaled heavily. "Probably not, but perhaps it won't make matters any worse."

As the Qirsi drew nearer, Torgan thought he recognized one of the leaders. He couldn't remember the man's name, but that was far less important than his sept, and the merchant racked his brain trying to attach an a'laq's name to the face before him.

"There are so many of them!" Jasha muttered. "Eight fours at least. Maybe ten. Do you think they sent out that many for us?"

Torgan concentrated on that face, saying nothing. He was so close to remembering.

"Torgan?"

He raised a hand, to keep the lad from saying more. It was right there, at the edge of his memory. . . .

"E'Menua!" he whispered at last.

"What?"

Torgan closed his eyes. "Demons and fire," he said. "It's E'Menua's sept."

"Who's E'Menua?" Jasha asked.

He just shook his head.

"Talk to me, Torgan. They're getting close."

Any hope he might have had left was gone now. He could hardly bring himself to speak. "E'Menua is the a'laq of a large sept that often keeps to the central plains. I should have known these riders were his."

"You've had dealings with him before?"

"Some, none that was particularly unpleasant. But he has little affection for any Eandi, be they warriors or merchants, and he's said to be a fearsome warlord." Torgan looked at the lad. "You should have run when you had the chance."

Before Jasha could respond, one of the warriors just behind the two lead riders hurled a spear toward them so that it rose in a high arc and then plunged to earth, stabbing into the ground just in front of them, exactly between the two carts. Torgan's horse reared, as did Jasha's, and both merchants fought to control their beasts.

"Damn them!" Torgan muttered. This was part of what made the Fal'Borna so dangerous. They were as skilled with weapons as any Eandi army, and yet they also wielded Qirsi magic. They were said to be fearless in battle, and merciless as well. Torgan could only assume that he had but moments left to live.

The riders came to a halt just a few fourspans from where Torgan and Jasha waited for them, stirring the dust, so that a dun haze drifted over the merchants.

"Both of you, throw down your blades!" one of the leaders said, hefting a spear of his own.

The merchants exchanged puzzled looks. Forty Fal'Borna warriors were worried about their daggers?

"Our blades?" Jasha said.

"You heard me! Throw them down now, or we'll kill you both!"

There could be no mistaking the man's tone: He meant what he said.

Torgan glanced at his companion again and shrugged. He pulled his old dagger from his belt and tossed it on the ground by his cart. Jasha did the same.

One of the Fal'Borna ran forward and retrieved the blades.

"Now, down off your cart, Torgan Plye!"

He wanted to ask what would happen to his wares, his cart, and his horse, but he was familiar enough with the Fal'Borna to know already. His beast would be well cared for; his possessions were forfeit. Slowly, he climbed down off the wagon and stood before the Qirsi, his feet planted, his arms hanging at his side. He should have been terrified, but a strange calm had come over him. He had feared that he might weep, or that his legs wouldn't support him and he'd wind up groveling in the dirt. He did neither.

"Who are you?" the Fal'Borna asked Jasha.

"My name is Jasha Ziffel. I'm a merchant. I come from Tordjanne."

"What business do you have with Torgan?"

Jasha shrugged. "He's my friend."

"Have a care, Eandi. Do you know what it means to declare yourself friend to one the Fal'Borna have named an enemy?"

"Yes," Jasha said. "I know."

The Qirsi eyed him briefly, looking impressed. At last he nodded. "Very well. Off your cart, then."

Jasha climbed down and stood beside Torgan.

"That was foolish," Torgan said under his breath, as several of the Fal'Borna dismounted and began to search the carts.

"It was the truth," Jasha whispered back.

"No, it wasn't. We're not friends, Jasha. You think . . ." He stopped, casting a furtive look at the Fal'Borna leaders, who, at least for the moment, were ignoring them. "You think the worst of me," he went on, dropping his voice even further. "You're with me precisely because we're not friends. You don't trust me enough to leave me. That's some friendship."

"Do you have others?"

"What?"

"Other friends. Do you have any?"

Torgan opened his mouth, closed it again. After some time, he shook his head.

"Then, I'd suggest you accept my offer of friendship and keep your mouth shut."

"Be silent!" one of the leaders said, glaring at them.

Torgan could hear them rummaging through his wares, and none too gently.

"If you tell me what you're looking for, I might be able to tell you," he said. "And that way you won't have to destroy my goods."

One of the leaders, the one Torgan had recognized from afar, walked over and stood just in front of him. He was a full head shorter than Torgan, but the look in his eyes could have brought snow on the hottest day of the Growing season.

"Do you know why we've been hunting you, Torgan Plye?" he asked, his voice a match for those pale eyes.

Torgan held the man's gaze for as long as he could—no more than a heartbeat or two—before looking away. "I have some idea," he whispered.

"Then you should understand that I'm eager for your blood. All of us are. We're just waiting for you to give us an excuse to spill it. Do I make myself clear?"

He nodded, not daring to speak.

The man stood before him a moment longer, then grinned coldly and spun away. Only then did Torgan begin to breathe again.

The Fal'Borna searched the two carts for what seemed an eternity. After some time, it occurred to the merchant to wonder if the Qirsi knew about the baskets, if they were, in fact, searching for some indication that he had encountered the Mettai woman. He didn't ask, seeing danger in the question regardless of what they knew. He remained silent, staring at the ground, waiting to die. At last, when it seemed that every item Torgan carried with him must have been broken or dented or ruined in some way, the warriors walked back to their leaders and announced that they had found nothing of significance. Torgan would have laughed aloud had he not been certain that the Qirsi would kill him where he stood.

"So, what now?" Jasha asked.

"Now, they kill us, you fool!" Torgan whispered.

But Jasha was looking at the two Fal'Borna leaders, who were approaching them.

"Now, we're going to take you back to our sept, where you'll face the judgment of our a'laq."

"You're not going to kill us?" Torgan said, without thinking.

"Not yet, Torgan Plye," the Fal'Borna said. "Not yet." He started to walk away. "The two of you will ride with us," he called to them over his shoulder. "Our warriors will see to it that your carts reach the sept."

Torgan felt someone push him from behind and glancing back, found himself face to face with a young Fal'Borna warrior.

"You're to follow the Weaver," the young man told him, his voice flat.

Torgan nodded and started walking slowly after the leader. Jasha did the same.

"We should be dead by now," the old merchant said quietly.

Jasha glanced at him. "Are you complaining?"

"Of course not," Torgan said, scowling at him. "I just don't understand. You heard the leader. They think I killed all those people in S'Plaed's sept. To the Fal'Borna, that's more than enough to justify a summary execution."

"Maybe they're scared," Jasha whispered.

"Scared? You mean of me?"

"Of the pestilence. Of whatever killed the Y'Qatt. They may yet kill us, Torgan. But they're going to want to understand all of this first. That's our one hope."

It made sense, and after a moment Torgan nodded. "Then, should I tell them what I know, or would I be better off keeping it to myself?"

Jasha just shrugged. "I don't know. But choose well. Our lives are most certainly at stake."

The sun had begun to set and a bank of clouds rolling in from the west had cast a grey pall over the day when the riders finally returned. Cresenne was still working and Bryntelle remained with the other children, leaving Grinsa with little to occupy his day. He'd been in the sept for only a short time, but already he had grown bored with the leisurely life afforded him because he was a Weaver. Not knowing what else to do, and unwilling simply to sit outside the a'laq's shelter, he had wandered off, following the stream that wound past the settlement.

He hadn't gone far, though, and was already on his way back to the sept, when he heard the beginnings of the commotion raised by the war party's return. He hurried on to the middle of the settlement, where he found Q'Daer and L'Norr already speaking with E'Menua. Two Eandi men sat on mounts behind them, eyed closely by several warriors, who also remained on their horses.

One of the men was young—he couldn't have been much past his twentieth year. He had yellow hair that he wore closely shorn, and a youthful freckled face. He remained watchful, but he didn't appear particularly fearful, not like the other man.

He was older than his companion, and larger as well, broad in the shoulders and thick in his middle. As a younger man he might have been formidable, but now he merely looked ponderous. He'd lost one of his eyes years before; the scars on his face were old, brown and weathered like the rest of his skin. His one good eye, which was as dark as the ocean on a stormy day, darted about as if he wasn't certain where to look and feared everything on which his gaze lingered. Based on all he had heard earlier in the day, Grinsa guessed that this older man was Torgan Plye.

When E'Menua spotted Grinsa, he gestured for him to join their discussion. Grinsa walked to where they were standing.

"Where have you been, Forelander?" the a'laq asked, sounding annoyed. "We've been waiting for you."

"Why?"

"You are a Weaver in this sept. I expect you to join us in discussions of matters of such great weight."

Grinsa wasn't certain what to say. A moment before he'd been lamenting his lack of responsibilities. Now it seemed that he had some, and had been shirking them. A quip leaped to mind, but he kept it to himself.

"My apologies then, A'Laq. How may I serve the sept?"

E'Menua stared at him briefly, as if wondering whether Grinsa was goading him again.

"As you can see," he said after a moment, "we've found Torgan Plye, of whom you heard us speak earlier. Q'Daer and L'Norr searched his cart and found nothing unusual. And as of yet, none of their riders have fallen ill. We intend to question them now, before putting them to death."

Both of the Eandi paled.

"You've already decided to execute them?" Grinsa asked.

"Yes, of course. They're enemies of the Fal'Borna."

"But you don't know if they did anything wrong!"

The warriors gaped at him. Q'Daer and L'Norr eyed him coldly. Even the merchants, who had barely taken notice of him until now, were staring at Grinsa as if he had challenged the a'laq to a knife fight. But it was E'Menua's expression that told the gleaner just how seriously he had erred. His large eyes burned like coals in a fire, his cheeks had shaded to crimson, and his sharp chin quivered, as if it was all he could do to keep from striking Grinsa down where he stood.

"In my z'kal!" he said through clenched teeth. "Now!"

Grinsa didn't dare argue. He merely turned and started toward the a'laq's shelter.

"Bring them!" he heard E'Menua say. Grinsa didn't look back to see who the a'laq had spoken to, but he assumed E'Menua had given the order to the other two Weavers.

Reaching the a'laq's shelter, he stepped inside, then turned to face the entryway and waited. He didn't have to stand there for long.

E'Menua threw aside the flap of rilda hide that covered the entrance, stepped into the shelter, and struck Grinsa across the cheek with the back of his hand. Grinsa had expected him to do something of the sort, and he made no effort to block the blow. He staggered back, nearly stepping in the fire, but he managed to stay on his feet.

"If you ever speak to me in such a way again, I'll kill you! I am a'laq of this sept and you will show me the respect I am due! How dare you question me in front of my people like that!"

His cheek still throbbing, Grinsa said nothing. Best, he thought, to let the a'laq vent his anger.

"You may be new here, Forelander. You may feel that you're not one of us, that you intend to leave Fal'Borna land at the first opportunity. I don't give a damn! You will address me properly, or you'll be dealt with just the way a mutinous Fal'Borna would be. Do you understand me?"

"Yes, A'Laq. It wasn't my intention to give offense."

To his credit, E'Menua appeared to accept Grinsa's apology.

"What exactly was your intention?" he asked, sounding calmer.

"I'm not really certain," Grinsa admitted. "It just seems to me that you may not be justified in executing those men."

"They have been declared enemies of the Fal'Borna, Forelander. They—"

"A'Laq?" came a voice from outside.

"Wait out there!" E'Menua called. He looked at Grinsa again. "Once someone is named an enemy of our people, his fate is decided. It's something you'd do well to keep in mind. I have no choice in the matter. These men have to die."

"Even if they've done nothing wrong."

"Torgan brought the pestilence to S'Plaed's sept."

"So S'Plaed claims," Grinsa said. "But what if he's mistaken? What if we can prove that the merchant did nothing wrong? Is Fal'Borna justice so unyielding that it would condemn an innocent man?"

"Why do you argue so? What is Torgan to you?"

It was a fair question, one that he'd been asking himself since he first began arguing for the man's life earlier that day. "The merchant means nothing to me. But I had a friend in the Forelands, a man who committed no crime, a man who'd be dead now if Eandi justice worked as Fal'Borna justice does."

E'Menua bristled. "Are you trying to provoke me? Do you wish to see just how far I'll go in punishing you?"

"No, A'Laq. I only want to see justice done."

"The Tesserate has declared that this man and any who help him are to die. You would defy them?"

"Of course not," Grinsa said. "But why did the Tesserate decide this?"

"Because S'Plaed has told them that Torgan attacked his sept with the pestilence."

"And if you were to learn that this wasn't true, wouldn't you be bound to tell the Tesserate?"

"I'd be pitting myself against S'Plaed."

"Is that worse than allowing an innocent man to die?"

"You judge us," the a'laq said darkly. "You have no right."

"I'm not judging you. I'm trying to understand you."

E'Menua regarded him for some time before finally giving a small shake of his head. "You are a most difficult man, Forelander. The truth is I don't know how to answer your question. Openly opposing the a'laq of another sept, even one that has been weakened as S'Plaed's has, can be dangerous. And it may do little good. The Tesserate may not listen to me—S'Plaed has a good deal of support in Thamia. So do I, but in this matter I'd be taking the part of an Eandi."

"A'Laq?" came the voice from outside again.

"Just a moment!"

"I ask only that you keep an open mind, A'Laq," Grinsa said. "I don't wish to see any man—Eandi or Qirsi—executed without cause, and I can't imagine you do, either."

"An open mind," E'Menua repeated, looking skeptical.

Grinsa nodded.

"Very well." He looked past Grinsa to the entryway and called for the others to enter.

Q'Daer and L'Norr stepped into the shelter, each of them guiding one of the merchants by the arm. The Weavers glanced briefly at the a'laq, but then stared at Grinsa. The shelter was dimly lit, but he felt certain that the welt on his cheek showed clearly, even in this poor light. No doubt both men would delight in seeing it.

E'Menua sat at his usual spot, and gestured for Grinsa and the other Fal'Borna to do the same.

Torgan began to sit as well, but Q'Daer stopped him.

"You stand, Eandi. Both of you," he added, looking at the other merchant.

"Tell us what you did to S'Plaed's sept," the a'laq demanded.

Torgan hesitated, licking his lips and looking so unnerved that Grinsa found himself wondering if perhaps the merchant was responsible for the deaths there after all.

"I did nothing," the man said at last, his voice quavering.

"You're lying."

"No! I've done nothing wrong! I went to the sept, I sold some wares, and I left! That's all! I swear it!"

"Why did you leave so quickly then? S'Plaed says that you were in a great rush to be away from his sept. It seems you knew some great calamity was about to befall them."

"No, it wasn't that! I had just learned . . ." He stopped, licked his lips again. "I had just heard . . . some bad tidings. I wanted to be away from there, away from everyone. That's all."

The a'laq glanced at Grinsa and raised an eyebrow, as if to say, *You see? I told you he was guilty.*

"Do you think we're fools, Torgan?" E'Menua asked, facing the Eandi again. "Do you think we can't tell when a dark-eye is lying to us?"

"No, of course not. But I swear to you—"

"He is lying."

Everyone turned to stare at the other merchant.

Torgan looked like he'd just been slapped. "Jasha!"

"He did do something to S'Plaed's sept, and what's more, he knows exactly what happened at C'Bijor's Neck."

Torgan launched himself at the younger man. "You treacherous little bastard!" He knocked Jasha to the ground and was on him immediately, his hands around the man's throat. "This was your plan all along! You want to destroy me!"

Q'Daer and L'Norr tried to pull Torgan off the young merchant, but Torgan was far bigger than both of them, and apparently as strong as he was large. Jasha's eyes were wide, and his face was turning bright red. He clawed at Torgan's hands, but to no avail. Just as Grinsa began to fear for the young merchant's life, he heard a sharp snapping sound. Torgan let out a howl of pain, rolled off of Jasha, and clutched at his right arm.

"I can just as easily break your neck, Torgan," E'Menua said calmly. "So can every other Weaver in this z'kal. Don't make us kill you."

"You're going to kill me no matter what I do," he said, bitterly. He nodded toward Jasha, who still lay on the floor, his chest heaving. "All thanks to this snake!"

"You have to tell them now, Torgan," the younger man said, still gasping. "That's why I did it."

The old merchant looked away. "I don't know what he's talking about."

Jasha lifted himself onto one elbow. "Your only hope is to tell them everything. Believe it or not, I may have saved your life."

"Shut your mouth, whelp! My only consolation is knowing that they'll kill you, too."

"Tell them, Torgan."

The merchant clamped his mouth shut and pressed his lips thin.

"Do you know what mind-bending magic is?" Grinsa asked. Instantly, he wondered if he'd stepped in where he shouldn't have. But when he chanced a look at the a'laq, he saw that E'Menua was nodding.

"You're not Fal'Borna," Torgan said, as if seeing Grinsa for the first time.

"Answer the question," the a'laq commanded.

Torgan exhaled. "Mind-bending. Yes, I have some idea what it can do."

"In that case," Grinsa said, "I shouldn't have to tell you that we can make you tell us. You can refuse us all you like, but in the end, we'll find out all that we need to. The question is, do you want one of us using his magic on your mind?"

For a long time, Torgan just sat there, cradling his maimed arm, shaking his head. "Damn you all," he finally muttered. "Damn every white-hair in the Southlands."

"What did you do to S'Plaed's sept?" the a'laq asked again.

"Nothing."

E'Menua closed his eyes and ran a hand through his hair. "Torgan—"

"Nothing that I meant to do," the merchant said, his voice dropping to a whisper.

"What does that mean?"

"Start with C'Bijor's Neck," Jasha said.

Torgan glared at him, and for a moment Grinsa thought that he might attack him again. But then the merchant nodded.

"What's all this talk about C'Bijor's Neck?" the a'laq asked. "That's an Y'Qatt settlement. They're not Fal'Borna."

"No," Torgan said. "But that's where I first encountered the Mettai woman."

E'Menua blinked once. It almost seemed that until that moment, he hadn't actually believed this talk of Mettai magic. "Go on."

"She was selling baskets. The most beautiful baskets I've ever seen. Perfect weaving, colors that take your breath away. She could have gotten . . . well, she could have gotten anything for them. Instead, she sold them for far too little, and seemed pleased with the bargain she struck.

"I convinced the man she sold them to—a man named Y'Farl—I convinced him that he'd paid too much for them, and he sold them to me. I left the village soon after, and steered my cart westward intending to find septs where I could sell the baskets, and the rest of what I carried. But that night . . ." He trailed off; swallowed and shook his head. "That's when the pestilence struck, though I didn't know it at the time. It looked like . . . like a battle, like the village was under attack. There was fire everywhere—Qirsi fire. And smoke, and shattered houses. I didn't know what had happened. I thought maybe it was marauders. At the time, it didn't occur to me that it could be the pestilence."

He shrugged. "So I moved on, fearful of remaining near the Neck. Eventually I found S'Plaed's sept. That's where I learned of what really happened in C'Bijor's Neck. I just wanted to get away. I still hadn't considered the possibility that the Mettai woman and her baskets might have something to do with all of this. I just knew that Y'Farl was dead, and that I had missed dying myself by mere hours. So I sold the baskets at a low price and left. That night, the same thing happened to the sept. The fire again, and the rest of it. That's when I started to wonder about the woman and those baskets of hers."

He looked at E'Menua, and then at the two Weavers. Finally, his gaze came to rest on Grinsa. "I didn't mean to do it. I didn't even know what I'd done until after—until I watched the sept burn."

For several moments, all of them were silent. Grinsa could hear children laughing outside. A horse whinnied, and the wind moaned in the wood holding up the shelter.

Eventually E'Menua stirred, as if shaking himself awake. "Tell us about the woman."

"No, Torgan," Jasha said. "Don't tell them anything more. Not yet."

The merchant frowned. "What?"

But Jasha was already eyeing the a'laq. "What are you going to do to him? You've heard his tale. You know now that he didn't intend any harm. He bought some baskets and then sold them again. He's a merchant. It's what he does. You can't punish him for that."

"He killed half of S'Plaed's sept," E'Menua said, his voice hardening. "Now it seems that he had a hand in killing the people of C'Bijor's Neck, as well. What he's told us changes nothing."

Grinsa opened his mouth to argue, but quickly stopped himself. Instead he faced E'Menua. "May I have a word, A'Laq?"

But the a'laq shook his head. "No. Not about this. He will tell us what he knows of the woman, and then he'll be put to death. He is an enemy of the Fal'Borna."

"And what of me?" Jasha asked.

"You're to be executed as well. You've ridden with him and protected him, all the while knowing what he's done. You deserve to die as much as he does."

"Dead we're of no use to you," Jasha said. "But if you spare our lives, we can help you find the woman."

The a'laq stared back at him, stony-faced. "We found you. Another sept can find the woman."

Q'Daer and L'Norr exchanged looks.

"Forgive me, A'Laq," Q'Daer said, looking as if he expected E'Menua to strike him at any moment. "But other septs might not know her. We can bring glory to your sept. Every Weaver in the Tesserate will know of you and of your warriors."

"I've spoken on the matter." His eyes flicked in Grinsa's direction. It was only for a moment, but that was enough. "These men are to die."

Suddenly, Grinsa understood. "You're doing this to punish me, not them," he said.

E'Menua glowered at him. After a moment, he waved a hand at the young Weavers. "Leave us. Take the Eandi and go. But not far. I'm not done with them yet."

They glanced at Grinsa, but Q'Daer and L'Norr did as they were told. A moment later Grinsa and E'Menua were alone once more.

"Do you want to hit me again?" the gleaner asked.

"I should."

"Then do. But don't kill those men. You know as well as I that they don't deserve execution."

The a'laq shook his head. "You have much to learn about Fal'Borna ways, Forelander." He passed a hand over his brow. "Torgan brought the pestilence to S'Plaed's sept, and for that S'Plaed has demanded vengeance. That's within his rights as a'laq."

"Even if it wasn't Torgan's intention to hurt anyone?"

"Yes, even so."

Grinsa shook his head in turn. "That's just wrong."

"You have no right to judge us." The a'laq said this quietly, without any of the anger he had shown earlier. "The Fal'Borna have lived this way for centuries. We don't need strangers from the Northlands coming here and instructing us in their notions of justice."

He was right. Grinsa could see that. The Fal'Borna lived in a hard land, one that would sometimes require hard laws. They had survived centuries of warfare, and no doubt that too had bred a certain kind of justice. Who was he to challenge traditions a thousand years in the making?

"You make a good point, A'Laq. Forgive me."

E'Menua narrowed his eyes. "I haven't known you long, Grinsa, but I understand you well enough to know that this isn't your final word on the matter."

Grinsa smiled. "No, it's not. S'Plaed may be justified in demanding vengeance, but don't you and the other a'laqs have a right to protect your people?"

"Meaning?"

"That Mettai woman is still out there. Until she's been found, no Fal'Borna is safe. And since none of you knows who she is or what she looks like, you still need the merchants."

"You're arguing as the Eandi do."

"Occasionally even dark-eyes make sense," Grinsa said with a shrug.

E'Menua laughed. "Now you sound like a Fal'Borna."

"Does that mean you'll spare their lives?"

"It means," the a'laq said slowly, seeming to make his decision in that moment, "that I'll delay their executions until the woman is found. I'll even have Q'Daer heal the dark-eye's arm."

"That seems just, A'Laq. Thank you."

E'Menua had grown serious again. "Don't thank me, Forelander. Not yet. The woman is the only proof we have that Torgan and his friend are telling us the truth. If the woman is found and executed by another sept, then these men will have done nothing to prove their innocence or earn my mercy. They have to find her, which means someone from this sept has to go with them."

It took Grinsa a moment. He didn't think of himself as being from any sept, but clearly E'Menua did.

"You'd let us go?"

"Only you."

"I can't leave Cresenne and Bryntelle."

The a'laq shrugged, as if the matter were of no importance to him. "You plead for their lives. You ask me to go against Fal'Borna law. Fine then. If you truly want them spared, you must do this."

Grinsa remained stock-still, not knowing what to say.

"You'll want to think about this, perhaps speak of this matter with your . . . your wife. I'll expect an answer in the morning."

He could barely hear E'Menua for the roaring in his ears. *If you truly want them spared . . .* At last, he nodded, stood, and stepped outside. The sky was darkening and a strong wind blew out of the west, carrying the scent of rain. The two Weavers stood just before him, glaring at him but saying nothing. Grinsa tried to step around them, but Q'Daer moved to block his way.

"Not so fast, Forelander," the young Weaver said.

Grinsa shook his head. "I don't have time for this right now." He tried to walk past again, but Q'Daer put out a hand to stop him.

"That's too bad. It's time you started showing the a'laq and our sept the respect we're due. The a'laq has chosen to let you live, despite the way you speak to him, so I can't kill you, much as I'd like to. But I can show you what happens to strangers who challenge the authority of the Fal'Borna."

Grinsa eyed the man briefly, and then glanced at L'Norr. The other Weaver stood just beside his friend, but though he wore a hard expression, he wouldn't meet Grinsa's gaze. It seemed this was Q'Daer's fight.

Facing the first man once more, Grinsa shook his head. "You're not going to show me anything, Q'Daer. You haven't the magic and you haven't the strength." He was certain of the former, less so of the latter, but he didn't let the younger man see that. "And as I said, I won't waste time on this foolishness right now."

Q'Daer's face reddened and his hand strayed to the blade on his belt. "I should kill you where you stand!"

In the Forelands he simply would have walked away. That would have been the smart thing to do. But this was a different land, ruled by a different set of customs. And though new to the Southlands, Grinsa had already learned a great deal about Fal'Borna ways. He had the welt on his cheek to prove it.

He reached for his magic and broke the man's blade before Q'Daer could pull it free. The young Weaver's eyes widened at the muffled chiming sound of the shattered steel.

"You bastard!"

Before he could say more, Grinsa hit him, backhanded, just as the a'laq had struck him. Q'Daer staggered back a step as Grinsa had, but he didn't fall. That was fine. Grinsa didn't wish to humiliate the man; he just wanted to put him in his place.

Before Q'Daer could throw a punch of his own, Grinsa stepped past him. "I serve the a'laq, not you," he said evenly, eyeing the man over his shoulder. "And I don't take lessons from ignorant whelps. Next time I'll break more than your blade."

The two merchants were standing nearby, their eyes wide at what they had just seen. But now, as he stared at Grinsa, Torgan's expression changed, shock giving way to desperation.

"Did you save us?" he called as Grinsa walked away, still cradling his shattered arm. "Will he spare our lives?"

Grinsa glanced back at him, but he said nothing and he kept walking. When he reached his shelter, he could still hear Torgan shouting after him.

Chapter 20

❖━I━❖

She hadn't meant to come here. She hadn't realized where she was until she saw the bridge, and then it was too late to turn back. North. That's where she'd intended to go. There were more Y'Qatt settlements around the upper Companion Lakes—Porcupine and Bear. After leaving C'Bijor's Neck, Lici had every intention of finding them. Somehow, she hadn't.

She'd crossed the bridge before, after leaving Kirayde, and it hadn't even occurred to her to go back. She'd had a purpose then—it drove her, like a wolf snapping at the heels of rilda. Maybe passing by twice was too much to ask of anyone.

That was what she told herself, sitting in the heat of the Harvest sun, squinting against the glare, the day so bright it seemed to rob the land of color, leaving the grasses and rocks and the occasional tree looking stark and flat and dull. The old nag snorted and stomped her foot impatiently, but still Lici remained motionless atop her cart, unable to decide.

She was tired. The time had come for her to begin the long ride back to Kirayde. No one lived forever, not even Mettai witches. Perhaps that was why she was here. She'd never have another chance to see Sentaya. She didn't need the Sight to tell her that. Her days were nearly at an end. Vengeance was hers. Whatever purpose had sustained her in these last years was ebbing away now, leaving her grey, like the world around her. Colorless, lifeless. But when she closed her eyes and thought of Sentaya, the colors were vivid. She could taste the food and smell the wood smoke. And she didn't want any of it. Life that real, that sharp, was too much for her now. Grey suited her. Death, or the promise of it, had drawn her here, and though she was ready to embrace the ending that awaited her, she had no desire to step back into that brilliant living world that still existed in her mind. Yet she couldn't bring herself to turn away. She just sat, staring, waging war with forces she didn't quite understand.

"I didn't mean to come here."

Saying it aloud was like asking the gods for leave to pass the village by, to turn around and find another way across the wash. It didn't help. The pull of the place was too strong, even for her.

She clicked her tongue and snapped the reins, and the old horse started forward, shaking her head as if to scold Lici for taking so long. Lici steered the cart across the bridge and, once she was on the other side, turned northward.

At least this time I got it right, she thought, and cackled at her cruel joke, at the poor girl who'd gotten it wrong so many years before. There were tears on her face by the time she reached the village, or what was left of it.

The houses stood just where she remembered them, shattered and charred, crumbling from years of neglect, green with mosses and vines. She reined the nag to a halt and sat, listening, shaded now, cooler. The sound of the wash, the smell of the pines.

And she was a child again, hurrying through her chores with Kytha and Baet, running to Sosli's house to see if her friend could play, tromping through the rain and snow to the small sanctuary on the eastern edge of the village. She remembered falling out of a tree near the wash when she was only six, and breaking her arm. For just an instant, she felt it again, her old, brittle bone aching with remembered pain. She could see the healer's knife glinting in the dim light of his home, the blood seeping from the scored back of his bony hand. She could feel his hands on her skin, as he probed the bone with deft, gentle fingers. The relief as her pain ebbed away, her wonder as she actually felt the bone knitting back together, his smile at what he saw on her face.

Broken bones, scrapes and cuts, even burns. These Mettai magic could mend. But not the pestilence.

If she followed the road it would take her past her old home. She held a vision of the house in her mind, clear and substantial. But sixteen fours had passed, and she was but a child when last she saw it. Who could say what it really looked like? Did she really want to know? Was there any point in disturbing memories that had served her for so long? Or was it already too late for such concerns?

Without truly intending to, without really thinking about it at all, she clicked at the horse again and started forward once more.

No, the girl within whimpered. *Please. I don't want to see.*

Lici ignored her. When had she become so cruel, so merciless?

At first she didn't recognize it. That small thing? That wreck of a house? But yes. That second one beyond it belonged to Sosli's family. Of that she was certain. So this one had to be hers.

Please. Get away from here.

She stared at the house, or at least what was left of it. The front door was gone—only a pair of rusted hinges gave any indication that it had been there at all. There were large holes in the front and side walls, and looking into the house, she could see bright spots where daylight poured through the remains of the roof. And like fragments of an old rhyme, recollections of this house in which she'd spent her earliest years came back to her. Some she welcomed, as she would warmth from a fire or the scent of her mother's newly baked bread. From others she recoiled, though, of course, she could hardly welcome some without accepting all.

She could hear the little girl sobbing now, but try as she might, Lici couldn't make out what she said. In another moment, the sound had vanished, replaced by distant cries and the moans of the ill and, finally, by the distant rumble of an approaching storm. She didn't need the girl to tell her what was coming, to warn her away from this place. She was desperate to flee, but the time for that had passed. If only she had listened before.

Her torch sputters with each gust of wind and hisses in the rain. She's crying, fear of the dark and the storm and the pestilence robbing her of whatever courage she might once have possessed. Her knees and shins ache from all the falls she's taken.

Still, she stumbles on, desperate now for any sign of a village or even a single house. Anything to relieve the relentless darkness of the wood.

It starts to rain harder. Licaldi can hear the thunder growing nearer by the moment, growling like some great beast stalking her through the wood. She glances repeatedly at her torch. There can be no mistake: The flame is dying.

The path leads her up a steep incline, and several times she almost loses her footing. Just as she reaches the top, a bright flash illuminates the forest. Mere seconds later a clap of thunder makes the earth shudder.

Suddenly, though, Licaldi doesn't care about the storm, or her failing torch, or her sodden clothes. Not far from the crest of the hill a faint light shines, half hidden by the trees, dimmed by the rain.

Licaldi breaks into a run, shouting for help and waving the torch over her head. A lone house? No. A village, larger than her own. Its houses look solid and comfortable, as if they have been built with a night like this one in mind. Most of the windows are shuttered, the doors closed. But as Licaldi continues to yell, making her way toward the marketplace, shutters and doors open, revealing white-haired men and women who peer out at her warily.

A Qirsi village! Gods be praised!

Lici shook her head and made herself look away from the house. Gazing toward the wash through a web of branches and tree trunks she could see the water sparkling like shattered glass. A flock of finches twittered and scolded in the branches overhead, and the trees whispered as a breath of wind brushed her skin.

She picked up the reins again and began to turn the cart, taking care to steer away from the house, so she wouldn't have to look at it again. It was far quicker to take the road through the village and the old marketplace, but Lici was eager now to be gone from this place. The last thing she needed was to drive her cart through the heart of Sentaya.

She was only halfway around when she stopped again.

The door is shut, the windows closed tight. Maybe, she thinks, they're all right after all.

But she knows better. She pushes the door open. Utter darkness, save for the deep orange glow of embers that settle noisily in the hearth. The smell of sweat and vomit reach her and she gags.

"Mama?" she whispers through clenched teeth. "Papa?"

No answer.

"Kytha? Baet?"

A glimmer of lightning brightens the house and Licaldi screams at what she sees. Both of her sisters are in their beds, their sleeping gowns and blankets soiled. Licaldi's father lies on the floor beside Kytha's bed, curled into a ball, as if too weak to make it back to his own bed. Kytha and Baet might well be sleeping, so peaceful do they look. But her father's eyes are still open, fixed on some spot on the ceiling.

Licaldi takes a step backward, turns away, and retches.

When her stomach is empty, and her throat is so sore she can barely draw breath, she goes to find her mother.

She knows just where to look. If Mama isn't in the house with Papa and the girls, she's by the stream, where she would have gone to get water for the others.

Licaldi staggers out of the house and makes her way down to the wash. Mama is lying on the bank of the stream, in much the same position Licaldi's father had been in. Licaldi hurries to her, crying out "Mama, Mama!" like she did when she was small, even younger than Baetri. Baet, who's dead.

Incredibly, her mother still lives, though only just.

"Licaldi?" her mother murmurs, as Licaldi kneels beside her.

"Yes, Mama. It's me."

"Did you bring healers?"

Licaldi touches her mother's cheek with the back of her hand. Her skin is aflame. Lightning flares, and Licaldi catches a glimpse of her mother's face. White as bone and though her eyes are open wide, it seems that they see nothing. It won't be long now.

"Did you, child?"

"Yes, Mama. I brought healers."

Mama smiles and closes her eyes. "Good girl," she says, the words coming out as soft as a sigh. "I knew you would."

"You there!"

Lici's eyes snapped up and she shuddered, as if released from a spell. Perhaps a hundred fourspans down the lane, an Eandi man sat atop a peddler's cart much larger than her own. He was far younger than she, with an ample gut and a full shock of red hair that poked out from beneath a leather wide-brimmed hat. The wood of his wagon was a pale, warm tan, and the beast hitched to the front was a large bay, fit and strong. This was a man of some means, a man who had done well for himself.

Grateful for the distraction, she smiled, and raised a hand in greeting.

The man flicked his reins and the bay started forward. Lici drove her cart in his direction, so that in mere moments their carts were side by side.

"Are you all right?" he asked.

"Yes, fine," she said. Too quick with her response, too much brightness in her voice. "I used to live here," she said a moment later. "Many years ago. I was just . . . remembering."

The man nodded. "You live nearby, then?"

"Not very, no. I've been abroad for some time now." She gestured vaguely back at her cart. "I've baskets that I've been trying to sell." She noted that his eyes strayed toward her cart. Perhaps, if he was headed in the right direction, she could interest him in some or all of her wares. "And you?" she asked, offhandedly.

He met her gaze again, and smiled. He had a handsome face, despite the fleshy chin and round cheeks. "I came this way hoping to find some Mettai goods, some Y'Qatt blankets, things of that sort. Things you don't often find in Tordjanne. But it's proving harder than I expected."

Mettai, Y'Qatt. This was why the gods had steered her back into Sentaya. This was why she had ignored the little girl. This was why she had chanced those memories, sharp enough to draw blood. She needed to proceed carefully, though. She couldn't seem too eager to be rid of so many fine baskets. And somehow, before he left with her wares, she needed to place the spell on them.

"Mettai and Y'Qatt," she repeated aloud. "You're rather particular, aren't you?"

He grinned again. "I can afford to be. Any merchant can show up in a Tordjanne marketplace with the same tired goods and make a decent profit. That's not good enough for me. I've made a reputation for myself by selling not only the finest goods, but also the most unusual." He narrowed his eyes slightly. "You think me a braggart."

"You don't lack for confidence."

"I merely tell you what I know to be true. There are such merchants in these lands, as well. Surely you've heard of Torgan Plye."

Lici shrugged and shook her head.

"Well, take my word for it. If you want something on these plains, you go to Torgan Plye. And if you want something in Tordjanne, you come to me."

"And you are?"

He smiled and removed his hat. "Forgive me. Brint HedFarren, at your service."

"My pleasure, sir. I'm called Lici."

"The pleasure is all mine, kind lady. It seems you're new to the peddler's life. At least I assume so, since you don't know of Torgan. How did you come to be driving a cart so late in life?"

She gave him the same answer she'd given so many others: She wanted to see the land before she died, and so had taken to trading, using the gold she earned from selling her wares to pay for food.

"And you've managed to steer clear of the pestilence?"

"Thus far. It seems I've been fortunate."

He nodded, regarding her once more through narrowed eyes. "You're Mettai, aren't you, Lici?" he asked her at last.

"I am."

"And you say you're selling baskets?"

"Yes, sir."

"May I see them?"

She gestured back at her cart. "Of course."

He eyed her for another moment, before climbing off his cart and walking to the rear of hers. She heard him draw aside the cloth that hung over the back entry to the wagon, and she waited. Let him look at them. Let him realize what a treasure he'd found, and then let him fix a price in his head. Not too long—he'd notice if she waited longer than was reasonable—but long enough.

Finally, she climbed down out of her seat and walked to the back of the cart. Brint was merely standing there, holding a basket in each hand and staring at the others.

He glanced at her as she stopped beside him. "You made these yourself?"

"Yes. Dyed them by hand. No magic."

The man smiled. "That was my next question."

"It always is with merchants."

He nodded, examined the basket in his right hand. "You do fine work," he said after several moments. "Another merchant would tell me not to say that, but I think you probably know it already."

"Yes, sir."

He reached in and pushed a few baskets out of the way, exposing still more. "How many are there? Do you know?"

Lici shook her head.

"What have you sold them for?"

"Too little," she said, without thinking. He looked at her, and she added, "I'm not skilled in such matters. I weave baskets. That's where my talent lies." She straightened. "I've gotten two sovereigns for many of them, and have traded food and such for others."

"Two sovereigns is a good price."

"Is that what you'll pay?"

Brint laughed. "I didn't say that." He regarded the contents of her cart again with an appraising eye. "No, I won't pay two. But I would be willing to buy all the baskets you have left for one sovereign apiece."

"One is too low."

"If this were a marketplace, I'd agree with you. But it's not. I'm of-fering you the chance to sell every basket in your cart, right now, at a de-cent price."

"And then you'll turn around and make a fine profit on each one."

"That's my intention, yes. But I'll be transporting them, putting them out each morning and packing up those that are left each night. You'll have nothing to do but return to your home and count your gold. Surely that's worth something."

Once more, as in Runnelwick and C'Bijor's Neck, and every village in between, Lici sought to find the balance between striking a convinc-ing bargain and ridding herself of the baskets. But she was tired, and this young merchant seemed the perfect tool for delivering her curse to the last of the Y'Qatt villages.

"Yes, it is," she said with a sigh. "It's worth quite a bit. But I la-bored over those baskets, and I can't let them go for quite so little. So here's my offer. One sovereign for each basket, plus ten more for the lot. Neither of us knows what that will come to per basket, but I'm sure you'll be making out well, and I'll feel that I got a bit more for all my work."

Brint appeared to consider this for several moments. "Very well," he said at last. "One for each basket and ten more for the lot." He started to climb into her wagon, but then stopped himself. "Forgive me. May I?"

"Yes, of course." But inwardly, she winced. He was in a hurry now—no doubt he wished to be moving on before nightfall. Lici had con-cluded, though, that the night would be her best opportunity to use her magic on the baskets. She could pretend to be going in his direction, but his cart was finer than hers, and his was the stronger horse. She'd never be able to keep pace with him.

He emerged from her cart a moment later with several baskets in his hands. "This is eight," he said, stepping to the back of his cart. "I'll leave it to you to keep count."

"Yes, all right."

He placed the baskets in his cart and was back in hers a moment later.

"So were you born in Tordjanne?" she asked, waiting for him to climb out again.

"Yes."

"And you live there still?"

"It's home, if that's what you mean. I can't really say that I live anywhere in particular." He crawled out of the cart again. "Eight more."

"Do you have family?" she asked, watching him walk to his cart and place the baskets inside.

"I haven't a wife and children. Not yet at least." He pulled himself back into her cart. "I have brothers," he called to her. "Three of them. And my mother is still alive."

"All of them in Tordjanne, too?"

"Yes."

"Where?"

He emerged again. "Ten this time. Do you know Tordjanne?"

"I've spoken of it with others. Merchants and the like. I have some sense of the land."

He nodded, stepping past her to get back into her cart. "Well, I grew up near Fairdale, on the river. My father was a woodcrafter and my mother made baskets." He came out again and smiled. "Though none were as fine as these. Ten more."

"And your brothers are merchants as well?"

"No."

He put the baskets in his wagon and climbed back into hers. She could hear him moving freely now. He'd be finished in another moment. The sun was low in the west, but not low enough. Not yet.

"So they're in Tordjanne still?"

"Who? My brothers?"

"Yes."

"That's right. I'm the only one who left the woodlands. The others followed my father into woodcrafting."

"What made you leave?"

He emerged one more time, laden with baskets. "Gold," he said. "This is the last of them. Eleven. So how many is that?"

Lici thought about this for just a moment, closing her eyes, as if tallying up the number in her head. "Fifty-three," she finally said.

Brint frowned. He put the baskets in his cart, then turned to face her. "I don't think that's right."

She made her face fall. "No? I'm afraid I've never been very good with numbers."

He shook his head, removed his hat, and raked a hand through his hair. "You might have mentioned that when I left it to you to count them." He exhaled heavily and began to count the baskets in his cart. Several moments later he faced her again. "I count forty-seven."

She took a step toward him, frowning in turn. "You're certain?"

"Quite," he said. "But you're welcome to count them yourself."

She walked to his cart and began to count, pretending to lose her place twice before finally turning to face him.

"Yes, you're right," she said, smiling. "I'm terribly sorry."

He smiled in return, though clearly it was forced. "That's all right. I believe I owe you fifty-seven sovereigns."

"Fifty-seven. That's right."

He hesitated, and immediately Lici knew why. Perhaps there was a way to do this without delaying him any further. Merchants commonly carried great sums of gold, and with road brigands quite common throughout the Southlands, they generally had several secret caches hidden within their carts. Clearly Brint was no exception to this. He would have to retrieve her payment from one of these, but he would be reluctant to reveal the location of even one of his caches, even to her.

"Perhaps you could leave me alone for just a moment?" he asked.

"And risk having you drive off with my baskets?" She shook her head. "I'm old, but I'm not a fool."

"No, of course not! I merely . . . I need to get you your gold. That's all."

She crossed her arms over her chest. "Well, I'm going to wait right here while you do."

The merchant made a sour face, but after a moment he nodded. He dropped to the ground and crawled under the cart.

Lici bent down too, placing her hands on the ground as if to brace herself. "What are you doing?"

"Getting some gold," he said impatiently. "Please, can I have a moment of privacy?"

"Yes, of course." Lici stood, and as she did, she grabbed a handful of dirt.

She quickly pulled her knife free, cut the back of her hand, and began the familiar chant, keeping her voice to the barest whisper. At the same time, she caught some blood on the flat of her blade and let it trickle into the earth she held in her hand.

Her spell was more complicated than most—just as it was more powerful than most. But still, she had long since committed the words to memory.

"Blood to earth, life to power, power to thought, magic to dust, dust to curse, curse to pestilence, pestilence to baskets, baskets to magic."

Saying this last, she threw her hands toward the opening to the merchant's cart. Dust flew from her fingers, dust that had been blood and dirt. It glittered briefly in the failing sunlight, before settling on the baskets. It coated them like light snowfall for just an instant, then vanished, as if absorbed into the osiers.

"I'm sorry?" Brint called to her. "Did you say something?"

"No, nothing." She licked her blade and sheathed it, then licked the back of her hand.

A few moments later, he crawled back out from beneath the cart, a small leather pouch in one hand, the back of his shirt and trousers stained and covered with dead leaves and twigs.

"Here you are," he said, handing the pouch to her. "Fifty-seven sovereigns. You'll want to count it I'm sure."

Lici didn't care to really, but neither did she wish to raise his suspicions. She stepped to her cart and poured the coins out onto the bare wood, making a quick count. Satisfied, she returned the coins to the pouch and faced him again.

"Thank you, sir. I hope the baskets bring you all the profit you seek."

"I'm sure they will. The plains people always pay well for Mettai baskets."

Lici blinked. "The plains people? I thought you were heading toward the lakes."

"No, the plains."

"But there are no Y'Qatt on the plains."

"Well, there are a few. But I'm not sure I need to go looking for the Y'Qatt. Not anymore."

"But you said you were! You said you were looking for Y'Qatt and Mettai!"

He smiled, though he was looking at her strangely. "Well, I found a Mettai, didn't I? Those baskets are quite beautiful. I'm sure they'll fetch a good price in the septs of the Fal'Borna. And as for the Y'Qatt . . ." He shrugged. "We're well into the Harvest now. I need to be heading west and then south, back to Tordjanne. I don't want to be abroad when the Snows come."

"No! You don't understand! You have to find the Y'Qatt! Those baskets—" She stopped herself, grabbing handfuls of her silver hair. "The Y'Qatt will buy those baskets," she went on a moment later, trying desperately to sound reasonable. "They love Mettai baskets."

"I believe you," Brint said. "But I'm sure they'll sell on the plains, too. Or in Tordjanne."

"No! You can't sell them on the plains! Not to the Qirsi!"

The merchant took a step back, frowning once more. "Why not?"

She opened her mouth, swallowed. "I hate them," she said. It was the only thing that came to mind. "I don't want my baskets going to the white-hairs. The Y'Qatt—they're all right. But not the rest! You can't let the rest have them!"

"I'm sorry, but they're not your baskets anymore." He turned away and started toward the front of his cart.

Lici hurried after the man, grabbing him by the arm. "I want them back then!" She held out the pouch of coins to him. "Here! Your gold! I don't want it anymore! Just give me my baskets back!"

He pulled his arm loose and walked briskly to his horse. Lici followed and tried to push the pouch into his hand.

"Get away from me!" he said, shoving her away with one hand.

She stumbled back, but quickly righted herself.

"I'll give you more gold! I have twenty sovereigns! You can have them, too!"

He scrambled up into his seat and took hold of the reins.

"All of it! I'll give you all my gold! Everything I have! Just don't take those baskets to the plains! I'm begging you!"

Brint didn't answer. Lici rushed forward and grabbed his leg, digging her fingers into his calf. *You can't go!*

"You're hurting me!" he shouted, kicking at her, trying to free himself from her grasp. His foot caught her in the chin, but still she held fast to him. He kicked her again, harder this time. She let go and fell to the ground, addled for the moment.

"I . . . I'm sorry! I didn't mean to hurt you. But you . . . What was I supposed to do?"

She shook her head, sobbing now. "Please!" she said. "Don't go! You're doing something terrible!"

He stared down at her, looking confused and scared. "I'm just a merchant. I sell and I buy. How much harm can come of that?"

"Death!" she said, her voice rising. "Death of thousands! And ruin! Entire villages destroyed!"

"You're mad!" He snapped the reins and his cart started forward.

Lici pulled her knife free and clawed at the ground, picking up a handful of dark earth. She cut a deep gash across the back of her hand and let the blood drip into the dirt she held. "Blood!" she shouted, raising her hand over her head. "Earth and power! Power to fire!" She lowered her hand and stared at the mud she held. That wasn't right. What were the words? She knew how to do this. She had just done it. "Earth to magic," she began again, raising her hand once more. "Magic to fire. Fire to . . . to that man." Her hand dropped to her side, and once more she began to cry. "Death!" she shouted after the merchant. "Death and ruin! I've seen it! You'll see it, too! Mark my word, you'll see it, too!"

But Brint didn't stop. Lici sat on the ground watching him drive his cart away from the village, her baskets in his cart, her curse following him like a storm cloud. How many would die? Who could say? It would carve through the Fal'Borna septs like a Mettai blade through flesh; it might even reach the J'Balanar. Her magic couldn't tell one Qirsi from another. It could kill any of them, all of them. All except the Y'Qatt, who lived to the north, near the lakes.

"You're a fool!" she shouted after the man, though he had turned a corner on the road and she couldn't see him anymore. "You don't know what you're doing!" Then she raised her face to the sky and screamed until her throat was raw and her voice was gone.

Eventually she must have passed out, for she found herself lying sprawled on the ground some time later. The sun had set, and only a faint sheen of daylight clung to the western sky.

She sat up and looked around her. Darkness oozed from the abandoned houses and empty lanes, like blood from some ancient wound. An owl called from far off and some creature—a fox perhaps, or a wildcat—growled low and harsh from the brush beyond her old house.

"You lied to me."

She started at the voice, her heart pounding in her chest. A figure loomed beside her, dark, insubstantial.

"Mama?" she whispered.

"You told me that you brought healers."

"Is that really you?"

"You lied."

She peered at the form, trying to make out a face.

"I was scared," she finally said. "I'd gone the wrong way. I didn't know what else to do."

"You lied to me!" the voice said again, loud and shrill.

Even as Lici flinched away, she felt herself growing angry. She wasn't the little girl anymore. She was old and tired, and she had done far worse in the years since leaving Sentaya.

"Yes, I lied," she said, sitting up straighter. "It was too late for all of you. I told you what you wanted to hear."

"And now you've condemned thousands to a death as terrible as mine."

"He said he was going to the Y'Qatt! It's not my fault that he lied to me!"

"Isn't it?"

"No!" She launched herself at the dark form, trying to take it by the neck. But there was nothing. She was grappling with air, flailing about in the dirt and leaves. Lici stopped herself and sat up again, her chest heaving, tears on her face. "Mama?"

Nothing.

"I didn't mean it."

She heard whispers coming from nearby, and, forcing herself to her feet, she started toward them.

"Mama?" she called. "Papa?"

The whispers seemed to fade, as if to draw her deeper into the gloom.

She halted, refusing to play their game. "Baet? Kytha?"

Was that a giggle? Were they teasing her?

"Come here!" she said, trying to sound stern.

She heard them on her right now, closer to the house, and she hurried after them.

"Let me see you! Show yourselves!"

Now they were to her left. Not in the house, but on the far side of it. She strode toward them, tripped on something, pulled herself to her feet, and trod on. It was so dark. Lici could barely make out the houses and trees, and soon found herself walking with her arms outstretched, to keep from walking into anything. But the voices continued, gentle and elusive, coaxing her on. The lane was behind her and to the left. Or perhaps it was more directly to the left. She wasn't quite certain.

But there was laughter before her, not playful anymore. Mocking.

"Stand still! Who are you?"

No one answered, but Lici thought she heard footsteps on the dry leaves. Slightly to her right now, and still ahead, always ahead. Arms reaching, fingers splayed, eyes wide, sightless, straining in the dark, she followed.

He had long since crossed the bridge and had put nearly a league between himself and the wash when he finally slowed, allowing his horse to graze on the long grasses. His hands still trembled, though not as they had before.

"Damn crazy woman."

The horse looked back at him for an instant, chewing loudly.

He had forty-seven baskets to sell. Fine ones—quite possibly the best he'd ever seen. He'd gotten them at a good price, and would probably manage to sell each at twice what they had cost him. That was what mattered. The rest was nothing more or less than the ranting of a mad witch.

Death and ruin. It was laughable. These were baskets, not blades or spears.

But they come from a Mettai.

He'd been searching for her people. Isn't that what he told her? Blood magic. It sounded strange and dangerous, and just slightly alluring. Selling Mettai goods, even things as harmless as blankets or baskets, was always profitable in Tordjanne. People there didn't quite believe in blood magic—most of them had never seen a Mettai. But they wanted the goods. They wanted to be able to point to something in their home and say, "That was made with blood magic." Here on the plains, merchants paid less for Mettai goods that they suspected had been made with magic rather than by hand. But in the Eandi sovereignties, especially those that were farther south, items made by magic often sold for more, simply because people there wanted to believe that they were buying something . . . well, magical.

But what was blood magic, really? Was there blood on these baskets? Is that what she was saying?

"She was mad," he said, scolding himself. "That's all."

Brint snapped the reins, forcing his horse into motion, though he sensed that the beast would gladly have eaten more.

He'd sell the baskets at his first opportunity. There were septs all around here and Qirsi villages along the wash. He wouldn't get as much for them in these lands as he would in Tordjanne, but he'd get enough. And then they'd be gone, and with them the memory of that old woman.

He absently rubbed his arm where she'd grabbed him. For an old woman, she had been uncommonly strong. Or simply desperate.

Fifty-seven sovereigns. He should have just done as she asked and given her the baskets back. Probably she was just deluded, but at this point he wanted nothing to do with her or her wares.

Brint was headed toward a bend in a narrow tributary of the Silverwater. He often met other Eandi merchants there to share what food they had, to speak of prices in the various marketplaces, to share tidings from other parts of the land, or simply to swap tales and sing songs. It was here that he first met Torgan Plye several years before. For all Brint knew, Torgan was there tonight. He never was sure who he might encounter at the bend, but usually at least a few merchants gathered there on any given night. And this evening was no different. Topping a small rise as the sun stood balanced on the horizon, he saw that there were already five carts in the bend, and as many figures seated around a small fire.

At first opportunity. He made the decision in that moment, with a clean conscience. Surely the woman was insane. That was why she said all the things she did. He would remember the crazed look in her dark eyes for as long as he lived. He'd recall the smell of her breath and the feel of her bony fingers digging into his arm and then his leg. That was why he couldn't keep these baskets for even one night. But for other merchants, men and women who hadn't encountered the old hag, they were simple baskets—beautiful, brilliantly made, and reasonably priced. He'd be doing them a favor, even if he did manage to turn some profit.

As he drew nearer to the bend and the merchants' fire, he recognized a few of the people there—a woman from Stelpana who was known simply as Lark, for her fine singing voice; another man from Tordjanne, whose name he'd forgotten, and Stam Corfej, who came from Aelea, but now spent more time in Qirsi lands than in the sovereignties. Good people all, successful merchants. They'd know the quality of the baskets, and they'd have no trouble selling them in the Fal'Borna septs that roamed these plains.

Stam turned at the sound of Brint's cart and raised a hand in greeting.

"If it isn't Young Red," the man called, removing his pipe from his mouth. "You'd better have food to share. We're a bit spare tonight."

Brint grinned. "I've plenty," he answered, halting by the other carts and climbing down out of his seat. "And wine, too."

Lark nodded. "Then you're certainly welcome."

"I've wares for you to see as well," Brint said. "Fine ones and at a good price."

"Offering bargains, are you?" Stam said skeptically, winking at the others. "And which one of us will be fortunate enough to be giving you gold?"

Brint pushed aside the cloth that covered the back of his cart and began gathering baskets in his hands.

"I imagine it will be all of you," he said. "There's plenty to go around."

Chapter 21

So, if you don't go with them, they'll simply be executed?"

Grinsa nodded, afraid even to look at her. He'd left her once before to save the life of a man falsely accused, and it had nearly destroyed them both. Now they were the parents of a baby girl, trying to make sense of a strange land, held captive by a hostile people. How could he consider such a thing? That's what she would ask him; that's what he was asking himself.

Cresenne sat beside him, her eyes locked on his, and she asked, her voice as even as the plain, "What are you going to do?"

"What can I do?" he said. "I'm going to let them die. I can't leave you and Bryntelle. Not here; not now."

She raised an eyebrow. "So you'll just stand by while two men are put to death without cause?"

"They're strangers to us. Innocent people die every day. I can't be expected to put our lives at risk for every one of them, can I?"

Cresenne took his hand in her own, and lifted it to her lips. "Not every one, no."

He looked away, his gaze wandering the shelter until at last it came to rest on Bryntelle, asleep in a cradle by their pallet. "That's right. There's only so much one man can do."

"Even if he is a Weaver."

He faced Cresenne again. "What does that mean?"

"It means, this isn't you."

He frowned. "I don't understand."

"Oh, come now, Grinsa. 'They're strangers to us'? 'Innocent people die every day'? You've never thought such things in your entire life. You've just convinced yourself that you can't leave us here, and you're trying to make peace with that."

"And you'd have me do different?"

"I don't want you to leave. You have to know that." She ran a hand through her long white hair. "But I also know that you'll never be able to live with yourself if these men are killed while you have a chance to save them."

"Who says I have that chance?"

She smiled, though the look in her pale eyes made his chest ache. "This is you we're talking about. If you decide to try, you have a chance."

He gave her hand a squeeze. "It's not that easy. In fact, I'm not sure it can be done. E'Menua wants to prove a point."

"Another test?"

"In a way. Only this time he wants me to fail. He's tired of me challenging him. I think he wants me to try this, and to return to him humbled, chastened. And Q'Daer and L'Norr just want me to go. I think they'd be happiest if I didn't come back at all." Grinsa shook his head. "I'm not sure I should give them the satisfaction."

"But E'Menua must want this Mettai woman stopped."

"I have the sense that he's not worried about her, or maybe he just expects that another sept will find her. No, I really think this is about him and me." He rubbed his cheek where the a'laq had struck him. "Did I mention that he hit me?"

"I saw the mark. I assumed you'd tell me about it eventually."

He grinned. The bruise felt tight and sore. "There's not much to tell. I argued with him in front of the other Weavers, the two Eandi, and a large number of warriors. He ordered me into his shelter and hit me."

Grinsa was still smiling, but Cresenne looked deadly serious. "You're lucky he didn't do worse."

He shrugged and looked away. "I suppose."

She bent lower, searching for his eyes, forcing him to meet her gaze. "I mean it, Grinsa."

"I don't think he's any more powerful than I am."

"That's not the point," she said. "And you know it. In any test of magic you'll stand alone against four of them. Strong as you are, you won't survive that."

"I know. You're right." He twisted his mouth. "While we're on the subject, I should also tell you that I hit Q'Daer. He challenged me after

I left the a'laq's z'kal, said he was going to teach me to respect Fal'Borna ways."

"And you hit him?" she asked, her voice rising.

He rubbed his hand. It was sore, too. He felt as though he'd come through a street brawl. "It seemed like a good idea at the time."

She shook her head, looking frustrated. "Why are you trying to antagonize them? Is there some purpose to it, or is it just some Weaver thing?"

He had to laugh. "Some Weaver thing?"

She smiled reluctantly and shrugged. "You know, 'My magic's bigger than yours.'"

"No," he said, still laughing. "It's not some Weaver thing." He shook his head, his mirth fading. "Really, I'm not certain what it is. I can't help myself. Q'Daer is dangerous, I know. But I think I can handle him. When all is said and done, this is about E'Menua. And I honestly don't know why I keep defying him. The others are so quick to defer to him, even when he's wrong. I can't bring myself to do the same. So I fight him. I don't know; maybe I'm hoping that he'll get so angry with me that he'll just let us go."

"I'd say he's more likely to get so angry that he'll have you killed. That's more in keeping with Fal'Borna custom, if you ask me."

She had a good point.

"But maybe you're on to something," she went on a moment later, sounding thoughtful.

"What do you mean?"

"What did he say he'd do if you found the Mettai woman?"

"Nothing really. He said he'd allow the merchants to live until she's found, but I think that if we can prove their innocence, and bring glory to the sept by finding the Mettai woman, he'll spare their lives."

"But he said nothing about you?"

"No," Grinsa said, understanding coming to him at last. "Nothing, at least not along the lines you're suggesting."

She grinned, her eyes dancing in the candlelight. "I haven't suggested anything. A concubine would never be so presumptuous."

"If we propose a bargain like this, and he agrees, I have to go with the merchants and find this woman. There would be no way for me to back out."

Cresenne nodded, her expression sobering. "I know. But if he agrees it might be worth it."

Grinsa leaned forward and kissed her on the lips, a kiss she returned passionately.

"I don't want to leave you," he whispered, resting his forehead against hers.

"I don't want you to go. But I don't want to spend the rest of my life among the Fal'Borna, and I certainly don't want Bryntelle to grow up knowing only these people. In the last few days, I'd actually started to consider that we might stay here, that we might not have a choice in the matter. But now, with this, I don't know anymore. You'll never be happy here; that much is clear. And I'm not sure I can be, either."

"Bryntelle is happy," Grinsa said. "You told me so yourself."

She smiled. "Yes, Bryntelle is happy. But this isn't the life I want for her, and I know you feel the same way."

"And what about you? You have a friend now. F'Solya, is it?"

"F'Solya is a friend, but even she doesn't know what to make of us, of what she's hearing about our past. We're not like these people, Grinsa. We both know that. So let's do what's necessary to get away, and be done with this a'laq and his sept."

They kissed again, and then Cresenne took his hand and led him to the small pallet, where they undressed and quietly, tenderly made love. After, as they lay together in the soft light of the single candle, Cresenne said, "I don't want you dying for these people."

"I don't want that either."

Her smile this time was fleeting, brittle. "I'm serious, Grinsa. I know you. You'll do anything to find justice for these men. You'll think nothing of risking your life to save theirs. And I'm telling you—I'm asking you—don't do it. If you fail, you fail. They'll be put to death, and we might not get away. But at least you'll be all right. At least you'll come back to me."

"What you're saying is I should remember that I'm doing this for us, and not for them."

She took a breath, then nodded.

"I'll try."

Cresenne smiled again, and this time it lingered. "I'm sorry. I shouldn't have asked it of you."

"It's all right."

"No, it's not. That's not the kind of person you are. You can't do what I just asked of you any more than you can simply let these men be killed. I just . . ." She shook her head.

He touched her cheek, making her meet his gaze. "I was serious a moment ago. I don't want to die for these merchants. I'll come back to you—to both of you. You have my word."

"And what if E'Menua doesn't agree to these terms? He doesn't care whether these men live or die, but he seems to care a good deal about keeping us here. If you insist that he agree to this, he might just say that you can't go at all."

"Yes, he might. Or he might be so certain that we can't find the woman that he'll take the bargain a step further."

Cresenne winced. "If you fail, we stay with the Fal'Borna for the rest of our lives."

"Right."

She stared at the candle briefly, slowly shaking her head. At last she shrugged and faced him again. "Then that's the risk we take. There are worse fates."

"You're certain?"

"What choice do we have, Grinsa? It all comes back to this: You can't stand by and let those men be killed. So we'll make this demon's bargain, and hope for the best." She rested her head on his chest and closed her eyes. "I hope these men are worth all we're risking for them."

Grinsa wanted to assure her that they were, but the truth was he knew precious little about either of them. In the end, "So do I" was all he could offer her.

The following morning, Grinsa made his way to the a'laq's shelter. It was grey and damp, and a chill wind still blew down from the north, making the shelters of the sept quiver and snap. The horses stood in their paddock looking miserable, their heads and tails hung low.

As usual, the two young Weavers were outside E'Menua's z'kal, though neither of them appeared too happy to be there. They wore heavy, fur-lined skins around their shoulders, with hoods thrown over their heads.

L'Norr watched him approach, his eyes bright, alert. Q'Daer wouldn't look at him. There was a welt on his cheek, similar, no doubt, to the one

Grinsa bore. Grinsa nearly laughed when he saw it—they looked like twin sons of some brute of a father.

"Welcome to Harvest on the plains," L'Norr said, as Grinsa drew near.

"It's like this a lot?"

"Until the Snows come. Then it'll be exactly the same, except colder."

A fine time to be abroad in a hostile land.

"I need to speak with the a'laq," Grinsa said.

L'Norr seemed to read something in Grinsa's tone, because he merely turned and entered the shelter. For a moment, Grinsa and Q'Daer stood together outside, avoiding each other's gazes, saying nothing. Then L'Norr emerged again and nodded to the gleaner. "He's waiting for you."

"Thank you."

Grinsa entered the z'kal. It was warm within. E'Menua sat by a small fire, and beside him sat an attractive woman with long white hair and a piercing gaze. There were small lines around her eyes and mouth, but otherwise her skin was smooth. She eyed Grinsa as he stood before them, but she neither smiled nor spoke. Sensing her powers, Grinsa realized that she was a Weaver as well. This had to be D'Pera, the a'laq's wife.

"You've made your decision, Forelander?" the a'laq asked, drawing Grinsa's gaze.

"You could say that. I have a proposition for you."

E'Menua's eyebrows went up. "A proposition?"

"I'll do this—I'll go with the merchants to find the Mettai witch who threatens your people. And if I succeed in finding her, you not only spare the merchants, you also allow Cresenne, Bryntelle, and me to leave your sept."

The a'laq seemed to ponder this for some time. D'Pera still said nothing, but she watched her husband closely, the way a sea captain might eye a bank of storm clouds.

"And what if you fail?" E'Menua finally asked.

Grinsa knew the a'laq would get there on his own, so he gave the only answer he could. "If I fail, we stay with you."

"And you agree to be joined to a Weaver."

He shook his head. "No, that's not part of the bargain."

"Then there is no bargain."

Grinsa spun away and stepped toward the entrance to the shelter. "Fine."

"Fine?" E'Menua repeated, stopping Grinsa on the threshold. "You'll just let those men die?"

He faced the a'laq again. "Their lives mean nothing to you. Why should they mean anything to me?"

"To be honest," E'Menua said mildly, "I'm not certain. But I know that they do." E'Menua seemed so calm, so sure of himself, that Grinsa had to wonder if he'd been expecting this proposition all along. Had he and Cresenne been that obvious?

"I won't marry another woman. Ever."

"Apparently you believe you're in a position to dictate terms to me," E'Menua said. "You're not. I'll allow you to leave if you succeed, but if you fail, you'll live among us Fal'Borna, accepting our customs and laws as your own. That's the only choice I'm offering you. You can go under those conditions, or you can remain here as you are now."

A voice in his mind screamed for him to leave the shelter, to find some other way to win his freedom from this man and his people. There was just so much he was willing to risk, and he had long since grown weary of having E'Menua outthink him at every turn. Had it not been for the two merchants, he would have simply walked out into the rain. But though the two Eandi meant little to him, he couldn't throw their lives away. Cresenne, who knew him so well, had told him as much the night before.

"You won't breathe a word of this to Cresenne, and while I'm gone, you'll do everything necessary to keep her and Bryntelle safe."

E'Menua's expression didn't change. "And if I don't agree?"

Before Grinsa could respond, D'Pera laid a hand on the a'laq's arm. They shared a look, and after a moment the a'laq faced him again.

"Yes, very well. You have my word that she'll be safe, and she won't be told of our agreement." He hesitated, but only for an instant. "She's bound to learn of it eventually, though."

"Only if I fail," Grinsa said. "And I have no intention of failing."

The a'laq nodded and laughed, though good-naturedly. "Very well, Forelander." He grew serious once more. "You'll take Q'Daer with you, as well as the merchants, and all four of you will have mounts."

"Does it have to be Q'Daer? Couldn't I go with L'Norr instead?"

E'Menua grinned. It seemed he knew of their dislike for one another. Perhaps he'd even heard of their encounter the previous day. "Q'Daer is the older of the two," he said. "It's his place to make such a journey."

Grinsa nodded. He didn't relish the idea of being stuck with the young Weaver for so long, but he was learning quickly that Fal'Borna customs left little room for negotiation. And however much he would have preferred a different companion, he knew that Q'Daer would be far less happy about it than he. There was some small consolation in that.

"All right. You'll provision us with food and gold?"

"The merchants will. They've ample stores of both, and if we have to give you a bit more food, we'll make certain that they compensate us."

Grinsa could see the logic in that. "Someone will tell me when the others are ready to go?"

"Of course."

The gleaner nodded. "Very well. Thank you, A'Laq."

He started to leave, but E'Menua spoke his name, stopping him.

"You may not believe this," the a'laq said, as Grinsa looked back at him, "but I hope you succeed. If what the dark-eyes say about this woman is true, she must be hunted down. And if it's our sept that manages to kill her, it will increase our standing in Thamia."

Perhaps he should have been grateful to the a'laq for saying this, but all he could think was that he didn't give a damn about the glory of his sept. "I'll do what I can," he said, and left the z'kal.

The rain had grown stronger, as had the wind.

"The a'laq will be wanting to speak with you," Grinsa said to Q'Daer as he stepped past the man on his way back to his shelter.

"What about?" the young Weaver called after him.

Grinsa didn't answer.

He found Cresenne on their pallet, nursing Bryntelle. She sat up as he entered the shelter, her eyes searching his face.

"What did he say?" she asked.

"He agreed to our terms."

She frowned, laying Bryntelle against her shoulder and patting her back. "Just like that?"

"He wasn't completely happy about it, but yes, he agreed."

Cresenne shook her head. "I don't believe you."

"Cresenne—"

"Tell me all of it, Grinsa. You're leaving me alone with these people, and that's fine. I as much as told you to. But I deserve to know all of it."

He sat, exhaling slowly. "It's nothing we shouldn't have expected. If I succeed in finding the woman and, I suppose, killing her, we're free to go and the merchants will be spared. If I fail, we stay here."

"And?"

He started to answer, but she held up a hand, silencing him. He could see her piecing it together. At last she began to nod.

"And you take a wife," she said. "That would be the one other thing E'Menua would want. You have to be joined to a Weaver, don't you?"

"It's not going to come to that."

"But that's what he wants."

"Yes," Grinsa admitted, feeling as if he had betrayed her. "I can go back to him if you want, tell him I won't be going after all."

She shook her head. "No. You're right: We should have expected it. They were going to insist on this eventually anyway. Otherwise there's no point in making us stay." She smiled bitterly. "You're most valuable to them as a studhorse."

"I'm not certain how to take that."

Cresenne laughed, but a moment later she was sobbing, tears coursing down her smooth cheeks. Immediately, Bryntelle began to cry as well. Grinsa put his arms around Cresenne and kissed the top of her head as she fussed over the baby.

"I don't have to go, Cresenne," he whispered. "There are other ways to get away from here."

But she shook her head. "It's not that. I mean, I don't want you to go, but we'll get through it."

"Then why are you crying?"

She shrugged. "It wasn't supposed to be like this. We came to the Southlands to get away from the fighting and the danger and all the rest. I just wanted to make a life here, and instead we're being forced apart again, just like before."

He stroked her fine hair. "I know. I thought it would be different, too."

She wiped the tears from her eyes impatiently and looked up at him, kissing him gently on the lips. "You should be getting ready to go. I imagine they'll be coming for you soon."

"They can wait, if they have to."

"No. The sooner you get going, the sooner you'll be back." She forced a smile. "We'll be all right." She held up Bryntelle, who had also stopped crying. "See? We're better already." She kissed him again. "Go on. Get ready."

He nodded, though he didn't stand just yet. Instead, he held out a finger to Bryntelle. She took hold of it in her tiny fist and leaned forward, trying to put all of it—his finger and her fist—in her mouth.

"We'll find her quickly," he muttered, staring at the baby. "I swear we will."

Cresenne nodded. "Good."

He forced himself off the pallet, grabbed his travel sack, and began to fill it—a second knife, his flint, a length of rope, a change of clothes, an overshirt, a skin he could use for water.

When he was done, he sat again beside Cresenne, his shoulder touching hers, but neither of them spoke. They watched Bryntelle and they waited. Before long, someone called for him from just outside the z'kal. He and Cresenne shared a look.

"Gods keep you safe and guide you back to us," she whispered.

"I love you."

They kissed one last time. Then he stood and left the shelter.

The rain had slackened, but the wind still blew and the sky remained dark and hard as slate.

Q'Daer and the two merchants were already mounted. They had brought Grinsa the great bay he and Cresenne bought in Yorl. He tied his travel sack to the saddle and swung himself onto the mount.

He looked around briefly, expecting to see E'Menua come to see them off. But the rest of the sept seemed to be ignoring them, as if they were strangers, or wraiths.

"We have everything?" Grinsa asked, meeting Q'Daer's gaze.

The young Weaver barely looked at him. "Yes," he said, kicking at the flanks of his grey horse.

Grinsa didn't follow. Instead, he called the man's name, forcing him to halt and wheel his mount.

"It wasn't my idea to have you come along," he said. "It was the a'laq's. If I had my way, I wouldn't be doing this at all, and I certainly wouldn't be riding with you."

Q'Daer stared at him a moment. Then he nodded, and started off again, northward, into that harsh wind and away from the sept. Grinsa and the merchants followed.

For some time, they rode in silence, Q'Daer some distance ahead, Grinsa next, and the two merchants just behind him. Finally, the younger Eandi asked, "Aren't you and the other white-hair afraid that we'll try to escape?"

Grinsa looked back at him. After a moment, he formed an image of fire, and then thrust it into the mind of the man's horse. The beast reared, nearly unseating the merchant, who clung desperately to the reins.

"Language of beasts," Grinsa said, facing forward again. "We both have it. You're welcome to make the attempt, but I assure you, you won't get far."

The merchants dropped back a few paces, falling silent once more. A short time later, though, the older merchant pulled abreast of Grinsa, eyeing him closely.

"Who are you?" the man asked.

"My name's Grinsa jal Arriet."

Torgan shook his head. "That's not a Fal'Borna name. I'm not even sure it's a Southlands name."

"It's not."

"It's true, then. What they said about you in the sept. You're from the Forelands?"

Grinsa glanced at him. After a moment he nodded.

"How did you come to be living with E'Menua's sept?"

"Just lucky, I suppose."

"They don't like you much. Obviously, Q'Daer doesn't. And I don't think the a'laq does, either."

"No, I don't imagine so."

"So why do you stay with them?"

"Is there something you want, Torgan?" Grinsa asked, his patience wearing thin. "Because I'm really in no mood to satisfy your curiosity right now."

"I want to know why you're doing this. My life is in your hands. So is Jasha's. I'm sorry if I'm disturbing you," he went on, sounding anything but contrite, "but I'd like to know a bit about the man who may end up determining whether we live or die."

It seemed a fair point.

"I'm with them because I'm a Weaver," Grinsa said. "They want me to become part of their sept; my wife and I want to move on. If I can find the Mettai woman you've told them about, they'll let us go."

"That's it? This is some kind of test? A way of proving yourself?"

"It's a way of winning our freedom. That may not sound like much to you, but we've come a long way to make a life for ourselves in your land, and we're not willing to let the Fal'Borna destroy that for us."

The merchant didn't look pleased, but he nodded once.

"We're on the same side in this, Torgan. You may not think of me as the perfect ally, and certainly I had no desire to have my fate tied to yours, but we're in this together now, and we'd best make the most of it."

"Yeah," Torgan said, "all right. As you say, we haven't much choice in the matter." He looked Grinsa in the eye. "You argued for our lives when no one else would. I suppose that's worth something."

He dropped back again, allowing the other merchant to catch up with him.

Grinsa continued to ride alone, his eyes fixed on the north horizon. There were hills ahead to the west, and he knew that there were mountains to the north beyond the plain, but he couldn't see them for the rain and clouds. Eventually, Q'Daer halted and waited for the others to catch up with him. He pulled a pouch of food from one of the sacks tied to his saddle, took out a piece of what appeared to be dried meat, and handed the pouch to Grinsa.

"We're cold," Torgan said. "How much longer do you intend to ride in this weather?"

Q'Daer smiled, though there was no warmth in his pale eyes. "As long as this weather lasts," he said. "And then we'll have some other weather to ride in."

"We've a couple of hours left before sunset," Grinsa said, biting into a piece of meat. It was good—better than he'd expected. "We'll ride until it starts to get dark."

He handed the food to Torgan.

The merchant shook his head. "We should stop before then. We'll need time to set up some kind of shelter and find wood for a fire."

Of course. The longer this took, the longer the merchants would stay alive and the better their chances of making an escape. In this respect, Torgan and Grinsa were anything but allies.

"Leave that to us, Eandi," Q'Daer said. "Your only concern is finding that Mettai witch you've been going on about. And the sooner we do that, the better for all of us."

The merchants each took a piece of the meat, and then Torgan started to tuck the pouch into his travel sack.

"Give that to me, dark-eye."

Torgan glared at Q'Daer. "It's mine. I bought it in Stelpana."

"It may have been yours once, but now it belongs to the Fal'Borna." The Weaver held out a hand. "Give it here."

"And if I refuse?"

Torgan's mount reared, just as the young merchant's had earlier. This time though, the rider was thrown. Torgan landed heavily on the wet grass and lay on his back, too stunned to move. Q'Daer was off his mount an instant later, a knife in his hand. He strode to where the merchant lay, picked up the pouch of food, which had landed beside Torgan, and stared down at the man.

"Next time, I'll break your arm. You may have hopes of being spared, or perhaps you think you might escape. But until the a'laq tells me otherwise, you're a prisoner of the Fal'Borna, and you'll do exactly as I say." He reached into the pouch and pulled out another piece of meat. Then he smiled and placed it between his teeth. Looking up at Grinsa, he held out the food. "You want more?"

Grinsa shook his head.

Q'Daer shrugged and walked back to his mount. "On your horse, Eandi," he said, as he climbed back into his saddle.

Torgan struggled to his feet and tried to get on his horse. He couldn't. Finally, the other merchant dismounted and helped him up. Soon after, they were moving again. Once more, Q'Daer rode a fair distance ahead of the others.

"We can help each other."

Grinsa looked over and saw that Torgan was beside him again.

"It sounds as though you want to get away from them as much as we do. So let's work together."

"No," Grinsa said. "I left my wife and daughter with the sept. I'm not going anywhere. And neither are you. I can't get away unless you help us find that woman. So that's what you're going to do."

"You told me before that we're allies," the merchant said sullenly. "But you sound like a Fal'Borna to me."

"Maybe I was wrong before. Maybe we're not allies. But I'm not Fal'Borna either. I'm alone in this." Grinsa knew as soon as he spoke the words that this was true. The merchants were concerned only with staying alive; Q'Daer was Fal'Borna. And he owed loyalty to no one except Cresenne and Bryntelle. "I have no allies," he said, as much to himself as to Torgan. "I have no need of them."

"You think you can do battle with the Fal'Borna by yourself?"

Grinsa shook his head. "I have no intention of battling the Fal'Borna. I'm going to war against a Mettai witch. And so are the two of you, so I'd get used to the idea. You want to live through this? Then you'll help me, you'll stop antagonizing Q'Daer, and you'll lead us to that old woman. Otherwise you're corpses. It's as simple as that."

Torgan glowered at him another moment, then fell back to join the other merchant.

"Serves me right for trying to talk sense to a white-hair," the Eandi muttered.

Grinsa didn't bother responding, or even looking back. His eyes were fixed on the young Fal'Borna Weaver riding ahead of him. Q'Daer was the real threat. The merchants might have been willing to risk an attempt at escape, but Grinsa knew that he and the Fal'Borna could stop them. The young Weaver, though, was another matter. The a'laq had told Grinsa that he hoped they'd succeed in finding the old woman. But what if he lied? What if he cared nothing for sparing the Eandi and stopping this Mettai witch, but remained determined to keep Grinsa in his sept? For all Grinsa knew, Q'Daer's purpose in riding with him was not to help, but rather to keep him from succeeding.

As if reading his thoughts, Q'Daer looked back at him and, after a moment's hesitation, gestured for Grinsa to ride forward.

"Come, Forelander. Join me. You don't need to guard the dark-eyes. They'll go nowhere without us."

Grinsa glanced back at Torgan, who was watching him closely. Then he kicked at his mount and joined the other Weaver. He even chanced a smile.

"I wouldn't have thought you wanted anything to do with me," he said, pulling abreast of Q'Daer.

The young man shrugged. "We both lost our tempers," he said. "Live with the Fal'Borna for a while and you'll realize that this isn't so uncommon." A smile crossed his lips and was gone; he still refused to look the gleaner in the eye.

"Well, I apologize for hitting you. I'm not sure why I did it. It wasn't at all like me."

"Perhaps you're more like the rest of us than you care to admit."

Grinsa nodded and gave a small laugh. "That may be," he said. "But still, I am sorry."

The man nodded in turn, glancing at him for just an instant. "Apology accepted."

It all seemed quite pleasant, far more so than Grinsa would have thought possible. And yet something in Q'Daer's bearing gave him pause. He didn't know the Weaver well, but he had always been a good judge of people, and he could tell when someone was hiding something.

So he smiled and nodded, and acted as though their conflict had been settled. But he kept a firm hold on his magic, and he was conscious suddenly of the dagger that he wore on his belt. He had taken the measure of the man's power, and he thought that he could prevail in a battle of sorcery, if it came to that. But he wasn't going to take any chances, not with so much at stake.

There was an old saying in the Forelands. Always keep your enemies at arm's length. Closer, and their blade might find your heart. Farther away, and your blade might never find theirs.

They stopped and made camp by a small stream that curved through the grasses and rich dark soil of the plain. Clouds still hung low over the land and daylight gave way to night in ever-darkening shades of grey. They found enough wood among the trees growing by the rill to build a warming fire, and they ate a small meal of smoked meat and bread.

The dark-eyes said little. The younger merchant watched Grinsa and Q'Daer keenly, as a grouse might eye a circling falcon, but Torgan had retreated into himself. He merely stared at the fire and ate what was offered to him in sullen silence.

Since apologizing for their earlier encounter the Forelander hadn't said much either; Q'Daer thought it possible that Grinsa considered the matter settled, which suited his purposes quite well. But they would have to speak some time if Q'Daer were to begin to gain the man's trust. He had also decided hours before that he couldn't allow the Eandi and the Forelander to become too friendly. It would have been quite natural for them to begin working together; Q'Daer didn't want that.

"Tell me, Grinsa," he said now, with a glance at the merchants. "Are the dark-eyes of your land similar to these two?"

The Forelander had just taken a bite of meat, and he paused briefly in his chewing, his pale eyes flicking first to the Eandi and then to Q'Daer. After a moment he finished chewing and swallowed.

"They're like some men I knew in the Forelands," he said evenly. "They're different from others."

"That surprises me. I'd heard that you had friends among the Eandi of the north, that you fought alongside their kings and nobles. Yet these two fight among themselves. At every turn they show themselves to be cowards and liars. They may have killed thousands. And you want me to believe that they're just like your friends in the Forelands."

Grinsa shook his head. "That's not what I said. You can find honorable men in any land, regardless of the color of their eyes." He gestured vaguely at the merchants. "I don't know these men very well, but I sense that they're not too different from some of the people I knew in the Forelands. Just as you're not."

Q'Daer's eyes widened slightly. "Me?"

A smile touched the man's face. "Yes. You remind me of several Qirsi I knew in the North."

"Friends of yours?"

Grinsa shrugged. "Some. As I say, there are all sorts of men, of all races."

Torgan continued to ignore them, the firelight reflected in his one eye. But the younger merchant had been listening, and now he said, "Sounds like you're no better in his view than we are, Q'Daer."

"Shut your mouth, dark-eye," Q'Daer said.

The Eandi shrugged, then took another bite of meat.

"Is that what you meant?" the Fal'Borna asked Grinsa.

The Forelander cast a hard look at the merchant, but then turned to face Q'Daer, his expression easing. "I meant nothing beyond what I said. You seem to think that people here—Eandi and Qirsi alike—are quite different from the men and women I knew in the Forelands, and I'm just telling you that the differences aren't that great."

Q'Daer nodded, though he wasn't quite satisfied with the man's answer.

"It's been a long day," Grinsa said, standing and retrieving his sleeping roll. "I'm going to get some sleep. I'd suggest the rest of you do the same."

Q'Daer watched Grinsa and the merchants arrange themselves on the ground around the fire before reluctantly doing the same. He wanted to stay awake, to keep talking so that they couldn't sleep either, but he knew he was being foolish, like a petulant child. Somehow the Forelander had managed to make himself the leader of their little group. Somehow the young merchant had managed to twist their conversation. None of this was going the way it was supposed to. He would have to be more careful in the days to come.

Q'Daer stared up into the darkness and listened to the fire settling beside him. After some time he began to grow calmer, his thoughts clearing like the sky after a passing storm. He still considered Grinsa a threat to all that he wanted, but with E'Menua's help he had glimpsed a way past the danger.

Before leaving the sept, while Grinsa said farewell to his woman and child, Q'Daer had spoken with the a'laq. D'Pera had been there when he entered E'Menua's z'kal, but the a'laq sent her away. Q'Daer had only seen him do this a few times before; the last time had been following the storm in which Q'Daer's men perished.

"You dislike the Forelander," E'Menua had said, once they were alone.

He saw no point in denying it. His cheek still throbbed where Grinsa had struck him. No doubt E'Menua could see the bruise, and even if he couldn't, others had seen what happened. There were few secrets in a Fal'Borna sept.

"Yes, A'Laq. I dislike him."

"Why?" Immediately, E'Menua shook his head and held up a hand to silence him. "It's all right. I know why. In your position I might hate him, too."

"My feelings aren't important, A'Laq. He's a Weaver, and his presence here strengthens your sept. He and I will find this Mettai witch and stop her."

The a'laq nodded once and smiled. "You are truly Fal'Borna, my friend. I wish your father had lived long enough to see the man you've become."

"Thank you, A'Laq."

E'Menua motioned for him to sit.

"I know how difficult a time you've had since the storm," the a'laq said, when Q'Daer was settled on the other side of the fire. "I know that you fear you've fallen out of my favor."

Q'Daer lowered his gaze. "L'Norr is my friend, and a good man, A'Laq. I believe either one of us would be a worthy husband for U'Vara."

"I agree with you. But I think you're stronger than he is. I have sons, so I don't expect that either of you will ever rule this sept. But I want a strong husband for my daughter."

"Yes, A'Laq."

"I also want the Forelander to stay here."

Q'Daer's mouth twitched. "Yes, A'Laq."

"You have every reason to want him to leave, I know. And that means that you have every reason to want him to succeed in this endeavor with the dark-eye merchants. He and I have struck a bargain. If he succeeds, I'll allow him to leave. If he fails, he stays and agrees to be properly joined to a Weaver."

It was just as Q'Daer had feared. Despite the a'laq's kind words of a moment before, he felt his hopes of being joined to U'Vara slipping away.

"I understand, A'Laq. You want me to make certain he fails."

E'Menua raised a finger, his eyes narrowing. "It's not quite that simple. I want this Mettai witch dead—I fear this curse of hers. But I don't want Grinsa to prove that Torgan and his friend are innocent, and I don't want the Forelander to be able to claim credit for killing the witch." E'Menua's pale eyes shone in the firelight. "I want you to succeed where he fails. Do this and I promise that you will be joined to U'Vara. The failure of your hunt will be forgotten." His expression darkened. "Fail me again, and I'll see to it that you never marry."

There had been nothing for Q'Daer to say but "Yes, A'Laq."

He left the z'kal, and a short time later he led the Forelander and the merchants away from the sept.

They'd ridden a long way this day; it was hard for him to believe that his conversation with E'Menua had taken place only a few hours before. It seemed like days ago.

He didn't know yet how he would do all that the a'laq had asked of him. A part of him simply wanted Grinsa dead. His cheek didn't hurt much anymore, but the humiliation of being struck by the Forelander still burned his heart like a brand. He knew, though, that he couldn't kill the man without incurring E'Menua's wrath. And he had to admit that he looked forward to seeing Grinsa defeated and humiliated in turn, compelled to accept E'Menua's authority over him. He would enjoy seeing Grinsa's woman forced to relinquish her place at his side so that she might become some other Weaver's concubine. He might even claim her as his own. And once he was joined to U'Vara, he would hold a place of honor in the sept, above all Weavers save the a'laq himself. Grinsa would be under his authority as well as E'Menua's. Then the man would pay for what he had done, not all at once, but a thousand times each day for a thousand days and more. Q'Daer would enjoy that immensely.

Chapter 22

THE LANDS BETWEEN RAVENS WASH AND SILVERWATER WASH,
SOUTH OF THE COMPANION LAKES

ain and wind, grey skies at dawn and dusk, starless, moonless nights. In the days since leaving Kirayde, this was all Besh and Sirj had known. Everything they carried with them was wet—their clothes, their sleeping rolls, their food. None of it had been spared. It occurred to Besh that the gods might be punishing him for his arrogant belief that he was still young enough to undertake such a trek. *You think you can do this?* they seemed to be saying. *We'll show you how wrong you are.*

The two men weren't walking particularly fast. Sirj took the lead each day, and he always set a reasonable pace. No doubt he could have gone faster had he been on his own; it was as though he was reining himself in. And still the old man suffered. It had been too many fours since last he covered such distances on foot. His legs and back ached. His feet were blistered. The slightest incline stole his breath; walking downhill jarred his ancient knees. He was cold and weary all the time.

Sirj was responsible for none of it, of course. He had gone out of his way to carry far more than his share of their food and water, to set a reasonable speed, to take upon himself the labor necessary to gather wood and build fires and cook meals. Yet still, Besh directed all his anger and misery and frustration at the younger man. He couldn't help himself. After just the first day he had come to realize what a fool he'd been, believing that he could have gone in pursuit of Lici on his own. Pyav and Elica had been right: He was too old. Had Sirj not been with him, he might well have perished that first night, when the rains set in and the air turned frigid.

But rather than being grateful, Besh found himself growing resentful. He knew why, of course. The man's mere presence served to remind him of his weakness, of his inability to fend for himself. He was acting like a sullen child, but he couldn't help himself. He barely managed to grunt a thank-you when Sirj returned to their camp with an armful of firewood or when he spooned another helping of stew into Besh's bowl.

For his part, Sirj didn't appear to notice, or if he did, he gave no outward sign of minding. He took Besh's care upon himself, as if it were just another chore among many. He rarely spoke, perhaps knowing that Besh wanted no part of a conversation with him, but occasionally he hummed softly to himself. On those rare occasions when he did say something, he was always respectful and courteous, until this too began to bother the old man. *I'm being an ass*, he wanted to shout. *Why in Bian's name don't you treat me like one?*

On this day, they were in open country, cutting across a plain of thick grasses. There had been small clusters of trees by Ravens Wash, and there would be more at the Silverwater, but here there was no shelter from the rain and wind. Besh was shivering with cold again. Still. He realized that he was muttering curses under his breath and he laughed at himself, drawing a backward glance from Sirj.

"Are you all right?" the man asked him.

"No, I'm not all right. I'm cold and wet, and I'm sick to death of being both."

"You want to rest?"

Besh took a long breath and shook his head.

Sirj faced forward again, but a moment later he stopped and swung his travel sack off his shoulders.

"I said I didn't want to stop," Besh said, continuing past him.

"And I decided that I did."

Besh kept walking, seething now, not knowing why. *Isn't he allowed to rest?* Ema's voice. *Does he need your permission to have some water or eat a bit of salted meat? What kind of man have you become?*

At last he made himself stop and look back at the younger man. Sirj was sitting on a stone a short distance away, lifting a skin to his mouth, his travel sack on the ground at his feet.

"You're certain you don't want any?" he asked, holding out the skin.

Reluctantly, Besh pulled his own sack off his shoulders and lowered it to the ground, though even doing this much felt like surrender. *In what war? He isn't fighting you.* He pulled out his own skin and drank from it.

• "I'll lighten my own load, thank you," he called to Sirj between sips.

Sirj shrugged. "You should eat something, too."

"You're my father now?"

The younger man laughed and shook his head, but at last Besh saw a bit of frustration in his lean face. "Fine," Sirj said. "It was just a suggestion." He muttered something else, which Besh couldn't make out.

"What was that?"

Sirj shook his head a second time. "It was nothing."

"Don't you put me off like that! I heard you say something, and I want to know what it was!"

Sirj returned the food and water to his sack, shouldered the burden again, and started walking in Besh's direction.

"Well?" Besh demanded.

"I said, 'Elica was right,'" the man said, stepping past him.

"Right about what?"

He didn't answer. Besh packed his water, threw on his sack, and hurried after him.

"Right about what?" he called again.

"I'd told her before we left that I expected you and I would become friends before long. She had warned me that you were nothing but a stubborn old fool, and that no matter how patient I was, you'd never treat me with anything but contempt. But I insisted that she was wrong. Turns out I was."

"So I'm a stubborn old fool, am I?"

Sirj stopped and turned to face him. "Yes. I believe you are."

Besh stopped as well. When Sirj had treated him kindly, Besh had responded with anger. Now that he finally had cause to be angry, he couldn't manage it. After a moment he nodded and looked away. "Well, at least you've finally figured that out."

"What have I ever done to you, Besh?"

He twisted his mouth sourly. This wasn't a conversation he wanted to have. "You haven't done anything. I'm sorry I've been this way. I'm cold and I'm tired, and I just want to get this over with so we can go back home."

Sirj just stood there, until at last Besh gestured for him to get moving again.

"No," the younger man said. "This isn't about you being cold. You've treated me this way for years. And now I'm asking you what I've done to deserve it."

Besh passed a hand over his brow. His stomach growled, and he wished he'd eaten something when he had the chance. "Elica asked me the same thing the day before we left. Truth is, you never did anything wrong."

"And yet you've been punishing me for all this time."

"Yes, well, when Annze finds herself a husband, you'll understand."

That of all things brought a smile to Sirj's lips.

"Now, go on," Besh said, waving him on again. "I'm not getting any warmer standing here talking about this nonsense."

Sirj eyed him a moment longer, still smiling. Then he nodded and started walking once more.

Besh soon realized that one of the reasons he had treated Sirj so poorly since leaving Kirayde was that he'd dreaded having to make conversation with the man. But even now, after they'd reached something of an understanding, Sirj seemed content to walk in silence. Perhaps they were more alike than Besh had been willing to admit. Hadn't Elica tried to tell him this as well?

Late in the morning, they came within sight of the Silverwater. Besh had made them follow a southerly course, thinking to start their search for Lici in the area around N'Kiel's Span and whatever was left of the old woman's childhood home. Now, though, Besh began to question his original plan. People were dying in the villages north of here. If they wanted to stop Lici from doing any further damage, that was where they needed to go.

Better then to turn north before crossing the wash. Otherwise they'd be covering much of the distance in Fal'Borna land.

"Wait," Besh said.

Sirj stopped and looked back at him.

"We should turn north, toward the Companion Lakes."

"I thought we were going to the span."

"That's what I'd intended, but I think I was wrong. She's been heading north, spreading the illness in Y'Qatt villages around the lakes. That's where we should be."

"But . . ." He shook his head. "Never mind." He started walking again, northward this time.

A few hours before, Besh would have left it at that, not really caring to hear the man's opinions, or at least having convinced himself that he didn't. But after their conversation, he felt that he owed Sirj more.

"What were you going to say?" he called.

Sirj didn't stop. "It doesn't matter."

"Yes, it does."

Still the man kept walking.

"Please," Besh said. "I want to know."

Sirj halted and turned. He regarded Besh for some time, seeming to wrestle with something. Finally, he looked away, toward the river. "I was just going to say that we're here now. It can't be more than a half day's walk to the banks of the wash. As long as we've come this way, we should do what we planned." He met Besh's gaze again. "Don't you want to see where she lived? Isn't it possible that you'd learn as much from seeing her home as you have from reading that daybook you carry with you?"

"You're right," Besh said after a moment's pause.

Sirj appeared genuinely surprised.

"Well, you are."

"I know," the man said. "I just didn't think you'd admit it."

Besh had to laugh.

With the wash in view, and Lici's home village less than a day away, Besh found his weariness sluicing away, and with it his discomfort. He didn't expect to find much in the village. For all he knew, Sentaya had never been resettled and its buildings had been left to decay. But having read Sylpa's journal, he almost felt that he had heard Lici's tale with his own ears. He did want to see it.

It seemed that Sirj did, too. Or maybe he sensed Besh's eagerness, for he quickened their pace. Before long they could hear the wash and see that its waters were running high with all the rain that had fallen. Soon, they could also see the bridge curving gracefully over the current.

"N'Kiel's Span," Besh said, pointing.

Sirj glanced back at him and nodded, smiling like a child. "I've always wanted to see it."

They reached the banks of the wash well before dusk and immediately turned north toward the span, halting just before it. For some time they just stood, staring at the ancient stone, watching the water course by beneath it.

"I thought it would be bigger," Sirj said eventually. "I suppose I should have known better, but still . . ." He shrugged.

"I thought the same," Besh told him. "So many battles were fought here, and yet it's just a small bridge."

Before Sirj could respond, a horse whinnied. Both of them spun toward the woodlands north of the bridge along the east bank of the wash.

"Did you hear that?" Besh asked.

Sirj nodded. "Is there a village near here?"

"Sentaya used to be. But from what Lici told Sylpa, I didn't think anyone survived the pestilence when it struck."

"That was a long time ago. Others may have settled here."

"Perhaps," Besh said. But a moment later, he drew his blade.

Sirj did the same, and they started toward the trees. A path led from the end of the span to the forest, and they followed that. The mud was marked by some cart tracks and hoofprints, but certainly not as many as one would expect had there been a village nearby.

As he walked, Besh strained his ears, but he heard nothing more; no voices, no animals. His heart was pounding and despite the cold and the fine, cool mist falling on them, he felt sweat running down his temples.

"It's probably just peddlers," Sirj said. But the way he kept his voice low, one might have thought they were creeping toward the camp of road brigands. And perhaps they were.

Besh said nothing.

A moment later, their path entered the wood. It was far darker among the trees, but Besh could still make out the lane and the cart tracks carved into the mud. Indeed, here, sheltered from the rain by the leaves and limbs overhead, the tracks were far clearer. There were three sets at most, two leading farther into the forest, one leading the opposite way.

"There's no village here," Besh said. "Not a living one anyway."

Sirj just nodded, his dark eyes watchful, his lean frame coiled as if battle ready.

On they walked, until, topping a small rise, they saw something that made Besh's blood turn cold. A short distance off, in front of the ruins of an old wooden house, stood a horse and cart. There was nothing remarkable about either. The cart was old and weatherworn; the nag was white, with a mane the color of a Qirsi's eyes. But Besh recognized them immediately. So did Sirj.

"Those are Lici's," he whispered, scanning the wood and the remains of the houses.

"Yes," Besh said, uncertain as to whether to flee or shout out her name. In the end, he decided to do neither. "Come on," he said, starting forward again. "Let's find her."

"Wait, Besh," Sirj said, facing him. "What are we . . . ? Are we going to fight her?"

He shrugged. "That depends on what she does. We might well need her help controlling whatever magic she's set loose upon the land, so I'd rather not have to kill her. But if she gives us no choice, then that's what I'll do."

Sirj stared at him, as if he'd just suggested that they declare war on the Fal'Borna. "You could do that?"

"I gave my word to Pyav—a blood oath—that I'd find her and keep her from doing any more harm. I'll do whatever I must to honor that oath."

"All right," Sirj said, sounding a bit awed. "Then I'll help in any way I can. But I wish I'd brought my ax."

Besh grinned. "I think we're more likely to need magic."

They continued up the lane, past wrecked houses and small, fenced-in plots of land that might once have been gardens but were now overgrown. Eventually they came to what must have been the marketplace. There were several old shops, all of them in disrepair. There were even a few old carts and the pale bones of horses. But no Lici. They followed the lane past the marketplace and through the rest of the village, until they were in the forest again.

Besh stopped. "We should turn back. She wouldn't have come this far on the road without her cart."

"She's not in the village."

"Maybe not. But she's nearby. Her horse looks healthy—she hasn't been here long."

Sirj nodded. "Should we split up?"

Besh took a long breath. "All right. You stay near the wash; I'll check the woodlands east of the village."

"Right," Sirj said. They started away from each other. "Call for me if you see anything. I'll do the same."

Besh began to wind among the trees, searching for any sign that Lici had been there, straining his ears for any sound. His hands trembled, and his knees threatened to give out at any moment. Already he wished he and Sirj hadn't agreed to search for the woman separately. He quailed at the notion of meeting up with Lici alone. The irony wasn't lost on him— at another time he would have laughed at himself. One moment he resented Sirj for having come with him; the next he wished the younger man were there just in front of him; he truly was acting like a child. But just then he couldn't bring himself to appreciate the humor.

A faint mist drifted through the wood and occasionally a gust of wind stirred the branches, bringing a cascade of water from overhead. Again and again, he thought he saw a figure moving furtively from tree trunk to tree trunk, as if hiding from him, but each time he convinced himself that he had imagined it. He took care as he walked to keep the sound of the wash on his right—on a day like this it would have been so easy to lose his way. He also tried to tread quietly, not only so he could listen for Sirj, but also because he didn't wish to alert Lici to his presence.

Seeing nothing unusual, he turned and wandered a bit farther from the river. Soon he reached a small hollow, and after just a moment's hesitation walked down into it. Doing so, he flushed a grouse, the bird exploding from the ground with a rush of wings and feathers. His heart abruptly pounding, Besh paused and leaned against a tree, his eyes closed.

And standing thus in the silence of the wood, he heard her.

At first he thought that her voice was coming to him from far off, and he considered going back for Sirj. But peering through the mist, he was amazed to find that she was only a few strides away. She sat at the base of a tree, staring straight ahead, her knees drawn up to her chest. She was whispering to herself. Occasionally she'd give a small shake of her head, or raise her voice slightly, as if in anger. But she gave no sign of knowing that he was there, and for several minutes he merely watched her, too fascinated to do anything more.

Her white hair was ragged and damp. Her face had a pinched look; the lines that time had carved in her skin seemed deeper somehow, as if she had grown ancient in the days since she left Kirayde. Besh stared at her, trying to catch a glimpse of the dark-haired beauty who had captivated him so in his youth. But she was gone, her place taken by this creature that sat before him. Even her eyes, which once had sparkled like emeralds, now looked dull and empty, as if the magic had drained from her.

Perhaps he should have gone back for Sirj—just moments before he'd been terrified by the thought of facing the witch alone. But seeing her now, he realized that he was no longer frightened. She didn't look like a demon, or even a powerful Mettai witch. She merely looked old, and he sensed that she was barely aware of her surroundings. More to the point, he'd sworn an oath to Pyav that he would stop her, and he'd given his word to Elica that he wouldn't let her husband come to harm.

Stooping, never taking his eyes off of her, he dug through the leaf litter that covered the forest floor and picked up a handful of dirt. Then he pulled his knife free, cut himself, and mixed his blood with the earth. If he needed magic, he'd be ready, far faster than she could be.

Taking a breath, he started forward again, stepping carefully, watching her, trying to make out what she was saying. But even when he was close enough to hear some of the words, he couldn't make sense of them.

Still she spoke, seeming to look right through him. And Besh took another step toward her, and then another.

With the third step she finally saw him. Her eyes snapped up to his—and perhaps there was yet power in them after all, for he grew cold under her gaze. She scrambled to her feet, keeping her back pressed against the tree. Too late, Besh saw that she also had her knife out. Her left hand was balled in a fist, and blood seeped from a cut on the back of it. No doubt there was dirt in that hand. And blood.

He wanted to shout for Sirj, but he didn't dare. What a fool he'd been.

"You!" she said, nearly shrieking the word. "You get away from me!"

Immediately she fell back to muttering under her breath. Besh was certain that she was whispering a spell and he expected to die in the next moment. But nothing happened, and she continued to speak, all the while staring at him, her eyes wide and wild, like those of some creature caught in a hunter's snare.

"Why are you here, Lici?" Besh asked, his voice quavering.

For just an instant her vision seemed to clear, and Besh had the sense that she could see him again.

"Mama brought me out here," she said. "I think she was angry with me. I didn't mean to lie to her, but what could I do?"

"Mama?" he repeated. "Who's—?" He shuddered. "Do you mean your mother?"

She didn't say anything. Besh found himself looking around, as if expecting to find himself surrounded by wraiths. He'd heard of people meeting their dead, although usually this happened on nights when neither moon rose. Had her mind failed her completely, then?

"When did you lie to her?" he asked, keeping his voice even, gentle.

She shook her head slowly, her gaze drifting to the side.

"Is this Sentaya, Lici?"

The woman looked at him again, her eyes narrowing. "I know you," she said. "Who are you?"

He licked his lips. "I'm Besh. You know me from Kirayde."

"You're not one of them," she said after several moments, raising her voice once more. "You're one of us. Did you see him? The other one? The one who took the baskets?" She rushed forward suddenly and grabbed Besh's shirt with her blade hand, nearly cutting his face with her knife as she did, though it seemed to the old man that she wasn't even aware of the weapon in her hand. "You have to stop him! He's taking them to the Fal'Borna! They'll all die!"

"Wh-what baskets?" he asked, trying as best he could to keep from breaking free and running from her.

She smiled, a sly look creeping over her face. "I found a way," she whispered, her foul breath hot on his face. "They wanted me dead. They wanted us all dead, but I found a way."

"What way? What do you mean?"

She leaned closer to him, so that her mouth was just at his ear, as if they were lovers. "Baskets," she whispered. She pulled back to look at him, and nodded.

Besh shook his head. "I don't understand. What baskets? Who are you talking about?"

She opened her hand, revealing a dark clump of clotted dirt. For a moment she stared at it. Then she looked at Besh again, smiling. "Magic," she whispered. "Blood to earth, life to power, power to thought—"

Without thinking, he grabbed her wrist and gave her hand a violent shake, so that the dirt fell to the ground.

She glared at him and yanked her hand away.

"I know you!" she said again. "You're that dark-eyed boy who used to stare at me." She spun away and started running from him. "You don't know that they'll all die!" she shouted as she ran. "You don't know it! Maybe he'll just take them back to Tordjanne! Maybe they won't ever see them at all, and then it'll be all right!"

Besh ran after her, his mind racing. *I found a way. Baskets. Magic.* Was that how she had killed so many Y'Qatt? Had she placed a spell on the baskets she wove? Was she, in effect, poisoning them?

He was so intent on the questions swirling in his mind that he barely noticed when Lici dropped to the ground in front of him and began to claw at the earth with her hands. An instant later, though, he saw her knife flash across the back of her hand and he halted. He still clutched the bloodied earth in one hand and his knife in the other, and he began to whisper a spell, readying himself, unsure of what she intended to do. She glared back at him, and he realized that she was speaking, too.

"Blood to earth, life to power, power to thought, *earth to blades*!" With these last shouted words, she threw her handful of mud at him. And before his eyes, the clod of dirt flew apart, becoming a swarm of tiny steel knives.

Besh had spoken most of his spell, and now, with hardly a thought, he did the only thing he could. "Power to thought, earth to stone!" He made a sharp motion with his hand, releasing the dirt as he did, so that it spread before him in a dark wheel.

Lici's tiny blades struck, but by then Besh's wheel had turned to stone. With a sound like the chiming of a hundred small bells, the knives bounced away harmlessly. Most of them, at least. Three got through his shield; two buried themselves in Besh's shoulder, the third hit him just below the chest.

The old woman spat a curse and grabbed for more dirt. Besh stooped and did the same, ignoring the agony in his shoulder. Instead of cutting his hand again, he pulled one of the small knives from his flesh and wiped the blood on the soil in his hand.

"Blood to earth, life to power, power to thought," they said together, eyeing one another.

Both of them hesitated. He wanted to stop her, to keep her right where she was so that he could question her further. She wanted him dead. He couldn't attempt any spell without leaving himself open to her attack. She seemed to sense this, because a moment later she was grinning like some ghoul in the gathering gloom.

"Earth to fire!" she shouted suddenly, hurling the dirt at him.

Bright, angry flames burst from her hand, as if she were the goddess Eilidh herself. Besh froze, held fast by his terror, knowing he had no answer for this magic. At the last moment, he threw himself down and to the side. Much of Lici's fire passed over him, but not all. Seeing that his sleeve and trouser leg were ablaze, he batted at the flames, desperately trying to extinguish them, knowing that she might well be readying herself to cast yet another spell.

When at last the flames were out, he climbed warily to his feet. Lici was watching him still, her eyes bright and wide. Her fist was clenched again and fresh blood flowed from the back of her hand.

Realizing that he still held his own dirt, and that he was still in midspell, Besh wasted no time.

"Earth to swarm!" he cried out, throwing the dirt.

Immediately, Lici was beset by a host of yellow and black hornets. Just as he had hoped, she swatted at them, the dirt and her knife falling to the ground. She screamed and grabbed her blade again before scrambling to her feet and fleeing. Besh started after her, ducking past the hornets as he did.

As she ran, Lici tried to bend and scoop up some dirt, but she stumbled, righted herself, and ran on without managing to get any.

Besh didn't bother with more magic and so closed the distance between them. At last, he caught up with her and grabbed her arm.

She spun toward him, the knife flashing by his face, just narrowly missing his eye. Suddenly his cheek was burning with pain and he could feel blood flowing down over his jaw and neck.

Seeing what she had done, Lici stopped struggling to break free of his grip. She just gaped at him, her eyes wide again.

"You were speaking of the Y'Qatt, weren't you?" Besh demanded, breathing hard. "Before. When you spoke of the baskets, of finding a way. That's who you meant. The Y'Qatt."

She nodded.

He didn't attempt to stanch the flow of blood. Lici seemed transfixed by what she had done, and Besh wanted her to remain so.

"You put a spell on your baskets, one that would make them sick. Is that right?"

"I can't talk about this," she said, her eyes still riveted on the wound she had dealt him.

"Yes, you can. I know what they did to you. I've been . . . Sylpa told me."

Again she shifted her gaze, meeting his. "You've spoken to Sylpa?"

"She told me what happened. How the Y'Qatt wouldn't help you. How they even threatened to kill you if you wouldn't leave their village. That's why you did it, isn't it?"

Her expression hardened. "She said she wouldn't tell anyone! She promised!"

"She was concerned for you. She sent me to find you."

"She had no—" Lici looked past him, her eyes narrowing again, her grip on the knife tightening. "Who's that?"

Besh glanced back and saw Sirj a short distance off, watching them, his blade drawn as well.

"He's a friend." He faced her again. "Just as I am. Believe it or not, Lici, I am your friend. I want to help you. But you have to stop killing them."

Abruptly, she was crying, tears streaming down her face, her wails echoing through the wood.

"I didn't want this!" she screamed. "He said he was going to the Y'Qatt, but he lied to me! He lied! He lied! He lied! He lied! He lied! He lied!"

"Who lied to you, Lici?"

"He's taking them to the Fal'Borna!"

And suddenly, finally, Besh understood. He grabbed both of her shoulders. She didn't fight him this time. Not at all.

"Do you mean to tell me that there's a peddler out there who's taking your baskets into Qirsi land?"

The word came out as soft as a dying breath. "Yes."

"Blood and bone."

"What is it?" Sirj asked, walking toward them.

Lici dropped to the ground, sobbing still, muttering once more.

"She's been spreading the pestilence with her baskets. She puts a spell on them, and then probably sells them in the marketplace or trades them with merchants. That's how she's killing the Y'Qatt."

Sirj stared down at the woman, disgust and fear chasing one another across his face. "She's a demon," he whispered.

"It's worse than that. She says that now a peddler is taking her baskets into Fal'Borna land."

"Gods save us all! How many?"

"A good question." Besh squatted down beside the woman. "Lici, how many baskets does he have?"

She didn't answer. Besh wasn't even certain that she had heard him.

"Lici?" he said again. But then he shook his head and stood once more. "I'm not even certain it matters," he said quietly. "One is too many. Ten could kill thousands."

"So we have to find him."

Besh looked at him and nodded. "I agree."

"And what about her?"

What about her, indeed. Besh had told Pyav that he could kill her if that was the only way to stop her. But now, seeing her for what she was—crazed and pathetic—he no longer believed that he could bring himself to go so far. "I don't know."

Sirj eyed the cut on Besh's face. "She did that to you?"

"Yes."

The younger man nodded toward the tiny blades jutting from his shoulder and body. "And those?"

"You think I put them there myself?" Besh demanded.

Sirj ignored him. "Those wounds need to be cleaned and healed."

"I'm not good at healing magic."

"I am."

Besh hesitated.

"You can't travel far with those wounds," Sirj said, his voice gentle, as if he were speaking to a child.

At last the old man nodded. They moved off a short distance and Besh sat on the ground, all the while keeping watch on Lici. Sirj turned his attention first to the witch's conjured blades. The one that remained in Besh's shoulder came free easily, but the other had struck between two ribs. As Sirj pulled it out Besh winced, inhaling sharply through his teeth.

"I'm sorry."

The old man just shook his head. He pulled his shirt off, and allowed Sirj to work his magic. Besh continued to watch the old woman, but she didn't move, or even look at them. It seemed she had spent all her power and passion in their brief battle. Besh knew just how she felt.

I'm too old for this, he told himself once again.

Very smart to think of this now, when you're leagues from your home. He could hear Ema's voice, see the look of amused disdain on her face. He let out a small laugh.

Sirj frowned. "What could possibly be funny?"

"It doesn't matter."

The young man shrugged, and a moment later he sat back on his heels. "There. I can do more later, once we've made camp for the night. But that should hold you for now."

Besh moved his shoulder, then dabbed at his cheek. "That's better. Thank you."

Sirj nodded, a small smile on his lean face. He stood and helped Besh to his feet. Besh pulled his shirt back on, but beyond that neither man moved. They just stood there, looking over at Lici.

"We're taking her with us, aren't we?" Sirj finally asked.

"I don't see another way," Besh said, his voice tight.

But Sirj just nodded again and Besh realized that the younger man hadn't meant the question as a rebuke.

"What's to keep her from slipping away while we sleep, or taking that blade to our throats?"

"We'll sleep in shifts," Besh said. "And we'll have her cart with us. She won't leave that behind."

"The Fal'Borna don't care much for our kind."

Besh nodded, knowing that this was true, knowing as well that there wasn't much they could do about it. It was quite likely that the merchant who had her baskets had no idea what his wares would do to the Qirsi who might buy them. What choice did Besh and Sirj have but to go after him?

"Nobody cares for the Mettai," Besh said, eyeing the old woman, noting the dark smear of blood on the back of her hand. "But we have to do this anyway."

Blood to earth, life to power. More than words. More, even, than a source of magic. *Who are we, Grandfather?* Remembering the question from so long ago, Besh knew at last what he should have told the boy. *We are the land*, he should have said. *We are its blood. Our power flows from the earth, and it, in turn, gives strength back to this land in which we live.* The Mettai had been shunned for centuries, hated by dark-eye and white-hair alike. And finally Besh understood this as well. The Mettai were a bridge between the two races. Once, had the Mettai of old seen themselves in this way, and had they understood just how much evil would come of the Blood Wars, they might have found some way to forge a lasting peace, one that would have saved countless lives. Instead, for century upon century, the Mettai had served to remind Qirsi and Eandi alike of all that they hated about each other, and, perhaps worse, of all that they had in common. The Eandi looked at the Mettai, and they saw how close they were to being like their enemy. The same was true for the Qirsi. How could Besh's people not be despised?

And yet now, once again, they had an opportunity to save lives, quite possibly thousands of lives.

"We have to do this," Besh said again. Trying to convince himself, as well as Sirj.

"All right," the younger man said. "Let's be on our way, then." He looked around the forest, which was growing darker by the moment. "I don't think we want to be near this village when night falls."

They walked cautiously to where Lici still sat on the ground. She was no longer crying, but she had begun once more to speak to herself, rocking slowly, her voice low. Stopping before her, each of them offered the woman a hand.

She stopped her mumbling, looking up first at Sirj and then at Besh. "I know you both."

"Yes," Besh said, taking her hand in his. "We're Mettai, just as you are."

Characters

✦⊱✦

Kirayde (a Mettai village in the northern reaches of Stelpana)

BESH, an old Mettai man, a member of the village's Council of Elders

EMA, Besh's wife

ELICA, his daughter

SIRJ, Elica's husband

MIHAS, Sirj and Elica's elder son

ANNZE, Sirj and Elica's daughter

CAM, Sirj and Elica's younger son

PYAV, a blacksmith, head of the Council of Elders, addressed as "eldest"

LICALDI, also Lici, an old Mettai woman

SYLPA, Lici's foster mother

OJAN, the village miller

KORR, Ojan's father, a member of the Council of Elders

MARIVASSE, the village herbmistress, a member of the Council of Elders

TASHYA, a member of the Council of Elders

Lowna (a Fal'Borna village on the Companion Lakes)

JYNNA, an Y'Qatt girl, orphaned in her home village of Tivston

S'DORYN, a Qirsi man

N'TEVVA, S'Doryn's wife

T'NOTH, a Qirsi man, friend of S'Doryn and N'Tevva

T'KAAR, a Qirsi man, brother of T'Noth

A'VINYA, T'Kaar's wife

U'SELLE, a'laq (leader) of the village

ETAN, a young Y'Qatt boy, orphaned in his home village of Tivston

VETTALA, a young Y'Qatt girl, orphaned in her home village of Tivston

HEV, an Y'Qatt boy, orphaned in his home village of Tivston

PELDA, an Y'Qatt girl, orphaned in her home village of Tivston

SEBBI, Pelda's younger sister, orphaned in her home village of Tivston

The Merchants

R'SHEV, a Qirsi merchant on the plains of Stelpana

D'CHUL, a Qirsi lutenist and merchant on the plains of Stelpana

TORGAN PLYE, an Eandi merchant from Tordjanne

Y'FARL, an Y'Qatt merchant in C'Bijor's Neck

JASHA ZIFFEL, an Eandi merchant

BRINT HEDFARREN, an Eandi merchant from Tordjanne

On the Plains of the Fal'Borna

GRINSA JAL ARRIET, a Qirsi man, originally from the Forelands

CRESENNE JA TERBA, Grinsa's wife, originally from the Forelands

BRYNTELLE JA GRINSA, Grinsa and Cresenne's daughter

S'PLAED, a'laq of a Fal'Borna sept in the northern plain

E'MENUA, a'laq of a Fal'Borna sept in the central plain

D'PERA, E'Menua's wife

U'VARA, E'Menua and D'Pera's eldest daughter

Q'DAER, a Weaver in E'Menua's sept

L'NORR, a Weaver in E'Menua's sept

F'SOLYA, a Fal'Borna woman

I'JOLED, F'Solya's husband

H'SHEM, a Fal'Borna warrior

Sentaya (once a Mettai village along the Silverwater Wash)

KYTHA, younger sister of Licaldi

BAETRI, also Baet, youngest sister of Licaldi

SOSLI, a young girl, a friend of Licaldi

About the Author

David B. Coe is the author of nine epic fantasy novels, including The LonTobyn Chronicle, a trilogy that won the Crawford Fantasy Award for best work by a new author, and the Winds of the Forelands quintet. *The Sorcerers' Plague* is the first volume of the Blood of the Southlands trilogy. David is already at work on volume two, *The Horsemen's Gambit*. He lives with his wife and their two daughters on the Cumberland Plateau in Tennessee.